In additions to an e-book catalogue, other print editions by Bruce S. Larson include the collections:

WITHIN AND BEYOND: The Realms of the Sun

NIGHTMARES AND OTHER VICES

WITHIN AND BEYOND: The Storm

ZOMBIE DOMINATION

and the novel

BEYOND APOCALYPSE

GRAIL

ICE AGE

BRUCE S. LARSON

GRAIL:
ICE AGE
by
Bruce S. Larson

Published by
World Line One Press

ISBN: 978-1-945207-12-9

OF HARLOTS AND SHAPES
Foreword by Cristopher DeRose

The first time I read a story detailing the dark adventures of one Joshua Grail (or Mr. Ice, as he was known in the early days) it was when I was publishing DARK MATTER MAGAZINE. I lucked out enough to get the Grail stories "Harlots" and "Shapes." The door, as they say, was open. All Grail had to do is walk through it. And he did, and as a fan of Bruce's work as well as Joshua Grail, I am glad the decision was made to join us.

Over the years, Bruce has gone from contributor to colleague to collaborator and, most importantly, a damn good friend. His level of writing has inspired mine and has reminded me that it's not always a bad idea to look over your shoulder to see who's gaining, because it can very well be a friend you're more than happy to run with and watch succeed. I like to think of us as a sort-of Don Felder/Joe Walsh duo. That will probably come as a surprise to Mr. Larson. But then I think that Felder and Walsh don't know, either, and I get over it.

I think of Bruce as being part of the New Weird, and this collection you now hold exemplifies that. Grail's world can lunge from the shadows his world holds close around its shoulders or it can sidle up and draw blood when you're not looking. It's unpredictable, and if it's not in your line of sight, it's probably up to something you'd rather not think about. Grail comes from a dark elite. He has a code of values unique to his persona and profession as he navigates the places outside the realm of streetlights and safety. Thankfully, brave souls like his creator can report back from the front lines and bring the stories back to us chickens who let the others deal with the things that dwell deep in the shadows.

As the stories have progressed, the world Bruce has created has become a rich, complex vision, full of monsters great and small, but related to us with a human face and psyche that brings us further into that world. It may not be pretty, but it doesn't have to be and is under no obligation to be anything else. Sometimes things aren't as clear as we would prefer them to be, and no one understands that more than our weary anti-hero, Joshua Grail. No need to thank him. Chances are, he wouldn't stick around long enough after the job to hear it, anyway. Grail's not rude (necessarily), he's just got things to do he knows you'd rather not think about, let alone talk over with him.

But if you're ever in the Pacific Northwest, maybe looking for Bigfoot and/or Wildboy, and you come across a certain writer instead, buy him a round. After dealing with Grail for as long as he has, it's the least we can do for him.

Cristopher DeRose
Los Angeles, 2017

REFLECTION AND RECOGNITION
Acknowledgments by Bruce S. Larson

He is called Joshua Grail, or simply Ice. One friend witnessed the character's genesis and evolution. Mr. Erik England read the earliest drafts of many stories in this book. He was at day one of the Ice Age. A nod of Grail's granite brow goes to Mr. E. to recognize those days, our continued creative exchanges, and the (brighter) future.

Mr. Ice appeared in online and print magazines, and even a few Year's Best volumes. For each editor's faith in my writing, I am forever grateful. When you get an acceptance, or perhaps just solid advice for a story's improvement, it can make your day. Actually, it may be the banner day for your year. The publications listed below started what grew into this collection. Join me to thank the people who brought readers their first trips into the dark world of future monsters and human menace. Have no fear. Most on the list don't bite.

Cristopher DeRose
DARK MATTER
"Shapes"
"Harlots"

S. Joan Popek and Diana Moreland
MILLENNIUM SCIENCE FICTION & FANTASY
"Rats"
"Direction in Shadow" (retitled "Social Contract")
"Public Service"

Patrick Swenson and Honna Swenson
TALEBONES MAGAZINE
"Inherit the Earth"
Interior illustration for the story by Bob Hobbs.

Daniel P. Medici
VAMPIRE DAN'S STORY EMPORIUM
"Freaks"
Cover illustration for the story by the Wallace Brothers.

CONTENTS

01
SHAPES

A shadow is darkness given form. Once a thing has form, it can change, twist, and evolve. Engineering evolved so that humanity's structures dominated the face of the Earth. Epic towers now cast darker shadows in geometric, artificial shapes over a lightless world. Above them rolled a shroud of black clouds that never parted or drifted away. Any light from the sky was a reflection from below.

In the past, dark progeny of avarice and industry was cast out and buried in deep places. Altered life and toxic forms changed, twisted, and evolved. They emerged to cast dark shadows of their own. An adaptation to exploit and remove Earth's corrupt masters is to use us as prey. Yet, with our numbers so vast, we survive. For now.

Naturally, we still prey on each other. The shapes of victims stay familiar. Criminals change, and vice versa, until the same basic shapes chase themselves. A woman walked along a desolate avenue. The majority of traffic now moved among and within the towers where people can afford the fare. The woman walked on a surface street. She puffed heavily against her respirator. Another, larger woman followed her. That woman breathed the caustic air with naked lungs. A well-honed shard appeared from under her sleeve. They both ran.

The smaller woman ran over a grating and woke the hunger below it. The thing's head was massive. It exploded from its nest and knocked the grating and pursuer into the air. It snatched the chasing woman from her sudden, hapless flight. Her body disappeared into the angular jaws. They would perfectly match a giant snake's jaws, but for the rows of shark's teeth. The first woman screamed. That called the thing's attention to her. The monster curved its enormous neck in mid swallow. The jaws opened again and shot downward.

I pushed the screamer aside. My first shot only blew a hole through the thing's sweeping palate.

Slower velocity! Lower angle.

The second shot blasted it backwards. The beast's shattered skull slapped the dusty pavement like butchered meat. I breathed heavier. Then I lowered my gun. I'm another shape moving violently within the shadows so that most of my fellow humans live a little longer. For a fee, of course.

"So," I asked the woman peering around me at the dead monster, "how much do you have on you?"

Skyscrapers stood dwarfed by super-towers, each a world to itself. They pierced the constant, black clouds that gave a ceiling to airborne traffic. I walked on a fairly well-lit street flanked by rows of concrete pillboxes and armor-plated shacks. Those buildings looked like a jagged step to bright shops and offices on the second floors of the towers behind them sealed in thick panes of artificial diamond.

I saw the hints of various colors through the glassy shielding. Gray dominated my hair, skin, and eyes. Brown did the same for John Slate. A similar choice of attire outfitted Police Detective and Monster Killer. We both wore long coats, heavy boots, and scowls. Other than height, mass, and Slate's respirator mask, we might've appeared as the same shape reflected in a smoky mirror.

We met under a weak cone of light from an ancient street lamp. He looked up at me and gave a nod. Up close, he looked more hardened than his holographic image when he called.

"That thing you put down on Admiral Street, Ice," Slate said behind his mask. "It took us an hour to haul out and bag."

"I'm glad you had enough motivated officers for the job." I replied.

"I don't. I never do. That's why I holoed. There's something stalking this district. Eating merchants." He cocked his head at the concrete and metal shacks. "And killing the street-level economy."

"Nice to know someone is considerate to the human loss." My comment annoyed him, more.

Slate pulled off his mask. "I am, Ice! That's why I'm hiring you!"

"Well, if we're going into business, you should know Ice is only my street tag."

"Yeah, Joshua Grail. I've got your name and license number. I've got everything on you. Don't worry."

I stayed quiet. I hope he didn't literally have everything on me. That could be difficult for us both. My silence provoked him to press further.

"Look, kill this one, and maybe I can help you sometime."

"Yeah, maybe." I replied.

Slate glared at me for a moment. He tossed me an uncoded infomere and left me to my work.

Slate's report showed the monster's *bite* stripped away flesh and muscle and left striated bone. Ick. It also held an interesting, little fact. Someone stole routing codes and downloaded the credit registers at each crime scene. Crime. It's good as any word for human slaughter. Yet, monsters aren't tech-literate. They don't even think—I hoped—beyond basic impulses like *kill, eat, kill again*. However, some people have an impulse to steal. Is the thief a remora, a scavenger carefully following the monster's tracks? Or something new?

Time passed to slightly later. The clouds hung, still as dark. Outside one armored convenience store, hastily pasted slap-screens beamed the lies *Sale! Real Meat! Half-Price!* The shadow of a man and some other thing fell over the bright letters.

Inside the cluttered store, *Nietzsche Pops* and other foods were of no interest to the man with well-oiled, black hair. The fabric of his neo-modern dress suit flared with pink flames. I focused on what quickly pranced at the end of the reigns he held. A bipedal, raptoresque monster slightly larger than a typical human male, but much more powerful. Its long, triangular head and similar pink hue tugged its lead. It yawned. Multi-sectioned jaws opened beneath forward facing eyes like petals on a flower. A *bloom* emerged from its throat made by a succession of smaller, internal jaws good for rasping away more than hollow calories from bones.

Interesting.

There was a story in how he found and trained the thing, and how he became a murdering freak, himself. I didn't think I would have the time to ask him before the beast yawned again. Man and monster stopped in front of the large, welded box at the center of the store. The word *cashier* had been burned above an eye slit and iris hatch.

"May I help you?" The question came from the temporary cashier in the box.

"Give me your access codes, Sweetums." The pink man said. "Or I turn her loose."

"Uh, I can't do that."

"You can if you want to live, silly beast." The man jerked the reins and his living weapon snapped its vicious head to the cashier box.

"No, sorry. That's against company rules." I swiftly flipped up the box's side, and then level my gun at them.

Faster still, the monster bolted with the man in tow holding the reigns. I fired. The shot blasted a condiment isle asunder, but missed them. The man screamed anyway. I guessed because mustard and garum spatter clashed with his jacket. He and his pet burst through the outer doors. I chased them outside. I found nothing in the street.

Sound! Overhead!

I looked up. The monster swiftly climbed the side of the building rising above the store like a giant, primrose gecko. Its talons gripped the glassy surface. The man in pink dangled below, clutching the reigns as a lifeline. Yeah, interesting. He glanced down at me. He freed one hand to yank out a small-caliber automatic and then pepper the street with pistol fire. I darted back inside.

The building the monster scaled was tall, but no super-tower. They would have to cross its roof before climbing higher, or to attempt a leap to another of the stepped roofs. I gave pink boy credit to realize he would not survive the attempt. No matter what they did, I had to stop the monster from killing again.

Atop the roof, the man's oily hair was now slumped to the left like a drop of tar slowly falling. He held the reigns with a devilish smile as his matching monster crouched by elevator housing. The lighted arrow pointed up as the car rose. They wait pensively for the doors to open.

"Soon, Jellybean." I heard him say with amplification from the sensors imbedded in the muzzle of my gun. I had also tapped the security cameras.

The arrival bell never sounded. Gun blasts from below sent them both sprawling. I climbed through the smoking hole in the ceiling as they recovered. The elevator doors slide open in front of them. I had taken the express cargo lift and then the stairs. The

4

monster charged with her petal jaws opened wide bearing a whirl of horrific teeth. They obliterated as I fired explosive rounds.

"No!" the pink man screamed as his pet's headless body lurched free of its reigns and collapsed.

He fired. His shots were guided more by emotion than skill. I lunged left and shot back. His body suffers the inverse of his pet. The pink jacket and torso slapped the dark, grime-covered roof. Dark red streaks flowed into pools across it.

I took a breath and glanced at the hole ripped through the heavy fabric of my coat sleeve. He got closer than I thought. I pulled out two automated collection bags, and tossed them near their indistinct remains. For a time the pink man and the monster he somehow trained were a synthesis of this new world. A union of the oldest impulses of man, and the latest version of primal survival. But, sometimes, new species run up against older, established beasts unwilling to let go of their niche, even when it's corrupted.

That, and I could hardly let them keep killing the innocent.

I wondered if there was justice in evolution, however artificial or natural the environment. It was time to call the cops, and tell them it's safe to come out again. At least here. For now. Life continues to adapt, twist, and reshape, even in darkness.

02
RATS

Rats. They remain one of the few natural species to survive Earth's ecological holocaust. It seems they have always been here in some form. They have survived by not being particular about what they eat, such as each other. Those thoughts surfaced as I looked at the luminous, holographic bubble that held my client's image.

"This is one of my most profitable apartment buildings, Mr. Grail." He said that with pride as his projected head floated over a stream of sewage in the center of the hall. If he was blind to that, then the stench wouldn't have changed his perspective. "But the living spaces are overrun with vermin, and some archaic law says I've got to eliminate them."

"Then maybe you should mop the place." I offered, and sidestepped a pile of accreted muck.

I had lowered my scan strength across the spectrum to spare myself more disgust. My natural senses revealed enough. Motion detection would forestall any ambush. I heard my targets running in the sluice water just ahead of us in the darkness. Typically, I killed larger pests, such as the hungry freaks that crawled from the pits of corrupted science.

"Why would I pay for sanitation work?" The owner asked. The shrill tone of his projected, effete voice made the idea sound perverse. "The other conditions are legal, but what isn't today? Except breeding."

The glow from his projection cast down an adjoining hall where a dense swarm of rats flowed over itself as they surged back into the shadows.

"Obviously the new tenants don't follow the rules." I said.

"And feed off garbage and each other." The building owner looked down toward the rats from his safe, disembodied view. "Strange how the world has changed but some species stay the same."

"Yeah," I said as he floated in the air seemingly buoyed by the vapors from his legal, open sewer.

My eyes were not the only ones to see contempt. The rats churned on the edges of shadows like magma under the Earth of yore before it burst through the surface. Larger, older eyes peered through cracking walls. They burned with swelling anger. The old man probably wondered if I was muscle to roust squatters or collect back rent. But I didn't think an enforcer would wear thigh-high protective boots and a well-worn overcoat. Yet the sighted, steel shaft popping in and out of my coat as I walked obviously wasn't a walking stick. The old, brown man entered the hall from his apartment after catching my own glare through the walls.

The term *old* was now more of a visual description. Skin tone and many other aspects of appearance were, for a price, negotiable with a genetic esthetician. Medical science had also separated age in years and from physical degradation over time. Access was to such treatment was mitigated by finances. Having more meant you looked less, in years. Obviously, the people of this building had to settle for less in treatment, and thus suffer more through their years.

"Did you hire him to kill it?" The old man asked the owner's hologram with familiar disgust.

"Ignore him," the owner said and did so himself.

"Kill what?" I asked. Killing is what I did, after all.

"The thing that's been eating us tenants." The old man said. "Sucks dry anyone who tries to use the john."

"Is that true?" I asked.

The old man fixed his eyes on me. They are the only things still round on his taught, bony frame.

"Statistics show mortality has been higher in this building." The hologram replied, slowly drifting forward.

"Dead renters don't eat into your wallet?" I asked, sharply.

"With a population of over a trillion, Mr. Grail? Tenants are dying to get *in*." The owner looked almost gleeful at the thought.

"So your lucre keeps flowing." The old man said defiantly. His eyes darted from the hologram and back to me.

A large drop of sewage dangled into the holographic bubble from the ceiling. The owner's projected face roiled with extreme disgust as it oozed through. A tinge of umber mingled with the filmy skin of the projection medium.

"In my sealed office I don't have to deal with any of it." He said as the glob splashed on the floor beneath him. "And all you're paid to worry about is the rats, Grail. The filth finds its own way out."

His hologram disappeared with a small pop and flash.

"No kidding." I said.

"Look, kill it anyway," The old man said as a command and also a plea. While most people avoided looking up at me and my glare, his cloudy eyes focused on mine with sharp determination.

"Go back in your room," I said. "And watch where you step."

He did so, slowly. I looked across the sewer that was once an apartment hall. Filth, decay, and some unseen monster. The place was a microcosm of planet Earth. Welcome to the future.

"Excuse me." A woman said meekly from behind a cracked door. "Could you check on Raymond, next door? He hasn't been out in days. I would, but he's so formal about manners."

Next door, a desiccated corpse sat on a toilet. Busy rats cover its legs and lower arms. Raymond. So formal you couldn't crap in the hall like everyone else. You turned a blind eye to the darkened world, and it ate you. I scanned his corpse. The green light from the beams annoyed the rats. They must sense vibrations in the plumbing when the monster moves through the pipes. It kills, and they eat what remains. A macabre symbiosis. But now that the human prey is avoiding the plumbing, the system is bound to break down.

"Aiahhg!"

The scream came from the old man's room. Hunger made things bolder.

The apartment door shattered when I rammed it. Inside, the old man swung a rickety chair at hideous, fluid-like tentacles swooping at him from the bathroom. They snatched him up anyway. The blasts from my gun cut him free. His frail bones hit the floor. I helped pull the convulsing bits of tentacle from his throat. More lanced out at us.

"Behind you!"

He shouted and I reacted too late.

I screamed angrily as a tentacle pierced my left shoulder. Impaled, I tossed a small, smoking cylinder into the toilet where more tentacles gushed out. The cylinder spewed a corrosive that burned the monster's arms into charred, flopping worms. Nothing like a little acid to wash away your troubles. Something rumbled under the floor. The monster was gone, for now.

I yanked twice to pull the dead tentacle from my bloody shoulder. Brave rats darted out and started to gnaw the wriggling meat as it hit the floor.

"Are you—?" The old man asked, and then coughed.

"I'm fine," I said. "I will be. Can you tell me where this building's reclamation tanks are kept?"

You are what you eat. If you eat fluids, you might find plumbing a nice place to reside. The rent is likely cheap. After a med-patch and equipment swap, I looked at the massive water tank in the basement storage vault. Countless pipes joined it at all angles to conduct flow in and out of the monster's home. Effluent in, filtered water out. That was the idea. Insurance might replace this ancient unit with one that worked better. I placed charges, and left the vault for the stairwell. I covered my ears.

One, two, three—

The vault doors flew from the wall in a beautiful fireball. Unfortunately, a putrid wave followed. In the vault, the blown apart tank revealed a horrifying mass. The monster looked like gargantuan stomach covered with flailing tentacles. The whole, horrid thing writhed.

Tentacles whipped toward me in rage. Others shot up from the water-covered floor. My flame-thrower answered. I knew if I could keep the beast in place long enough, then opportunity should turn its former allies into hungry executioners. And soon I heard the squeal of the cavalry. Rats erupted from the foul water and swarmed the monster, oblivious to the flames. I stopped and watched thousands of ravenous vermin spew out of the broken pipes to join in the hellish feast.

Eat hearty, I thought. *There's plenty for everyone.*

Eliminate the monster, and then the natural balance should return. Organic law should work even in this environment, even for all rats. The building owner bolted from his overstuffed floating chair when I blew the vault door to his pristine office. Now, I had a job for him.

The old man could not contain his joy of the moment. I stood next to him as he steadied the flashlight beam on the owner who could barely hold the mop while looking fearfully back at us.

"The mop," I said. "Push it."

The owner looked petrified at feeling the filthy water flow into his shoes. He was no hologram, now. Reality felt wet and dirty, and smelled like raw violation.

"I hired you to kill rats, not to harass me!" The owner screamed at me, his former employee. The frustration from not being separated, safe, and in control was as great an emotion as his fear.

"Push the mop." I slid out my own cleaning tool, and curled a finger around the trigger. "Remember, I'm licensed to kill monsters."

Suddenly, the owner found motivation to start mopping the place. Maybe things will be a little cleaner around here. Even livable.

"I suppose we still have that rat problem." The old man said.

"Not for long. But right now, that might not be a bad thing," I said and turned to leave. "They'll eat just about anything."

Behind me, the old man looked at the owner edging closer to the shadows. He took the light off him and called after me.

"Hey, wait. Let me guide you out. It's pretty dangerous around here in the dark."

"True enough," I said. "Monsters are everywhere."

03
HARLOTS

The more things change, the worse they get. At least that's the new axiom for planet Earth. The sky is black. The air is toxic. The streets are ruled by the twisted beasts that have eaten all the muggers and gangs. For whatever reason, most people don't want to die. That wish to live creates my job: killing monsters. I've been called many things in different times. In this life the tag 'Killer' is as apt as the fearful slander whispered behind my back. In this perpetual nightmare the monsters never sleep. The shapes of the beasts are constantly shifting, yet certain monsters are classical. Some things remain the same.

"Hey! You're on time. Thought you'd keep me waiting. Y'know, play me like a tease." The voice from the dark said. The man who bought my services would not come out into the filthy alleyway for good reason. "Uh, did you see it?"

"No." I answered. "It's playing hard to get."

"You won't find that attitude in here. C'mon in. The thing'll get hungry soon enough."

I stepped down through shadows into his dank place of business. Only a burned-out and battered overhead lamp indicated the doorway. Inside was a cramped and oppressive hallway. The fat man, Queban, squeezed his way between two rows of plastic doors, the same kind on portable latrines. Only, these doors had the locking bolts on the outside. I followed sideways in Queban's oily trail of smoke curling over his slicked down hair. Once, organic leaves were rolled into cigars. Now, what smoldered in the brown stub on his lip was anyone's guess. However, his occupation was obvious. A few doors were opened. All the clientele were too busy with Queban's employees on the rickety cots to notice our passage.

"So your ad said your name is Joshua Grail." Queban raised his voice as music grew louder as we neared its source. "But the punks I heard talking about you called you Ice. Which is it?"

"I don't much care what you call me, as long as your payment clears."

"Okay, then." Queban stopped and turned to me. His round, oily cheeks arched in a flippant smile. "How about I call you—"

I looked down at him with a narrowed glare.

"Yeah, okay. Ice works, fine." Queban shrugged. "And so the thing outside is starting to eat my business. First it was just a couple of johns now and again. But then it took a couple of my girls, and a good business protects its capital, eh? Right now, nobody will even change the light bulb outside."

Queban squeezed by an opened door. A pair of wraith-like arms grabbed at him from inside the humid stall.

"Queban? Please just kill me. I can't do it anymore!" The girl pleaded. Her age was impossible to tell from her taught, wasting features.

Queban shoved her back inside. He then threw his weight against the door to slam it shut. "You can die when your contract expires!" He shouted and locked the bolt.

"When will that be?" I asked.

"Ha! Never. Anyway, if the thing shows up, kill it! You'll get paid when you perform, too."

Ahead, the hall opened into an aged club. At its center was a small circular stage built like a tiny, lurid amphitheater for the tiny, lurid people occupying half its seats. With me close at his back, Queban popped out of the cramped hallway like a bullet and bumped into his hired muscle.

"Geez! You guys should lay off the 'roids." Queban spat, and reassumed his head-forward gait.

"I don't use 'roids" I said.

Queban's bouncer replied with a sneering smile, and then followed his boss like a good dog. I looked across the skin yard. Another of Queban's girls danced on the stage. Above her a holographic sign read-out the competing bids for her private show.

"So you're the big Killer that Queban hired?" I heard behind me.

I turned and looked down to face the drab and haggard woman sizing me up. "And you're his official greeter?"

"I'm Silky," she said. "Show me some graft and I'll do more than smile hello."

"Sounds like you enjoy your work."

"I don't have a choice. None of us do. You think we like it here? Look at Gingy. She's just fourteen!" Silky motioned to the girl on the stage.

I noticed Queban's bouncer take an interest in my new conversation from across the club.

"But what do you care?" Silky asked like a challenge. "You're just another john. Except your date is in the alley."

"I am no john." I grated over the canned soundtrack. My professional and personal pride was not typically in play when I took a job. I kill monsters for money. It's a simple idea that's hard to pull off. So I'm usually regarded with fear, not arrogant scorn. Silky was getting annoying.

"Yeah? Then fix this." Silky tossed her head to the hallway. "You've got the license. Use it."

Silky was well informed. A clause in my license states that for the greater good I can do bad things in pursuit of killing a monster. It's based on the fact that people fear the hungry freaks more than mourning the loss of property, their neighbors, or their liberties. Or maybe it was just the government that decided to give my profession that power from their own fears of facing down the terrors at street level. Whatever the reason, I can do almost anything to anyone if it's justified. I'm a better shot than most, so I use my professional ammunition discount more than the legal loophole she pointed out.

"Sorry. I kill monsters." I said.

"Then kill Queban!" She hissed through clenched teeth, leaning aggressively towards me. "Someone has to. Why do you think I brought that thing here?"

"You brought it? How?" I didn't believe her. Only once had I seen a monster trained by a human. Usually they just regard us as food.

"Yeah. I found it when it was little. It grew." Silky seemed to wilt, dropping her shoulders. Maybe seeing some of her friends die from her supposed pet pulled heavy on her conscience. Maybe she was just changing her tactics with me. "I thought—"

Queban burst in between us. "I knew it! I knew you caused this! You filthy—!"

The bouncer hovered close in the background. Queban's fat, wet hand slapped Silky to the ground. I pulled him away from her on instinct.

"Zee-Zee!" Queban screamed.

The bouncer lunged at me with a serrated dagger in the air. I threw my forearm into his face. His nose snapped and exploded with blood. The rest of the struggle was rote. I twisted his right arm holding the knife out of its socket, and hurled him over my shoulder. He hit the floor in pain, but not broken. Out come our handguns. Mine was much bigger and aimed first. My weapons are built to kill monsters hardened in the acidic pit the world fell into. The single blast shook the club. Zee-Zee's fragments showered Gingy and her audience in flecks of dark red and bone.

Now fear appeared. It gave Queban rare speed but stunted judgment. He bolted away from me down the hallway. I chased him, both trying to save his life and also wanting to snap his neck. He tripped on the short stairway and stumbled into the squalid alley. He cut his face on something tall like a spike-edged lamppost. Queban wasn't alone, and this time I was too slow. Through the doorway I saw him look up in terror. The lamppost moved in swift concert with seven others. Queban was snatched from the ground before he could scream. I leapt into the alley to see him dangle high above the ground. Queban's body seemed to spasm violently as the monster ate him.

At first, quick glance it looked like a towering spider. Instead it was some mutated arachnid cousin more closely related to the amblypygi, the tailless whip scorpion. It could have just been a new sequence of synthetic genes amping a nightmare to epic scale. Queban's cigar fell to the ground in a contrail, forced from his mouth by froth. For a fraction of a second the hideous thing loomed before me with the remains of its prize hung from sickle-like jaws and flexing pedipalp arms. I fired. The blasts rocked the walls of the alleyway.

I returned inside. Silky knelt on the floor cupping handfuls of her blood as if to keep it from mingling with Zee-Zee's spread across the floor.

"They're gone." I said. "I missed. Queban is dead."

Silky's hands became wet, red fists thrust above her head. Her bleeding face contorted in hacking laughter. The reasons were different than I imagined, but she was happy.

One day later, after a retouch at a medical kiosk, Silky took a new girl to a room in the darkened, oppressive hallway. Silky wore one of Queban's suits drastically recut for her own frame.

"You can leave when your contract expires." Silky told the girl, and steadily guided the reluctant victim into her cramped cell.

"You're going to keep them here, too?" I asked from the door to the alley. My own contract was unfulfilled.

"Queban was a lousy husband, but inheritance laws are wonderful to widows." Silky answered with her arrogant scorn also rejuvenated. "Besides, a good business needs its capital. Right?"

Silky smiled defiantly.

Most monsters kill for food. Hunger is a motivation I always understood. Queban severed life from people more slowly than but just as certainly as a monster's jaws. He fed off the cravings of the corrupt people that crept into this pit. Now Silky planned to do the same. That had always been her true goal. Better to be the spider than a victim bound to the web.

If I killed the monster, this business would bloom again. If I walk away the beast will still feed on its human prey, indiscriminant to innocent or oppressor. The problem was the predation of both monsters. One killed faster than the other. I needed to stop both horrors. I grabbed Silky by the arm.

"Hey! What are you doing?" She barked. "You want it rough, you pay first!"

"Yesterday you asked me to fix this problem." I said hauling her into the alleyway. "But then it was only a ruse to eliminate Queban. I need to kill the monster you brought, but it moves too fast. I need something to distract it."

I released Silky. She flailed and stumbled forward. It didn't take long. Silky screamed when reunited with her pet. She ran. The gigantic arachnid thing didn't seem to recognize her before it snapped her up and in half. The blasts from my gun lit the inside of the brothel hall in violent white flashes. The monster's blasted remains painted the alley walls with grotesque graffiti. I stood next to the monster's ravaged corpse. Some of its legs curled slowly towards its massive, overturned body. One severed leg twitched farther down the alley. The brutal symmetry was broken.

I walked over to the brothel's door. Some of the braver women were in the hall looking out. I reached up to the battered lamp over the doorway. The worn socket screeched but accepted the new bulb I put in. Stark light flashed over the women's faces.

"It's over." I told them, and walked away from the opened door. "All contracts are finished. All of you can leave. Now."

04
PUBLIC SERVICE

Cleanliness is next to affluence. I left tracks along a white floor. It and the gleaming white halls and ceiling were constantly shined and sanitized. Only people that prowled the maintenance channels ever saw the cleaners. Those unlucky few, like me. My ad and ID tells you I'm Joshua Grail. The important part is my license to tag and kill monsters, and if I'm free for hire. The mall cleaners were always on duty. They were small, gliding disks emitting disinfectants, occasional bursts of gamma rays, and a pleasant, fresh scent. They killed stains and microscopic life. I dealt with bigger things. Much bigger things that make people disappear. I typically leave a mess.

Modern opulence is sterility. Here, not even artificial plants violated the deliberate starkness. The only life was shoppers walking and floating between stores, and scurrying out of my way. The place indulged the new fad of actually traveling out to buy needless merchandise. So far, there were only a few places like this. However, monsters are everywhere. Hungry and powerful, they strike from shadow, oblivious to the pain they inflict. Only the vigilant survive, most of the time. That wasn't so for some shoppers on level twelve. One victim was a politician's husband. So the bureaucracy hired me to find and kill the thing. I'm their revenge masquerading as public service. No mask could have hid the obvious unease my presence created. I am unwelcome in this sterile and false sanctuary. The bloody memories of yesterday stained my work clothes. The armored fabric of my long coat never completely concealed my weapons.

Most of the privileged shoppers and submissive storeowners hoped I'd disappear like the monster if they averted their eyes and pretended to ignore me. They saw little difference between me and the thing I hunted. We were both uncomfortable realities in this artificial world. At least I have a line of credit. That could be good news for the food court. I followed my scans of the monster's path to the fire escape door mandated for public safety. Yet it appears this monster had learned to work cheap locks. That's bad news if I don't find it before lunchtime. Mine, not the monster's.

The door opened to solid black. A cone of light beamed from my gun muzzle revealed a flight of stairs. Something very heavy made an impression in the landing. I emerged onto street level. Black yielded slightly to shadows and yellow hues of the aged street lamps. The coarse air vibrated with the noise of the global city. Yet this block was desolate and eerily still. The monster could have driven off the local population. That drove it to hunt upstairs. I stalked its traces into an alley. I saw it. My weapon's fire would not shatter the ominous still. The reptilian beast with its dexterous claws and jagged teeth was dead already.

Noise!

A sudden presence met the end of my gun barrel. The noise was only a man coughing. The man stood, but seemed as devoid of life as the mall and this dim street.

"Kill me. I don't care," he said and coughed louder.

I became aware of others like him throughout the alley as my scanner dumped their locations into my brain faster than my natural senses. I lowered my gun. The scan continued deeper into the man before me. Monsters take many forms. Like stains, some are very small.

"What's wrong with us?" A woman asked. I was stunned for a moment to see she held a small child balanced on her hip. Her eyes begged for an answer, even from a massive stranger dressed for violence. "It started about a week ago. Spread fast. I don't get it."

"You're all sick," I answered.

"Sick?" Many repeat the word like it was an unknown concept. It is, today. That is, if you can access a medical kiosk and pay.

"You've been infected by a mutated segment of RNA, presumably from the monster. Its twisted biology probably created the same disease that eventually killed the rest of it." My answers only magnify the group's bewilderment. "Your own DNA is breaking down as your ribosomes unwittingly use the viroid in replication. Your genes are slowly being deleted. You're all dying."

The group stirred. They understood that concept, and most obviously didn't share the fatalism of the man next to me. It distracted them from wondering how a mere Monster Killer could interpret what his scanners recorded inside them, or why the settings would be set so deep. As a biological irony, the disease slowly killed its host, but its side effects killed chemical population restraints. Of course, people will be people no matter where they reside. Nature took its course in this alley, as well. It was how the human species came to overpopulate Earth. Once.

"I'll get help. Wait here." I said and left. I figured that some would probably trust me and stay. The others will be too sick to move.

Monsters roam anywhere. Their hunger breached diverse barriers and walls, so my Killer's access pass let me into many restricted places. Deep inside a government tower, I walked a hallway nearly as wide as the mall. The photophores imbedded in all the surfaces were much older than the ones in the mall, making the light here far dimmer. The sign proclaiming my destination was larger than the office itself. Perhaps the office shrank over time, but no one could move the sign. The chiseled words *HEALTH MANAGEMENT SERVICES* rose across an imposing block of synthetic marble.

"You stumbled into a blank zone, Mr. Grail. Or do you prefer the street tag, Ice?" Director Schiff replied to my transmitted query as I entered and before I even spoke. "It's marked uninhabitable, so it's been deleted from our service corridor."

The chromophores on her face broadcast colors like a diva's stage make up. Her hairstyle capped the display like an ancient helmet. She sat overstuffed in a uniform that fused a doctor's coat and business suit. A cluttered blur of holographic citations and diplomas projected from the walls behind her.

"But there are people living there." I said. "I've spoken to them. They all need medical attention."

"People?" Schiff questioned, and consulted a projection of names, numbers, and locations that popped on over her desk. "They have no registration. No habitat. No means of revenue. In short, they don't exist."

Now, like the people in the alley, I was confused.

"Is reality outside your service corridor, Schiff?" I asked. I had no chromophores, but my anger was obvious. "Those people are dying! The infectious agent may not stay in your blank zone."

"It is an unusual situation." Schiff shrugged and her body threatened to burst her uniform. "The plague will probably wipe itself out. Or we'll move when it affects a zone that warrants our intervention. One with tax payers, or under contract."

"That's what makes someone worth your time?" It was obvious more than her sterile desk separated us.

"We need to know that our services will have a return on expenditure," Schiff explained, calmly. "My office is a privatized contractor, Mr. Grail. We are alike. We both do a job for a fee. However, I buy the right to provide public service. And, naturally, my shareholders expect a return on their investment. I do thank you for correcting the area's habitable status. I'm sure our affiliate agencies will do that as well."

Schiff smiled, and turned aside. Our meeting was over. I walked back to the door. My frustration burned through.

"We do differ, though. In another way." I said. "My license gives me a lot of leverage. I guess killing monsters is a job more important than most. And I don't answer to shareholders, or almost anyone. I'll return for you later, Schiff. Be sure your own accounts are in order."

Schiff finally wore a concerned expression. Her chromophores dimmed.

I returned to the alley. This time I came armed with an old-fashioned inoculation gun. It was loaded with what I hoped would rewrite these people back into existence, from their genes up. My medical expertise might reveal more about me than I wanted current reality to recall. I've had other jobs and might recall a time when humanity ruled the world, not hungry freaks. Now, I stalked the shadows to elude the memory of my own failures. Perhaps those long buried monsters would come stalk me in my sleep. Yet, I had little choice but to act if I wanted to remain human. I had to first undo the harm these people suffered. The mother presented her little girl to be injected, first. If I had crafted the right cure, she would see her daughter live, at least a little longer.

Or not. I heard the whine of approaching turbines. Beams of white light lanced by the alley entrance, and grew stronger. We rushed to see the giant machine fill the street as it approached. It was a huge version of the mall cleansers, a modern street sweeper. Our heartbeats matched the vibration from scouring beams vibrating and irradiating the pavement and anything else before it. Civilization has decided to return to this zone in full, automated force. The real estate company's logo of a star swirling like a circular saw blade beamed from the huge machine's flanks. The technology of its automation and merciless function has changed, but the armored hull had lasted the ages. Even my weapons might not find a chink and stop it. All I could do was yell. Very loudly.

"Run!"

We fled. The corpse of the dead monster obliterated before the blast of the sweeper. The mechanical beast sucked up the fragmenting tissues into its blinding maw, and then exhaled sterile vapor through its grated top. I followed the last fleeing people. The sweeper detected our motion and began a deafening barrage of advertisements with holograms of properties beamed from its hull. But with no credit or ID signal, it won't stop.

"Please state price range!" echoed off dead walls.

The sweeper's sensors didn't hear my expletive reply.

We ran for a block and reached a street where someone must pay rent because the streetlamps were working. Most of the alley people ran well while being sick and breathing corrosive air. Epinephrine is wonderful. The sweeper's lights flashed in the distance as it turned down a street for more dirt, debris, potential buyers and/or victims.

"What now?" the mother asked while trying to comfort her crying child.

I hesitated to offer my answer. "I think there is a, well, a government office that could help."

One without shareholders, I hoped

Some of our human caravan disappeared back into the shadows. They had reason to flee there before they came to the alley. Most others made the pilgrimage from the desolate to the merely threatening. We ascended well-worn granite steps outside the *OFFICE OF HUMAN RESOURCES*. We entered through a hissing airlock. I did not expect to step out of it and then into another world. Inside was a steep slope of equally worn steps. The noise from a thousand conversations broke against our ears. We looked across a vast beach made of multicolored, living sand. A small wave of need carried us, here. We were one of many to wash against this shore.

Inside, the smells of industry, food, and refuse drifted up from a repopulated, ancient ruin. The current inhabitants paid no attention to the relics they surrounded. Only the latest immigrants with me noticed the stalactites of dust and airborne sediment hanging from marble arcades high overhead. People flowed or collected around the spiral columns supporting that inverted landscape. Human beings composed this sprawling, city within the city, not structures. Thriving market places spread out from two, tall doors before the actual office. This civilization outside those doors was just the people waiting in the lobby.

"Here," I said to the mother. I dropped a glistening capsule into her palm. "It's an infomere. It has games and an encyclopedia. I intended it for your daughter, but it looks like you'll need something to trade. Parcel it out."

"What about my daughter?" the mother asked. "See was born without a permit."

I drew a deep breath and looked out across the expanse of lobby. "By the time you reach the office, she'll be tall enough so that no one will bother to ask questions."

I turned to leave. Some offered a fractured chorus of gratitude. Others questioned if thanking me was appropriate.

"I'm not finished, yet." I answered, and entered the airlock.

Schiff looked at me with surprise. Seeing someone over the same issue twice in one day was a complete unknown at her office. It had been a long day. It was time it was over.

Godforsaken. If anyone still prayed, that would be the word to describe where I took Schiff. The permanent darkness colored the air. Schiff nervously clung to a dying street lamp. The corroded metal stained her white coat.

"Monsters are everywhere." I told Schiff, although the reality was suddenly quite clear to her. "They have many different forms. I used another kind of viroid to delete your files from this district's dataframe. You have no credit. No identity. Here, you don't exist. It won't be hard for you to re-establish yourself from a com-link uptown. All you have to do, is walk home."

The idea terrified Schiff. She tried to speak. Her face scowled, and then melted into a strangled plea. Her chromophores went as dark as the clouded sky. I entered a building stairwell from the sidewalk. Behind me, the armored door slammed shut. I, too, would walk through the darkness, but in another direction. Somewhere, hunger had penetrated again. There, too, the screams suddenly fell silent under the permanent shadows.

05
DREAM OF REASON

Who are we in our dreams? We are not what other people see in real life. Many conscious eyes have looked across me and not seen what is truly there. Many inhuman eyes have glared at me. I am the last thing many have seen. I am not the destroyer of worlds, but I am a hunter. And, therefore, a killer. Am I different to human and non-human eyes? Perhaps, what I see in myself is most important. Or not. When I dream, I see the surreal world around me. In a sense, I am looking inside my mind. Or not. Although in worlds real and imaginary, I face monsters.

I found myself standing in the middle of a rustic, arching, wooden bridge built over a wide, placid stream. I knew what wood is in this dream, although I had rarely seen it. In fact, images of times far gone created a world I never walked. Seed down floated in the air. Stands of alders swayed in slow rhythm on each bank of the stream. Soft light illuminated everything. There is a gentle sun in the morning sky.

A thought occurred to me. I was certain it was my own, yet it felt from another mind in a past age. *I don't know why I still come here. It's always the same, but forever changing.*

A winsome woman with very long, blonde hair appeared on the bridge in a pale summer dress. The change of seasons was now a historic note on the calendar more than change in weather or wardrobe. Oddly, the woman always kept the front of her body facing mine.

"It's lovely here isn't it?" The woman said. She then took my hand. "You should come to the shade."

Walking backward, she led me off the bridge. I followed her reluctantly. We came to a flat, sandy stream bank.

"It's lovely here isn't it?" she repeated.

She encircled her arms around my neck and pulled herself up to kiss me. I felt tranquil. I moved my arms around her slender form. And then jerked backward in shock. I pulled her sideways and backward by gripping her left arm and the thick, tendon-like tendril attached to her back. It swept down from her spine and into the stream. My seducer became suddenly, strangely blank and rigid.

The stream roiled. A giant, spiny rockfish surged out of the water. Its mouth opened as it rushed straight at me. Above the maw, the tendril attached to the woman connected to its brow.

Time slowed. It can do that in dreams. It only seems to in waking life.

Other thoughts came to mind. *Fear. I still feel it.*

The shadow of the monstrous fish slowly fell across me.

It can all be over, if I just stay still.

If I had been clothed in the dream to that point, I was unsure. Suddenly I was well aware of what I wore. It felt heavy. My gray overcoat and the weapons it covered now hung over me. Time resumed. The rockfish nearly engulfed him in its horrific jaws.

No!

I threw my coat open. I aimed my shotgun and fired. The blast obliterated the attacking giant. It was gone. Blood coated the bank and mingled with the stream. The woman, the monster's lure, lay collapsed on the sand with the tendril severed. She raised an arm to me.

"Nn—Noah?" she said in a low and weak voice.

"Noah?" I asked and kneeled beside the remnant of the odd creature. Flecks of blood covered her face.

"You must s—save—" She became ashen white, and still.

I noticed the tendril stretched back under the rippling stream. I pulled it like a rope out of the dark water. I hauled an attached body onto the bloody sand. It was me, naked and with a body ravaged by my gun blasts the moment before. People have said that you can't die in your dreams. They lied. Your past can hunt you in dreams. There, time has no real movement. Or maybe they show your future. Or maybe, I reasoned, it was just a nightmare. Nightmares have one advantage. In them, you can wake up from death.

In the next moment, I did wake up. The dark place was familiar. But it was slashed by familiar pulses of green light. My wrist com signaled a new client needed me.

Time to get up, get dressed, and go to work.

06
NOIR

Snake eyes. In the age of monsters, something serpentine with two, or maybe three or more eyes threatens a murderous hunger. Snake eyes also means two dots on a pair of dice, even today. You might wonder that if walking on a dark street risks your life, then why gamble in other ways. People don't need to gamble their money on games of chance. Yet the old promise of sudden wealth and thrills without imminent death keeps gambling a viable enterprise. It happens in legal halls and illicit backrooms. So does people being killed and eaten. Fear of sudden death and the hope of stopping it keep me in business and taking risks. My job is a needed enterprise. Welcome to the future.

The welcome to my latest job at an illicit gambling hall was a low snarl by its proprietor, Leo. He became more sociable—or not—and added: "Monster freaks are getting worse than vermin!"

Leo said it as if *I* was the freak and not its answer. Perhaps he thought my profession of monster killing was in league with the freaks we fight and kill so people like him can complain another day. Running a covert business might skew his imagination to thoughts of other hidden commerce. Leo was the definition of *thug* in any industrial age. His body was large. His well-oiled hair was as flat as a slick on water across the top of his thick skull, yet unkempt and curling around his neck like a dead octopus. His tight, shiny, black suit was tailored to fit, once. Now its wrinkle abating cloth worked overtime to appear pressed while Leo moved in quick, jerking movements. Leo's attitude cooled as if a thought struck him and he was momentarily numbed from the impact.

We walked through a wide hall with collection of antique gaming equipment. Two other thugs loitered in the hall. Roulette wheels, card whirls, blackjack, and craps tables all sat ready for missing crowds. Obviously, the old games were still effective at entertaining and creating thrills. The card compartments and old magnetic tech hidden inside them were also still effective at fixing the odds.

Not every aspect of the hall was about gambling. Other machines were as addictive to some. Old-style virtual e-mersion booths offered fake experiences of violence and other vices. The rippling titles offered *Kill the Monster! Kill More Monsters! Kill All Monsters!* The booth with the most wear beamed *Love Your Neighbor's Monster.* I wasn't sure if I should just shoot it as prophylaxis for idiots in real life. Other booths didn't trust bloodlust or imagination to attract users. Cartoon and human characters solicited entrants with smiles and other entreating gestures.

I'd never seen an animated mouse assume such positions.

Blatant gambling returned with a line of archaic slot machines at a right angle to the booths. These never had a slot or used coins. To jerk the handle or slap the wheel and see a kaleidoscope resolve into a winning shape, you needed to let them access to your financial accounts, while they lasted.

Another attraction stood off to the side of more gaming tables. She leaned against a baccarat table and ran her fingers along its edge. Her black hair and clothes were styled like a twenties flapper, except that the dress ended well above her knees. Leo pretended not to notice, but his heart rate and blood flow indicated otherwise. Her caress of the tables was more alluring than the flagrant holograms, perhaps because she was real. I covertly scanned her to be sure. I was in a place that institutionalized avarice and stared at by a living personification of sensuality. Perhaps it was good that I was heavily armed. You never knew how things evolve.

"The monster is back here. Damn ugly. Big." Leo kept walking at the same, quick pace to a doorway at the back. I thought the monster must be sated or somehow contained. People rarely charge into their lairs just to save time. I noticed someone had already met the beast. Leo stepped over a dark smear of haphazardly mopped fluid. I frowned as I thought about a mop as final resting place for the only surviving remains. The smear was human blood.

"Hard to find good help," I said looking at the smear.

"But not marks, thankfully." Leo said. He noticed that I stared at the smear. "That was Mallet. He worked for me."

"I see you're busted up over his loss."

"I'm busted up losing business," Leo snapped. "But you're going to fix that. And quick."

I wasn't sure if Leo's words were an expression of confidence in my skill or a quickly spat threat. I'd be paid either way. But if no other people were at risk, the job might take more time than it needed to, after that comment. My meter was running.

"In here," Leo jerked his head toward the rear doorway.

Beyond the door was a dank hallway. To the left, the hall continued to a missing wall torn down to access an old city conduit now filled with shadows. I stared down it, expecting something to stare back at me. The monster was not there.

"Backdoor to freedom," Leo said.

"To the street?" I asked.

"Yeah."

"Then it's the entry point of your monster," I told him.

"Huh," Leo shrugged. "I'll install a scanner. And a gun."

"You should install a wall." I said.

"No way." Leo shook his head. "I need a place to run. Always have a way out."

"To the street?" I asked again.

Leo stayed silent, but checked his belt where his handgun rested perhaps on considering my point.

"Your job is in the vault room," Leo said and turned to a door on the right.

Inside was a big thug. He didn't need his loud, plaid jacket to stick out. I realized I'd never seen a bright, plaid jacket, and understood why. The thug guarded a vault door pocked with bullet impacts. The ricochets had slashed the concrete walls. The large vault it sealed was likely a converted, walk-in freezer. I hoped but doubted the small arms fire did more damage to the thing trapped inside. On the wall by the vault door dangled a bullet-riddled control panel with an old palm reader. It hung on old wires that trapped old insulation and fresh rat crap.

"My boys shot up the control panel poppin' off at the thing. Dumb Ass here shut the vault door on it."

Leo didn't point, but the large, bald, and plaid-wearing thug bristled at the insult. If he had a name other than Dumb Ass he never said it. He never said anything.

"Then Dumb Ass saved your lives," I said.

"Yeah, well, now I can't reopen until the vault does." Leo growled. "Can you do it?"

"And kill the thing inside," I said. "I'll bill you for both. But Dumb Ass and friends stay out of my way."

"Fine. Good luck." Leo said, and he and Dumb Ass left.

I located the live wires and tinkered. It looked as though I could reattach the intact CPU behind the panel to power. That should work, I hoped. I had asked for space, but no one stopped the main attraction from the hall from sauntering into the vault room. The dark-haired woman leaned on wall beside me. I kept focused on the panel. She started working, too. Like a wire, she was long and lithe. Her black nails fingered a cameo broach on a red-ribbon choker adorning her subtle neck. The cut image was not something I noticed.

"Leo says they call you Ice." She said. "That's a nice name. Smooth and slippery. Mine's Noir. Can I hold your gun?"

"No," I said and felt an electric arc through my fingers.

Noir leaned against the wall close by and nearly draped herself across me. "Afraid it'll go off if I touch it?"

"It might blow a hole through you," I said, twisting the last wire in place.

Noir took her hands and folded her fingers into the shape of a pistol. She blew on the index fingers as the barrel, slowly. Then she caressed them her ebony painted lips, slowly. Not that I noticed.

"Don't worry," Noir said. "I'm bullet proof."

"My guns fire shaped explosive projectiles surrounding a unilquantium armor piercing core. Not bullets."

Noir slid down the wall with her arms pressed flat against it. Her descent was serpent smooth and silent, as if friction didn't want to defy her skin or expensive dress. Although, there was generated heat. I didn't look straight at her, and fought the urge. And to stop my cheek muscles from pulling my stony face into a smile.

"Sounds... penetrating." Noir breathed.

"Yeah," I inhaled. "You have no idea."

Noir slid closer as I worked to prop the panel back against the wall panel. "So, yours must make a bigger boom than Leo's."

"Leo shoots smaller targets," I said.

Noir stood. Her attention switched to the next room.

Breeeet! The panel made a high-tone as it came to life.

"I can be a monster too, you know." Noir said. "You should get out your gun."

"You got that right," I said and stood. "Tell Leo I need—"

I detected Leo's treachery, and calmly turned to face it. Leo and two fresh thugs in more demure jackets stood next to the doorway with guns drawn. Noir slid next to me.

"His palm print and codes." I finished saying.

"Told you," Noir said.

"I'm not done," I said. "The thing is still in the vault."

"Yeah, we got enough heat for that, now." Leo paused to consider his words weighed against his memory of the monster's size. He then nodded affirmation to himself.

"So why hire me if you were just going to kill me once the door opened?" I asked.

"You Killer guys all got skills," Leo said, "and do you know how much an electrician costs? This way I pay nothing. A Monster Killer dying on the job will ring true, even to cops. Besides, Noir likes you too much."

One of the thugs moved closer and raised his gun. .40 caliber. Small bore.

"If you open fire now she'll die, too." I said.

"True," Leo said. "But my point is more about keeping discipline than property."

"Ouch," Noir said and flipped off Leo.

"Sounds more like ego protection," I added.

"Whatever," Leo shrugged. "What's in that safe is more valuable than her. I'm not risking anyone making off with it."

I raised my hands with palms up. The thugs smiled. So did I.

"Now move next to the vault door," Leo said.

His thugs in front of me collapsed and hit the floor, asleep. Noir dropped to her knees and snatched up a thug's dropped pistol.

"What the—? What just happened?" Leo yipped as he looked at his suddenly unconscious muscle littering the floor.

Noir aimed her recovered gun at Leo. I reached into my coat and pulled out the canister attached to the tube down my sleeve. Bright words on the canister beamed *Nap Fog Plus. New! Improved!* Below the words, animate labeling showed a smiling man hit by a small cloud who then fell unconscious. The animation repeated as I tossed the canister.

Leo ran. I heard him bark orders to more thugs. I sighed. They wouldn't get close enough for a nice tranq mist with fresh, potpourri scent. I pulled my heavy, Aquila handgun. Compared to most automatics, it's a small missile launcher.

"C'mon out, Ice!" Leo yelled. "We're cool. We just want you gone, now. We won't shot if you don't!"

I told Noir to stay. Of course, as soon as I showed myself outside the backdoor, Leo, Dumb Ass, and another, thinner thug opened fire. But Noir and I had no other way out other than bolting passed the door and being shot at anyway. Then we could face other monsters down the conduit while being easy targets for Leo's guns. I also didn't want to find out if they had grenades or bigger noise makers. Luckily, I'm fairly quick. Being able to sense finger tension on triggers helps with timing. I leapt to the side as Leo and friends squeezed. Several shots went high, but five hit my torso. The small, automatic rounds went through my coat but bounced off my sheer body armor, good for most teeth, claws, and standard goon rounds.

When their salvo failed, Leo and his thugs took cover behind a blackjack table. My return fire was louder. The two shots struck and obliterated large chunks of wall over their lousy cover. The debris hit them behind the blackjack table. I fired and it blew up in front of them.

"Geez!" Leo yelled.

I ducked next to a roulette wheel as Leo's two goons gave haphazard return fire. I considered a new definition of *crime wave* as they all dove and rolled behind a craps table. They had to hope there were more tables than I had ammo. This was clear when that table became shards in the air and splinters in their skin when my next rounds exploded. Leo's thinner thug didn't want to play those odds. He leapt up and fired at where I was the previous second.

"Sterno!" Leo yelled after the man with amplified dread.

I fired one round. It hit Sterno at center mass. Leo's most courageous and stupid hood blew apart. A red spray flew across the hall. The sudden, horrific cloudburst hit Leo and Dumb Ass. Leo screamed and shook off some of Sterno from his face.

"Okay!" Leo screeched as his senses mostly returned. "You win! We quit!"

Leo tossed his gun towards me. Dumb Ass did likewise. I kept my gun leveled at them as we all stood. They came closer with hands up. Then Leo shoved Dumb Ass toward me and bolted into the backroom. Dumb Ass shrugged with an apologetic expression. Then he squinted as if expecting a loud noise and tried to punch me.

My spy stud recorded the events in the vault room. Leo entered, panting. Noir stood holding the recovered gun behind her back. Leo took note of her with a nervous glance.

"Say Leo, did you mean any of that stuff before?" Noir asked.

"Nah, it was just to throw him off," Leo said.

Noir leveled her gun at Leo's head. First, he looked at the muzzle with shock. Then, his face drooped with resigned recognition.

"Too bad," Noir sighed. "I sure wish I had Ice's gun."

Leo's face flashed true terror.

We heard the shot in the hall, but Dumb Ass and I were otherwise engaged. Noir placed her left, stiletto heel on the right arm of Leo's fresh corpse and stuck the gun against the wrist.

"Hold still honey," Noir said to her dead boss. "You're heavy but I need your palm."

There were more shots. In the hall, I evaded Dumb Ass's attack. I was kind enough not to simply fire and make him join Sterno as a brief, crimson cloud. He swung again. I imagined the meaty fists doing damage. I wasn't kind enough to stand there and allow it. I dodged the blow.

Inside the vault room, Noir pressed Leo's bullet-severed hand against the repaired control panel screen. The vault opened. She quickly lifted Leo's hand to the darkness inside it as an offering.

"Monster?" Noir said as she peered into the vault. "Here, babe. You ate Mallet, not me. I know you like me. You can eat Leo, now. I just want—"

Dumb Ass swung again. He zeroed in better on his target, my head. More red splashed the ceiling, but only from the edge of my gun creasing his skull. Dumb Ass fell with a *thud!* On the floor, his eyes were open but rolled back. He'd wake up and likely have one major clean-up chore nursing a headache and bandage. He survived, again.

Noir didn't share the thug's fate. I heard her scream. Maybe the high shriek held tones of disbelief mated with utter, naked fear. I bolted into the backrooms. Even fast, I was far too slow. All I found was Noir's choker on a bloody scrap of ribbon next to Leo's ravaged body. Traces of Noir and the beast lead straight down the conduit. I followed. The passage was tight, but I forced through to the ripped open grating flanked by dumpsters nearly a block from the gambling hall. I emerged in an alley filthier than most that met a noisy, indifferent street. The trail took a right angle up the side of an older skyscraper. The flexcrete tower was high for human scale. However, surrounding, glassy super-towers piercing the constant black clouds had aged it to a dwarf building. There was no residual heat. The beast was gone. Traces showed it had scaled the building's rough, eroded sides. It was well adapted to city life.

At the start of the upward track, a large sack of diamonds sat burst open as if having been dropped from a distance. Noir must have held it in a death grip all the way from the vault. It was that important to her. No matter how the world changes, some baser instincts stay the same. Sex. Greed. Hunger. In some, they grow in size. Some want more than what they have, or need. They want so much, it consumes them. For Noir, something else did that, literally.

I looked closer at the diamonds. They were not compressed carbon. They weren't truly diamonds. They were data crystals. I guessed that from recalling old pages in another archaic data storage format: books. Today, no one thinks about the technology of holograms. They weave artificial entities around and above us. They are as common as the air we breathe. And as degenerative to our minds. Mostly. Old hologram tech stored information. Lasers cut micro images into the interiors of crystal media. The images held information. Only specific lasers could retrieve that data. These crystals probably held identities, true and false, bank records, blackmail data, and whatever else crime networks could use to punish and profit off people. Few sets of eyes could recognize the crystals. Fewer people could hack the files. The data wasn't formatted for present technology. Most likely, a gangster, hood, or sanitation worker with a degree in engineering found an old set of data crystals and laser reading unit in a layer of urban sediment. That person deduced its operation. Later, the finder, or a friend, or a bright thief sold the ancient tech to create an unreadable, undetectable, underground information network. Smart. I'm sure the police would think so, as well.

Some of my systems transmit information as curls of RNA that enter my brain as new memories. Other systems relay data in a style familiar to many eras, as numbers, words, and graphics. I used a synthesis of data collection and communication technology. Not one part of it could read the crystals. That would require a curious engineer. I was a well-worked Monster Killer. My own systems generated the potential path of the fleeing predator now far away. It had also logged pleas from potential clients surely less murderous than a certain dark lady.

No one would find Noir. She killed for greed and gambled her life. She lost. Anything left of her would be gone before me or another Killer shot the thing that ate her. Dumb Ass, or someone else, would patch the gambling hall and the monster older than the beasts in the shadows would come alive, again. I would keep stalking the things sating their hunger on the victims of stacked decks, and any chaste people taking the high-stakes risk of coming home.

Reload. Roll the dice.

07
FREAKS

Reality is inverted. Ecology has met apocalypse. It's something to keep in mind when walking modern streets. An ocean of perpetual black floats above the city paved Earth. Massive skyscrapers cut dark, rolling clouds into sharp channels. The blackest channels slowly eat away the towering glass and steel shores. That is not what is eaten far below. Most of this stratified civilization drifts at the bottom of the global maze. Monsters strike in the cracked streets and blind alleys. They eat the slow and stupid, the smart, the strong, and all else who are unlucky in one second of a lifetime. I kill freakish beasts adapted to the global city so many of the soft and all too human prey can live longer. My license reads Joshua Grail. Where I walk, survival is perverted. Welcome to the future.

It was late night. Black as day, naturally. I had done my job inside one of the towers. The interior gleamed, except where my explosives rounds had blasted leg shards and tissue of a fleshy spider-like thing with chainsaw jaws. The beast had found an empty storage chamber in a large, lobby couch. Then it just waited for people to come sit down beside it. Eventually, I came along and blew the spider thing away. I bagged the body, registered the bounty, and dropped the heavy bag into a refuse shaft. The janitors, living and robotic, would clean the floors, walls, and crystal lighting fixtures. And they might want to vacuum inside that comfy couch, after the coroner collected the shrunken and desiccated remains.

The tenants I saw were probably moving out, even though I made their floor safe, for a while. Those that stayed would be glad when I left. Inside this horizontal world, my large frame and spattered trench coat met frightened glances and arrogantly turned heads. Most people here never saw a rough surface or a spot that wasn't color coordinated and carefully placed among art or advertising. It didn't matter that I spared them a terminal moment on the comfy couch. I violated the polished world. At least the spider thing kept out of site.

The tower's security system pulled my name from the directory of Biological Aberration Eradication Specialists. We are licensed, arsenal toting exterminators. Or simply, Monster Killers. My class of worker is the cheap solution for hungry nuisances with audacity to creep up from the streets and eat leaseholders. I assume all humans taste the same, despite elevation. Although I doubt monsters share culinary information.

I was one byte of information processed by the security system, a complex program called a Specific Intelligence. It calculated I had the best chance of making the statement that only one Monster Killer is needed for one monster to make safety true. $1+1=T$. Simple logic. And it works, most of the time. Specific Intelligences processed vast amounts of data, but additions to their code kept them from being self-aware. In theory. Today, society considers artificial sentients another form of monster. Human-like interfaces dropped from favor long ago when they acted a little too interactive in true human affairs. Some even wanted odd things like greater opportunities, equal rights, and recognition for creative works. The subsequent SI's were faceless, voiceless, and focused solely on task. They managed several super-towers, and were my occasional employers. This one actually paid me for my work, promptly. Plus it added a bonus for validating its deduction. I appreciated the kind thought.

Still, job done meant time to leave. The elevator gave an almost negative-G ride to the street's dust and shadows. My wristcom flashed green. I activated its holograph. I could display the image across my retina, but I was tired and grouchy and didn't want another person inside my head.

For a moment the holographic bust of a man who appeared to be a standard-issue, second-story citizen floated above my wrist. He wore clean clothes. Clean skin. A stranger. I didn't want another job. Even with enhancements, both biological and otherwise, I can get fatigued. Fatigue can get me eaten. This night I wanted sleep and the usual nightmares. I dropped my arm to my side and waited for the caller to disconnect. On his display, he could only see my distorted reflection in the polished elevator walls and the long row of lights indicating the car's fast trip, downward.

"J. Grail, or do you like Mr. Ice?" The man asked.

I was silent. He pressed on.

" "Um, could you come to this address? I—"

"I'm not interested." I said. "Lock yourself in something strong and call the cops. They're cheaper, anyway."

"Everyone else, including your colleagues, is either dead or employed tonight. I'll pay you double if you come."

His tone was a strangely entreating. The typical attitude held that street life should come running for any bone the towers throw out. I have enough ivory stored to afford contempt, but my true motivation was to make myself horizontal on a cot.

"No. Call in the morning." I said. "If you still can."

"Well, all right then. Tomorrow morning." He sounded pleased. "I'll wait for you there."

His dangled image vanished. He seemed strange. This man wasn't arrogant, or frightened. I decided to meet him the next day. I was curious. I survived curiosity better than most cats. Then I wondered if any cats survived on Earth. Maybe they live in a tower zoo, next to the silicon processor, and klarschlange.

The elevator car scanned safe. As I waited for the rapid descent to end, I leaned back. Eventually the elevator doors would open and I could start for home. Until then, I could rest.

Morning. Black as night. I arrived at the site sent to me by last night's caller, Mr. Gray. The warehouse there was ancient. I knew of it, but thought it abandoned by both man and monster. The sagging building somehow escaped destruction to make room for a small part of the massive foundations needed for the towers jutting into the ashen sea, overhead. Inside, the rusting warehouse was empty. Its weakly lit interior was a small vacuum among the dense flow of humanity around and above. Mr. Gray seemed to fit the odd scene. He was a small man. He had waited outside long enough for the leeching dust that drifted down from the clouds to coat his skin and clothes. It robbed him of all color. Not that there was enough light to see color. He wore no respirator. The same dust should have also aggravated his throat and lungs. Somehow he resisted coughing, as if he was used to the inhaled irritants.

Gray still smelled nicer than the sheen of slog I had pushed through to hack an unexpected bounty, en route. Gray sidestepped the bigger drops from the end of my overcoat. He did not walk away. He scanned clear of enhancements. Nominal genes. He also didn't register fear or contempt from my long downward stare and violations of his personal space. He continued to be placid and accepting, as if the only difference between us was nearly two feet in height. This was a very strange man.

"I wasn't aware this warehouse had an owner." I said as we approached its center.

"It does now." Gray said without the expected pride of a property owner. "And there is definitely something big beneath it. I really don't want anyone else to die. You can destroy the entire structure. If you wish."

"You're sure this site has no squatters?" I asked. "People have kept away since the monster arrived?"

"Oh yes!" Gray chirped. "There is no one around it. No one at all."

I found that odd. People are every monsters' food. They usually don't need personal space, just a full stomach. We came to a large trapdoor. If the beast were above us, it or we would be dead by now. I withdrew a gun styled like a large, autoloading pistol. My choice of method disturbed the odd Mr. Gray. His brow furrowed when I reached for the trapdoor. I'd never seen anyone disappointed when a monster was about to die. Or was it actual fear for my life?

"I don't think you should risk confronting it," Gray said. For the first time I heard a hint of nerves in his voice. "I thought you'd gather more information, first. Perhaps you should use a gas. A large volume of poison gas."

"And risk creating another poison-resistant monster? There is a reason I use these tools, Mr. Gray." I brandished the gun.

"A large bomb then?" Gray offered in a pleading tone.

"Too loud."

There are other reasons behind my confrontation style I didn't explain to him, in case he was a psychologist and could understand them. I opened the trapdoor and descended as Gray appeared to struggle for a phrase to stop me. The end of the gun nosed through the dark ahead of me. The hollow point of my present-day spear relayed and magnified motion, sound, and scents through nanoscopic connections in my skin. The sensations are indescribably heightened when I fire. Failsafes are supposed to act as buffers. They almost work. Perhaps I should check for a software issue. Nevertheless, to pull the trigger is to feel as if part of me explodes in blind rage at the monster. A part of me does, but not the weapon. Revenge, for love lost. Time and hardened sorrow bury those emotions. Almost.

I focused on my task and data. I prowled the rotting basement and detected remnants of human filth and debris. There was no sign of what drove the people away. The rats looked comfortable and uncaring. Mr. Gray seemed eager for me to annihilate this place. Insurance money, or—

Motion!

A rusted length of pipe flew out at me from a shadowed doorway. The concrete wall had blocked my sensors. I retaliated at the charging target. One shot. A bright, sharp flash and deafening boom. The explosion ebbed. Infrared imaging and FRACDAR revealed the blood mist and shattered remains as they fell to the soiled floor. The method of attack was bizarre. Monsters come equipped with weapons more devastating than old pipe. My weapon OS reassembled scans of the body fragments into the best approximation of the attacker's form. The resulting model played across my mind's eye. It held a misshapen, humanoid form. I scanned the scattered tissues and blood for deeper analysis. It was human!

I reeled and wondered why the person attacked me. Then I wondered how, even on this Earth, could a person's physiology become that twisted. I knew it couldn't be a birth defect. Pregnancy is banned on the streets. Prophylactic compounds in the water enforce population control. Perhaps the wealthy can pay a colossal fine if they used private water and ignored the law. However, medical scans would likely monitor gestation from zygote to newborn for defects. My scans flagged artificial strands in the attacker's genome. But the alterations were insane, not therapeutic.

As I swept for other threats, recollections of history gave me the likely genesis of my attacker. I recalled vids of tower dwellers gawking and looking away from people remade into similar horrors. Those people posed on a base for display. Decoding our genome allowed the human tapestry to be unraveled and reworked. Once needles and threads fixed tissue tears. Advances created microscopic looms that worked within cells to remove malignant strands and repair or add fabric to bodies and genes. Though, in the quest for cures and perfection, sometimes a stitch was misplaced, a reject formed. Some found a use for weaving aberrations, and perfected the flaws. With time and technology, that became easier and thus more likely. Aesthetic debate eventually took place on a living, human canvas. There were plenty of volunteers to be a public curio. It was supposed to be a temporary state. The consequences proved longer term. Cubist nightmares were freed from the canvas to roam the streets begging for food. Some called them the first monsters. I thought they were all eaten by the real ones.

A thin edge of light cut through the darkness. It beamed from the slit of a closed doorway. I open it. Beyond the metal door was a cavernous room. It held an underworld populated by forms stranger than all the paintings of Bosch viewed in high fever. Cubist people stirred. A murmur rose. Twisted limbs flexed. Elongated faces expressed caution like a shouted voice. Geometric shapes that were once bone and skin bent and straightened. Swollen folds parted to reveal curious eyes and organs. Living masses slid alive as if a wax frieze now melted. The cubists slowly began to roll, walk, and undulate. Some lurched instinctively to guard other odd shapes. They seemed to be lying across the floor, waiting for some mass event and not a lone stranger. There was no fear of me, the armed intruder, only surprise. I was shocked. These people must have kept hidden for decades. A giant face on stunted limbs approached me.

"Congratulations, Killer. You found us. Now do your job." It—he challenged.

"Do what?" I asked, and lowered my gun.

"Start killing!" The cubist man's giant expressions contrasted with the flailing of his childlike limbs. "End your nausea with your guns."

"You want me to kill you?" I realized the attacker with the pipe was part of a larger picture.

"No, I want to live like this for the rest of my life." The cubist's immense expressions magnified his sarcasm and anger. "Do it!"

"Look, spare me the attitude—"

"Freak? Say it." The cubist screeched. His voice was becoming weak. His lungs and larynx were not in proportion to his mouth. "We know we're all monsters in your eyes."

"So far, you alone are beginning to create that impression." I glared down at the misshapen man I would have felt rare pity for a moment ago. I could exterminate this entire enclave and collect a bounty for each. Away from the warehouse, few people would care that is was mass murder. I had not yet traveled that far into the darkness. I put my inner rage in smoldering check, and my gun inside my coat.

"Mister Grail! Bool!" Gray shouted from the doorway.

As Gray rushed to me and the giant face named Bool, another cubist man approached. His ribcage flared out like butterfly wings. The vestiges of his arms curved as if to form a halo when lifted above his head.

"You weren't supposed to find them until afterward, if at all." Gray said to me with disappointment.

"You hired me to kill these people?" I asked with naked contempt.

"Yes." Gray answered without guilt. "Zero here is my father." He embraced the man with grotesquely elongated ribs. "I was born after most of these people were, well, reborn. They raised me to be their agent with the outside world. I found places for us to live and hide. I've tried to protect them as best I could."

"Then why hire me?" I shouted. I found Gray's calm acceptance of actions more bizarre than the shapes of the surviving cubists.

"We thought you'd be faster and more thorough than mass suicide." Zero answered.

I looked at them all with mingled surprise and disgust.

"Is that so hard to grasp?" Zero asked. "Look at us. We live as outcasts from human society and the prey of monsters."

"So instead of living like rats and dying like cattle, we've taken destiny into our own hands." Bool furthered. "Those of us who have hands."

"But there are treatments—" I began.

"That made us like this!" Bool flailed his small limbs in protest. "And even if we could afford a reweave, we would still bear a stigma and be back on the streets. We have nothing!"

"You're wrong." I answered. "You, Bool, have a great deal of despair and self hate."

"Don't get sanctimonious with us, normal!" Bool screeched through massive, clenched teeth.

"You organized this mass death, didn't you?" I asked Bool.

"Yes! Could you live like this?"

"I don't live like this. You do."

"And so—!" Bool began.

"Take a nap." I interrupted him with a mist sprayed from a small cylinder labeled *NAP FOG, PLUS: From screams to silence in less than a second!* I kept it part of my hysterical client/crowd-control kit. As advertised, Bool collapsed into sleep.

I turned to the mass of cubist people gathering closely around us. I did not want to intimidate my antagonists, nor bring sudden death. I wanted to find the right words as I fought through the shock threatening to wrap the experience in disbelief.

"There are treatments that can help you. That work." I said to the confused glances and defiant stares. These strange people actually made eye contact. "You may carry a stigma for anyone who learns your past, but each of you still has the potential do something that the people who remade you didn't. You can look to the future. You can find a better life for yourselves. It's a better place than this."

I turned to leave, but saw Bool's unconscious form. I knew he'd wake up, unchanged. I had to leave a stronger impression.

"You came together and survived for a long time." I said. "You share a common goal. It doesn't have to be death. As long as you are alive, you are more than food for a monster, any kind of monster."

Outside the warehouse, I waited with the remains of my attacker neatly collected by an automated body bag. A municipal disposal unit descended from the transit lanes above to my location. The craft was twelve dented cylinders surrounding a rusted oval. The craft's levdrive hummed while it hovered. An empty cylinder rotated to face me. It opened with a hiss of foul air.

"Mr. Grail, wait!" Gray called from behind. His voice echoed through the empty warehouse. "I thought—"

"Keep thinking. It beats the alternative." I said and dropped the body inside the open cylinder. The bagged corpse was small compared to the space reserved for the city's typical predators. There was an echo as the black bag hit metal.

"But some still agree with Bool." Gray dropped his head. His mind was conflicted and confused. Choice can do that. "I have a duty to execute their wishes."

Gray's actions seemed clear to him hours ago. Now he wrestled with a decision that would affect his and many lives.

"Then you can hire another Killer, or you can buy food and medical help. You and your people still have a choice, Gray. Convince them to think it through. Oblivion is just another monster's gut. I, for one, refuse to be eaten."

The disposal unit grew impatient of my neglect to register the bounty and sounded three low tones. I didn't do it. I knew unregistered kills were scanned. Perhaps the person would then be identified. Certainly the scans would find human DNA. This zone's perpetually updating census trackers would note the human death and its location. A police drone would investigate the site. That, and my own call, might bring help before another Killer did what I refused to do.

The disposal unit shot back into the moldered air. I also turned to leave. I could not kill the beasts at war in Gray's mind. He walked slowly back inside the warehouse, still in conflict. I walked away through the forbidding streets. It was not yet noon. Somewhere there was another monster in a dark place. However, there were other Killers working. Hopefully those with little conscience would stay busy and away from here. I felt like avoiding the usual nightmares, and headed home.

08
SOCIAL CONTRACT

The city. It's everywhere. All natural land is covered or devoured. *Terra firma*, as it was, is forgotten. Geology gave way to hidden and collapsed layers of construction. *Terra urbana* is humanity's current world. A cycle of build, rebuild, and then build more buried the planet. People filled the ever-rising floors. People who can afford life above the streets, anyway. Everyone else must live in the crannies and shadows among the towers. Ecology, of a sort, asserts itself in the dark. Freakish things from the buried, polluted places come crawling. They take and eat humans in the dark niches. I stalk those predators. I can't say the job keeps me off the street because I work at street level, mostly. Like most people, monsters can't pay the elevator fees.

My license offers the name Joshua Grail. It allows me access to hidden and forgotten places. At times those sites are as strange as the things I stalk. Yet many are like tombs or charnel pits. They make me turn down the chemosensors that amplify my standard-issue human nose. Death has its own, strong odor. So do the sewers of a massive population. This I discovered on a notable day. I walked to the mouth of a cavernous drain intake. No water flowed anywhere. These deep channels are now merely caves. Water is too precious to flow freely. However, hunger raced out from here in a form fast and savage. I came to make it still. I considered the irony that humanity left caves to conquer and then nearly destroy the Earth, and now we're back fighting hungry beasts in the darkness. I approached the beast's lair just as many hunters did so, long ago. Alone.

The monsters of this age didn't rise from evolution's random path, but from the id of science cast into the sewer. They were fruitful, and multiplied. That sewer went unchecked, and its monsters flooded the world. Perhaps we should call this age *terror urbana*. Either way, welcome to the future.

I can use a synthetic vision called FRADAR linked to my eyes from my weapons' sensors. My unseen augmentations are personal secrets beneath my thick skin. On this hunt I opted for an old-fashioned means of detection. A light on the end of my rifle blasted a bright cone ahead of me as I crept through the artificial caverns. Light can be a weapon in dark places and blind eyes adapted to blackness. My link with the rifle let me feel the beam sweep across the curves and cracks of the cold concrete walls as tactile sensation. Painted and etched graffiti and crude drawings sprawled across the tunnel sides. They are not illustrations of spears or antelope. They were warnings to turn and run. In addition, one interrupted note of defiance. The line of paint indicated something grabbed the artist from behind. Part of his hand still gripped the spray can tossed down the tunnel.

Farther in, more parts of other artists, homeless souls, and hapless passers-by formed a small dam in the dry channel. I stepped through a field of cracked bones. Only human bones. We are the most available prey on Earth. I considered another irony that there is limited strength in numbers when the population surpasses one trillion, or two. Three? It's easier to ignore your neighbor's disappearance when it gives you an extra square inch to stretch. For some people, anyway. Someone called me to come kill this thing. Such is modern civic duty.

I don't need heightened senses to taste the stench at the tunnel intersection. Or hear the beast move. The light beams struck the monster's clawed feet. Intensifying the light has no effect on it. The thing has no eyes. Twitching bat-like ears sweep across the top of its massive head. Stabbing, high tones drown my rising heartbeats. Its body held the shape of a compact *Allosaurus*. There were modern improvements. Webbed claws formed menacing scoops beneath its gaping mouth. Serrated teeth jutted out at imperfect angles. All those savage tools united with an indomitable will to survive by eating my species, and now possibly me. It charged.

I fired. The blast outshined the light beam and rocked the tunnel. The monster's head shattered into blood mist and ballistic chunks. It fell. Dark red spattered the graffiti, the dry channel bed, and me. Survival of the fittest doesn't apply if the gun's caliber is big enough. I took a deep, involuntary breath of the rancid air as I backed away from the contorting claws. My sensors amplitude returned to normal. It had lowered to adjust against the light and loudness of the rifle shot. Still, my ears rang. The monster's huge ears were now just fleshy pieces.

For a moment, I relaxed. Stealth protocols eased. Then I jumped at another high tone as a green light flashed from my wristcom. I'm glad potential customers did not see my two meter plus frame twitch. At least my finger stayed cool on the trigger. I blinked and nanoscopic projectors put the face of a worried man in my field of vision. I switched from a live feed on my end to a display of my exterminator's license to block him seeing the fresh carcass. He looked queasy enough.

"Mr. Grail, are you working now?" The man asked impatiently. "I want to hire you. Now."

"You're in luck," I said. "I just became available."

I met my new client, a Mr. Sperren, at his dank factory. We left the dark clouds for a high roof lined with aging, tubular lamps. Their bleaching light seemed to die before it hit the wet floor. We walked among large pipes the same as any era. The plumbing and equipment became progressively more complex as we walked farther into the warehouse shell. Vats, smaller drums, throbbing plastic tubes, leaking, rusty pipes, valves and pressure gauges flowed together like three-dimensional Celtic art.

"I produce reproductive inhibitors for the government's Population Control Board," Sperren told me. "Half the water districts in this precinct use mine."

"Something to be proud of," I said dryly as I watched obvious pride light his face.

"And profitable. Even if I'm forced to employ a certain number of human workers with the automation."

Sperren motioned to a small group of people in protective garb monitoring gauges. Others pushed drums on lifting sponsons that floated the mass above the floor. There was something about pushing large objects. People assumed an angular posture as if the act was arduous, even when technology made the burden weightless. Some of the workers glanced at me with nervous relief, or grave pity.

"Problem is," Sperren continued, "workers are being eaten. And that's delaying my shipping schedule. So, the faster you can get this done, the more I'll pay."

"Start the second hand." I said. I knelt down to a loose floor drain with splotches of blood mingled with moisture.

"The what?" Sperren asked.

I didn't explain. I waved my wristcom over the drain to scan the blood and deeper tissue traces. This method is less agitating among people than aiming sensors on the end of my gun. The information flowed into my brain through my nanosys and slightly illegal RNA tech. No need for numbers with a mental download that's the same as your own thoughts. Analysis and cross-referencing become new memory.

"Your monster is either serpentine or can change its shape. The tissue traces under this grate indicate the monster butchers its victims for transport. The blood in this duct doesn't match with any of the victims on file."

"You must have some nice imbeds." Sperren said with a smug smile. "The blood must be what's left of the first Killer I hired."

"Any reason you called me next?" I asked and pretended to ignore his correct guess on how I gained my insight.

"The guy was either screaming your name or an ancient swear word when he died."

I rubbed blood between my fingertips. "Nice to have references."

"I hear they call you Ice, as well." Sperren said. "What's the story, there?"

I stood and looked down at him with a stone-faced expression. "Street name. Because I smile so much."

Sperren obviously doesn't get the joke but nodded and then looked back at the grate.

"Right," I said. "I'd better get to work."

Sperren showed me where to enter the drainage pipes and darker sites below his operation. He then left in a gait that gained speed with each step. I was alone again. Above the entry hatch, a sign read: Supply Line Access—WARNING! Today the word *warning* meant *enter and die*. Something was leaving the lines to kill. I was going into them. Whoever said intelligence gets you the big bucks? The handle protested as I turned it. Once more, into the darkness. Because of the confined space, I used sidearms. They fire the same explosive shells as my long guns, so I foresaw no problem in stopping this monster.

My quarry was particular about where it ate. If I found that place, I'd find it. I crept down the dark, cramped conduits. Scans indicated the path in the tubular world, but I only had to follow my nose. I came to an intersection. Bingo.

The monster rested across the junction. It was weird among the menagerie of people eating freaks. They rise from genetic chaos as unique beasts. That was the theory. It was not what I faced. This thing was a large, silent ball of dark-steel scales. Or dagger blades. The blades had cockroach-like heads with vicious jaws. It was a moving colony of some new species, a group of like-kind monsters. Together the blades formed a collective beast. The blades slid across each other as a wingless swarm that defied gravity. Now it was about to defy me.

The sliding stopped. It—they—noticed me.

My gun was already in hand as the colony monster rose into a bear shape composed of quickening daggers. I blasted a hole through them, killing dozens. The top half of the monster split into four tentacles. My caseless but loud rounds cut two in half. Flash and noise shields protected my senses and sensors from the blinding gun flashes. I saw the knife-edged swarm flow into a squid shape. I pulled another gun and fired at dagger-arms attacking from every direction.

Too many! Too fast!

Dagger tentacles grabbed me. Pain! Instantly they penetrated through my armor-weave clothes and into my legs and torso. A butchering cloud engulfed me. Lacerations twirled deeper into my skin.

Sensory amps: Off!

The daggers gathered into a tight, compressing mass. I fired my guns in useless convulsions. The swarm of blades wasn't the cause. Near death triggered a painful fail-safe. My belt and weapons harness fired a powerful electric field.

My body burst through the factory floor on a churning eruption of bloody daggers. Workers ran for cover from debris and scattering blades from the swarm. The insect-like monsters raced back through the crater.

The electric shock proved my salvation—just. They would have cut through the battery lines as they did my coat, clothes, and first two layers of skin. The bravest workers walked through the blood to my tattered body.

"Dear, Gates! Is he alive?"

"Get a med-cab! Now!"

I tried to speak. "No. No, hosp—"

Darkness, again. Red. Shreds of dark purple. Black. Slashes and deep cuts crisscross my memory as well as my body. I stitched together a memory from the continuous recordings of my sensors and memory RNA in my own gray drive. Luckily, the little beasts didn't penetrate my skull.

First, the workers sponsored me outside. The sky was dark and seething, like my brain. A med-cab dropped from the transit lanes that shoot between decaying skyscrapers. Impossibly higher towers rose above them and cut the black clouds. The automated med-cab snatched me into its cold belly like a great, hovering carrion beetle. In its metal gut, preservative gels coated me instead of stomach acid. They also lubricate the pneumatic stretcher. The med-cab spat me into the battered warehouse bay that serves as a modern emergency room. A filthy conveyer belt brought me through the mouth of the retracting door. My head bumped the feet of the preceding patient.

Inside, an old monitor displayed WELCOME TO DISTRICT GENERAL—REMAIN CALM in placid pink. It then flashed: RUNNING I.D./DIAGNOSTIC SCAN. And finally: UNABLE TO IDENTIFY. UNABLE TO ACCESS PROOF OF INSURANCE. SORRY. PATIENT REJECTED.

I was summarily shrink-wrapped and dropped through a trapdoor. I slammed atop a pile of fellow rejectees. I hoped they were all cadavers and not waiting for someone to claim them or give proof of coverage. That shrink wrap can itch.

For me, the unconscious black soon turned into mere darkness. Despite my rigid cocoon, I sat up. Other biological failsafes had triggered during the attack. Like the RNA tech, they are slightly illegal but necessary in my line of work. Otherwise, I may end up like my colleagues among the bodies in the pile. Later, a slash of light exploded wider. The body bay doors opened. Two talkative workers in soiled jumpsuits started perfunctorily loading bodies into a large dumpster. Advertising on its side beamed: VOLUME FUNERALS. WE BURY THE MASSES!

"And so my wife says—" One worker began.

"Oh, geez!" The man's partner yelled, and then slowly lifted the shrink wrap I had torn off and tossed aside.

49

"Maybe we should call somebody." The married worker said, and nervously peered across the vault.

"Let's just get out of here, before it comes back!"

It was only me in the shadowed corner. I borrowed clothes from my fellow corpses before I departed, alive. No one had my size. Still, the tight-fitting attire was better than traveling as a crosscut nude sporting metal accessories. I went home to rest and get clothes and weapons. Home is a cot tossed inside a buried chamber repurposed as an armory. A small, shrouded laboratory lies at one end. I kept my background in science as another secret. The floor is more paved-over layers of built-over sediment an archeologist might enjoy digging through. Only a few meters of space survive beneath the vaulted ceiling of this forgotten, gothic cathedral. My wounds filled and healed. Soon enough, it was time to go back to work.

I walked along a desolate, weakly lit street on my return to Sperren's inhibitor factory. The hull of a decrepit, centuries-old Cadillac pulled beside me. An electric unit long ago replaced its engine, but an audio system recreated the rumble of internal combustion, as far as the engineer could imagine it. A fellow Killer drove the relic. Skrymshaw leaned out and smiled. Dental plaque obscured the ornate design-work cut into his oversized teeth. A fuzz of hair grew back over his tattooed scalp. I was fairly sure both designs were some form of seascape. Maybe. Like Skrymshaw himself, the artist was not the best to hire for the job.

"Ice! Been lookin' for ya, big man." Skrymshaw bleated.

I kept walking.

"Now hold on there!" Skrymshaw continued. He stretched farther out of his Cadillac while driving. The old, maybe ancient tires kept bumping the curb as he spoke. "I can slip you something extra on bounty, Ice-man, Ice-baby. That plant you're workin' at, might be good just to blow the place."

I stopped. "Why?"

Skrymshaw stopped his car. "That monster. A bitch! Chews norms and Killers."

"There is a way to stop the monster and save the workers and plant. I'll find it."

"But," Skrymshaw shrugged with his exposed shoulder. "Might be more money if you do blow it."

"Why?"

Skrymshaw cocked his head and flashed his ornate, oversized teeth. "Just sayin'. Do it and people be happy. Graft slides your way. Dig?"

I step beside Skrymshaw's rumbling hulk and loomed over him as he hung from the driver's window. "More than money rides on this. People are in the balance."

"*Oookay. Nooo* prob." Skrymshaw smiled, shrugged, and slid inside his car. He motored off. I imagined more smog from his ride drifting into the corrosive air.

I returned to the inhibitor plant. I talked with Sperren next to massive tanks filled with his liquid wares. His aversion to my plan was nearly as huge.

"If you can't do kill it, then I'll—" Sperren began.

"I told you, we can't kill this monster by ordinary means." I said. "But your reproductive inhibitors can be altered to halt its growth. We then use them to flood its hiding place."

"Look, just poison it!" Sperren became hostile.

"I don't know if a current poison would kill it. Monsters drink our toxins. And I bet its accelerated reproduction will spawn resistant members before the dying ones drop." I pointed to his precious tanks. "The solution is right here, right now."

"Losing the shipment would ruin me! Insurance doesn't cover voluntary loss! My contracts would be nullified!"

"The problem will only mushroom, costing you more tomorrow." My voice carried over the din of the pumps. "And today, more people will die!"

"Forget it! I'll hire another Killer. One that will do his job with his mouth shut." Sperren stormed deeper into his universe of pipes.

Slowly, I turned and left.

Another trip later, I remained standing despite the offer of a decrepit chair. A thousand conversations reverberated over cubicle walls. Hundreds of other such makeshift offices stretched in all directions. And this was just one floor of the police precinct.

"I studied the file you sent." Detective Sergeant J. Slate said. "I've never seen a monster like this." His brow wrinkles into thick folds of brown.

"Neither have I." I looked at his concern with relief.

"The monster is composed of individual organisms? Bugs?" Slate asked. On his desk, a holograph projected the image of one dagger from the swarm.

"That have formed a mobile colony," I added. "All can perform the roles of any structure needed: teeth, eyes, arms. Each seems to contribute its experience to adapt to new problems. Quickly. Far too quickly."

The holograph magnified the dagger's head. A vicious, insect face with chainsaw mandibles spun, slowly. Another detective looking over the wall twisted his face in disgust.

"They survive as a whole," I said. "Where the individual thrives. They form the ultimate social contract."

"And if your calculations for its growth are correct, this could be what finally nails our society into the coffin." Slate stared as a holographic swarm replaced the individual dagger. The swarm grew to cover his desk and continued to surge. "We'd better stop it, now."

"I'm glad you see it my way." I released a long, deep sigh. I think I'd held it since the hospital.

The inhibitor plant's walls were aged, corrugated plates. They contrasted strongly to the distant but oppressive, seamless towers surrounding the plant. I walked with Slate and a small group of police technicians who wore hazardous-material suits and sidearms. Sperren stood defiantly ahead of us.

"Your inhibitors have been commandeered," Slate told him. "My men will execute their orders, now."

"You can't do this!" Sperren bellowed.

Slate glared back at him. "I'm a cop. I can do whatever the hell I want." Slate pointed to the plant entrance. His men moved toward it. "Anyone gives you a problem, shoot—"

The plant blew into a colossal fireball. The shockwave threw everyone backwards. We landed amid smoking debris. Waves of scalding steam and filthy water struck next. A few bodies rolled in the onslaught.

I rose to my knees. "There were still people in there!"

Sperren looked at the destruction. Flames curled where pipes and tanks had stood. A smile bent his blackened face. "Uh, at least I can collect insurance on this."

I stood and then ripped Sperren off the wet ground. I angrily swayed him with each grating syllable: "You did this?"

"No! I swear I didn't!" Sperren screamed.

"Then who?" I demanded. "Who did?"

"I don't know!" His fear scanned as genuine. So was his initial shock at the destruction, despite realizing its benefits.

"Who did you hire after me?" I yelled point blank into Sperren's face.

After my answer, I found and then watched Skrymshaw saunter toward an alleyway. A sheen of oil coated him and his massive rifle.

"Monsta, gon' kill you good." Skrymshaw sang to bait his prey. "Monsta!"

I grabbed Skrymshaw's neck from behind a shadowed dumpster and tossed him backward. I snatched away his rifle and used it to slam him against the alley wall. Slate pressed his gun over Skrymshaw's left eye. I kept my sensors on scan for whatever he stalked farther down the alley.

"Tell me who hired you to blow the plant, Skrymshaw!" I pressed the rifle harder against his body. "Or die."

"Easy, Ice." Slate says. "Skrym knows confession cuts prison time."

The veins on Skrymshaw's head bulged and rippled his scalp tattoo as he choked out his answer. His oversized teeth threatened to pop from his gums. "Ooo-K-kay! Molder K-Chemicals. Rivals to Sperren. Wanted his K-contacts with Water Distri-Kt. Dig? Monster eqKualed opportunity."

I released Skrymshaw and then pushed him down the alley. He stumbles backward facing me. With Slate covering Skrymshaw with his handgun, I tossed the rifle back to the startled Monster Killer.

"Now earn your bounty." I told him.

Skrymshaw scuttled deeper into the alley.

"Your letting him go?" Slate looked at me, puzzled.

I held up the ammo clip I detached from Skrymshaw's rifle. "He'll have one shot, chambered."

We heard that shot boom in the alley darkness and saw the flash. Nearly instantly, we heard Skrymshaw scream. His screaming became gargled then hollow as something ripped through his throat. Then, silence.

"You've got a way of making things final." Slate said. His reproval was clear in his glaring eyes.

"There were people in that plant." I said. "And I see things through."

I took out my own gun and followed Skrymshaw's path into the alley. Blind alleys are good places for monsters. There is only one way in, and once it's caught your scent, no way out. Some people have dark alleys in the minds. They don't care about human life beyond themselves, or about the consequence of letting monsters thrive. Who are the monsters, I wondered. A pool of Skrymshaw's blood and oil reflected my image on the ground.

Movement!

I spun. A huge, armored beast sailed in mid-leap. Its arms terminated in sickle claws outstretched from a chest of jutting spikes. I fired two, rapid shots. Each shell hit the beast at an angle, but detonated. More blood and bone splinters sprayed the alley. The thing crashed against the wall. Impulse. I fired two more shots to blast the body away from me. Even with sensors and amped senses, the monster had the drop on me. Funny how we can change the odds in mid-heartbeat. But I didn't hear any laughter, just dead silence. Then came the ringing in my ears.

I hauled out the fragments of monster and Skrymshaw's ravaged corpse in vacuum-sealed body bags. Slate had left. He let me face the beast alone. It would not come bursting out of its plastic wrap. Its life was done, just as the dagger swarm and sewer beast. I looked at both black bags. Considering the link between monsters and humanity brought to mind a near-forgotten Hindu tale where Shiva, the destroyer, saved humanity from a dragon devouring the world by feeding the monster its own tail. It ate itself. Humanity had come full circle. We gave rise to monsters that devour us. They thrive in our global, urban dominion that consumed the world.

I see a familiar flash of green from my wrist. The cycle, the contract, has yet to end.

09
INHERIT THE EARTH

I am Joshua Grail, at least on the day in question. I work in the city. I have no choice. In my time it wraps over the face of planet Earth and climbs skyward as massive towers piercing rolling, black smog. The dark clouds robbed the blue sky and stars from eyesight. Most people don't want to see me, especially not in the rising towers. Typically, I prowl the shadowed streets below them. It's where most eyes live, but some of them are not human. When those eyes catch sight of a hapless person or senses track the scent of fear, I, or someone like me, follow the sudden end to the screams. Some see us as vengeance. Others view us Monster Killers as opportunistic fools. Whatever the perspective, we are in demand.

Some people call me *Ice*. What they perceive as coldness is less from dispassion and more from staying focused, and alive. I am a hunter but could just as easily be prey. I may have deep, burning reasons to seek and kill monsters in the dark and slightly brighter places. I can't change my past, but I can end things that rip away peoples' future, or at least give them time to run. Most days, my profession is a solitary slog. It's not the job I considered for my life's work. This future is not what many people imagined. Yet it is exactly what some people say we deserve. I might claim to reserve such harsh judgment for what I hunt. That would be a lie. Yet I am large and heavily armed, so most people don't ask what I think. No need to risk a disagreement.

Collectively, we humans agree to destroy what treats us as food. On one day more odd than most, I had companions. They smelled traces of blood spatter and small slivers of flesh in the folds of my overcoat. The scent drew the first few from their dark hiding places. The carrion flies were new, at least around here. They weren't a swarm, just enough to be pests. I wondered if they were a synthetic abomination like the things I hunt, or a resurgent species of *Diptera* defying extinction. Their speed and erratic flight made them hard to scan. Good survival skill. Whatever their origin, they were at home in the dying, urban landscape. The buzzing dots followed me for the faint odor and the greater prize it promised.

I created carrion from larger hungers in the darkness. But if my sensors failed or my aim was off by millimeters, the flies might dine on my remains. I wondered if future generations of flies would take a taste to living tissue. I doubted they had the time. Someone would see the flies as something to fear and call for their end. Too bad. I figured we could use the help in cleaning the cracks through the global city. I thought I might save one or two flies in a little jar. Or maybe I'll get the contract to burn them. It was always hard to know how your day was going to end. Our own species held surprises. We were a swarming mass, just slower and meeker than what crept from the same darkness as the flies.

Sometimes hunger comes into weak, city light. At least some electric power was still making it to the streetlights where I walked. The few, decaying city blocks were a blank zone, or hole. It was a dangerous region abandoned by service providers, such as health workers, plumbers, or sanitation crews and prostitutes. It was a good place to hide, if not survive. What did prowl here usually ate anyone seeking respite from the law, or more dangerous groups. My sensors drew me to the area. The screaming brought me to an alley. My autoloading shotgun-styled weapon slid fast from under my coat.

Bingo.

The hungry thing ahead dug through a dense pile of trash. Behind the useless barricade screamed a panicked woman once hidden in the deep frame of a basement window. Steel replaced the glass long ago, and the thing's nose wasn't fooled by the barrier of urban detritus. The beast was an opportunistic predator. It must typically feed its bulk on garbage. It hewed away and gulped down chunks of rot as it dug for the woman. Stout jaws sheared metal fragments between razored molars. A heavily muscled neck pitched the fragments away as its giant claws ripped and crushed debris. Tiny eyes retreated under lids of thick, umber skin as it pushed deeper. It smelled me as I ran down the alley and turned to face its attacker.

The beast didn't hesitate and charged with jaws and claws wide open. Powerful hind legs gave it surprising speed. I didn't hesitate either. The charging hulk disappeared behind the yellow blast of my gun. The fired shell struck and detonated. The monster's head blew apart. Its claws snapped backward. The headless body slapped hard against the pavement. The clock began a new second. The flies found the fresh tissue splattered across the alley walls. More of them buzzed to the shattered neck of the warm carcass. I flipped out a collection bag. The woman was still screaming behind a thin wall of trash.

I finished the job started by the monster and knocked down the remaining trash in front of the woman. Her legs kicked away from me. She wore a high-priced environmental suit I've only seen in advertisements. I wondered how a street person could get that kind of expensive clothing. The woman couldn't retreat any farther into the blocked window well. Shadow hid most of her, but the FRACDAR scans overlaid on my field of vision revealed her rounded frame pressed against the steel and brick. My sensors also gave me odd biological readings. Two beating hearts. Maybe she had fooled my sensors and was no woman, after all.

I backed up and barked with gun leveled at her: "Get out and stand! If you understand!"

She did so, trembling. My scans of her were now direct and clear, but the oval shape of her abdomen explained the strange readings. I lowered my gun.

"I see why you were hiding. Not just from the monster. You're pregnant."

There was only one reason a lone and pregnant woman would hide in a devastated and potentially lethal area like this.

I sighed. "Your pregnancy, the child, is unsanctioned, right?"

"What—what are you going to do?" She asked.

I glared down at her and took a deep breath. The alley really stank.

"Please don't turn me in." She said with trembling voice.

Flies buzzed around me. I knew they were not the only annoyance I would suffer that day.

"Please...!"

I saw a complex of rising towers over the tops of decaying buildings along the street where I stood. Black clouds rolled among the monolithic skyscrapers, and elevated highways snaked between them. Occasional, high-altitude traffic that needed no surface flashed beneath the clouds. Street level was far below the summits of the towers. My mind was high above them, but I need to bring it back, quickly. Official judgment drove down the street. The modern cop car was a floating vehicle that served as armored personnel carrier and disposal truck. I never intend to be inside either compartment. The search for a certain missing person had brought the police to my site. Their arrival could have been a favorable coincidence. Collection pods won't descend to this zone, nor will any traffic. The cops could register my bounty, and collect the monster's body. However, the law's arrival was no happy event for the young woman shielded within the building behind me. I had promised her that she would not enter the truck. There were prisons for unregistered mothers. Without substantial fees paid beforehand, motherhood was a crime. It was supposed to be impossible with inhibitors in public water. Yet so were odd or maybe persisting species like flies. Nature liked surprises. Currently, I was not a fan.

There was a time when mothers were revered and not seen as arrogant. That was before the world's population reached over a trillion, before humankind burned the face of Mother Earth, and before the monsters came. But the attitudes of avarice remained constant. Laws declared that no more people could be born to take away what the existing population held so jealously. The living stole the legacy of the unborn, and declared them as never to be. At least not without paying those currently alive for the privilege of enduring modern Earth. For a fee, parents could buy official sanction to subvert these laws. As a reflection of society's priorities, a birth permit cost substantially more than a license to kill.

The air vibrated from the black sponsons levitating the police truck over cracked asphalt. Five officers in blue and white coveralls and full-face respirators jumped from a side hatch. I motioned down the alley. They groaned and walked to the bagged monster's body. One officer noticed flies buzzing about and gripped his sidearm. He looked at me to see if I did anything about the weird, tiny offenders. When I didn't, he joined his fellow officers cursing at him to help them lug the body to the truck. The words EVIDENCE/DISPOSAL glowed on the rear hatch. The driver's hatch hissed and swung open. Sergeant John Slate stepped onto the truck's running board.

Slate had worn the same overcoat since I'd first met him. It was still more stylish than mine, if just as weathered by abrasive air. His skin was a slightly lighter tone than the black cap of close-cut hair over his skull. Slate's pigmentation was no fashion statement, as are many alternating shades of skin today. His accusing stare was more subtle than mine was, and therefore more dangerous. Slate was a professional acquaintance and occasional ally. I tested the strength of that alliance in our exchange that followed.

"Ice! Glad you're here." Slate finally said looking down from the running board. "See anything odd?"

"That," I motioned to the bagged carcass wrestled from the alley by the jump-suited police. "And cops actually breaking a sweat."

The face-covering respirators hardly muted the curses directed at me as the large, rear hatch opened. The police pulled chains and hooks from inside the chamber and fastened them to the bagged monster. They yanked free lengths of chains to raise the carcass on pulleys. The manual system loaded the heavy body while the anti-grav tech supported the whole truck. The officers obviously understood the contrast in technology or its lack at their expense. I understood their ire. Someone higher on the chain of command decided arms and backs were cheaper than more anti-gravs, or just one electric motor.

"See any odd people?" Slate continued.

I resisted the obvious reply, and merely stared back at Slate.

He paused, considering my gaze. "I see. Funny. But you realize harboring a fugitive is—"

"Fugitive? Cut the crap." I snapped, and killed any pretense.

"What are you so hacked off about? Kid's not yours is it?" Slate asked.

"Of course not. And what kid?"

"Right." Slate lifted his own respirator to his face and took a breath of its filtered air as if to commiserate with his straining officers while enjoying the privilege of rank. "Not that you'd need a deep scan to notice an unregistered mother to be in a hole like this."

"Just keep your scanners and dogs at bay, Slate."

The police crew turned their plastic covered heads to me as they strained to push the body inside the truck. I wasn't making any friends of them.

"Careful, Ice. You may be a tough man, but you're one man." Slate warned.

"I've survived this long."

"Sometimes with a little help." Slate flipped his respirator aside and glared harshly at me from his perch on the truck.

I stayed silent. Surprisingly, my emotions were making our encounter into a conflict. The bridge between Slate and me was in danger of collapsing like many of the decrepit walls around us. I attempted to balance our respective pride and preserve any respect and opted for a statement of truth.

"It's the written law I don't trust." I said.

"Okay," Slate nodded. "And you see me bound to it. Maybe you even think you're protecting me. Fair enough. But I'm not your problem. Not your biggest one, anyway. So you'd better hope your rugged individual act is enough to get you and anyone else you're guarding to a secret birthday."

"Why?"

"Someone really doesn't want that kid born." Slate coughed. "One anonymous account has hired half this precinct's free Killers, and probably not to hunt monsters. Still thinking you can go solo?"

"I have little choice." I took a breath and flinched at a darting fly.

"You don't trust things getting lost in bureaucracy?" Slate asked.

Slate offered me a way out by suggesting he could protect the young mother by burying the case under stacks of electronic files and even physical ones. But someone with significant funds was working to find her. It would take a lot of ready cash to lure one Killer away from taking lucrative bounties, and this account had paid for several Killers. I was a bit annoyed I had not made the list for easy money. Big graft could also buy processing speed for severs holding the forms. Money still made the world go 'round, even when veiled under smog.

"You know that same money will move things faster, even in your precinct." I said. "And like you said, you're bound. You can't stand alone. I can."

Slate was quiet for a moment. He then shook his head. "Then, good luck, Ice. I'll be around. So will the truck."

Slate entered the cab. Two officers walked by me with sideward glances through plastic.

"Tough man," one officer said.

"I guess he'd better be," her partner added.

They entered the cab and closed the hatch. The rear hatch slammed shut. Its metal ring echoed across the desolate street as Slate and his officers drove away. I waited for the police truck to round a darkened corner before returning to the hidden woman. I entered a ransacked first floor. The buildings were so ravaged that not even squatters risked stepping inside them. I walked cautiously through the ruins with my senses and sensors on perpetual scan. The young mother and biological outlaw still crouched silently where I had left her. Her eyes were wide with fear as I stepped behind the partially collapsed wall. Her concern didn't wane after recognizing me. Other than being tall and massive with unkempt gray hair hanging beside a face like rock, my steel-blue eyes always searched for weakness. It was a habit, but not always a bad one.

"I'll help you, but I need the truth." I said. "Who are you, and why are you here?"

"I'm—I'm Barbara." She paused, and cradled her stomach. She obviously felt caught between being frightened to tell me anything and wanting to vent all her secrets. She sat on a metal crate and drew a shallow breath. "I was running, obviously. I didn't think anyone would follow me here."

"Not even cops?"

"No. I'm hiding from them, too."

"It's not as if you can hide the evidence if they catch you." I took a deep breath and was instantly sorry I did. "I can detect you've ditched all com-tech and internal trackers."

"I only know the direction to run." Barbara looked off as if hoping her direction had been accurate.

"Sometimes that's all you need." I said. "You've been underground until now?"

"Yes. There's a network." Barbara stopped suddenly as she caught herself saying that aloud. "But, ah, with the baby so close to birth I contacted my father. He said I could come home, but my shuttle was intercepted en route. Somehow my mother must have found out and had it diverted. Or worse. There was a man, big like you at the park and ride. My friends helped me escape. I don't know what happened to them."

"Well, they're not here." I said and wondered if the big man was a professional acquaintance or mere thug. I hoped for thug.

Barbara flexed her fingers against her distended sides. Her pale skin seemed to lose all color. She shut her eyelids so tight the pressure must have caused her to see phosphenes flash within her eyes.

"Why would your mother try to stop you from making it home?"

"My parents divorced long ago. But together they still control Conglomore V.V. It's a virtual and vertical real estate company. Very lucrative. There's a lot of building sides and holograms. Data gaps. And flash ads."

"I've noticed."

"You might not have noticed every ad they run. But they probably hit you. Some are pulsed infra-cognitive tweaks when you open a screen, a box, or bottle. They use any way to hit your brain. Even down here."

"Nice to be wanted. But aren't there enough brains to hack for everyone to get a slice of the profits? What's that got to do with your baby?"

"Mom is a control freak. I mean a real freak. By law, contract, and gene-lock, only family members and descendants can own company stock. When the baby is born, and when it's sanctioned, then a percentage will go to him."

"And baby's proxies will side with its granddad?" I asked.

"Yeah. Patrilineal equilibrium. Whatever. It would cost a fortune for mom to contest."

"Cheaper just to make the inheritance—the heir go away." I said. "Especially since the conception is still illegal, and unregistered."

"Yeah. I bought anti-contraceptives from a pusher. They actually worked. I wanted to get at mom, but I didn't think it would get this bad. I thought my dad would fix it. I ran from him to be with David, the baby's father. It'll cost dad, but he can still fix it."

"Where's David, now?" I asked.

"We had to move to a lower level. He was—" Barbara drew in a deep breath and then coughed through sobs. "Killed. He was killed."

"And your mother is ruthless enough to kill you?"

Barbara glared at me. "Yes. Why would that shock you? You're a Killer."

I glared back at Barbara. She looked away. "I kill monsters, not children."

"Of course, I'm sorry. I just—" Barbara pulled her legs up to her body and hunched her head and shoulders down as if to wrap her body around her unborn child. Brown locks of hair escaped from her matching cap and fell as a curtain around her face.

"You wonder if you've done the right thing and what to do now."

"Yes. The baby is the only thing I have left of David. But how can I bring a child into this world? Down here, it just seems so horrible."

"Yeah." Flies buzzed around me. "But the rent is cheap. And somebody has to pay it."

Barbara gave me a nervous nod. Her opened mouth threatened to betray her. Then she blurted out the question on her mind while wincing at the potential answer.

"Why do you care? I mean, about me? You know there's a price on me, and my mother would pay out a lot. Why bother protecting me? At least—I mean, that's what you're doing. Right?" She waved away flies after a confused moment and then recognition that they were living, flying things and not something tossed up by an odd breeze.

"Rest for a minute," I said. "The flies will follow me."

Not all the flies followed, but Barbara nodded off anyway. Perhaps her dreams would be soothing compared to thoughts of this hole and losing David. Yet not all memories fade. Some of mine I never wanted to lose. Some I could not fully retrieve. I withdrew a small holograph disk from a deep, inner pocket. Its center disappeared beneath an image of the past: another young woman, harder looking than Barbara even through all her current sorrow. This woman gave an almost brutal stare at the camera. I smiled. I knew her well. A happy ending was never written for us. I suppressed thinking of names to prevent deeper wounds from reopening. In time, memories of people become sensations and some of them bring pain.

I wondered about another life, another woman, and another fate torn away. I imagined this other woman in soft clothes. I saw her hug and play with a baby that never was. For a moment, the two women merged. Just as quickly, the merged image flew apart as if the differences were too great even for imagination to unite in a brief, temporary thought. Although I stared at the hard face on the hologram, the image of the other woman and child lingered. I wondered if such a happy scene occurred between Barbara and her mother years ago. What must she think of such memories now? Some memories become liabilities, like Barbara's own past. Danger is everywhere. No one can be invulnerable from attack from a shadowed beast or from inside the mind. You can never be free of liabilities. Or old feelings of loss, or stokes of anger. A fly landed on the holograph, oblivious to the image it obscured. It died between fragments of the disk that shattered in my hand.

The scans were clean. Rather, nothing that could eat us was around. Still, I took out my long gun and armed its artificial neurology with a thought from my own. Barbara and I exited the building to the desolate street.

"I boosted a message through to the com-node outside the hole." I told her. "Your father's limo will rendezvous with us three blocks north. They're afraid to come closer. We need to get moving. The others will find us soon."

"Who? Others?" Barbara squeaked.

"Your mother has hired a squad of Killers," I said with a calm tone masking my own concern. "We may need to make a stand."

Barbara's resolve died. She slumped toward the gritty pavement. "I don't want more people to die, just so I can live!"

"It's no longer just about your life. You decided to create another. Now it's about mine, too. And I also intend to make it home. Such that it is."

"Why are you doing this?"

"Because I have, too. That was decided when I didn't pull the trigger on you, myself. That's what passes for altruism down here." I grabbed her closest arm and almost gently pulled her back to her feet. "Let's go."

Barbara moved at my side as fast as she could. I knew it was not fast enough. Looking up and ahead, I noticed a dot veer from the airborne traffic coursing through gaps in the towers. It could only be an illegally descending, private transport. I bet it wasn't a limo, but it was coming here. We only had time enough to hide.

A reinforced second-story window allowed us to view our pursuers. I started working on a battle plan as I watched my fellow Killers jump from a rear ramp as their transport slowed over the street. Barbara's mom paid enough to override the machine's property protection protocol. Or they put a gun to the head of the pilot. Human liabilities, again. The Killers fanned out. Two were large, pale men. The one woman appeared woven from ebony cable. The fourth Killer wore a suit of armor more expensive than the vehicle that brought him. (I'd like to see the mortgage on that weapons unit.) The exiting competitors now shifted from bravado and gun hugging to the actual act of finding their quarry. I hoped they didn't know about me, yet.

"Do you know them?" Barbara asked, and recoiled from the window. "I've seen *that* big guy at the park and ride!"

I lined up her fearful stare with one of the men. "Damn. He's called Tanner. The slow one with the fat gun is Moore. He's as stupid as his gun is wide. I'm surprised he's survived this long. The bald and jet-toned woman is Kohn. Kohn is greedy. If monsters could bribe her, she'd never pull the trigger. Stipe is inside the tin can. Obviously he relies on technology, and far too much. The one you know slipping on dark goggles, Tanner. Now, Tanner—yeah, Tanner."

"What are our chances?" Barbara asked stepping farther away from the window.

"Let's move."

The optical studs I had pressed into the walls and ceiling spied Moore's cautious entry into the hallway. The flies confused him, but he was smart enough to read the direction of their flight and realize they might guide him to something of greater interest. Moore stalked with his jaw dropped open, but slapped it closed with a twisted frown after a fly darted in to test the waters. His cheap scanners taped to the end of his cannon marked the trail of blood on the ceiling. He walked slowly across the decrepit office hall transfixed by the blood trail flicked minutes ago from my hand. He barely noticed the old holes smashed through the walls, or the weakened floor section concealing another hole straight down to the subbasement. His bulk might help him survive bar fights. Maybe a big bite or two. Here, it caused him to crash through the floor after the second step over my trap. The echo of his plummeting expletives ended when his body slapped against the foundation floor.

Other optical studs showed me Kohn exit a stairwell and enter a room, gun first. Her eyes peered through open sights. A smile spreads across her sinuous face. My coat and all its accessories hung over a broken pillar. One shotgun was propped before it. Two of my heavy sidearms hung in outer pockets. Kohn knelt by the column. Scans told her the safeties were a weak, RNA-based protocol. They would be easy to hack if they weren't merely a ruse of the real security ready to blow off her fingers and slightly more. Fooled by the ruse, she reached over to caress the shotgun. It was a good make. Better than her assault weapon. And so were my jamming emitters. Her living senses proved better. She heard me behind her, but not before my gun pressed against the back of her skull. Kohn was greedy, but not stupid. She froze at the touch of the metal.

"Life or death. Choose, Kohn. Either way this hunt is over for you."

Kohn slowly shrugged her shoulders, and raised her now empty hands. "Hey, no problem, big man. Half fee is better than none. Eh, J—*ugh!*"

A pistol whip ended Kohn's repartee, and the electrical backlash building in her gun belt she intended to arc into me. I wondered what her dreams would be like.

The investment of all Stipe's past bounties glistened silver even in the low light. His armor was hardly camouflaged. Neither was his pride in it. A devilish smile curved beneath the helmet's retractable faceplate. His sensors picked up heat, or motion, or both and displayed them across his eyes. My data reading was less obvious. So was my movement. Stipe prowled closer to a position over his target that moved in the rooms beneath the floor creaking under his metal boots. The hum of a building energy field added to his acoustic signature. I even heard a hollow voice confirm 'CANNON LOCKED' from inside his helmet. Stipe aimed his bloated, silver arm at the target below the floor. I took cover. An aperture opened on his gauntlet's forearm plate. A linear inferno of plasma lanced downward. Flames curled at the edges of the floor's instant crater. Stipe took aim again.

Shells from returned fire punched through the floor and exploded against Stipe's wearable fortress. He stumbled, more from surprise. He fired another plasma lance and incinerated more floor. More shells blasted through in response and detonated against Stipe, the ceiling, and in mid air. Stipe ignored his targeting computer. A good thing, since I was skewing its sensors through an offensive suite of operating system monkey wrenches fired quietly from my own weapons' OS. (I had thought *they* were expensive.)

Stipe unleashed a dual barrage of waning infernos from both gauntlets. The return fire of explosive shells finally stopped. Stipe had vaporized enough floor for a clear view of his opponent, or what is left of the smoldering corpse. Stipe didn't need his scanners to recognize Moore from his partially melted cannon. Not that Stipe cared whom he just killed. At least not right away.

"Poor bastard, Moore. Hey, is that rig insured?" I ask behind the barrel of my shotgun as I stepped from my hiding spot across the hall.

The name and shape of my weapon was traditional. It fired more potent rounds than groups of lead balls. Like Moore's shells, they might not penetrate Stipe's armor but they will give the joints and servomotors some problems. The hum from Stipe's gauntlets began again, but it droned on without building. He aimed and fired anyway. Only static arcs flickered at me in mild anger.

"That's the problem with E-weapons and premature discharge, Stipe, the batteries go flat. And then so does the owner."

I fired. I hit Stipe's shoulder joints first, and then blasted his mid-section hard. Naked concussion ripped across the alloy with intense flashes of yellow-white. Two shots apiece blasted his knees. All during my fusillade Stipe lurched backward with each detonation until the suit's joints seized up and all he could do was scream. I needed to conserve ammo. Tanner was coming here, by now. Hitting Stipe with an I-beam fragment and knocking him down through the blast hole wasn't necessary. Or maybe it was. Moore's gun cushioned his fall, or made the impact worse. The *CLANG!* was thunderous. The impacted floor collapsed and an avalanche of urban ruins and ego plummeted farther into darkness. Another echo of metallic thunder and clattering debris reported the end of the violent fall. Stipe wouldn't get back up as Moore had. Not until somebody, or something, dragged him out for whatever reason it wanted to open the canned human.

It was time for us to get out. I gathered Barbara and guided her from the ruin.

"Scan's clean. Let's move." I exited first, and we slid along the building front. "If we can get—"

Rocks. Little bits of rubble that weren't there before. And familiar. I spun to shield Barbara. One of the small, camouflaged mines exploded. My bulk shielded her from most of the explosion. She was only stunned. I helped her up quickly and pushed her back through the doorway as a second mine exploded. It sent shards of itself and asphalt into my thigh and lower back. Barbara stumbled but did the smart thing and kept running back inside. A bullet punched through my right shoulder. Tanner was too close behind me, so the bullet's explosive head detonated against the building and not inside me. Still, I fell flat.

Tanner didn't need to stalk us. He let his competitors take the hits and laid in wait for us to expose ourselves. Tanner stepped over me and drew aim on Barbara with his cut-down assault rifle.

"Tanner!" I screamed. I drew another gun but fell forward while trying to raise it.

"Wild." Tanner said looking down at me. "The mines and bullet should've busted you down for good. I don't get it."

"You don't have to get it. Just get out of here!"

"No way." Tanner fired a second round. A third. Both bullets blasted small craters in the pavement in front of me as I rolled. Tanner walked inside. Torturing prey was a side of him I hadn't seen. A large bounty can do strange things to a person. I tried to reach the building wall. Tanner set off more mines. Their concussions hammered me. Tanner was right. I should just die. But like Stipe, I've made some expensive investments. The ones I paid for dearly were less obvious on the outside.

Tanner had to work harder than he expected. The will to survive made Barbara elusive. She finally made the mistake of entering a room with no exit. Tanner followed. Barbara pulled and aimed the pistol I had given her. Tanner smiled as she pointed it at him and quivered.

"Can't do it, huh? First time's a bitch." Tanner took aim.

The floor beneath him exploded.

Tanner fell through the sudden hole. He cried out as flooring shards drove deep into his legs on impact. His goggles flew off and spun away when he hit, but I had to kick his gun away. I looked down at him as he grimaced. I pressed medi-blisters across my shoulder wound with my shotgun barrel. I thought he would be more surprised. Maybe impressed. Instead, Tanner head-butted my groin. He then charged into me and slammed us against a wall. It hurt. I had dropped my shotgun some paces behind us. We engaged in a pathetic wrestling match of bleeding hulks attempting to grasp limbs slick with sweat and blood. I grabbed Tanner by the neck and left arm and pulled him away from crushing my mid-section. His right arm beat against my ripped-open thigh. My knee struck his shoulder. He stumbled backward. I'm sure Tanner and I could run clinics on hand-to-hand fighting. That was before we began shooting and blowing pieces off each other. It messed with your focus. Tanner threw a left hook into my gut just off target of my liver. I buckled, anyway. I dodged his kick and punched his butchered leg. He cried out and fell back. I kicked him, hard. He rolled against the same window where Barbara and I watched him arrive with his now fallen competitors. The fight wasn't finished. Tanner climbed a wrecked desk and holes in the wall to stand. He turned with a small pistol drawn from his belt to face my retrieved gun leveled at him.

"We can deal, Ice." Tanner gasped. "We split—"

"No deals."

"C'mon! She can't be paying you near enough!"

"She isn't paying me anything."

"What? Then why?" Tanner's anger tightened his grip on his gun.

"You wouldn't understand. You only kill for pay."

"And sport. Why do you do it? Some high-minded purpose? You think you're saving lives? Walk the street! Are monsters the only ones eating people alive?"

"So it's okay to turn your guns on a defenseless person for a fee, just as you'd kill a monster for the bounty."

"I kill, Ice. So, yeah. You—!"

Tanner's words were a ruse. His aim was steadily reaching the level of my head. The sounds of my gunshot and shattering heavy glass were instantaneous. My bullet ripped through him and window. His body fell with the glass shards toward the street below. He was two stories above the street. Too many stories. Somehow, Tanner was alive and arced his body to try to survive the fall. The altitude shattered that hope. Impact. Velocity and old pavement did something many monsters never could. It killed him.

I looked at the bloody shape that was once a powerful man. Medics could take the remains and preserve the viable parts and living cells. If Tanner had resurrection insurance, a hospital could rebuild and replace the shattered bones and crushed tissues. But brain trauma meant Tanner was gone. Even so, resurrection meant generating new grey matter overwritten with dated neural imprints and saved copies of old m-RNA. A living zombie would walk out of the hospital with family comforted by the falsehood their loved one had never died. Sooner or later, the tics and oddities caused by a new brain with a copied mind stamped-over it would start. Then family and friends would then need to decide to accept or abandon their manufactured Lazarus. Even if I had made the emergency call, no one would have answered it in this hole.

Barbara's calls drew me slowly upstairs. Together we made our way back to the street. I limped out of the building and gained strength with each step, but this time Barbara took the lead. Outside, she stopped and stared at Tanner's body.

"Did he have any children?" she asked.

"No. He could never afford them. Barbara, get back in the building."

"Why?" Barbara broke into tears at my order.

"Just do it, now!"

She did. Too late. Slate's police truck already rounded the corner as she entered. I had no idea how much farther I could go. I respected Slate. I didn't want to fight him. And I couldn't fight all the cops in the world.

Slate eased my tension over the truck's loudspeaker: "Relax, Ice. Guess who I've been talking to?"

The ride was smooth. The back of the truck wasn't so bad, other than the smell. At least Barbara and I weren't locked in the EVIDENCE/DISPOSAL compartment. We rode in the personnel cab. The police squeezed around us gave Barbara odd looks that were easy to see without the plastic respirators covering their sweaty faces. A pregnant woman, live and in person, was unique to them. Barbara seemed almost a different breed of humanity and not the once-common sight. Her pregnancy made them stop and think, especially the female officers.

Slate had come through, again. My mistrust for the law and bureaucracy was apt, but my faith in the one, honorable man whom I could almost call friend was rekindled. Slate found and forced Barbara's father to pay all fees and penalties. He likely also donated to the police pension fund. The payments retroactively made Barbara's future baby a legitimate member of society. Although I wondered if the future heir would like that title.

We rode in the truck for almost a full minute. Then the hatch opened. We saw well-dressed human statuary with rifles surrounding a sleek, black limousine floating at an intersection of crumbling asphalt and smooth, even pavement. We were out of the hole. The limo's turbines whined and gave an auditory quality to the nervous stare of the man awaiting Barbara by an entry ramp beneath a gull-wing door. I didn't blame Barbara for her first impulse: run to the limo and safety. She stopped and turned back to me as the armed *chauffeurs* approached her.

"Thank you, Ice—Mr. Grail." Barbara said over the turbines. "I want to, uh, help you. A lot."

"Give your father my number. We'll talk."

"I want my child's name to stand for something. You have a first name?"

"Yeah. But name him David."

Two rifle-bearing chauffeurs whisked Barbara up the ramp and into the limo. Her father waved like a politician on campaign. Maybe he was. The remaining chauffeurs followed him and piled inside the sleek limousine. Its doors sealed and the black and vastly expensive vehicle shot cloudward. Barbara and her future disappeared into the transit lanes high above the streets.

"All those guns. No guts." Slate observed.

"True family love." I added.

"So you didn't want the kid named—"

"No." I cut off Slate's barb.

"When you can handle it, I've got a contract for you."

"Tomorrow." I said.

Slate looked at my wounds and nodded.

Tomorrow. Same place as yesterday. But I owned a new coat, some new skin, and the weapon of choice was a gas. Using poison risked creating another resistant strain of something. But I didn't know how else to destroy a growing swarm of flies. I told Slate I wasn't going to account for every last, tiny body. He said I should try his job for a day. Thousands of days ago, someone claimed the meek shall inherit the Earth. There were undoubtedly a lot more flies to deal with back then. What will future children, legal and otherwise, like David deal with tomorrow? Yet with all our human liabilities and everything we've done, we keep our hold on the Earth. So who are the meek? Has the inheritance come to pass? I guess we will see, maybe in a new tomorrow. I snapped down the lid on the little jar trapping a few of the carrion flies I found. They were a natural species, after all. They just need proper registration, or a less obvious home. I would also be in that shadowed tomorrow. And not alone.

10
FEAR

Freedom stays alive, as long as you do what you're told. That phrase arcs in on itself, just as many towers appear to if you stared up at them from street level. The illusion rises from the tallest ones reaching higher than other buildings from past ages. In bygone times, city buildings ended at some point and never truly scraped the sky. Today, many towers pierce the sky, or at least its dark replacement. Permanent, black clouds flow around as an inverted ocean cut into channels. It's quite dark, high above. Colors have a limited altitude. Vibrant ads on screens and dancing holograms can only capture attention at the angles humans eyes are comfortable reaching. The ascending towers create rigid, deep canyons with the streets at the bottom. If you look ahead for a sense of horizon, the perspective of tower walls pinches the distant lights and images into a bright blob. What the ads tell you gets lost. You could see that as a kind of liberation. Maybe.

Not all the artificial canyons have bright ads or adequate light, because not all zones squeeze together people with disposable income. But almost everywhere has people. Some streets have more shadows and less noise. Until someone screams when something attacks. I attack the things causing the screams. Tower canyons are not the only artificial fact of modern life. Monsters creep out of our less than bright legacy and eat us. Most people object to becoming torn prey. That creates a market for killing monsters. It's my job. And I don't need to advertise. But my own ad might read: Joshua Grail. Your hope for walking home or waking up tomorrow.

Even in an urban world oppressed by too many people, we hope for the future. Or I could just be an idealist. My weapons serve the public, but I am a freelancer. That's the idea. On this day, the concept came under fire. The police know my name. For me, that knowledge has brought profit, and acted to save overworked officers time, limbs, and lives. So I've always paid attention when authority called. It never occurred to me to test if I had the freedom to ignore it.

I entered a familiar police precinct. Horrified screams. Gunshots. The constant roar of motion above and through the streets. All of that noise was just from the first few rows of detectives' cubicles. Holograms played audio and chaos on every desk throughout the warehouse-sized chamber. I walked through the maze and caught glimpses of felonies in miniature flanked by projected files with the names of victims, suspects, and alphanumeric tags for actors possibly not human. It was a sea of moving images and the pained expressions of the watchers. Algorithms filtered the data and deleted suicides, non-violent crimes, and those suppressed by local patrols. The remaining carnage was remanded before fatigued, human eyes. I had no doubt the cops here thought the filters were broken or a myth. Information collection and surveillance systems grow outdated. The police state is now one of frustration.

Darkened human nature and inhuman predators thrived. Both caused horrors that disgusted even these detached watchers. The police have many merciless ways to react. Now it seemed that included me, with or without my approval.

"That Municipal domain clause in your license? I'm exercising it now." A police lieutenant named Papas told me without looking up as I stepped inside his office. It was merely a raised cubicle with thin walls. Nevertheless, his power was higher than all those down the three stairs from his desk.

Papas was obviously used to using that power and giving orders. I was not used to being low on the food chain.

"I've worked with cops before." I said. "In cooperation, but not impressment."

I could just about smell Papas' annoyance bubbling up. I mentioned one cop I could almost call friend. "Sergeant John Slate has—"

"Slate. A good cop." Papas interrupted me. "Dedicated. Actually likes people. It's what makes him slow."

Papas let out a bitter sigh. He still hadn't looked directly at me, but I didn't think he was reading the holopages in front of him, either. Most people don't want to glance at me for long. It's not merely my size or the spattered, heavy trench coat covering the guns beneath it. I'm typically viewed as a menacing intruder or violent reprisal. Most people are glad I killed the thing that terrorized them. They are sad it ate a loved one, and hate the fact they couldn't the avenger. Still, they are frightened by the person who kills the beast. The difference between the monster and me is that I don't eat them. As far as I know, most people still don't prey on their neighbors. Not to eat, anyway.

I wondered if Papas was thinking of a sandwich as he stared sideways at all the flickering files and names stacked high into the air from his holograph. I was sure you could compress the images, but maybe you couldn't with the police system. A new file flashed on at the bottom. Papas sat and sweated. His physique was squat, like a once stocky man who has suffered excess gravity for too long. His thick hands smoothed over his slick, balding head. Such a condition must be by choice today, or he has no time to visit a medstation. His expression was one of mental constipation. No doubt, the gravity he suffered was his job.

"Yeah, well," Papas continued. He locked his eyes directly on mine, unafraid. "Slate wrote you bounties. This one is mine, and you'll do it. I've wasted enough time with you, already. You've heard of the Henderson Tower Butcher?"

"Yeah," I shrugged. "The media says that's a serial murderer. Not a monster."

"The media is screwed. I think it's a monster. I'm giving you the job. I want him—it—down by tomorrow. Simple enough."

"Do I call you if—" I began.

"Just bag the body!" Papas grimaced and jerked his head as if tearing away a small chunk of meat. "My techs will take it. Your bounty is on file. Along with a review of your license."

Papas reached to his side and then tossed a small gelatin capsule, an infomere, through the holograms across his desk. He then gestured to the exit. My audience was over. He gave me a job and a threat to my license as inducement. He was covering his ass and putting mine in a bureaucratic sling. Nice. I picked up the infomere and left.

On the way out, I stopped to bother mere Sergeant John Slate across the sprawling precinct. I've had never thought of him as an underling, but we all have our bosses. It seemed we both had the same one, for now.

"Papas?" Slate's brown face wrinkled in a frown tight enough to force the color out of it. "Hard ass. Just do the job and quietly walk away. That's all I can do for you." Slate returned to his own stack of case files with his back to me.

"Papas didn't just call me." I said anyway. "He summoned me here. He gave me an infomere, not a transmitted file. Looks like he wanted to do this with minimal records."

Slate said nothing.

I took out an old, palm-sized interface unit from my coat and fed the infomere into its slot. Another one swelled out of its port as a copy of Papas' infomere. I tossed it onto Slate's desk and left. I didn't need to pressure him to read it. His natural curiosity would cause him to find the time. Now, I had a job to do. In truth, I was curious about this job Papas had pushed on me.

Papas' file did not justify the two, cubic milliliters of matrix in the infomere. It contained an archive of the Henderson Tower. It was an older building among the walls of gravity defying towers. There was a list of known Hall Walkers, prostitutes who solicited inside towers. They come from men and women who once worked inside them and still had security access. People with the right physical attributes, depending on their client's taste, could find new employment among old contacts and coworkers. It was safer than the streets, most of the time. Like every new niche, it attracted new predators. Recovered viscera confirmed Hall Walkers were the majority of the Butcher's victims.

The file related that a few people reluctantly admitted to hearing shrieks over break room coffee. No one had witnessed an attack. People disappeared, and then traces of them reappeared. Something was unknowingly tracking bits of them from a close-by lair. Yet most monsters learn to move or die, because Monster Killers like me find their lairs. And if the Killer fires his or her weapon in time, the monsters die. The Henderson attacks all seemed to occur during the same time of day: noon. Most monster attacks are seemingly random, motivated by hunger not the clock. Hunger's schedule depends on the size of the person the monster last ate. Papas' file put me in about the right place at the right time. I would likely find the Butcher. Papas assumed I would stop it—or him. Her?

Inside the Henderson Tower, most of the businesses had casual dress day. Well then, I should have fit right in. Right. People looked at me nervously. The security guards didn't ask to see my pass. So really, this place had no security. I soon found a trail matching the genetic files of two missing people. There was also a third unknown human. The trail ended at an air duct. That's a typical avenue for monsters, but this duct was odd. Its placement was at the center of the wall. My scans and building permits revealed the interior was rebuilt several times. Some old utility structures such as air reprocessing ducts were kept where feasible. I rolled a ball-probe through the duct's loose grate. My round spy's FRACDAR images relayed to inconspicuous enhancements linking me to my weapons and tech. The probe located an old, abandoned room hidden within new construction like a bubble in concrete. Papas' timetable was accurate. It was noon. There was a rattle through the ancient duct, and then screams.

The first cries were piercing echoes up the shaft. I was certain the voice was human, and not a sound mimicked by a monster to lure prey to a wounded meal or to help. The screams' pitch changed from sudden shock to what could be the horrified awareness of being tortured. Strangely, perhaps horrifically, if the victim was being tortured it might give me enough time to save the person. The hidden room was nine meters of dust-encrusted angles below. The probe's signal cut out, but I had to act quickly. I squeezed into the shaft with barely enough room to squirm forward. The screams continued. So did I.

I made an undignified entrance worming into the darkened room. My bulk crashed to the floor. The Butcher heard me, of course. He was a human male in a dated business suit. He had listened to my approach down the duct for several seconds. His victim was a woman strapped to a conference table. He kept twisting his long knife into her to make me think he was preoccupied. I couldn't act to stop his ambush with my weapons pinned inside the shaft. And he was on me as I crashed to the floor among boxes of forgotten supplies and dust from every office across the tower. The Butcher's long knife struck my right shoulder as I rolled. The blade was sharp, but my coat's armored weave stops sharper and larger teeth. Still, the impact hurt. The man dressed ready for work from the past was stronger than he looked and crazy enough to commit his whole body to the attack. He struck my shoulder again.

I pulled my large, autoloading handgun and clubbed him with its slide. It ripped a gash across his face and he reeled backward. We both rose and he sprinted to grab a large cleaver from a meticulously organized desk. Maybe he caught the glint of the scanners just under the gun barrel as he spun around with his bigger blade. The muzzle flash was certainly the last thing he saw. A boom echoed up the duct.

My weapons don't fire solid bullets, but explosive shells. It was hard to distinguish between the fragments of the attacker from the pieces of his female victim, but they can do that and far more at a hospital today. She would survive to reach one. The shock of my entry had made her quiet. She moaned on the bloody table as I broke her bonds, and then screamed again as one of my collection bags swallowed her into expanding, black plastic and bio-gel. I set it to preserve mode. I've only used that feature once for a fellow Killer I found after he failed to kill his target. The bag stopped bleeding and sustained life until surgeons could reassemble pieces and add new ones until insurance money and/or public largess ran out.

There was no hope for the truncated Butcher on the other side of the room. The old employment chip on his neatly organized but now blood-flecked desk identified him as Lewis Banks, CPA. I guessed his business died and he decided to live in his old office when kicked from his home. The loss of professional, physical, and emotional security eventually drove him insane and homicidal. Or maybe he was just a murderer who found an old suit in a closet. Whatever his story, Papas' monster was dead.

I sent word. A police recon unit was kind enough to burn a more comfortable passage to the Butcher's hidden room with cutting torches, even though an old stairwell gave access. Despite what Papas told me at his office, he came to the crime scene and took personal custody of the body. He gave me a narrow stare but it seemed leavened with appreciation as I waved off a medic and massaged my sore shoulder.

"There was never any monster, Papas." I said. "All the evidence pointed to a human perpetrator. You knew—"

Papas cut me off with a quick slash of his hand and look of disgust. "You've had basic biology! Before you saw him, could you be certain the freak wasn't a monster with some new molecular camouflage, or some parasite dug inside a streeter's brain?"

"No," The word was short but I answered slowly.

"You let me worry about evidence. Your license makes it legal. You're allowed to kill anyone jeopardizing your life or others during the commission of your services. What's not legal here?"

"Nothing." I grated.

"I'll sign your bounty. There'll be others." Papas walked to the torched opening.

I was certain there would be others. I already had met bad actors whose last image was the end of my gun. Still others saw my face disappear as a door closed to leave them on a dark street with nothing but fear. I had legal sanction as their executioner, as long as there was a monster, somewhere. Papas had an even broader interpretation of that clause in my license. Now that license was his to control because of the same law. I remembered the stack of file names growing on his desk. I felt an odd tug of gravity.

My wristcom flashed a familiar green. Slate's face appeared as a hologram when I cocked it horizontally.

"Finished?" Slate asked. His eyes seemed to look for Papas lurking at the scene.

"I guess. For now." I answered.

"Then meet me at Pier Seventy." Slate said. "If you'd like another bounty."

"Well, when you put it that way."

There was still nothing like a day at the beach. The stench is like standing next to a vast, open cesspool. Walls of corrosion-resistant alloy kept the black, foaming tides at bay. Sand was somewhere beneath the dark water, if it wasn't all dissolved. Maybe builders in the past fused it all into old-style glass for tower windows. There was only a width of street forming a ledge between the seawall and the crush of sky cutting buildings. The same corrosion-resistant alloy clad the pier and seawall. The large, docked ship was an older variant of steel. The relic's hull had seen many transits into the dark waves. Maybe too many. It almost appeared to be dissolving into rust as I stood with Slate and the ship's Captain Milfurst by the gangway. Finding the ship was not hard. It was the only hulk in the water. Pier Seventy was a historical name. It was also unique along this edge of city expanse. The pier shot across the water at a right angle from the rigid seawall.

It seemed impossible, but humanity still fished whatever it could find out of the surviving ocean to process as food or its likeness. We cannot eat the meager catch without first treating it for toxins and the occasional biological surprise. *Catch of the day* meant something different at the docks, now. It could mean a new disease. Something nearby thought it meant the ship's crew.

"No remains?" Slate asked Captain Milfurst. He seemed a person too clean and pressed for his oily coveralls. His captain's hat looked much newer.

"None. No blood. Nothing." Milfurst answered. "I might have thought it was desertion, but for the screaming."

"There's always screaming," I added. "The monster is in the deeper water by the pier's end."

"Next to shore? Are you sure?" Milfurst asked.

"That's the only place it could be." I answered. "Something running down the pier would leave traces of itself and the victims. With your ship's suspension field off, it's probably hiding beneath the ship. Or on board."

"No." Milfurst shook his head. "I screen of every inch of my ship, even the heads, in case the crew tries to shang equipment."

"Remind me to pee off the dock." I said.

"Do you swim?" Slate asked me with a sly smile.

"Nope."

"So how do we catch this thing, Ice? Depth charges?" Slate asked me using my street tag. He glanced over to the end of the dock and narrowed his gaze at the darkness. A ripple of wave caused him to step back and raise his hand, slightly, toward his sidearm strapped beneath his long, armor-weave coat. "Or maybe just leave you out as bait?"

"We have no data on this thing," I answered, and also listened to the ripples. "Usually a monster's size is within a range relative to humans. Not surprising when you consider they're adapted to a human dominated world. But this thing likes water. Maybe it's something new. And big."

"It's amphibious? Like something in the sewer?" Slate asked.

"Worse," I said. "Like something from the sea. Were there any attacks before this ship came in?"

"Hey! I've got nothing to do with this!" Milfurst threw his hands up and shoved them through the fetid air.

"I'm not saying you caused this, captain. I'm establishing a timeline." I said. "This thing might have moved out of an alley after noticing your crew. Or followed your ship and the catch from your fishing site. You took what it ate and now it's eating your crew."

"That's impossible!" Milfurst snapped. "We scanned nothing but the catch out there. There's no logs that—look that's crazy!"

"Ages ago, skyscrapers topped out before the clouds, and nothing crawled out of the john to eat people in their apartments." I gave a slow shrug. "So, take your pick on what's impossible, today."

"Yeah, well, I've still never seen anything bigger than kunan and krill out there." Milfurst glanced back at his ship before glaring at me.

"How long have you been a sailor?" Slate asked. "Not many left, today."

"Well—" Milfurst leaned backward and shoved his clean hands into his dirty pockets. His head bobbled as he considered how to answer Slate.

Slate cocked his left eyebrow with a hard glance at Milfurst. Slate's attitude shifted from one of offering assistance to investigation. He turned his head and spoke to his interface. "Clip last question. Merge context. Search." The answer came back through the link in his ear.

"You just bought this boat a few months ago! After you got tossed as a slide-fund manager." Slate looked back at the obviously self-appointed captain.

"This was a good deal." Milfurst shrugged. "The ship is almost fully automated. The crew—"

"Who is the real captain?" I asked with a scowl similar to Slate's own.

"I am! I own the ship and everything else. Look, I didn't call the cops to explain my investments. The Coast Guard says this is your problem. Fix it! Kill this damn thing!"

Milfurst charged up the gangway. It rocked under his angry climb, but he kept full steam until he reached the ship's deck.

"Black Beard's got a point." Slate said. "How do we kill it?"

"If it's big, it will be hungry again, soon." I answered. "So, yeah. I guess I get to be bait. Unless you have a better idea."

I hoped he did. No luck.

"We'll hook you to a very strong line." Slate smiled.

I sighed.

Later on, I tugged on that line of heavy cable. Around it was wound a reinforced power cord trailing from my insulated suit. I had a shock-field harness for protection if I'm knocked out, but this suit and the power linked to it would shock a whale. If any whales still existed. It would stun this predator if it hit me before I opened fire. The line would also haul something of me back if I miss the kill shot. Worst case, maybe doctors could save me like the woman at the tower. I stood alone on the pier holding my shotgun-styled long gun. Milfurst had spewed complaints about keeping his crew sealed below. The deck still needed swabbing so it wouldn't pit, but I needed the monster to have no choice in menu selection.

I did not wait long.

I had dropped a few ball probes to scan the water beneath the pier. The ones that sank died in the brine and other corrosives. Their FRACDAR was too weak to penetrate the murk, anyway. The floaters transmitted images washed over by black waves. There was a sudden big wave. The thing was hungry again. And it was huge. Its mass pushed a swell of water beneath the pier. I tensed. A huge, serpentine shape shot towards me. I fired. My shots butchered the thing. It thrashed violently. Then I saw the sucker disks! I didn't realize how massive the beast was because only one arm caused the swell. Another, huge tentacle grabbed me. My safety cable held, but I was suddenly airborne and being crushed.

I fired again while being shook. My shots went wild. I heard shells pock the ship's hull. My gun flew from my hands even as I clutched it in a near-death grip. The surge of electricity cooked the thing's arm, finally. Still, I was a mere gnat thrashed at the end of a spitting cord. The dark world was a blurred shadow. It held me even as electricity burned its arm and made a stench of seared tissues. It slammed me against the metal pier. That hurt. Bad. Worse was the sight that replaced the blur. Giant, orange eyes rose out of the dark water. Weak rainbows bled back to the sea as the pollution rolled from it and the giant octopus ascended next to the pier. Its skin was at first a deep red. Then it became a living kaleidoscope of rippling hues. The patterns flowed too fast to perceive. But I understood it was mad, and focused on me.

There was more pressure around my chest. My suit ripped and I felt the current course through me as well. It thrashed me again. I pulled all my strength together to yank the release before my thick neck snapped and my head flew into the water. I was flung from the suit but hit flat steel. More pain. The damage I had inflicted on the giant was equal to a bee sting. Maybe. I crawled away as eight massive arms wrapped around the end of the pier. One shot back at me. I rolled. Crawled. Stumbled. And then ran like a man out his mind. The pier shook and I fell.

Slate grabbed my shoulders. I was glad he was strong and in shape. He hauled me behind the sea wall. Black waves exploded skyward and hit the street. Sediment in the road seams fizzed into vapor. The octopus turned it full fury on the pier. Giant muscles tugged the alloy slabs. The beast couldn't bend the steel, but it ripped the end of the pier off its older pilings. Metal slabs shot into the air. Bolts snapped. The pier's end section fell into the churning water causing greater waves. Close to the road, Slate lost me in the black impact. Saturated and nearly blind, we both dropped into a shoreline emergency alcove built for the rare storm. Decontamination jets doused us.

The fishing ship listed sharply away from the pier. Its cable lines attached to the collapsing pier pulled taught. Large waves slammed the hull. The ship's crew released the lines. They snapped away like whips. The sudden lurch of the ship hurled the crewmembers backward even with deck gripping boots. The captain, or someone with sailing skill, reactivated the ship's suspension filed. The hull rolled to an even keel as waves raged around it. The surge of the ship's electromagnetic stabilizing field stunned the giant octopus. Its skin flashed brilliant red. I then noticed lesions pocking its body. It slid like an enormous starfish into deeper water. The ship pulled closer to the shore. The suspension field buffeted Slate and me like incessant vibrations. The remaining beads of decon fluid rolled off us in horizontal lines, except where our hearts beat them off our chests.

"Did you—" Slate inhaled, "scan that thing?"

"Yeah." My natural senses and several add-ons had gathered information deep within the beast while it rampaged. I was too preoccupied to pay attention, then. But I called up the collected data as I regained my breath. "You're going to love this. No red flags. No M-vectors or chimeric DNA. It's not a monster, Slate. It's a natural species."

Slate's eyelids widened to a size near the octopus' eyes.

The giant octopus destroyed the pier again, but this time in miniature as a hologram on Papas' desk. I stood with Slate in the lieutenant's elevated cubical. Papas watched the hologram with shocking incredulity. Apparently he never watched media streams. Even in this age of apathy, a giant beast destroying a large pier was news. Perhaps I overestimated the shock. Watching images was not direct experience. Unless you sold the m-RNA as a download. Even then, safety buffers prevent your brain from full immersion. It seemed Papas didn't need buffers. The calluses on his psyche were tougher. Still, I thought he would prove useful to approve the plan Slate and I waited to propose. We needed to act soon. The beast had a ready food source: anyone within arm's reach in the city. For this giant that was almost everyone.

"Damn big," Papas said when the hologram ended.

"I can't believe it's not a monster," Slate breathed.

"Matter of opinion," Papas countered. "But you drove it off. Good job. Now forget it."

"Forget that!" I pointed at the hologram as it replayed.

Papas swiped his hand across his desk and the images vanished.

"Yeah," Papas shrugged. "You got other bounties."

"That one is the biggest." I said. "It's a natural species. But it has an unnatural disease. A form of cancer."

"Cancer?" Papas raised his eyebrows in actual concern.

"Yes. Humans may not suffer it, now. But—"

Papas cut in. "Is it contagious?"

"No. It's unique to the—"

Papas cut me off again and added to my growing anger.

"Okay. Is its disease terminal?"

"Maybe," I grated. "But before then it may reach its brain."

Papas opened his mouth to cut me off again but I raised my voice and kept speaking. "If it loses all control and stays hungry, it becomes an even bigger threat! But we can use that hunger if we act quickly. The fish inside the ship are in preservation tanks. We can—"

"We've got a lot of threats on the streets," Papas said with a glance to his stack of holographic files as two new ones appeared at the bottom. "Coast Guard can get wet if they want to find the thing. You had your shot, Ahab. Now get back to work, here."

Papas' knowledge of the classics surprised me, yet he had to be educated to be a top cop. But his rank and power was not helping. Instead, it was in my way and his shift in focus would surely cost more lives.

"But I know how to stop it. And we have to." I didn't really want to kill the giant octopus. It was an amazing, massive creature. More important, it was natural. But it was doomed and I had a duty to save human lives. Maybe Papas held a similar ideal. Or not. Maybe his biggest concern was not human life but the number of files he needed to clear. He held power, but a different idea in how to use it. And my name rose to the top of his list for quick fixes.

Papas looked at Slate. "I know you got files to clear, detective sergeant."

"I do." Slate said. He left with a glance of caution over to me.

Papas looked at me. "So do you."

Brick. It was a building material used for centuries. Now it's an archeological relic. I usually find brick at the bottoms of dark, buried shafts that were once street-level alleys. But some brick survives in walls and buildings exposed to the acrid, city atmosphere. Construction workers stacked those bricks so long ago that people might confuse them with the ancient pyramid builders. If you could find the pyramids. They are not along the street I walked. It was a near forgotten stretch of road off the main commercial arterials. It harbored a different world one block over from the building-side holograms and bright lights. This street was an older, darker length of pocked and lonely asphalt. No vehicles traveled across or above this length of Othello Street for several intersections East and West. My boots made a louder noise against the grit than the airborne and surface traffic visible as moving dots cutting across the slash between buildings in the distance.

I had never been here. Papas sent me to find a monster reported to be menacing the area. Maybe he was telling the truth. I didn't think so. A little research said this was the home of the Othello Street Shadows. A street gang. There aren't many street gangs, today. If they stay around too long, they get eaten. Their bravado might as well be herb seasoning across their skin. I wondered if the Shadows were more like a helpful militia that took up the slack where city services failed. Or maybe they just robbed people. I figured the Shadows were why Papas sent me to Othello. I was more worried about running into a fellow Monster Killer who may be less than pleased seeing me if he or she considers this his or her turf. But I was sure we could cut a deal if we met. We may all carry an arsenal, but we also show colleagues professional consideration and kindness. Most of the time.

I tossed a *huv* into the air. It's a small hovering camera the size of a fly. I've seen living flies in the streets, but usually a buzzing dot indicates some human is watching you. I carry a pulse wand to drop flying spies if I feel demure. The huv gave me an overview of the unknown territory sent to my retinal screens. From overhead, the brick buildings appeared like sideways sediment under the pressure of successive, newer buildings. Those rose as steps to the epic, smooth towers that reached through the clouds. The huv dropped back into my pocket. I had a feeling others wanted access to them, as well.

I had to give the Othello Street Shadows credit. I did not intimidate them. That hurt, a little. They formed a moving circle with gang members ahead, behind, and flanking me. They were organized, had tactics, and all wore the same color scheme of dark blue and black. It was time I acted to gain the advantage. I did something they never expected. I spoke to them.

"So, ladies and gentlemen, there is a report of a monster around here. Seen it?"

Silence. Several looks of surprise rippled across the Shadows' chain of command. I followed them to the leader. She stood in the group of three behind me. I turned to face her.

"I'd like a clue," I said to the leader. She was a sinewy, blonde, and probably young woman. "It's better when I start shooting if the rounds head in the right direction. But I've got a lot of ammo. So—?"

"Only thing weird around here is you!" The leader fired at me.

"You exclude yourself from weird?" I asked.

The reply was a round palisade of middle fingers.

"Look, we own this place." The leader crossed her arms as her lieutenants nodded affirmation.

"Fine," I said. "I'm sure you're great landlords. But I'm here to kill something. If—"

"Us?" the leader cut in.

"Do I need to?" I asked.

There was another second of silence as the leader worked up a comeback. She obviously knew I was well armed and they had maybe a few stolen guns and sharp objects to back up all the clenched fists.

"Hey. I think *we* ask that question!" The leader said and stabbed her thumb backwards to point at herself.

"Answering it would be hard for us all," I said. "I think you know my kind. I know yours. Any truly weird kinds here we both need to whack?"

The leader took another moment of thought, and then answered. "Honestly, no."

"Okay then," I shrugged. "Have a nice day. And keep out of dark places."

"Uh, yeah." The leader waited a second to see if I actually turned to walk away. When I did, she stiffened and added. "Now get lost!"

I replied to the 1.75-meter, 56.68-kilogram warlord of broken asphalt in a way I typically never do. I smiled. The Shadows parted to let me pass and didn't follow.

One crumbling building width away, brick caught my attention again. Something on it moved. It was a moth. Large brown wings fluttered and revealed vivid blue circles that made false, flat eyes. Typically such *eyes* glared to warn off predators. However, this display was not a warning. It was a lure. That was easy to deduce, because as far as I knew, flies, some other species of insects, and a few nasty arachnids survived, but moths were extinct. The moth fluttered again to be sure it caught my attention. Slowly, I reached for my gun. I had found a true monster.

The fake, colorful insect was an *ipex*, a word formed from Incongruous Physical Expression. It didn't describe some modern, freeform dance. It described a seeming out of place physical trait manifested in the horror show of monster features. An ipex could be a human ear on alligator-like jaws or a pig ear where a shark's eye might look more fitting. Some monsters enjoyed either a freak of luck or some unknown manner of selecting traits out of their genetic chaos for useful things such as extra eyes, or lures that look like pretty moths. Just as with the first tentacle of the giant octopus, the moth was part of something bigger. The whole creature's reveal would come in the next heartbeat. Then, I would kill it. Or be dead.

A tendril extended from the fake moth to something else in the alley beside it. I moved toward the alley entrance and felt the instant of anticipation and the spike of epinephrine that tells you that no matter your resolve, the emotion you feel is fear. It all occurred in fractions of a second. Strangely, the alley debris vibrated. A cluster of compound eyes rose from behind an ancient trash can. They attached to a black slope that ended in an opening maw. The moth flew from the wall propelled by the tendril. It slapped my face and sprayed a toxin my enhanced system quickly neutralized. The maw erupted with teeth of chitin. The beast was a chimera with more than one, neat trick. The moth lured prey onto a nearly invisible membrane. Later analysis showed it appeared similar to huge dragonfly wings as supple as skin. The membrane slid the victims to the slicing teeth that hewed them into chunks for swallowing. It jerked me closer to the snapping mouth but I leapt back and rolled onto the gritty street.

The monster was surprisingly quiet for something the size of a dumpster that was no longer hiding. I made noise with two massive handguns. My eardrums would heal, but not the monster. The shells punched through its folds of black and mottled skin and exploded. The burn mark the moth lure left on my face stung again as blood and chunks of the beast showered the alley and street where I stood. Its mouth and membrane quivered. They stopped. I shook my head to flick off bits of monster spatter from my hair. One more people-eating freak was dead. And once again, I needed a shower.

One of the Shadow lieutenants came closer. He was a little rounder in the body than the leader yet somehow more gaunt in the face.

"You know, we really didn't know that thing was there." The lieutenant said.

"Yeah," I took a deep breath and holstered my weapons. "But you would have."

"There was a monster. A real one." I spoke to Papas via a link to my retina screen from my wristcom as I walked into the busier, brighter streets away from Othello. I saw a transparent display of Papas' round, peptic face across my right eye.

"Really?" Papas jerked his head. "But there is still a little gang issue, right?"

"Not my problem!" I barked and got looks from other pedestrians, even those engaged in their own apparent monologues.

"Don't play around." Papas sneered. "I send you. You do the job. You get paid. Same as ever."

"Not quite. This monster covered your ass. More bounties like the Butcher case and it won't just be me making complaints."

"Then they can call the cops." Papas said.

"Funny. Hilarious."

"Oh, I'm a laugh riot, Grail. Or Ice. That's what the streeters call you, right? Cold as a glacier. If you know what a glacier was."

"I do."

"And if you know what's good for you, you'll answer when I call."

I said nothing and cut the link. There were enough people uttering expletives to express my mood.

Throughout the planetary apocalypses both prevented and endured, some things stayed constant. One was that food served near an ocean view at least doubled in price. Some engineers had created a view that looked out across the expanse of dark waves and straight below to the ones hitting the artificial shore through a transparent floor. You could also see the sky, if you preferred a different hue of black. The restaurant was fused to an older tower stuffed with old money. Its structure stuck to the shoreline tower like a barnacle made from the modern versions of glass and steel. Oddly, the wealthy diners rarely noticed the black rolling abyss.

The restaurant caught the attention of something beneath the waves.

The diners noticed the shaking even before the loss of view caused by massive tentacles. The huge suckers were certainly odd. The violent tugging was disconcerting. The moan of the steel and cracking windows triggered terror. I watched a news feed of the disaster played across my retinas. The restaurant's bonding to the larger building was strong. The giant octopus was stronger. The restaurant tore away. The metal moans ended and the sound of shattering fixtures inside the falling, artificial barnacle merged with the screams. Octopus and restaurant hit the sea. The black water became an explosion of waves and thrashing tentacles. The impact of the waves against the surviving tower was the last sound as I cut the feed.

Soon after, I was back in front of Papas' desk. He smiled when I entered his cubicle. I glared.

"You ignored the threat." My words sounded as if a rasp worked across my clenched teeth. "It came back and killed again. Now you want to rush in and snatch up the glory? Maybe get a higher cubicle?"

Papas also ignored my rebuke. "You said you had a plan. I know it will be simple like a bullet to the head. How do we kill it?"

I swallowed my anger to finish the job. I clicked my wristcom to send data to his holograph and display my file. "Tissues left on the surviving pier showed pollutants caused an oncogenic reaction in its nervous sys—"

"Yeah, well?" Papas cut in.

I switched off the display. "Is the ship still at the pier? Still looking to unload?"

"Yeah. And?"

"We poison the fish."

Captain Milfurst was unhappy with the plan to use the remaining, unprocessed fish in his ship's automated guts. "What! No way!"

The brightly lit bridge was the only piece of the ship that looked modern, but with monitors, not holographic displays. Still, they were not rusting.

"The thing's got cancer," I said. "It's spreading to its brain. It's losing its mind. Soon it will come back here and sink your ship, and then move to other piers."

"If we don't kill it soon, more people die!" Slate added.

"My catch is worth eighty-five stems!" Milfurst screeched. "Forget it!"

I had been a little stressed. It affected my actions. I grabbed Milfurst's thick, oily coveralls. His deck boot holdfasts popped as I jerked him off the floor. I held him at nose length from my glaring eyes. "Your attitude stinks, little man!"

"It's here, now." Slate said almost calmly as he pointed to the sonar screens and the huge mass coming near. "It dies."

I told myself killing the octopus was the humane thing to do. Death from its cancer would be more torturous. Its genome would be archived and added to the thousand millions of species witnessed and lost from the shrouded Earth. We watched as a police forensics team poisoned the living fish. Seeing species of kunan in the holding tanks was a new experience for them, Slate, and me. There would be enough. The fish would swim out, confused. The giant octopus would catch and eat them as one big feast. Soon after, it would also die. We humans have become really good at killing all kinds of things. I suppose we always have been.

Those thoughts resurfaced hours later as I watched two workers load a particular body into municipal incinerator number eighty-five. Its existence justified the open space of the precinct's utility yard. The burning never stopped. The workers cursed the hatch lock for jamming and kicked it shut. The row of decrepit chimneys looked as though they threatened to collapse. They appeared made from some type of heavy brick. Smoke drifted from their cracked tops to the constant canopy of black clouds high overhead. Their substance looked the same.

"What are you doing here?" I hear Slate ask as he arrived behind me.

"Part of the job." I said.

"No it isn't. Your bounty is paid on this one." Slate looked at the incineration order for Lewis Banks on the old scrawl board, and then tossed it back into the attendant's booth.

"Why are you here, Slate? Can't be to stay warm."

"I read the file on the Butcher case." Slate paused. He seemed to reconsider saying what was on his mind. "Despite Papas' own report, there was no monster. Was there?"

"No. Lewis Banks was a standard-issue psychopath. Just another twisted human. Just a man. Papas tagged him a monster simply to save time. No technicalities. No trial. One file cleared. Just tag, bag, and burn."

Slate nodded. The ramifications were clear to him. Fire from a reopened hatch lit his grimace.

"Makes you wonder how far it will go." As I spoke, workers tossed bagged sections of the Othello Street monster into the incinerator. "Your union dues paid up, Slate?"

The incinerator hatch slammed shut. Lewis Banks was then just more ashes in the sky.

"What's Papas got next for you?" Slate's question was pointed.

"I turned him down. The municipal domain clause is valid only if I'm not already working a job. In the way I read it, anyway. Something will get hungry by tomorrow. And, I put the word out among my colleagues. Papas won't get many responses. Monster Killers like being able to choose what to shoot at and when to run. We don't like being manipulated and controlled. We're funny that way."

"You'd better be careful," Slate's eyes were bright in the firelight flickering through gaps of the hatches. "Papas can make life hard for you."

"I might be a little too slow tomorrow, and be dead before he cares. Then again, something might eat Papas."

"True." Slate almost smiled.

I turned to walk toward the gate.

"Ice." Slate's face tensed. "What Papas made you do, may make another Killer do, it's not that different from what you've done to people yourself, in the past."

I paused and took a breath. "You're right."

"So no one is safe, human or monster?"

"I suppose in a way, that's balance. But not my idea." I looked at him and shook my head. "My goal is to kill monsters. Yours, detective?"

"Old story." Slate turned from the incinerators. "Respect for the law. Maybe even bring justice to the oppressed."

"Good luck," I said without irony.

"All we can do is try."

"I'm for that." I gave a slow nod.

Slate nodded back and looked back at the incinerators. His body relaxed. "By the way, Ice—Mr. Grail, my union dues are paid up."

I kept quiet for a moment, before saying in earnest: "Glad to hear it."

I left Slate at the incinerators and returned to the pier. I watched the body of the once powerful giant octopus move at the mercy of the tide. Decay already ate at its great, still mass. The smoke of the incinerators still in my nostrils mingled with the cloying stench of the rotting beast. I fixed my stare on the huge and once angry eyes that were now clouded and dim. An ecosystem deep and far away had sustained this titan. Once that natural system collapsed, its power wrought havoc on the surface. Balance, natural or manmade, once kept even great monsters in check. But checks and balances must be maintained, or power can lash out with intolerant fury. The sea giant brought its fury to the human shore at the cost of its life, and perhaps the last part of a vanished world.

My wrist unit flashed the familiar green. Another monster was causing terror, somewhere. Time to pay my dues. Usually I saved lives by destroying abominations that should never have taken breath. I was sure the people I spared did not mind the scales tipped in their favor. For a time, I could end their fear.

11
CHILDREN OF DARKNESS

Part One
"Child of Hunger"

The future is like an unlit room. It has potential for terror or peace that stands revealed in light. On an Earth captured by black clouds giving permanent siege to the sky, darkness isn't the mere absence of light. Electric lamps offer a truce from uncertainty if not fear. Yet, there are many forms of darkness. It can persist in well-lit rooms of any size. Forms of darkness live where and when history is forgotten, or willfully perverted. Omens also take many forms. Creaks warn of support beams weakening and cracks growing larger. Stomping feet trample the sound and echo across an old, elevated warehouse where a group of uniformed children practiced the archaic art of marching. Much has changed on Earth since people marched under national banners, but not the laws of physics. A sharp snap quells the marching. The beams give way and the decrepit floor collapses. The children and shards of broken beams plummet into darkness. The children scream. Two large, serpentine eyes catch the light through the hole and watch them fall.

Several blocks from the warehouse, no eyes met those of the man known as Tuco. His eyes sat in a rounded face of young, but weathered skin like freshly cooled lava. This neighborhood of the planet-spanning city is his domain. His heavy boots clanged over an ancient street grating that other people avoided. Something below may hear the footsteps and stir. Tuco has no such fear. Although, sometimes at night the massive hunter feels as if he is plunging uncontrollably into darkness. He knows it is only the sensation of falling asleep. Still, he hates it. It is the only time Tuco feels helpless. It reminds him of the past. Once, Tuco was a scared, little boy who climbed lampposts for fear of the dark. Now he makes his living in dark places by killing things that others fear.

A high-pitched tone sounded from Tuco's wrist-com. He raised his forearm to a horizontal position. A holographic bust of a very nervous man in a glittering uniform projected over Tuco's wrist.

"Uh, hello," the man said. "Ah, geez! Are your rates reasonable? I need some help. There-there's a monster."

"Reasonable? Depends. How much time do you have to bargain?" Tuco laughed aloud on the street as people passed. The hologram projected the nervous man's sweat with perfect fidelity. Tuco laughed louder.

Transit lines quickly took Tuco to the warehouse and the man in the glittering uniform known as the self-appointed Commandant Bodhran. Curious and brave child cadets of Bodhran gathered around Tuco as he looked into the hole made earlier by the marching children.

"It's down there in the shadows," Bodhran pointed, and then quickly yanked his hand from the hole. "Some of my cadets are trapped by it."

"They're still alive?" Tuco asked and put on a set of sheer goggles. He peered back into the darkness. "It's their lucky day, eh? Monster must have a full belly. That gives me a little time."

Tuco removed his heavy jacket and dropped it on the wooden floor. It hit with a *thump!* He wore a repelling harness stretched across his wide chest with holsters for his two, massive handguns. He knelt and removed a bundle of narrow rope and three, thin rods from his jacket. He took the rods by their central knob in his right hand and flicked them. They snapped into a tripod. Some of the children jumped. Tuco smiled and tossed it over the hole. The three, narrow legs shot extensions that anchored into solid flooring around the jagged hole. Tuco attached a small pulley to the rope as the tripod adjusted its apex over the hole's center.

"So, you run this school?" Tuco asked Bodhran. He tossed the pulley with precision at the tripod's center. A metallic *snap!* sounded as pulley struck the tripod and automatically positioned itself at the center of the three, narrow shafts.

"Yes. It's a military academy. The first of the century, I think." Bodhran answered with pride.

"Military? That must mean rich, if all these kids are legal." Tuco cocked his left eyebrow and aimed a stare at Bodhran.

"They are, I assure you. I'm also sure the parents of my trapped cadets will pay you a bonus if you save them." Bodhran chimed.

"Maybe a bonus if I don't." Tuco laughed as he attached the rope line to his harness.

Bodhran's smile sunk. "Well, ah, wouldn't your own parents have wanted you back?"

"I can barely remember them." Tuco shrugged. He dropped the free rope through the hole. A slight hissing sounded as its fibers stretched and lengthened into the black. Tuco pulled the length between himself and the tripod. It contracted and tightened. "My father wasn't around long enough to make an impression. I do remember my mother, a bit. She brought food to our little home. Hardly anyone else was around. I guess she had to work a lot to afford having me. Irony, eh?"

"No school? Didn't you get an education?" Bodhran asked.

"You could say I had an interesting education." Tuco said as he looked below into the darkness. "I left home a lot to escape the loneliness and survived the streets. But I always came back when I got hungry."

"You needed structure and guidance, like I provide here." Bodhran chirped. "Do you have any children, Mr. Tuco? I can make some openings as a way of thanks."

"If I fail, you'll probably have a lot more openings." Tuco gave a low laugh to himself and reached his to his sides to adjust his weapons. "I could never afford the permits for kids, even with a steady wife. It's hard to think about a family when it's tough to keep myself alive. But that's why I'm paid well, eh? Especially you, today, because I noticed you called me before the police or medics."

Bodhran felt the stares of the cadets on him as Tuco smiled with a narrowed gaze at Bodhran. He replied with a pained, affirmative nod to Tuco.

"I know my mother did as best she could before she disappeared." Tuco said and then swung out over the hole. An audible creak came from the entire floor. Some cadets glanced to each other and crept away from the edge of the hole.

"She left you, sir?" a brave female cadet asked across the hole from Bodhran.

"No. She was taken." Tuco said as he kept his goggles aimed into the dark. "All the police found was blood and a torn sack of groceries."

"That's sad, sir. I'm sorry." The cadet replied.

"You think this monster below me has parents? Maybe some kids?" Tuco smiled at the child as he slowly began his descent.

"Well, I don't know, sir." The cadet replied, surprised by the question. "It's just a monster."

"Does it matter?" Bodhran asked, and then finally waved the children away from the danger.

"Never seems to," Tuco answered quietly as he dropped lower. Shadow now enveloped his legs. "Keep the lights on. It probably blinds your monster. Not so your Killer." Tuco's voice was distant with a slight echo in the chamber below.

Tuco glanced up and smiled at Bodhran, but all the elaborate commandant could see was a brief glint reflected off Tuco's goggles. Bodhran said nothing as shadow fully overtook Tuco. He considered Tuco's point if he failed. That could be better financially for business. Bodhran would not have to pay the Monster Killer. The cadets' tuition was banked. Their slots would open for more cadets with rich, fully permitted parents. Bodhran heard creaking. He looked at the taught rope line tugging the impossibly narrow tripod, and stepped away from the hole.

Tuco dropped farther in the black. He made a good living as a single man. He was never hungry, anymore. But the monsters were always taking prey, taking people. Tuco thought of his mother every time he shot a hungry beast into bloody pieces, and collected them into a self-sealing bag. He kept those thoughts of revenge to himself. Now, he focused on saving young lives caught in darkness.

The fallen children cowered together below him at the edge of the faint cone of light. Bruises and cuts marked their faces. Low whimpers escaped from the most frightened two. Near them, the serpent flexed its mammoth coils as it watched the annoying thing from above drop too close. Its human enemy saw all revealed in clear, high-definition FRACDAR from his goggles. The serpentine monster snapped its jaws open. Instead of fangs, rows of shark-like teeth launched at Tuco. He immediately released the rope's tension and dropped. The serpent's jaws slapped shut over the rope. The stream of light through the hole revealed the beast to curious and defiant young eyes above. They screamed. Tuco cursed the rope's manufacturer as it snapped.

Tuco plummeted free, but tossed up a small, cylindrical flare from his harness. The sudden burst of intense light stunned the huge serpent. Tuco hit the floor and rolled beside the monster's coils. He pulled his guns in mid-somersault. The monster arced its neck and lunged down at Tuco. He thrust up his guns. He saw only the beast's serrated mouth over him as he squeezed the triggers. Explosive bullets shredded the serpent's head. Tuco kept shooting until only bloody, butchered muscles struck him.

Reflexive contractions made the headless body squirm as Tuco fought his way from under the heavy, moving corpse. Once free, he stood and shook off the monster's blood. He took a breath as he watched the headless thing's writhing slow and end.

"*Requiescat in pace*, mother." Tuco said. He holstered his guns. "Tonight I come home again."

There was noise behind him. Tuco turned and only saw the generated images of the fallen children blurred by the monster's blood on his goggles. The violence of blinding flashes and terrible noise of gunfire created only more terror and confusion. They had no idea they were now safe and were still afraid and in pain.

"Don't worry little ones. I'm not here to eat you." Tuco smiled. He knelt beside the cadets and removed his goggles. "You are all too thin."

Later in the light above, Tuco carefully lowered the last rescued child to the solid edge of the hole. At the far end of the warehouse, medics carried the two more seriously hurt children up a stairway in medical cocoons.

"Don't worry, little one. It's safe. For now." Tuco winked at the small girl who was reluctant to let go of him even with the monster's blood still splashed across him.

She finally released her tight grip on Tuco. He lifted her over to the solid floor. Bodhran watched them with pointed interest.

"Mr. Tuco, you seem to have a way with children," Bodhran observed. "I have a proposition, if you have the time?"

Tuco massaged his bruised shoulder. "If you have the cash, Mister—what's your name, again?"

"Commandant."

Part Two
"Mother's Little Monster"

As Bodhran droned on, another Killer prowled a different part of the darkened city. In a shadowed alley between near ruins of apartment buildings, an old lamp gave weak light over the only opened door. A young boy emerged and placed a small dish beside two decrepit steps. Drops of the synthetic equivalent of milk fell over the side and hit the layer of dust drifted down from the black overhead. The distinction between purpose and abuse was already lost.

"Kitty, kitty," the boy sang. He then snaked back into the doorway.

In short time, a scruffy cat wearing a band of wire twisted into a makeshift collar arrived and lapped at the dish. The boy peered out in anticipation from behind a narrow slit of opened door. Other eyes appeared low in the shadows and reflected the weak light. The cat tensed. It turned to hiss at the sudden menace. Giant mantis arms covered in lizard skin snatched up the cat. The boy opened the door wider. He grinned wickedly as savage jaws devoured the cat. Blood spilled over the aged steps. The spat, wire collar followed. The boy made gleeful squeals as the monster swallowed.

The monster was no larger than the dogs that once played with children. Its body was like a featherless raptor with the grasping arms of a praying mantis. Its long and wide mouth stretched across a thick distortion of a crocodile's snout. Mottled, reptilian skin wrapped its muscled body. Its large, reflective eyes narrowed as it turned its head to the door. Thick, lizard lips pulled back over curving teeth as the monster made an imitated grin at the boy.

"Kitty, kitty." The hideous beast repeated like a deep-throated parrot. It crept back into the shadows. The boy closed the door.

Minutes later, forensic scans generated data to reconstruct the bloody act from fur, blood, and other evidence. Many new species of predators live in the shrouded city. The man called Ice is one of them. His full name is Joshua Grail, at least in this life. He picked up the cat's collar with the muzzle of his shotgun-styled weapon. The mangled band took a long journey up and finally hung before steel-blue eyes locked in a granite face. Stony features frowned. Like Tuco, Grail preyed on the monsters in the dark. No job was too small, but the beast here was gone. He had larger bounties to pursue, and walked back to the noise of the street. The presence of a young boy, perhaps six years old, was a rarity for the range incomes in this region. More surprising to Grail was the discovery of cats surviving into this age. He wondered how many of the felines lived around the alley. They were a natural species, and thus rare.

The next day arrived. There is no new cat to bait, but the monster's hunger had returned.

"Kitty, kitty" the boy drew a sigh. "Kitty?"

The beast left the shadows and approached the milk dish. Reptilian eyelids sagged. The monster's down-curved lips suggested a frown across its snout.

"Kitty, kitty," the beast chirped at the boy.

The boy looked down at the thing from the top step. He shrugged at what he knew as his playmate in their brutal game. The monster mimicked the boy's shrug. The boy smiled and made the classic gesture of sticking his thumbs in his ears and flapping his hands. The monster attempted to mimic the boy as best it could with its grotesque limbs built to snatch and kill. It stopped. Hunger led its shift in thought. The boy stopped playing and dropped his arms. He looked at the monster and his smile ebbed. A predator's eyes focused on the boy.

"Kitty, kitty," the boy said in hope of resetting the monster's mood.

"Kitty, kitty," the beast repeated. Its association with the words was a simple one. It moved closer to the boy. A hideous, false smile revealed its teeth. It expected the boy to hiss.

The boy slammed the door shut. He ran in panic into his home, screaming. "Mommy!"

The frightened boy hit large, adult legs wearing protective boots. He fell back. From the floor, he looked up the length of a gray, canvas trench coat. His eyes finally met a stone face armed with steel-blue eyes.

"Stay down." Grail told the child firmly, and lifted his shotgun.

In the next second, the monster smashed through the door with arms and jaws opened wide. The boy rolled behind Grail. The small beast blew back through the shattered door with sudden thunder. Its blasted carcass slapped against the alley pavement, dust, stains of blood and artificial milk.

The boy cupped is ears as he looked out the door's enlarged hole with wide-eyes. His mother handed Grail a small bundle of moldered cash. The bills hung like limp skin.

"This one's on me." Grail waves off her attempted payment, and hooked his weapon beneath his coat.

"It's not for the monster." The mother glanced at the boy. Her nervous eyes looked back at Grail. "It's to keep quiet."

"He's legal. I checked. His code is on file in the registry of heirs."

"I know." The mother presses the cash against Grail's chest. "But some cop might want to check that, too. The law says words on a screen aren't proof of sanction. They can confiscate him until some bureaucrat gets around to checking, and then some judge bothers to sign off on him. That happened before. I lost one of his birthdays. Just-just take it and keep quiet! Please."

Grail sighed. "It must have cost a lot to finance his license."

"It's why we live here, now." The mother said while still pressing the cash against Grail's chest.

"Then keep it. The city pays my way through here, anyway. But maybe," Grail shrugged, "just watch him more."

Grail gently pushed the mother's arm away. Her expression changed from anxious to outraged.

"So you're volunteering to sit with him while I work?" She shouted. "Good! I can quit his day care now. And you'll teach him, too. Right? You can take Charlie with you on your city paid time to shoot freaks!"

The maternal anger stoked Grail's own emotions, but they didn't flare into retaliation. His weapons and broad powers to kill now felt like constraints, not liberties. They were useless, here. He understood her frustration, but could not solve the problem. At least he saved the boy, for tonight.

"I'm sorry." Grail said. "I only kill monsters. Most of the time."

The mother glared at Grail as he stepped outside. The boy, Charlie, rubbed his ears as he watched Grail enter the alley. Grail's granite brow broke into furrows. Scanners relayed strange results across his retina. The monster's cells were in an accelerated mitosis. It was still growing. The monster might have been a child itself.

"If that's true," Grail muttered, "I'd hate to see its—"

Faint sounds behind Grail seized his focus. A heavy liquid struck the alley pavement from high above. Grail turned. The weak light of the old lamp reflected across large, reptilian eyes. The eyes were already higher than the tall Grail. They rose higher. The monster's giant mother stepped forward, almost silently. Grail's enhanced vision revealed its entire, nightmare form. She was a fusion of mantis and Tyrannosaur covered in thick scales of armor. Saliva streamed from opened, sickle-bearing jaws above Grail's head.

Inside Charlie's home, he stared terrified through the blasted door. He jerked back as huge claws snatched his savior into the air.

"Mom! Mommee! Run!" The boy screeched and then yanked on his mother's arm as she intently looked for a new place to hide the cash.

"It's all right, Charlie!" She stuffed the cash into a pants pocket. "He's—"

Grail is smashed through the wall at the end of monster claws. Debris sent the mother and Charlie tumbling into the front room.

Grail hit the floor. His coat crackled from a protective discharge of electricity. He leaned up and shouted. "Run!"

The monster bursts through the remaining wall. Charlie and his mother escaped through the front door. Grail rolled and fired at the charging monster. His shells deflected off the monster's armored hide. Teeth and slashing claws snatched at Grail in the cramped apartment. He clubbed the monster with his shotgun and knocked aside its thrusting head.

Outside on the forbidding street, the mother and Charlie reached the lamppost on the curb. Speeding traffic hummed past them in a blurred line. Grail exploded back-first through the apartment wall. His arc ended with a thud against the curb. Grail shook his head as the mother attempted to lift him.

"Get Up! Help us! Please!" she screamed.

The monster smashed through the new hole. Grail hurled a small cylinder at the monster that exploded in the air ahead of the beast. It jerked backward.

"Ammo drop! Now!" Grail yelled into his wrist-com. A large, black drum dropped beside him from its orbit in the overhead transit lanes.

The monster shook off the stun from the explosion, and sought the target of its wrath. It charged again as locks released on the ammo drum. Grail grabbed a rocket launcher from a circular weapons rack inside it as he ducked swipes of talon-scythes on huge, mantis arms. Grail thrust up his new weapon. Massive jaws swooped to engulf him as the mother and boy screamed. The monster's head disappeared in a deafening blast and flash of liquid purple. The beast's headless body lurched up and continued its now mindless charge into the traffic. High-speed ground cars hit the headless carcass. It bounced between the fast moving traffic of wedge and oval bludgeons. Horns blared as in traffic of long ago. Magnetic fields and flexible alloys prevented greater carnage for the drivers as cars hit the monster and each other. The blur of headlights slowed into a chaotic chain of bright dots. Low-level taxis, busses, and the odd personal transport formed the blaring links.

The battered Grail leaned against the lamppost still holding the smoking rocket launcher. Traffic police arrived from overhead.

"Are you okay, Mister?" The mother asked over the din of horns and thumps of distant collisions.

"Yeah, I'll be fine. But that one, that one will cost you."

A few peaceful moments later, Grail waited for specialized police. The monster's body was too big for typical removal. An Evidence/Disposal truck arrived through a path cleared for it. Officers in dirty rubber suits cut the battered and headless carcass into sections with invisible beams lancing from the rear of the truck. A wet, acrid stench wafted over the street.

Grail sighed as he registered his bounty with a faceless officer protected by an opaque helmet. Grail wondered what he saw through the glassy surface. Behind them, Charlie peeked over the jagged edges of the apartment's street-side hole. His mother's arms enveloped him, and she pulled the boy farther back into the shattered home. A shriek sounded from Grail's wrist-com, along with a familiar flash of green. He cocked his right arm horizontally.

"Mr. Grail, are you open to new business?" Bodhran spoke as a holographic advertisement played in place of his image. The projected words grew larger: *Sanctioned Parents, do you have a trying child without direction? Are you tired of expensive schools with no values? Contact: Commandant Bodhran. Direction is Salvation.*

Grail looked up the apartment. Charlie's mother hung a sheet to fill her missing wall as police considered the damage.

"Yeah. I've done all I can here."

Part Three
"Legacy"

Grail did not look far to find transportation on the crowded street. Soon after, he entered Bodhran's converted warehouse on a landing to a missing floor. The stairway descended to the surviving floor that sported a newly patched hole and Bodhran's academy. Grail took in the panoramic view of the recreated military training camp. However, only a few loosely organized groups of children used it. Others were scattered lazily about the facsimile-wood sheds intended to serve as barracks. All the camp's cadets wore green uniforms like Bodhran's own, but without the gold laurel on the shoulders and brimmed cap. Bodhran marched toward Grail. The only disciplined squad of cadets followed him. The children managed to march in tight formation carrying huge, black rifles. None of them appeared to be older than a teenager.

"Mr. Grail! Welcome, sir." Bodhran beamed as Grail stepped off the stairs. The squad of rifle-bearing cadets snapped awkward salutes behind him.

Grail looked at his greeters with cool suspicion. A typical, suppressed tension lived in his brain when he entered a site harboring a beast that attacked humans and might use him for food. Armed children were not what he expected, but nearly as odd as the shapes of monsters. He focused his stare at Bodhran.

"You said there is a monster here." Grail growled. "Where?"

"I apologize for the canard, sir." Bodhran bowed his head in a quick, darting motion. "May I call you Ice?"

"No."

"Oh! All right." Bodhran darted his head backward. "Well, Mr. Grail, I promise you'll be well paid. If you would follow me?"

"The meter is running." Grail eased and indulged his curiosity.

"You are direct. Good!" Bodhran snapped to a stiffer posture with a smile, but still found his hat lower than Grail's glaring eyes. "And, unlike the rest of the world, I have a direction in life."

Grail and Bodhran walked from the stairway followed closely by the rigid squad of children. Bodhran gestured purposefully as he spoke. Grail continued eyeing him and his surroundings with caution.

"You see, Mr. Grail, today, there is no sense of country or ethnic belonging. At present, there are no real independent countries. And you can adopt any racial characteristics you choose. Blue even. Our children are lost with no direction to guide them. I want to create a school based on traditional values, those values of generations past with strong division of purpose."

"Were your ancestors fence builders?" Grail asked.

"Ah, maybe." Bodhran paused to consider the question. "Anyway, to accomplish my goals I feel a military order is best. Eventually, our training will be complete with live fire exercises!"

Grail and Bodhran arrived at a group of historical holograms standing before cadets sitting on the floor. Projected leaders from past ages looked out beyond the children and gave speeches to lost audiences. Among them, individuals in pressed suits competed for attention with others in uniforms and armor. Some figures were stiff. Others gestured wildly. Swords and assault rifles stabbed the air. Fists clutched and waved papers. Shields and standards glimmered next to billowing lengths of bright fabrics. More holograms fused into a confused background of forgotten leaders. The impassioned flow of words merged in a low murmur across the watching children.

"The trouble Mr. Grail," Bodhran began again, "is that there is only so much that images and media stimulus can teach my cadets. They need flesh and blood to show them the pain it takes to succeed in the world."

"The world gives enough pain on its own." Grail said in a low snarl.

"Precisely! That's why we need to stiffen them. And that's where you have a purpose. Without real militaries today, there aren't true instructors in the arts of war. But as a Monster Killer you've seen enough action to curl the hair of a thousand little Caesars. By Chrysler, you'll teach them all new tricks!"

"Even the old dogs?" Grail watched a familiar and seemingly out-of-place colleague approach.

Another squad of children followed Tuco. Their formation was less rigid than Bodhran's cadre.

"*Hola*, Ice. How do you like my recruits?" Tuco smiled. "Not bad, eh?"

"They look too small for apprentices." Grail cocked his left eyebrow. "You're not using them to bait hooks, are you?"

"Ha!" Tuco's massive frame rocked as he laughed. "You should have been here, earlier! I was bait on a line."

"Instructor Tuco is the person who suggested you for employment, Mr. Grail." Bodhran chimed. "As you can see he's, ah, worked wonders with his cadets. But there is still much to do! With spirited effort, we can shape these youngsters into obedient units with purpose!"

"Obedient units?" Grail drew a deep breath. "So what happens after you've trained them?"

"We continue their progress into a new, decisive path." Bodhran straightened his back. "One that will benefit us all."

"And you have that path all mapped out, Bodhran?" Grail asked.

"You ask a lot more questions than Instructor Tuco." Bodhran rolled his shoulders. "But, yes, I do. Let me ask you, Mr. Grail, how do you deal with a monster?"

"You kill it."

"Well, my methods need not be so final, at least not at first. Enemies of a healthy society are everywhere. A little implication of force should cure the social invalids once our movement builds." Bodhran nodded.

"Threatening invalids with children. Sounds like a brave plan." Grail's eyes narrowed at Bodhran.

Bodhran's face slowly drew into a scowl. Grail remained calm. Tuco took in a long sigh and looked to the ceiling with a resigned expression, and then motioned for his cadets to march away.

"This goes much farther than personal bravery, Mr. Grail." Bodhran sneered. "But perhaps your own knowledge of that is less than billed. The future of this world is at stake. I'm strong enough to take a stand to stop it. Are you going to sit by while the planet falls deeper in the sewer? Where are your priorities?"

"Where they've been for some time, Bodhran. In that sewer is where I stop monsters from messing up peoples' day. Maybe you should join me there. It has a way of changing a person's perspective, like on the value of human life. When you see it can be so quickly taken, you tend to respect it more."

"It's obvious we are at odds. You may leave. It's too bad you don't see the same potential of the cadets that I do." Bodhran turned away from Grail with a face twisted in disgust.

"All I see are the future bodies of dead children. I've seen enough of those in the stomachs of other monsters. I won't let them be piled into a monument to one man's ego."

Bodhran spun and gnashed at Grail. "You should have just left, Killer! I will not allow you to spoil this operation, nor will I tolerate disrespect on my campus!"

Bodhran snapped his fingers. His rigid squad of children pointed their weapons at Grail in a near unified motion.

Grail casually rolled out a small cylinder from his right cuff and held it out to Bodhran and his cadre. Tuco immediately covered his eyes as Grail closed his. A brilliant flash blinded the rest. Rifles and children dropped to the floor. Grail then tossed the cylinder high. It exploded with a bright flash and *bang!* Bodhran stumbled and bumped into Tuco who instinctively shoved him back. Bodhran hit the floor butt first. High above, the heat from the exploding cylinder triggered a forgotten safety precaution. Ceiling fire sensors opened ancient valves. The old sprinkler system sputtered to rusted life.

Bodhran looked up at the rumbling pipework crisscrossing the ceiling with dread. "Dear Gates, no!"

An artificial rainstorm exploded from the ceiling. Sprinkler units spewed brown, rust-laden water and putrid stench. All of Bodhran's cadets across his saturating academy became a screaming, chaotic wave and ran for the exit. Bodhran gathered himself from the floor, but slipped in a deepening pool. He ran in a headlong gait after the stampede of cadets fleeing in the imitation downpour.

"Are you imps afraid of water?" Bodhran screeched. "I'm still the Commandant! I order you to hold your position! Come back, you little worms! No refunds for your parents! Come back!"

Grail stood like a glacier in the tumult. His long, wetting hair flattened to the sides of his head. Tuco wiggled a finger in his left ear and looked up at the ceiling.

"Of all the old, crappy systems in this place, this one decides to work." Tuco looked at Grail and sighed. "Would it have been so bad to make the children fighters? It was good money."

Grail looked at the field of holograms that now flickered and died in the brown rain. "Yeah. It always has been."

Their coats and garb keep the bodies of the two Killers dry. People they walked by considered their wet heads just another style choice as they made their way from the warehouse to a transit platform. Nervous passengers in the crowded rail car managed to give Grail and Tuco ample space in the center aisle. The view through the thick, filthy windows of gleaming glass building sides, dying neon and LED lights, concrete, steel, and shadow all blurred as the train launched to its next destination.

"So, you say someone like Bodhran was nothing new?" Tuco asked while squeezing water from his hair.

"Bodhran aspired to be just another one of his holograms." Grail said. "History can replay like those cheap recordings, for those who care to watch."

Tones chimed from a dented speaker. Then a muffled woman's voice spoke as the train slowed and stopped: "Welcome to Columbia, the Federation's former capital."

Grail, Tuco, and a crush of people debarked the train onto a vast, underground platform packed with still more people. The masses exchanged places in an almost civil collision of human tides. Grail and Tuco waded through the crush. The two men ascended the steps of a dead escalator and emerged onto a skyscraper-flanked street.

"I'll bet not many of those holographed leaders were driven out of business by fake rain," Tuco offered with a glance down the escalator shaft at the flow of masses.

Grail looked across the street where another, looser multitude flowed like a swarm of noisy ants. "You're probably right. But apathy can breed a nation of followers ready for any leader with a skewed vision of the truth. I always wonder when the voices *In Flanders Fields* might call again."

"Flanders Fields, Ice? What's that?"

"It's a poem. An old poem." Grail said and began walking from the train station. "It was written by a soldier in the First World War. It describes the voices of dead soldiers calling upon their countrymen to avenge them."

"You think that's a bad thing?" Tuco asked as he caught up to Grail.

"I guess it could be, if you become one more voice in the field."

"But you and I might be swallowed in pieces tomorrow." Tuco said. "I'm pretty sure you'd kill the thing that ate me. Vice versa, old friend."

"Thanks. But we face death on our own terms. We defy the monsters because others can't, or don't see them coming."

"Yeah. I like to think that when I burn a monster, somebody will go home that might not have made it back. Not that there is a shortage of people, but that's how I feel. You know what I'm saying, *compadre*?"

"I think I do. I don't think Bodhran did. That's why I wanted to come here. I'm looking for another observation of another war. There is a historical site nearby."

"What does this history look like?" Tuco asked as he and Grail cut through the street crowds shoulder to shoulder.

"It's called *The Wall*. It's an old, really old monument. It stands as an ominous reminder of the misuse of human valor, and the dubious quality of some causes. I wonder if the names on it would have called out to their generation, asking to be avenged. Or did they warn them, instead? They store it in this tower lobby, now. The air was etching away all the names on the black granite. But on the preserved sides, you could see your reflection as if it was their ghost staring back at you."

Grail and Tuco approached a set of thick, transparent sliding doors at the base of a tower. The doors open before them with a strong gust of filtered air. Inside, Grail and Tuco looked in different directions with perplexed expressions.

"So where is it, Ice?" Tuco asked with a palms-up shrug. "I'd like to see it."

People flowed around Grail and Tuco as they stood and looked across the scene inside a long, shopping promenade. Groups collected at the storefronts and balconies with bright signs and

110

holograms advertising every act and product a human could afford or pine for inside the glass-clad shops. The stores were stacked on top of each other in the tower's cavernous lobby. Large, brilliant red letters of a twirling hologram spelled JOE'S MEGA-MALL overhead in the air.

"It used to be here. Somewhere." Grail said, and then drew a resigned breath.

"Maybe your wall got buried in that field." Tuco said and then smiled.

Grail glared across the entire shopping center, but recognized nothing.

"Hey, Ice, that was a joke." Tuco looked curiously at his companion who still searched across the busy scene.

A long sigh escaped Grail. The sound was lost in the din of the rambling crowds.

12
KILLERS

Feral hunger filled the niches and cracks in Earth's global city. If you hid in the shadows, a hungry beast might take you. In the scarce light, other predators might find you. Monsters take many forms. Curious eyes spotted a large man with a bulge beneath his shirt and blank stare on his face. The man stared ahead at nothing as he walked by an alley. He took no notice of the violent silhouette on the alley wall. The thing that cast the shadow was twisted and hideous. So was the mind behind the empty stare.

The man with the blank face walked beside the wreck of a taxi once hired and then destroyed. It was not empty. Four human predators slid out and followed him. Their hands snaked into tattered pockets. The large man stopped. His right hand retrieved the bulge under his shirt. A huge, silver handgun emerged and reflected the weak street light. The stalkers held shivs and much smaller guns, all scaled for human prey. The silver cannon held by the blank-faced man was built to destroy more massive things. Each stalker looked at the blank stare above the gun. In the same second, the roles between predator and prey switched. The smartest member of the street gang realized this large and freakish man stalked them. He turned and ran. His three comrades attacked.

Up close, the muzzle blast of the silver gun was blinding. The running thug saw his shadow stretch in front of him with each shot. The gunshots killed all other sound from the city. The large killer's actions were fast and deliberate. His blank expression never changed. He never showed recognition of his brutal acts, or reacted to the explosive deaths of his attackers. The only change to his face was red flecks that also rained across the street and sidewalk. He took aim at the smartest, fleeing thug. The missed shot obliterated a section of reinforced lamppost. The smart gang member stumbled, but kept running. He turned down a side street, and didn't stop his flight.

The city air was harsh. Its assault drifted down from the permanent black clouds that ate the sky. The survivor needed to rest before his lungs bled. He hid in an alleyway and pensively peered at the street. Tentacles seized him from behind. He had breath enough to scream. The giant centipede legs made no sound as they raced across pavement. The segmented tentacles grip the screaming man like steel cables. Scent hairs led the hideous fusion of octopus and arthropod shapes to its home. A loose manhole cover capped its lair in the center of the darkened street. An unwelcome visitor waited for it. Another hunter flipped up the manhole cover. The steel-blue eyes of the contemporary exterminator called Joshua Grail, or simply Ice Mr. Ice, fixed on the monster He leveled his weapon at the beast. The sound of another massive, silver handgun killed all other sounds. Below the screaming gang member, scales and tissue explode. Acrid blood spattered him. He hit the ground still enmeshed in tentacles. Two more shots from the hunter loosened the crushing grip. The victim stopped screaming.

The monster's intended victim took nervous interest in Ice's weapon. He holstered the silver gun beneath his heavy coat. The gang member then looked up at his massive savior. The two-time near fatality realized this man was not the blank-faced murderer from the other street. Somehow, he relaxed in the tentacles.

"Thhaa—thanks, man!" The gang member spat out as Ice pulled the tentacles and loosened the dead monster's grasp. He unconsciously shouted to overcome the loud ringing in his ears. "You saved my skin! Thanks!"

"No problem," Ice answered. "It's part of the job. Sometimes."

With the density of Earth's population, few people enjoy empty space. Unless the rare space is wrapped in entropy and shadows. At such a place, a woman sat alone on an ancient bus bench. She could no longer afford medical reweaves for her body, and had begun to age in the city air. The constant din of traffic beyond and above her was familiar and free comfort. Her street was dark and filthy. Normally, it's all hers to behold. On this night, she gained a visitor. A large man with a blank stare sat beside her. Dark, red spots peppered his clothes and face. The woman squirmed and moved farther down the bench. She saw a glint of silver before the gun killed all noise, again.

Two hours later, several armored police officers formed a human wall around the bench and dark stain across the cracked sidewalk. The living palisade wore face covering respiration masks. Their rigidity and uniformity created the appearance of a row of assault rifles fastened to black posts. The armed barricade attracted massed curiosity with a more human appearance. The crowd was a mix of modern people of various walks of street life and a few floors above. Over half of the breathing mosaic wore their own respirators of various styles and quality. Some only coughed. That sound had joined traffic as common urban background noise.

Beside the bench, a black bag with the illuminated label POLICE EVIDENCE held the woman's remains. Detective Sergeant John Slate observed his forensic technician, Jane Tonson, slowly move sensor gloves over the bench and concrete. A tight Evidence Collection Suit sealed away Tonson's face and body. Slate's face was bare. His mask was tucked inside his overcoat. Slate's ancestors were proud warriors in Africa's past. Slate was a contemporary peace officer. His tense expression gave image to the internal battle between bureaucratic frustration and the fulfillment of justice. The unwanted presence of Oversight Psychoanalyst, and acting Specialist Judith Landers hovered near Tonson. She had rushed to the scene and came unprepared for the exposed street in a business suit and no respirator.

"What type of bent mind just offs somebody?" Tonson pondered aloud.

"A sociopathic individual progressing to homicidal acts," Landers answered. "Or someone whose mind was in a biologically or chemically altered state."

"Didn't someone say civilization is only a state of mind we all share?" Tonson asked as she read the glove-collected data displayed across the interior of her mask.

"I think that was me," Slate said. "And I was being sarcastic."

"So what state do we live in today, Sergeant?" Landers asked. "Anarchy?"

"Close. But I prefer to live in denial," Slate said. "That's why I chose this job."

Tonson let out a heavy sigh. "Slate, the bench is so fouled, I can't get a fix on the murderer's pattern. It will take a long time to sift and match the genome to the time frame."

"So we have no leads," Slate groaned.

"Tragic." Ice's comment came as a low rumble from the wall of armored police.

An officer in the palisade looked back at Slate. He nodded. Ice entered the circle and Landers' attention fixed on him.

"Mr. Grail, sir." Slate spoke in a tone hovering somewhere between convivial and exasperated. "Alias Ice. Alias a monster's worst nightmare. Alias a reason for a lot of my paperwork. Still, nice of you to drop by our outdoor convention."

"Why the dragnet after a couple street-level homicides?" Ice asked as he looked at the body bag. "I thought if there was a viable theory to explain a crime, it was considered solved."

"Yeah, the courts aren't looking to overfill their dockets more," Slate shook his head in disgust at the thought. "Unless the perpetrator poses an exceptionally grave threat to society."

"Or offs a wealthy politico." Ice said as he scanned the crime scene with his own, less obvious sensors. "This is the work of the same murderer who killed Council Member Quant on Wednesday, right?"

Slate cocked his head with a wry expression of both affirmation and resigned acceptance.

"Power to the elite state." Ice said as a friendly, verbal jab.

"Tell that to Quant. He was rich, but he took the train every day." Tonson said.

"He should have voted for better platform security." Ice answered. "He didn't."

"Do you see that as justice, mister, er, Ice?" Landers asked.

"Ice, meet Specialist Landers," Slate pointed at her without looking towards her. "Our precinct's recently attached psych analyst, or oversight shrink."

"The thought police?" Ice turned to Landers.

"Not quite," Landers said. "Though I am interested in what you think of this case."

"Why?" Ice asked as both he and Slate raised their eyebrows.

"You're a killer, too." Landers said. "That's why I had you contacted. You probably think like our perp."

Ice replied with a cold stare down at Landers.

"Maybe you'd like to rephrase that." Slate also glared at Landers.

"No offense, but you are a predator." Landers said and stepped closer to Ice. "Maybe you share a motivation?"

"I kill monsters." Ice's reply was slow and measured.

"And sometimes people who get in your way."

"So stay out of it." Ice turned and walked back toward the police phalanx.

Landers moved to intercept Ice, but thought better of grabbing his arm. "Look, you hunt monsters, so do I."

"Mine are motivated by hunger." Ice said without turning around. "They make better use of their victims."

"Come on, help us." Landers said as Ice left the curb. "How would you bait this killer?"

"Shut off transit access." Slate said as if talking to Tonson. "Keep everyone off the street. Make him hungry, and flush him out."

Landers turned to sneer at Slate who returned her gaze indifferently.

"Oh, sorry, Judith." Slate shrugged. "Just the ramblings of a trained *police* mind."

"Would you excuse us, Sergeant?" Landers huffed.

"Hey, no problem, *acting* Specialist."

Landers turned back to Ice, but only saw his head and shoulders moving through the crowd behind the reforming police line. "Damn it! We need more to stop him."

"Who, Ice or the perp?" Slate asked.

"Maybe both." Landers looked accusingly at Slate. "You sure it's not him?"

"Back off!" Slate snapped. "I've worked with Ice. He's no sociopath. Our perp is. They are not the same."

"Maybe, but the killer has chosen his type of gun based on the—" Landers looked at the body bag and paused as her mind seized on imagining the explosive trauma. "Well—"

"Detonation pattern," Tonson offered.

"Right," Landers said and tore her stare from the body bag. "Perhaps the perp has chosen Ice as his model."

"Yeah, like he's famous!" Slate grated. "That proves nothing. The gun is mass produced like toilet gauze. The weapons have internal OS and security programs. I can track just about every one of this make. But the perp's gun is filed off line. So quit groping the air to justifying your theory."

"Look, Slate. He isn't like most killers. I've read your files on Joshua Grail, A.K.A. Mr. Ice. The typical monster hunter gets a thrill shooting a gun just like a sex addict at an orgy. All their heightened hormones projected into one big bang. Ice is more dangerous. Based on your own assessment, his actions are considered and calculated. He has a reason for killing. Some deep seated, maybe long suppressed motivation. I think he that he believes he has some cause to serve. But what is it? Is it even real? You tell me, detective: am I right?"

"You're annoying." Slate growled. "Not everyone fits a model based on casual observation. Some motivations run deeper than a psychological fix. And some actions have no motivation. You itch, you scratch. That's it."

"But what causes the itch?" Landers pitched her eyebrows. She coughed from breathing the air for so long without a respirator.

"Irritation." Slate answered. "There's a lot of that around nowadays."

Slate returned to his precinct. He walked along a row of aged doors with opaque glass windows. The wall siding and doors were made to simulate wood, although what they mimicked was forgotten. A vast field of cubicles peopled with fellow police detectives spread out opposite the doors. Slate took pride that he had risen from the ocean-sized maze of the cubicles. Now, one of the many doors was now his own. Another detective emerged from the maze to chase Slate.

"Sergeant! Oversight Chairman Milikan is in your office."

"Really? How did he get there?" Slate raised his left eyebrow and stared at the detective.

"I, huh, I let him in. Sorry?"

"You will be, Dennis. Now go solve a crime and make me happy. As if that were possible."

Slate entered his office and removed his overcoat. He momentarily ignored the well-dressed, overstuffed man in the creaking chair in front of his desk. Milikan eyed the sleek, black handguns strapped to Slate's chest and quickly considered his words with greater caution.

"What can I do for you, Chairman?" Slate sat on his desk in front of his unwanted guest and locked eyes on Milikan's condescending smile.

"How is the Quant case progressing, Detective?" Milikan leaned back, making the chair squeak.

"Detective Sergeant. You mean the investigation of the latest street slayings?"

"Detective Sergeant, of course. Specialist Landers informs me—"

"Specialist Landers has put her time in," Slate gave a slight nod. "*My* investigation will proceed."

"Yes, well, there is concern over a certain monster exterminator. You won't consider him a suspect, and I'm concerned your friendship with him can become a liability."

"We are hardly friends. And there is no liability because he is not a credible suspect, at this time."

"Well, I'm glad you are least open to filing charges." Milikan smiled wider. "Certain pressures may require, as I'm sure you're aware, a swift resolution."

Slate paused. "I see the angle you're working, here. You need a suspect, and Landers has fingered one for you. Although I doubt she's smart enough to see where her theory leads."

"Detective, I'm certain you didn't intend any insinuation to me, or insult to a qualified colleague. We share concerns for—"

"Your concern is political." Slate said and a moment of icy silence followed. "I'm trying to find the real killer, and I don't care who that hurts or helps. I just want him stopped. Landers is a political appointee, like yourself. She reports to you, and you use her to find angles to crawl up."

"Watch your tone, Detective."

"I'd rather watch you squirm." Slate caused another icy moment. "I get that you want to replace Quant on the Council. But you need that hot platform to win an election. Carefully created public outrage is a good way to inspire apathetic voters. Or just enough of them to win. So if I can't find the real killer, you'll hang the murders on someone by sound bite and innuendo. Then ride your hollow wave into office. Maybe even throw in some police conspiracy you overcame. That angle is never out of style."

Milikan drew a slow, deep breath and wiped his palms against his knees. "You are committing serious insubordination. I'm warning you, I can have the contents of this meeting added to your service record."

"Well, Milikan, maybe there was a day you could've yanked my badge, but read the latest draft of the constitution. I can stuff you so deep into the system your lawyers will need subway suits to find you. By then they'll have to dig back out through all the dirt my dedicated public servants will haul out of your office. And they will. Compliance, following orders, is an act of loyalty more than rank. And loyalty is earned by respect, not false accusation. At least the kind that lasts. I ride my people, but they know I have their back. So put this in your press release: this investigation goes my way. Or you go down."

A loud squeak was the only sound Milikan caused as he rose from the chair and carefully stepped around Slate. Milikan then charged out of Slate's office. His grimace squeezed the red from his face. Slate stepped out and watched him bump through officers to the elevators.

"Hey," A fellow detective nodded at Slate. "How'd it go with Milikan?"

"Just fine. He seems like a reasonable man."

Slate watched Milikan push into a crowded elevator as the fellow detective focused on Slate with a curious gaze.

Back in his own office, Milikan dove into his padded chair. Projections within the window offered a distorted outlook on the city. False images of shinning new towers replaced old buildings. Dilapidated bullet trains on elevated platforms vanished behind the artificial foreground. Only their hum remained. The screen program showed fewer people than truly moved outside, and all visible were smiling and clean.

Milikan's holo-phone switched on to connect a voice-only communiqué. "Chairman, how did it go with John Slate?"

Milikan slowed his breathing, and replied. "Foul. He's actually a dedicated cop. He may even find the real killer."

"Should we reassess our plans?"

"No. Proceed anyway. I hate leaving justice to chance."

An abandoned office building corroded on a dark, desolate street. The marquee did its best to advertise England Business Plaza to any eyes that could read. The urban layers beneath the ruin hid the chambers of a buried cathedral. Its chambers now served as the rent-free living quarters of a certain Joshua Grail, A.K.A. Mr. Ice, A.K.A. Target 30721C by his unwanted guests, en route. Although when Grail rests, he would also like to be forgotten like glaciers.

A wingless aircraft dropped quietly in front of the dead plaza. A squad of five black-clad commandos exited its cabin. They hoped never to be remembered. All were completely clad in light and scan absorbing black. Thin equipment packs clung on their backs and machine pistols aimed ahead. Their transport rose and rejoined the transit lanes between the skyscrapers and super-towers rising like walls into the dark clouds. The commandos crept into the plaza. The muzzles of their weapons entered first. FRACDAR revealed details and topography without telltale light beams. All team members spread out and searched for stairs, a ladder, or other access into the unseen levels below.

"Got it!" Their leader chirped through their closed and scrambled channel.

The commandos assembled behind their leader. He knelt and slid a fallen door aside. Others shouldered their weapons to clear sections of flooring from a hidden stairwell. The leader took point and crept down the stairs. His team followed.

"Remember," The leader said in all earphones. "We plant the materials and then leave. Steal nothing. We were never here."

All the black helmets nodded in unison.

The five commandos slunk down the dark stairwell. At the bottom, the last member turned and crouched just inside the stairwell and guarded the *six* or rear of the team. The others penetrated the shadows across an ancient basement. A crater hole in the cement floor was invisible to sight but revealed in precisely arranged fractals. The hole offered precarious entry into a granite foyer. Ropes gave the commandos a safe descent. Their FRACDAR displayed the Gothic cathedral doors through pitch black. Small winches from their packs opened the heavy doors with no greater noise than a whisper. The commandos peered down a long, stone hall and floor of much newer concrete.

"Stop!" Commando Two froze. "It's a kill zone. There's no cover for ten meters. Let's get out!"

The leader turned to the wary team member. "Quit thinking so military! This a Monster Killer's lousy hole, not some politico's house. Scan forward. There are no electronic signatures. No security rigs. There's nothing biological bigger than a rat's ass. Nothing period."

"So where is the target?" Commando Two stabs his weapon into the dark hallway.

"Out working. If we waste more time, he might come home. Maybe you'd like to meet him?"

"No. Let's go."

Commando Two followed his team leader into the black.

"Do you scan a forward doorway?" Commando Four asked at the team's six.

"Hey!" Commando Three stopped.

"Quiet!"

"Number One, are you getting a reading? I'm jammed!"

"Shut up! Switch to passive reception. Go to I.R!"

"Some frequency is churning the whole O.S! Yo, Five, are you—!"

Footsteps echoed as Commando Four ran back to the hallway entrance. A black wall fell in front of the doorway. It seemed to compress the darkness beyond it. A faint staccato of machine pistol fire echoed from the stairwell. Four attempted to slide and avoid hitting the sudden mass as it crashed hard on the floor, but he struck it hard. The thunder of the impact quickly died against the thick walls entombing the team. Four recovered and all pushed against the fallen monolith with no result. Commando Three aimed his weapon at the new wall in frustration. The leader thrust down his gun barrel.

"No! You want to die in the ricochet. These walls scan too thick to penetrate with antipersonnel rounds."

"Who tripped it?" Three asked.

"Tripped what?" Two probed the seal of the new wall and doorway. "There's no power source. It just—just slid down!"

"There is an old-school actuator," the leader said. "It's called gravity."

"The jamming stopped as the wall closed." Three glanced around. "But I can't reach Five. Look!"

All weapons and eyes locked on a shaft of light that cut through the darkness from the left wall. Ice's voice echoed from the length of the narrow pipe allowing the light to penetrate.

"I'd say welcome, but I don't want you here. And I'm sure you'd rather be someplace else."

"I'll keep him busy until Five finds him." The leader said over their channel. "Keep looking for a way out."

The leader cautiously approached the end of the pipe. A false, calm and calibrated female voice projected from the helmet speaker. "Look, we weren't here to kill you. Our guns are just for witnesses. Let us out, and we'll leave in peace."

"You're peaceful, now." Ice answered from the chamber on the opposite site of the thick wall. The unconscious Commando Five was slumped beside him with a fractured helmet. "So is you're pal from the stairs. Still alive. I think."

"Damn!" Three shouted over the radio.

"Look, we can negotiate." The leader continued. "You could turn this into a payout."

"Waste of time. I've got bigger paydays on the street."

"If you just let us out. We leave, and you buy yourself time."

"I've got time." Ice said with confidence. "You don't. You can't get out. Your air scrubbers and supplies will wear out and empty. Then I'll call the cops. Their excavators will lift the stone. And you get a trip to the morgue's evidence locker. See you there. Actually, only I'll see you, there."

"Wait! We don't need to fight!" The leader switched his audio output to his actual male voice. "We have insurance! Surviving witnesses are retroactive beneficiaries!"

The light from the pipe disappeared.

Slate sat at his desk scrutinizing a holographic diagram of the murder scene projected from a small black dome. The incoming-signal tone beeped. Slate tapped the dome. The projected bust of Ice appeared.

"Yo, Ice. This is a switch, you calling me."

"Check your byte sack. I've sent an image of a streeter I saved from a monster. He was in a place and timeframe close to the killings. I would have sent it sooner, but some friends arrived."

Commando Five's unconscious form replaced Ice in the display.

"I see. Interesting friends." Slated noted. "I'll send a squad and invite them all to my place for interrogation."

"I'm sure they will prefer that to scratching away at stone. And each other."

Slate's holograph next flashed an image of the gang member Ice saved from the centipede beast.

"I rebooted my scan of the monster's victim," Ice said. "He registered two sets of fatigue residues. It isn't surprising that he was scared and running before the monster's attack, but from what—or whom—might be. He took a good look at my gun."

"The precinct S.I. took your bytes and just found an ident file on this guy." Slate said with a smile as a mug shot flanked by rolling text and data replaced Ice's image of the gang member. "He's kept a steady float between jail and the street. I'm surprised he hasn't been eaten."

"He almost was."

"If your guy saw the killer, he might give us an I.D." Slate took a deep breath. "We're generating a cross-referenced hologram using memory-RNA from a few victims. The ones whose heads were intact. But most were E.X. and shunt addicts, so it's hard to distinguish what's real memory without a common clue."

"Some people used to say all life is an illusion." Ice said with a smile almost creasing his stony face.

"Sometimes I feel that way. But I usually tell people to wise up before life bites them on the ass."

"Sage advice, Sergeant."

"Yeah, you get that after the tooth marks heel."

Slate entered a briefing room in his precinct. His overcoat was closed. Several armored officers filled the seats. Landers entered and stood in the doorway. As Slate stood at the front, a holographic image of the blank-faced gunman floated beside him. Slate's address to his seated officers was broadcast to holographs, visual screens, and voice channels in cruisers and cubicles across the district.

"Okay, we know what he looks like. This image crosschecks with window peepers brave enough to talk to us. Our cordon around his last hit means he's still there, somewhere."

"Sir, if we find him, do we arrest him?" One officer asked. A concurring murmur followed.

"Yes. But not at the expense of your personal safety. He's big. Probably pump-stitched. Use appropriate force. You have your orders and positions. Let's go nail this murdering freak."

The assembled officers snarled affirmation, stood and filed out of the squad room. Some turned their heads to nod approvingly at Slate.

"Nice detective work," Landers said as she approached Slate through the rumbling exit of armored police officers.

"It's my job, Specialist."

"Look, I know you think I'm Milikan's spy, but—"

"Think? No Landers, I know it. You report to him. Spy? Yeah, that took no detection to figure out."

Landers clenched her teeth. She spoke with building anger. "I do what's right! I'm good at my job. You may have his face, but have you deduced his motivation?"

"No. But I know mine. How about yourself?"

Landers remained silent as Slate followed his men. She ignored the backward glances and cutting grins. Anger, spite, and then resolve took turns influencing the thoughts behind her focused stare.

The street was still empty and forbidding. Landers walked on. The Evidence Collection Suit she now wore protected her from some aspects of the street. Yet, she began to reconsider her gamble of infiltrating the cordon. She couldn't find new evidence to support her theory that some, like Milikan, thought would help them. Alone on the street, with all its dangers real and around her, the success of others didn't concern her. Her survival gained importance, especially away from the other officers. There was no answer to Slate nor personal heroism to be found. She would concede this and anything else to Slate if she found him and he got her off the street.

Landers reached for her com-link. She heard a noise and looked behind her. A blank stare met her eyes. The large man with the large gun calmly walked several paces behind her. Landers ran. The massive killer followed her flight into an alley with deliberate and all too fast steps. Landers leveled her handgun at him from behind an overflowing dumpster and shouted.

"Freeze!"

The killer replied by firing his handheld cannon. The muzzle blast knocked Landers backward. The bullet obliterated a section of wall above her head. Landers fired back from the ground. Each shot hit the killer, pocking his torso. His expression remained blank. He failed to notice his wounds. Landers looked at the bleeding killer with wide, terrified eyes. He continued walking down the alley towards her. The pavement behind Landers exploded as she ducked into the side entrance of a decrepit stairwell. After several panicked steps, she stumbled out onto a pitted patio rooftop. Landers flipped up her respirator mask on instinct to breathe deeper. She coughed instead, and then felt pain.

Landers reached down her left leg and pulled out a fragment of asphalt imbedded in her calf. The pain distracted her from the killer walking out onto the rooftop behind her. She heard his heavy steps. She screamed, spun, and fired. Small craters erupted across the killer's stomach. He only flinched. Then he raised his gun at Landers. There was another deafening bang that killed all sound. The killer's chest exploded. His shattered body fell across Landers' bloodied legs. A huge silver handgun emerged from the stairwell shadows. John Slate grimaced as he lowered the weapon and stepped toward Landers. She resisted vomiting.

"You okay, Specialist?" Slate holstered his silver gun. It took up a large space beneath his overcoat. Two officers with heavy rifles walked out and flanked Slate.

"Uh, yuh-uh, yeah. You?" Landers replied. Her legs were still under the heavy corpse.

Slate winced as he massaged his right hand. "I think I just broke at least one hand. By the way, you're under arrest."

Landers wiped bloodspray and bone from her face, and then realized what Slate had told her. "What? Why?"

"Obstruction of justice and violation of police quarantine." Slate continued massaging his aching hand. "Your ego nearly got you killed, Judith. Or, maybe you would just rather resign?"

Landers stopped wiping her face and stared blankly at Slate.

Milikan walked out through courtroom doors. Lawyers that held thin, metallic squares like one-dimensional briefcases flanked him. True briefcases were long obsolete, but their use to defend clients from camera and questions gave the legal profession the shields they quickly employed when besieged by a mass of reporters and swarming media drones. Two lawyers tossed small, black balls into the air. They flew at the media drones that were forced to arc and dive to avoid collisions.

An aggressive reporter slapped away a briefcase and dove at Milikan. "Chairman! Why did you attempt to plant false DNA evidence?"

"There was no conspiracy to do that," Milikan replied.

"There was no conspiracy!" A lawyer shouted while thrusting the reporter back.

Milikan's mob continued down a marbled hallway. Above them the looping dogfights between drones and black interceptors continued. One black ball suddenly dropped with a puff of smoke from unseen countermeasures.

"What of the m-RNA evidence linking you to the public-relation firm's Proactive Assault Team?" A voice shouted from a diving drone.

"Faked, of course." Milikan and one lawyer said in perfect unison, and then glanced at each other.

The mob approached two rows of massive columns set on a cracking marble floor laid centuries ago. The columns rose high above the mob, but ended in broken tops below the ceiling. Milikan and his lawyers squeezed through the contracting mob to reach thick, clear airlock doors between the columns. The airlock opened with a gust of foul air over the crowd that kept contracting into a more dense mass trying to reach Milikan as he entered the airlock.

"But the P.A.T's testimony confirms the facts!" A reporter managed to shout despite crushed lungs.

"Coerced, obviously." A lawyer yelled through her shield.

"Look, you all know how powerful the police are." Milikan said as the airlock closed. "No one is safe anymore."

Milikan smiled and waved behind clear, although closed doors.

Ice and Slate watched the telecast projected on the hood of a sleek police interceptor outside the fortress-like precinct. On it, Milikan still managed a forced smile through pain as his lawyers squeezed into the airlock before the doors closed again and cut them in two. The telecast disappeared like a popped bubble.

Slate turned to Ice. "You always like to sum up things. What do you make of this?"

"You want me to make sense of electoral politics? I can't. There isn't any."

"At least we agree."

"Scary thought, Sergeant."

"You're telling me. I guess that makes us a civilization of two. So much for the *state* of mind."

"Looking for a revolution?"

Slate cast a questioning glance at Ice. "You volunteering to lead it?"

"No. I'm a Monster Killer, and you're a cop. Would you want a nation of bounty hunters, or a police state?"

"Maybe someone in the past knew how to deal with this."

"Several people did."

Slate knit his brow considering Ice's comment. "What happened to them?"

"They all died. Some were killed."

Slate raised an eyebrow while staring at the stone-faced Ice. "Is that supposed to be funny?"

"Ralph Waldo Emerson said: "The end of the human race will be that it will eventually die of civilization." Today, all most people have is other people standing around them to protect them from the things in the shadows—human, or otherwise. I'm not sure what Emerson would think, now."

"Keep working on it, Ice. It's when the thoughts stop that everything comes to an end."

"True enough. I guess that's when you're finally alone."

13
AFTER HOURS

Some describe me as an all work and no play sort of Monster Killer. I answer to the name Joshua Grail, or Ice, Big Dude with Loud Gun, screams for help, and the occasional stream of expletives. After a day of facing beasts looking to bite off your skull, and perhaps even saving a few lives, some Killers need to flip on the safety, holster their weapons, lower scanner intensity, and sit down. It's understandable. The job is intense. Our world, our job, is a circus under shadows. History shows circuses had weird acts and *taming* of captured beasts. Our beasts are uncaged and much weirder than a dancing squid. And mean.

At times, the world seems its own parody. Perhaps even ludicrous. Monsters prey on people. Their forms are various and deadly. Yet, now and again, some look ludicrous. The personalities of Monster Killers are also various. Some are indifferent. Others, courageous. All need time to loosen tension, perhaps reconnect with their humanity, or maybe just to blow off steam instead of the limbs of their neighbors. When relaxed—or intoxicated—their behavior can appear to be parody.

The darkened Earth is indifferent to dawn and dusk, so I can imagine nights or mornings spent after working hours. One job crossed the paths of colleagues at a public house. Well, it was more like a seedy bar. Actually, it was a nasty dive. Today, the circus needs no tent.

Tuco entered a bar—. He stepped into the street-side dive. He had a license to carry weapons on his massive form and commit carnage for the greater good. The bar likely did not have any license, yet may well cause greater devastation to humanity with shot glasses than what Tuco blows away.

Next to the door is a large window. Across it, faded, flaking stenciling for DAVE'S PAINT SHOP defied maybe centuries. The bar and stools were to the right as you entered in line with the window. Shadowy booths were opposite the bar along the wall. The interior was narrow, long, and smoky, although no one used vapor devices. Some said the smoke came in from the street and was too afraid to leave. Smart smoke. The proprietor stood behind the bar. He appeared to be as flaking and aged as the *DAVE'S* letters on the window. It was a style choice he thought matched his dive. He answered to Dave, although his name was Topher.

Tuco sat at the bar two stools down from the window.

"Usual?" the proprietor Topher/Dave asked.

"Well, man, I've never been here before." Tuco said.

"We only serve the usual." Topher/Dave placed a cracked tall glass filled with clear liquid in front of Tuco.

"The usual is fine," Tuco said and took the glass.

Tuco glanced down at a bowl of peanuts. Two small but sinister eyes looked back at him. Tuco slowly reached under his coat for his weapon that fired small, explosive-tipped bullets as fast as paint flew from a spray can.

"Hey, there's a monster in your peanuts." Tuco said.

"Yeah," Topher/Dave answered. "It keeps people from eating too many."

A woman whose face resembled a scrunched napkin leaned against the bar beside Tuco and spoke to him. "Say are you, y'know, a licensed guy?"

"I'm a Monster Killer," Tuco said and then took the whole pull from the glass. He coughed. "I think maybe that stuff is, too!"

Topher/Dave refilled Tuco's glass. The woman took it and sipped from it.

"I think you killed my sister's husband once," she said.

"Once?" Tuco said and motioned to Topher/Dave for another glass.

"They got him to surgery in time," the woman said. "Grafted on some new guts. He's thinner now."

"Well, I'm happy to help out." Tuco said and then threw back his new drink. He coughed.

"Say, could you kill him again?" she asked.

She tossed back the rest of Tuco's first drink and seemed hit by an electric jolt but caught herself before falling from the stool. Behind her, another equally attractive woman approached with hands on hips.

"No way, Shelly!" The second woman barked. "You got the last fresh blood in here. This one's mine!"

Tuco looked up into a mirror behind the bar at the reflections of the two women. He had not yet withdrawn a weapon. Thoughts of what to shoot first might have delayed him.

"Do you want Annie or me?" The first woman, Shelly, asked Tuco.

Tuco cautiously picked up a peanut while staring down the thing in the bowl. "How much would it cost for you both to leave?"

"A hundred." Both women speak in unison.

Tuco calmly placed his large, black automatic with its fat, extended clip on the bar. "I think maybe today is my lucky day, and you both just go away."

Both women gave Tuco snarky smiles and extended middle fingers. They turned and walked to the booths.

Another woman came from the door having watched the scene and scanned the dive. Her blonde hair reflected brightly in the dingy mirror and glass window. It was as tight against her scalp as the coating of ye olde matchstick tops. She looked equal parts Nordic ancestry and Viking spear. Her pale skin contrasted to Tuco's ruddy hue. He recognized her without looking up, but nodded when she sat beside him. The fellow Killer, Rafale, adjusted her weapons strapped around her taut body and hardly concealed beneath her armored coat.

"What's the matter, big guy?" Rafale asked. "You going soft? But, you were always soft on civilians."

"Civilians? What you a cop now?" Tuco laughed.

"Better. And better than you." Rafale replied and nearly smiled.

Topher/Dave slapped a drink in front of her. He did smile.

Tuco laughed harder. "Hardly! Nice to see you, Rafale."

"Tuco," Rafale nodded and took a sip. "Big, bold and bad ass. Where you been?"

"Killing things."

"We've missed you," Rafale said.

Topher/Dave nodded in agreement.

"I've never been here before." Tuco shrugged as he looked at Topher/Dave.

"You sure?" Rafale asked. "Enough of this and you'll think you're me."

She tossed back her drink and grimaced.

A very large, grimy, and flabby man squeezed out from a booth and rolled over to the bar. He almost collided with it as he leaned over to look at Tuco from Rafale's right side.

"Huh. Some tough guy." The grimy mass said with disgust. "He needs a gun to blow off dames. You tough without it?"

Tuco sighed. Topher/Dave nodded *no* with a stern look at the man. Rafale looked at the peanut bowl and smiled.

"Here, mister odors," Rafale slid the peanut bowl to the man without looking at him. "Have some peanuts."

The man reached for the bowl gesturing at the owner with a triumphant glower. "See, Dave, you don't own this place, I do!"

Tuco squirmed. Rafale put her hand on his gun on the bar. The grimy man grabbed a fistful of peanuts with force. The small monster leapt out of the bowl and onto the man's face before any entered his chasm mouth.

Mmmwwwaafffmrff! was the best scream the man could do as he reeled back with an angry tick-like octopus, or an octopus-like tick covering his face. He still held the peanuts, tight.

"You kill monsters?"

The voice came over the clamor as the large man reeled and crashed across the booths and down the bar. Several people bolted up to either try to help pull off the monster or punch and kick the annoying, grimy lout. Tuco looked perplexed and conflicted. Rafale smiled.

Rafale answered the question. "Sometimes."

Tuco looked over at who made the query. A young woman looked at Rafale. She had a shaven head and odd adornment. Safety pins impaled her face, even through her eyelids.

"I couldn't bring myself to kill anything, even a monster." The pin girl sighed through the metal.

"Uh, how humane." Tuco said.

Two similar men wearing shockingly clean clothes with argyle patterns and broad smiles approached Tuco and Rafale. Tuco blinked and then scanned them to make sure they were not illegal clones. Behind the men, the rescue/beat down continued.

"Say! My friend and I—" the man on the left began.

"Friend?" Tuco queried.

"Yeah, friend." Argyle left replied. "So we were betting we could pay you to kill everyone in this bar."

"How much?" Argyle right asked.

Rafale broke from watching the violent theater she started as it continued down the bar. She stared at the smiling argyle boys. Tuco glared. Their smiles melted.

"You two I'd do for free." Rafale said.

The argyle boys stepped backward and continued backing away in odd unity.

Shelly returned to the bar and breathed heavily. "Dave, d'you got, uh, something big and sharp?"

Topher/Dave nodded *yes*. He reached under the bar and then handed her an enormous clever. "Just keep the blood off the tables."

Tuco noticed a tall, weasel-like man reflected in the mirror.

"You guys, Killers?" The weasel asked. "I'll give you a hundred if you kill me."

Tuco stared to reply.

Rafale spoke first. "Cash up front."

Annie pushed the weasel aside and shouted to Topher/Dave. "Hey, uh, Shelly had the clever, and—"

"Did you get the monster?" Tuco asked.

"Monster? No." Annie gave Tuco a questioning look, and then focused back at Topher/Dave. "So, uh, you have a bucket?"

Topher/Dave made a wry face and lifted over a bucket. Annie took it and ran. The small bowl monster crept by Rafale and Tuco under their cautious stares. It slid back into its home under the peanuts. Tuco opened his mouth to speak. A grey haired and bronze tinged insurance broker cut in and sat at Tuco's left between him and the window.

"Can I buy you a drink, sir?" The broker asked Tuco.

"No."

The door opened. A medic completely covered in a hazardous materials suit entered with an emergency case.

"Someone call a medical unit?" the medic asked from behind the clear plastic square on his hood.

Topher/Dave shrugged, but motioned with his thumb for the medic to walk farther into the bar. He did so and made audible, rubbery ripple noises as he walked. The broker pressed closer to Tuco.

"So about that drink?" The broker smiled and leaned across the bar almost snake-like to address Tuco. "And another purchase you should consider is a comprehensive insurance plan."

"You should consider some peanuts," Rafale said as she reached over to push the bowl.

Tuco reached and grabbed the lip of the bowl to hold it fast. Rafale's hand became a fist. It then flew by Tuco. The broker literally fell silent after Rafale's sharp knuckles cut off his speech. Tuco raised his eyebrows and looked at Rafale.

"Hey, that guy tried to buy me a drink yesterday." Rafale said.

Topher/Dave handed Tuco and Rafale fresh drinks.

"Cheers, amiga."

Tuco raised his glass to his lips. A loud *BOOM!* from the back of the bar made him spill it.

A minute or so before Tuco spilled his drink, I climbed out from another kind of fluid. It smelled worse but might be healthier than *the usual*. My odorous cocktail was condensation and sewer seep. It flowed through the underground maze I traveled while on the clock. I popped up a manhole cover in the unisex john at the back of DAVE'S. You may ask why there was a manhole in a restroom. If so, you live in a much nicer locale. It's better than an open toilet in the middle of the street. (Yet, there is an argument for them when people hear nature's call but a hungry aberration owns the house plumbing.) The manhole was here because city structures ebb and flow like tides over time. A street became a floor as rebuilding rippled over whatever land survived when a super-tower foundation consumed miles of old city. What's beneath the super-towers? Maybe hell.

A man on a chipped and cracked toilet with his pants around his ankles observed my ascension. It was his groaning I had heard, not the monster's calls. He looked at me in terror. I can have that effect. Suddenly, his eyes looked away from me as he considered the sensation against his glutes. He became more terrified of what lurked right below him. He leapt up. An eye on a muck covered stalk rose from the toilet. The man was lucky it was a sensing tendril, and not a feeding one. I had tracked the thing to gauge its range and mass and get an open shot. Then it began tracking me. Nice that we found a cozy spot to meet. Now I could kill it.

Law bans using living monsters as weapons. Using weapons made from them is—I had never asked. I whipped out a necrodermic needle and stabbed the eye. I was certain the neurotoxin would kill it fast. The man pressed himself against the wall with his pants still around his ankles. The tendril thrashed. It fell dead. The rest of its bulk would do so, soon enough. Now *DAVE'S* and several other questionable establishments were safe. That is, safe from that thing. Then the huge termite-beast with a shark's grin came ambling down from a crack in the ceiling.

Monster two went straight for the man, interrupted. He might've suffered intestinal issues, but this was his lucky day. I fired. Monster two died explosively. The man looked at me again. His wide eyes blinked from drips of monster splatter.

"You're welcome," I said. "But next time use the sanitary lining."

Tuco heard the shot, spilled his drink, and came running. The man from the restroom hit him as he bolted out. He then made good speed out the bar while only holding his pants up at the crotch. Tuco saw me and lowered his gun while bursting into laughter. Without any other greeting, we walked back to where Rafale still sat. She raised her glass. I sat with them.

"Usual?" Topher/Dave asked me.

I glanced at Rafale's glass and scanned it.

"No, I'm feeling bold." I said. "Bring me some water."

Topher/Dave shrugged and put a glass for me on the bar.

"Another thing," I said.

I swiftly put a combat knife in the center of the bowl by Rafale who only leaned back and kept her drink steady. Two small but menacing eyes went dark. Three monsters down. It was a good day. Or so I thought.

Topher/Dave clenched his teeth and slapped his hands against his thighs in anger.

"Hey, amigo, he might have used his gun." Tuco said to him and laughed.

Topher/Dave shrugged and sighed.

"Okay. Hey, it's good to see you relax, Ice." Tuco said. "Bright side, now we can all have more peanuts!"

"Tuco, you know I like history." I said, arching an eyebrow while staring at the bowl.

"Yeah, compadre. So?"

"I'm damn sure those are not peanuts."

14
GESTALT

Monster: an unnatural predator that treats humans as prey. They are a hallmark of this age, and the reason for my profession. Some call we Monster Killers fools. Fair enough. But most people have better days when we kill things that would eat them at their job, or in their homes, or anywhere else. Earth's ecology is dark and imbalanced. Twisted. At times, human outlook reflects the ecology. On modern Earth, some people enter darkness to kill monsters. Others enter it and don't return. Some become part of the greater imbalance, and are twisted. They emerge to create darkness.

A monster was killed. I wasn't here. Not that I kill them all, just a lot of them. Usually monsters are shot to death with high-caliber, explosive rounds fired by a specialist in facing danger and difficult situations. This monster was not shot. It was beaten to death. And by a human. The monster was comparatively small. The man was comparatively huge. Usually, the dynamic is reversed. This time, the human body, however amplified, proved stronger than the hungry freak in the dark.

The scene of the monster's attack was usual. It occurred on a street flanked by buildings, skyscrapers, and far below the apex of super-towers cutting into the permanent black clouds. On this street, another man was looking for people. This man was of normal size. His reason to brave the streets was odd. He offered people hope. Then the thing came charging from the shadows. It bit into the prostitute who spoke with this normal man named Venn. The monster was an armored thing with sharp scales and heavy claws. Its description recalled the extinct pangolin. Instead of eating ants with a long tongue, this twisted copy ate people or their parts with long, curved jaws like serrated scissors.

The human giant came from across the red-light street. I would guess he was a regular, there. The giant pulled the beast from its victim. The giant began beating the beast with his fists. The pounding struck sharp scales that crushed muscle beneath them, and then bones, and then organs. The giant's hands became bloodied, and he became a sudden hero. Venn offered the giant a new job, to be a protector of his dream. The giant, called Shank, went with Venn to a secreted place he had built in the shadows. Many from the street followed Shank. It would seem a fairy tale, one with a hero slaying a monster. But on present Earth, more than the ecology becomes twisted.

Time passed. It does so in stories and the dark places I stalked. Though I might have wished for a monster attack instead, my chapter was added to the story of Venn and his giant. Venn hired me and promised a generous fee. His location was a bit far. Yet today, everywhere was another part of town no matter its place on Earth. Transportation remained a logistical challenge, especially for a stratified population the looks thicker than the planet's crust. Yet, if a person can afford the fare, one can move quickly from city section to city section and all dense, urban points in between. Some vehicles defy gravity. High-speed surface cars defy friction. Mass transit defies the weight of humanity moved in tubes and tunnels with so many crowded cars they look like clogged arteries. Yet the throb of humans never stopped.

I journeyed outside where technology is woven into smoggy air. Bright lights, massive tower ads, and floating holograms offering delirious joy for a fee became background glow. My last leg of travel assaulted the ears, not eyes. A centuries-old railcar clicked and clacked to my stop. I ventured into a region not forgotten by time, but by city maintenance 'bots and crews. Its location likely didn't generate enough capital to warrant upgrading, or even demolition and reconstruction. Yet.

I left the train to the relief of my few fellow passengers. I began walking to the address Venn sent. The sound from the departing train echoed behind me. *Clickety-clack! Clickety-clack! Clickety-clack!* Surprisingly few people walked ahead of me. Another echo followed as I passed a darkened lane flanked by dead streetlamps. *Click-scritch-scratch! Click-scritch-scratch! Click-scritch-scratch!* That sound was probably not distant, steel wheels over rail. I made a note to investigate after my current job.

Some buildings around me had makeshift patches to cover intrusions of entropy, looters, or something else. There were a few older buildings once prized for ornate architecture. Now they slowly died like desert ruins under inverted dunes of black. For humans, one benefit was cleaner air. It wasn't clear and sterile like the expensive bottled stuff, but most people might get by with using a respirator part time, or only a weekly lung vac.

The city had applied a clear, hard resin over most pavements as a quick fix to seal and then forget the region's streets. Some people sought such places to escape the human crush. Although the numbers of lives packed here would still shock past census takers. Still, there were a few relatively capacious areas shunned by locals. Why risk exploring when hunger may find you? Yet, some found small zones to repurpose. People had done that with zeal at Venn's address.

My virtual maps listed the long, wide access way between older skyscrapers and industrial buildings as an alley. Obviously, no one had commissioned an update for a long time. When I looked across the so-called alley, I thought the span between updates might be a century. It was much less than that. Some people still knew passion and invention. Through them, the alley had become another world.

History can be useful to understand where you hunt. I accessed the construction permit records and viewed the archived images over my retina, supplemented with some imagination. First, the records showed a wide, flat surface next to the street. That was the original *alley*. The flanking buildings, along with their landings and loading docks, kept rising and expanding. A succession of wedged, abutting mesas rose from layers of brick, concrete, and asphalt. Later, huge nozzles sprayed paving as hardening tsunamis. The luckless workers greatest concern was not accuracy. It was not slipping and becoming entombed. In time, the *alley* became a jagged set of overlapped terraces walled between similar, vertical chaos.

Recent order had claimed part of the urban ravine. The new world I saw with my natural vision flowed over the terraces. It obviously followed a coordinated design. An even symmetry of small, human-scale structures contrasted to the layered, angular chaos beneath them. Mostly scavenged materials formed the new structures, yet all were raised with precision and care. The enclave's buildings were solid, not ramshackle. The conscientious engineers had discreetly tapped the surrounding utility lines. Machines might receive energy from batteries or beams, but the aftereffects of human intake still needed pipes. The rough edges of the pipes' hole punched through the sidewalk didn't match the finer construction it served. I guessed the enclave held shops, homes, and anything else needed by this splinter society slid among larger buildings. It might have time to thrive in this zone of lapsing, official attention. The reclaimed alley was a small piece of civilization folded back on itself, or pioneers staking a claim within an overdeveloped but impersonal frontier.

Obviously, no one had filed permits for this enclave. The builders' audacity impressed me. I entered. A long row of small ground lamps lit a central pathway. Other light streamed from uncovered windows allowing vision both out and into the shop or home. Fewer people lived near the street. The population increased as I stepped to the next terrace. There was art and organization along the main path and side trails. These people were here to stay. I thought the rent must be cheap. I wondered what industry they had, or if they worked normal jobs and brought resources from outside. The view overhead was a crooked slash of black between the flanking buildings and skyscrapers. Their sides looked more massive and imposing over the enclave's roofs, even through a bright haze from the lights.

The place was oddly inviting, and culturally weird. Many of the people I saw looked friendly, as if strangers were a welcome sight. I detected a few looks of relief. I felt my constant motion and questioning stare did more to keep me a solo presence than being an outsider. There was one, common aspect of city life. The only drifting voices were from adults. Long ago, communities carried the sounds of children in daytime. In this era, birth is banned. Mostly. Chemicals in water inhibit conception. However, the potential still lives in most women, and I assume any man willing to undergo intensive procedures. Subverting or altering biology is the easy part. Today, having a child is an economic issue. For the poor, affording a birth license is a punishing tax that likely keeps them in poverty. For the wealthy, the cost is an inconvenience or mark of status. The financial burden carries a multi-purpose control. It restrains population growth, and restrains most of the population.

For this place to increase its people, newcomers needed to join the community. And so its culture mutated to be friendly. But how might new people change the community? Like genetics, every system can benefit from internal change or from incorporating it from the wild. At times, the change can be bad, such as a corrupted chromosome, a disease, or a monster. I came to address a malignant change. Perhaps people who knew that were extra happy to see me. I assumed Venn would greet me, soon. If not, walking a troubled area can lure out the monster. That idea came to mind as I noticed a man in the distance who stood above everyone. He took note of me and then walked in my direction. I stopped, anticipating a welcome or other action by the giant. My pause and searching gaze brought a question from a far smaller person.

"Hello! You're new. Looking for a room?" A woman with olive skin and close-cropped hair that rippled in orange hues asked. With a smile, of course.

"Not unless there's something unwanted and hungry in it." I answered.

"Um, okay." The flame-topped woman glanced off to consider my reply and shrugged to herself, but her kind nature remained. "I'm H'san. Just thought I might help."

"I was hired by Venn. Is he around?" I asked, and blinked.

"I'll send word. I didn't see a cab descend. That's our usual tip off to a new arrival. Sometimes with Venn."

"I walked here."

"You walked?" H'san's shock was immediate and obvious without the added flourish of simulated fire on her head.

"From the train. Cheaper than a cab, and more scenic."

"That's a really long walk to here!" H'san nodded with wide eyes and opened mouth.

"Longer without the train." I said, although I understood H'san considered *long* to mean danger, not distance.

A new voice was deep: "Long walk, back, too."

The giant had arrived. My scans identified him as human. I thought I might recalibrate them for accuracy, later. Physical size often brings physical power. It makes it harder to squeeze through tight spots, but more able to wrestle a surprise tentacle or survive crushing jaws fast enough to strike before finger squeezes trigger. My height makes me tall for any age. Towering, in some cases. Rarely have I met a person taller. More rare is a person obviously more massive, as in a rhino standing by a bull moose, to use extinct species as reference. Or, an explosive tipped .50cal round versus a solid, 12 gauge sabot slug. If I wasn't near, the pale, hairless man with hyper-developed muscles might seem a species unto himself. There was a more common word for that, but I was here for a monster that ate people. I was sure this giant did not do that. Reasonably sure.

"This is Shank. He's our protector." H'san's voice took a darker tone that contrasted to her brilliant hair. She seemed to doubt the words, and stepped back as if to use me as a barrier.

"Yeah, that's me," the giant said with pride. "I always meet the new meat."

"Meat?" I asked.

"Everyone's meat but Shank," said a normal-sized man in Shank's orbit.

Others followers hidden behind Shank spread out when he stopped. He had a lot of gravity.

"Nice you all have roles," I replied. "But I not meat. I'm here to stop you all from becoming food."

"A monster?" Shank shrugged massive and bare shoulders. "We don't need you for that."

"We got Shank." Shank's moon said.

"We do need Mr. Grail for that." Venn said as he arrived. His own dark hair seemed to catch fire for a moment as H'san's walked away. "Our current problems are bigger than one man."

"No one is bigger than—" Shank's moon began.

I cut him off. "Yeah, we get it. Now, where is the problem I'm here for?"

"Right," Venn nodded. "Thanks, Shank. I'll show Mr. Grail around from here."

"I think I should—" Shank began.

Venn cut in. Of course, with a smile. "I'll be fine, thanks. I think Tedloe has a sewer issue and wants your help."

Venn nodded to Shank and then actually took hold of my left arm and pulled. The rough canvas of my coat made a crinkling noise. Nice guy that I am, I followed Venn's lead. Shank flexed his shoulders. He and his moons turned and walked away.

Venn and I walked to the next terrace. He spoke his conviction and passion akin to an estate agent for hot properties turned evangelist. We have no evangelists, today. Property rises over your head, and far higher. As Venn spoke his arms seemed to occupy a different timeframe as if his brain had advanced to the next thought before the impulse to gesture for emphasis reached the nerves. As we walked, I kept scanning for a target through Venn's pitch and the many flanking smiles.

"I hope you like our *recolony*." Venn said and returned nods to a passing group.

"Recolony? That's a new one." I said.

"It's fitting. There is no more naked land, so we've built our new society in this cleft of the old."

"It must be hard to stay under the radar while making changes, even in a small zone." I said and almost smiled back to small group passing us on the lit pathway.

"It's a constant, cautious balance. Balance is why I hired you. I understand you are discreet as well as effective."

"Tell that to my police friends." I said.

Venn froze.

"Who I won't be calling about this place."

Venn took a breath, and began walking again. "Well, I also have—had a few contacts in the force before I started the recolony."

"I doubt you were a cop. Maybe a litigator?"

"No." Venn smiled and shook his head anticipating my reaction to his former job's description. "I was a supervisor for the district's psychoanalytic census department."

I didn't freeze, but was silent after Venn's sentence. I finally said "psychoanalytic census?"

"It's likely not something you've heard of, but it's something your government does."

"The government does a lot of things." I sighed.

"You mean, that you do or don't know about?" Venn asked.

"Both. And neither." I sighed again.

"Um, that doesn't make sense."

"But your job did?" I asked.

"It provided data, at least. So, yes." Venn nodded to himself.

"Then why leave it?"

"The data!" Venn's voice and flail of arms were in sync at those words. "I saw misery, and at the very least, growing apathy. I saw our remarkable biogenetic and medical technology applied as mere bandages, after the fact. But the apathy and psychological damage remains. We bandage fractured people in a fractured world. Then I saw a way I could lead or at least inspire a better society. One where people's psychology wouldn't need to be healed after trauma, but where mental health—all heath—was part of society's foundation."

"Sounds more challenging than what I do." I still had not heard screams, found traces of blood, or scanned an odd DNA sequence in dropped spit, anywhere.

"Well, if we make understanding ourselves and others, and the world as a whole, all part of the culture—of society's foundation— then we might build a much better world from the ground up." Venn's arms now sped faster as if to whip up his words. "We wouldn't need to apply mental and medical fixes after the fact. It would be part of the daily culture. The individual would benefit from a healthier community, and we all would benefit as one, healthy society."

"One, big happy." I said.

"Well, yes. Ultimately."

Venn directed me up a short stairway to a balcony rest spot made from aluminum peeled from an old warehouse and a fibrous material predominantly composed of cellulose. We overlooked a small, dim courtyard with a sparse gathering of people. We could hear voices but were too high to discern conversations. Venn leaned against a railing. The people less than a story below were relaxed. I wasn't. I watched a strip of pitch-black shadow just behind them. Then Shank entered the courtyard with only a few moons. He'd followed us at a distance and pretended not to notice us up in the balcony.

"You sound skeptical." Venn said. He stood up when seeing Shank.

"Maybe in time you can build your better world. Right now, you're dealing with people from the current world you want to change. Your foundation is at risk." I said, and stepped nearer the railing. "He's a prime example."

I didn't need to point out Shank, directly. Venn knew whom I meant.

"Genetics say he would be big." I said. "A little help makes him even bigger. His power draws others, and he becomes a center of his own, personal society. He walks here like a king. That's not healthy for your vision."

"You can tell that? I mean, his genes." Venn asked. "You can analyze them?"

"My scanners go fairly deep."

"I didn't see any tech in your hand." Venn glanced over me.

"And I don't see the com-link built into your senses, either. But it's there."

Venn raised his eyebrows as his own secret was exposed. "Um, yes. It keeps me informed."

"As an overlord?" I narrowed my gaze at him.

"Hardly." Venn shook his head. "No. As a guiding force. I use discussion as a means to address issues, so I need to know what to discuss and what the issues are. I need to be in touch with everyone. As much as I can."

"So, you're the nexus of your gestalt," I said.

Venn thought on the idea and then nodded approval.

"Your protégé, Shank, doesn't seem to enjoy talking."

"Protégé?" Venn looked at me with a hint of anger. "You're being funny, I take it."

"A bit. But you must've brought him here, and allowed the rift he's making."

"I did." Venn took a deep breath and made a slight cough. "He had skill as a plumber. And others."

"Plumber? That explains his body's pump stitching."

"It does?"

"Imagine having to fix a leak in a dark place in this world. His strength could be useful not just be for turning stuck valves."

"Makes sense." Venn nodded and glanced at Shank below. "And his gun."

I narrowed my stare at Venn, again.

"This was a bad neighborhood!" Venn shrugged and leaned back. "Worse than now. And I saw him smash a monster with his fists."

"Lucky break."

"A pun, Mr. Grail?"

"Unintended. But now he has greater power. He likes it. And so far I've haven't scanned traces of a non-human aberration. I might guess your intent of bringing me here was a psychological ploy. I'm an outside menace to check your internal one."

Venn fell silent. His head tilted forward in a slow collapse of neck muscles and pride. He stared at the ground, blankly. Embarrassment, shame, and failure mixed into his internal conflict. The same ethics that inspired his *recolony* now collided with a giant reality that threatened his vision. Venn's obvious gambit was to threaten Shank with another power with guns. Me. Yet if Shank couldn't be intimidated, Venn still wanted him gone. He struggled with the severity, or lethality, of Shank's eviction. As leaders, they would collide. Venn sought order through consensus. Shank was raw power. It was a classic tale, yet I didn't want a role in the potential tragedy.

"You might make a good psychiatrist, Mr. Grail." Venn said and took a slow breath.

"I'm good at the job I have. And someone needs me to do it, somewhere. Good luck, Venn. But my consultation, here, is over."

"If you could stay a little longer. I, of course, will pay. You're a strong individual, Mr. Grail. But your career keeps you isolated. You probably live alone. You likely—"

"And if you find a real reason to hire me, I won't take compensation in psychoanalysis."

"Um—uh—?" Venn was a man who liked words. They failed him as he saw his plan start to walk out.

"Look," I said, "get a lot of loyal guys and toss him. It's better as an inside job, anyway."

"Easier said than done." Venn countered. "He has—had his uses. He has his followers. Any confrontation within the colony might split or destroy it. I, um, I understood people like you could be hired to do certain things. Um—" Desperation took Venn directly to the point. "Do you know anyone else who will do this?"

"Here's a cheaper idea: send Shank out for soda. Hire a small army of street thugs. Or a big army. They might be able to take him. Maybe."

"Can you?" Venn pleaded.

"Maybe. But—hold on." I sensed motion in the shadows.

"What?"

I didn't answer. I saw a woman with a magnificent expanse of brown, curly hair like an airy cloud caressing her head. She was mere moments away from losing it. I jumped over the rail and into the courtyard and drew my massive Aquila handgun as I hit the ground. I raced step for step, second for second for her life with the thing attacking her from behind. Everyone else was oblivious. My sprint took me near Shank. He saw my armed charge. His face lit with a burst of fear and then rage from believing I was indeed Venn's betrayal. Shank felt all the simmering issues between them finally explode. But none of it was why I jumped down. Shank reached to grab my gun. I shoulder checked him aside. I aimed my gun and fired. The monster's chitinous jaws were just hitting the woman's skin on her neck. The bullet hit. The monster's head blew apart.

The woman with the brunette cloud needed care for small, imbedded pieces of metal and monster. She also had slight burns, and shock. But she would be fine, in time. Alive. Her friends attended to her, right away. I took closer scans of the monster. It looked like a biological compromise between a locust and an isopod. A replay of m-RNA showed its saw-toothed jaws were its last, forward segment split midline beneath sweptback compound eyes. Behind the eyes, a series of slits directed air across a powerful chemoreceptor good at detecting scents of prey through the foul, city air. The stunned people murmured as ears rang from the gunshot and minds caught up to what their eyes just saw. Shank stepped beside me.

"That was, uh, that was okay." Shank said. He looked relieved.

"Yeah!" another female voice called behind us. Applause and cheers followed.

Shank bobbed his head. He kept his eyes on the dead thing before us, but his face flashed shock. He felt the cheers were stolen from him. His eyes darted at me. His anger was returning. I kept my gun out as I scanned the monster. Shank's face slowly curled into a camouflage smile as people came to slap my back and thank me. Many looked at the creature's remains. Venn joined them. I took a breath and holstered my weapon. I didn't kill the people's joy by telling them this wasn't over. The results of my scans told me I would need my gun and maybe another, soon.

The applause died away and the people dispersed. Venn stayed and stared at the creature. He likely considered the danger it posed to his recolony. I removed a containment bag from inside my coat and tossed in front of the monster's corpse. The small, back square unfolded several times to form a long rectangle. The bag hissed open at the short edge facing the dead beast. It acted as a wide, flat snake to draw in the body. I helped it every few seconds with a gentle kick from my boot.

"I've seen monsters, before." Shank said, watching the process. "I was—am a plumber."

"Nice rates," I said. "You should find a place with more pipes. A nice, rich tower. Probably fewer of these to punch out."

"Yeah. I did that, once." Shank smiled. "No gun. So I don't need you, here."

"Really? The girl would be dead if I wasn't here."

"Okay. So you saved her. But now that thing is dead. Good job. Now leave."

"There are more of them," I said. "Their coming."

"How the Gates would you know that?" Shank challenged.

It was a new experience to see someone lower his head to sneer at me.

"The body. The thing's biology." I replied.

"I thought monsters were one offs!" Shank barked. "It's what they told us at I.T."

I was sure I.T. stood for Institute of Technology. I suppressed making an *IT* joke looking at Shank.

It was hard.

"Singular organisms created through spontaneous genetic origin." The voice was strong and female. The woman wore a paramedic's jumpsuit with the hood pushed down to free long, blonde hair. "The genesis in genetics."

Venn's focus shifted immediately to the woman. He smiled. His heart rate increased and so did his perspiration. Shank stood a little taller.

"We don't need you, Holly." Shank said. "Things dead. And we aren't dumping it off for re-sus."

Shank's tone was mocking, but he looked at me as if actually seeking confirmation. On keeping the thing dead, we easily concurred. I nodded agreement.

"I would've liked to examine the body," Holly said as the bag sealed closed.

"You're a—" I began.

"Scientist," she finished. "And what passes for our medic and surgeon. I'm Dr. Hollis, or Holly."

"I can copy the scans. They smell better, anyway." I said.

"Yeah. And he was just leaving." Shank added.

"Nope." I shook my head once in disagreement. "This thing was pregnant. *Was* pregnant."

Now Shank and Venn were in unison as they looked at me with incredulity.

"How is that possible? It—I'm sure it's no natural species!" Holly said looking at the monster's shape, now vacuum-sealed in black.

"It's not. But the creature had larvae folds beneath its plates and a parthenogenic aspect."

"So, the same aberration, the same anomalous genome." Holly noted. "It's basically monoclonal. Actually, *multi*-clonal."

"It could be a self-generating colony organism. If the trait is shared by the offspring." I said with dread weighted by bad memories. "This one bore a half-dozen copies. And each copy—"

"Crap!" Shank yelled. He grasped the horror. The recolony could be overrun.

"You learn that tech-term at I.T?" I asked.

Shank didn't know to growl or laugh. Venn and Hollis laughed.

"Okay. So, um, what do we do?" Venn asked.

"You do nothing." I replied. "I find and kill them all."

"Sounds easy." Shank said.

I arched my left eyebrow and glared at Shank. He glared back.

"One's behind you," I said.

Shank spun. I detected his massive heart pound hard enough to knock down walls. There was no monster. He turned back to me with a face twisted with rage that faded as he saw my hands slowly draw both of my large sidearms.

"You're going to have to leave," I said.

A giddy, half-stifled laugh escaped Venn.

"Right, here. All of you," I added. "The monster's kids have smelled blood. And their coming. Keep your people back, and get out of my way."

They left. Even Shank.

The thing that attacked the woman had struck from the shadows. Its hungry copies did not rise from the city depths. They came charging down the side of a tall building. I had detected their motion, but they moved too fast to prepare anything other than using the courtyard as a shooting gallery with me as bait. The risk was assuming they would follow a path laid out by the first menace. If not, I'd have to run to their next attack. Fast. At a distance, they appeared to be large, descending scales. As they came lower, the lateral bands of their armor were visible on one as it halted for and instant as another raced by it. The term *pack* usually referred to a group of mammalian creatures, not large arthropods. But these murderous, pill-bug monsters acted almost as a family of wolves, but wolves that had armor and traveled vertical surfaces faster than cheetahs once ran.

These beasts did not use spots for camouflage. Their shells absorbed active scans and didn't reflect signals. Their spike-tipped legs gripped a wide conduit fastened to a high wall that flanked the recolony. It was easier just to see them, but seeing them was hard beyond the recolony's haze of light. The imposing masses of skyscrapers beyond it made human eyes instinctively look away. I stayed focused. They monsters had a long trip down. They finally reached the recolony roofs. They scuttled in darkness and too soon into the courtyard. The scent of spattered blood from their original copy, or *mother*, had excited and drawn them here as I hoped. They didn't come to exact revenge. They had come to eat her corpse.

Whatever else they found would also sate their hunger. Like me. And unfortunately, there were more beasts than I accounted for. Bad. And soon, painful. I had time to pop in an extended clip into one Aquila and take aim. FRACDAR made the shadow a visible plane. The monsters raced through it. I opened fire before they hit the courtyard's weak light. Their armor was useless against armor piercing cores. On penetration, the explosives surrounding the cores detonated. Their devastated bodies flipped and spun from the explosions. Some of the giant bugs halted at the remains and carved out exposed tissue. They were the easiest to target, but more charged at me from behind them. I backed up, firing. The slide locked back on my left gun. Empty.

From the left, one set of jaws tore across my midsection. My coat, gun harness, and body armor spared my skin and organs from the assault, but the creature's power ripped away a wide swath of it all. Then the second set of jaws ripped into my exposed flesh. I spun. The slashing beasts were the final ones blown apart with the last rounds from the extended clip as my own blood and muscle shot out across the courtyard.

Pain.

Sensors are not my only augmentations. But even my amped biology has limits. Still, I was sure I would heal. Mostly. I dropped my guns. I needed to hold my guts in place. I needed help. I hoped Dr. Hollis—the weak light of the courtyard grew dimmer. I found myself on my knees. I slid on bits of shattered monster and my blood. Footsteps. A powerful hand lifted my head. Shank smiled. His joy was not that I had saved his life, but from the threat to my own. I heard Venn. I blacked out.

Today, popping something from a bottle remedied most ailments. If you can't swallow or parts of your throat are missing, visit a nearby med-kiosk or quick clinic. You'll be back home and smiling in no time. Or dead. Results in your neighborhood may vary. Don't travel in your neighborhood if you've heard screaming or are apt to blunder into darkened alleys. Tell your doctor about other people taken in your neighborhood, and if you've recently experienced limb loss or other side effects of modern life. If you can't afford medical care, your provider may be able to help with a single dose of strong narcotic and quick shove. Remember: do no harm to your credit rating. It can save your life.

Those and other, unfortunately non-hallucinatory ideas floated through my brain as I woke up. I saw Dr. Hollis over a curled obstruction. She was now fully suited with goggles and mask. The curled barrier was the tattered edges of my jaw-torn clothes and sheer armor peeled back from my wound. Other, bloody pieces sat tossed aside with bloodier sponges and used gloves. Dr. Hollis had used a very sharp scalpel, or laser shears. She leaned over my abdomen on my left. I could feel my arms dangling off the sides of the surgical bed. Hollis smoothed the last sheet of lock gauze into place. It bonded to the rest. They adhered to my surrounding, intact skin and drew tighter. The lock gauze would act as a large, flexible scab and hold my organs in place until I healed. I glanced around. The operating theater was a tight, rectangular room with cabinets that no doubt held whatever she would need to save her fellow recolonists.

And then I noted I was still alive.

"I can see you've amped your healing rates and augmented your biology in general," Hollis said without looking over at my raised head. She inspected her handiwork across my abdomen. "You shouldn't be awake. I gave you enough tranq to put Shank asleep."

"You should keep it for that." I croaked.

"I do. In my pocket, always." She glanced at me.

"Smart."

"What you did wasn't." Hollis lifted her goggles and pulled down her mask as she turned to look at my face.

"I did my job."

"Your job sucks." Hollis glanced at my dressed guts.

"Yup." I nodded once and hit the surgical bed. "But a lot of people won't die now. At least not by that pack beast."

"Venn has saved a lot of people from the street. From monsters." Hollis said. "Just in a different way."

"But one still showed up, here." I took a breath and regretted it.

"I guess that's why you're here."

"Right." I nodded and hit the bed again. "And why you carry the tranq with you. Do all the women?"

"Maybe not tranq." Hollis ran a hand across her left pocket. "Too bad you're hurt, and hurt bad."

"Yeah, well. I kill monsters, not attitudes."

"Well, good for you for having ethics." Hollis bobbed her head and looked at me with a flash of disgust. "But you jumped to conclusions very quick for a smart guy. I wouldn't ask you to kill anyone, just get rid of them. Shank is getting more powerful."

"Or people are getting more intimidated." I took the pain and rolled to my side to sit up as Hollis watched my stomach to see if everything held in place.

"Same thing," she said. "He threatens more than me, or Venn. He may destroy this entire place and the dream it's built on."

"I don't think that's his game." I said. "That would put him out of power, too."

"You're wrong." Hollis said sharply. "He really has no plan. No purpose. Not other than making himself a hero, to win popularity."

"Sounds like another politician."

"So do you!" Hollis snapped.

That hurt.

"Look!" Hollis pressed closer. "Venn is a man of ideas, of ideals. Shank is a strongman. Some think his strength will keep them safe. All they have to do is wake and sleep. The strongman will take care of what stalks their nightmares. He's a promise, and that's all. Now you've shown he's not enough. So what will he do to keep his power when you leave?"

I took a deep breath. It hurt. "Well, I guess I can talk to him."

"Talk?" Hollis whipped off her goggles and pulled her hood down.

"Think about it," I said. "Venn's reputation will fall apart if I just blow Shank's head off—not that you'd want that. Shank needs a reason to leave, and his people need to see him walk."

Hollis looked to the side as she thought about what I said.

"Where are my guns?" I asked and eased my legs down to the floor.

"In their holsters, there." Hollis pointed to a large cabinet. "You need them?"

"No. I think this is one time they are better left behind. But I don't suppose you have a shirt that fits?"

Actually, I took one handgun. It was a long walk to the train. Squeezing a trigger was easy. The aftereffects were hard. Shank needed to go, but I needed to be careful about how I got rid of him. I was still weak. I needed to make him weak. Or at least appear to be nothing more than mortal. The same method he lucked into to gain power would be the perfect weapon. Nevertheless, I would offer him a choice.

The local train station was only an arc of empty track near a sidewalk and darkened street. I was glad I stood there, alone. Yet I worried my plan had failed. Then a familiar, deep voice eased my concern.

"You're more stupid than I thought." Shank said coming up behind me. He reached behind his back and brought out my Aquila in his right hand. "You left your hardware behind. Most of it."

"I like it there. I like Venn's ideas." I said. "I'm just going to get a reweave. Then I'm coming back."

"No you're not." Shank's eyes narrowed at me and he smiled wide.

"You can't use my gun," I shrugged. It hurt. "In fact, you'd better drop it now that I've remote armed its security. That building e-field will blow the gun, and your arm. Well, maybe only your hand."

Shank shook the gun and then tossed it to the street. "Nice."

He massaged his right hand, but then reached around his back again and brought out a large, black automatic. I supposed he could hide a small armory behind him.

"But I also brought my own piece."

"I see that. I also detect it has lousy firewalls with an old OS that's still compatible with mine. And my hacks."

"Crap!" Shank squeezed the trigger to no avail. He threw his own gun across the rails in anger. "I should've just beat you down back at recolony!"

"You should've done a lot of things. But you still have options. I'm giving you and Venn's colony a choice. Freedom."

"Freedom from me, you mean?" Shank laughed. "They love me."

"Only some of them. Not the majority."

"Too bad for them!" Shank barked.

In the distance, the clattering sounds of the ancient train rolled through the background city roar.

"People get sick of tyrants, Shank. They will tire of you, even your most ardent fans. And you know there are more people like me. Some, not as nice."

"I'll beat them, too." Shank's defiance was as large as he was.

"Maybe not. So here's a deal. The train is coming. I'm going to get on it. Come with me, and you'll be safe."

"I'm safe anyway." Shank looked around with his palms up and shrugged. "Like I said, I don't need you. Or guns. I could even just call out my people and have them rush you. You wouldn't shoot them." Shank laughed. "So here's my offer. You come back and make nice. Make like we're friends. And here's a bonus: name who you want. I'll make sure you get them. Man. Woman. Both. Want some fancy food? I can get that, too. Just take it and then leave. If you stay, I'll have to crush you like I did that monster."

"Like when you stood with me in the courtyard?"

Shank sneered.

"You got lucky. Once." I said.

"That's all it took!" Shank laughed again. "Now I'm lucky every day. I'll give you one day. Take it. But come back to stay and I'll kill you."

"And maybe the people back at the colony who don't like you. Right?"

"Hey, they can always leave." Shank motioned to the approaching train.

"Venn won't leave. He built the place. It's his vision taking shape."

"Then maybe he'll die there!" Shank lurched forward. "His choice! The place is mine, now. So is whatever he had."

"Like Dr. Hollis?" I asked.

"Her. Anyone."

Behind us, the train rolled to a stop with a squeal of metal friction.

"There's your ride," Shank said. "Get on it!"

"One last chance, Shank."

"That's my line, twitch! I know you took one gun. But somehow I'll get to you. And when I do, it won't be a fair fight."

"Right." I stepped toward the train. "But soon you won't be fighting me. You will fight something else. Unless you run. I can sense them coming."

"Them?" Shank bellowed. "What's *them*?"

"The second pack. This one split off, earlier. They're even more hungry. I'll come back and kill them, but you should run. I'm not taking them on, right now."

"You lying sack! There isn't any monster here!" Shank's rage was overtaking his fear of being shot. He lurched closer to me as his veins became visible across his neck and scalp. "Get lost! Get out of here before I beat you into the rails!"

The automatic doors of the train car slid open with rusted protest.

I stepped towards them with one last glance at Shank. "Try not to scream."

Shank shouted expletives. I stood in the railcar as its doors screeched shut. The old train made that familiar sound as it pulled away with me and a few huddled passengers: *Clickety-clack! Clickety-clack! Clickety-clack!* Shank heard similar sounds soon after. These were not steel wheels on rails, but claws raking old asphalt covered in resin: *Click-scritch-scratch! Click-scritch-scratch! Click-scritch-scratch!*

I wasn't sure if the monster coming close to the train was a pack of giant isopods. I just knew they scarred Shank. What he saw was more reptilian, just as hungry, and much bigger. Shank fought. He screamed. He saw his blood. He saw red parts from under his massive chest. All of his parts disappeared like so many others into the darkness. After I killed the beast, his tissue traces might be flagged and separated from the monster's body. If anyone at the city incinerators paid attention.

Some at Venn's colony were shocked that a monster killed Shank. It didn't seem possible to them. Some would miss him, but probably not for long. They would blend back into the community. Venn would have another chance to build his new society, and for a while, be free of monsters.

15
IMMORTAL COIL

"Now, blessings light on him that first invented this same sleep!"
- Cervantes, *Don Quixote*, *Part II, Book III, Chapter 68.*

Mr. Quixote fought monsters. Yet his battles were with figments within his mind. Mr. Cervantes created *Don Quixote*. Thus, Mr. Quixote was also a figment, like a dream. In dreams, we become figments of our own imagination. Such a motif might appear as a serpent with its head coiled to bite its own tail. In dreams, our folded brains make what we see. Yet, what lurks in the unconscious realms might appear as something unfamiliar, as if it's infiltrated our psyche from outside the skull. That is similar to how monsters slide into places where they should not be and attack. Sometimes you feel attacked in your own dreams. Personal myth becomes a stalking presence in that theater you alone can enter. And the snakes and the windmills spin.

In one unconscious orbit, I stood before the rocky opening of a cave. Dead roots and bushes flanked me. That they were dead seemed normal. Where they had come from originally I—well, it was a dream. At least I was clad in my gray coat that would shield me from any thorns. I knew why I was there.

To face destiny. I thought, although I really hated the idea, even in a dream.

I entered the craggy cave tunnel with my weapon styled as a shotgun. Deep into the cave, light flickered across the rough sides. Ahead was a chamber, lit from within. Inside the chamber was a rocky pedestal. For whatever reason, if reason existed here, I could not see its top.

Thoughts raced through my mind as if others were writing a play I expected to be improvised. *I wonder what it looks like. Paradise is lost, and it holds the only piece left of the former world. Is that why it hides in a cave?*

A deep and slashing voice spoke behind me. "So now *you* have come. Such impudence."

On the pedestal, I could now see a strongly lit flower blossom. A massive serpent coiled around the rough-hewn base.

"You think you're a better man than *he* was?" The serpent raised its viper's head. It stayed coiled around the pedestal but still rose higher than my height and always kept its menacing eyes focused on me. Its voice became a shout. "You think you're a better than Gilgamesh?"

"No." I said. "But you are still the same lowly serpent, and I can learn from his mistakes."

The serpent's eyes appeared to flash sinister glee. I could hear manic laughter. Then it struck at me. Its sickle-sized fangs dropped from its upper jaw. Naturally, I fired my gun and blew its head asunder. The blast noise echoed down the cave. Blood, scales, and fragments of muscle dripped from the rocky ceiling and walls. I looked up from the headless serpent and saw the blossom it guarded. I took off my coat and hung it on a rock jutting from the wall. I focused my attention back on the blossom. I picked it up, carefully.

"Why would I want to live forever?" I asked no one.

Still, I heard a reply. My coat still hung on the wall. However, now it had a stretched face and limbs as if my flayed skin was sewn onto it. Yet there were no seams. The skin and coat were the same hide. My shotgun was now propped against the wall to the left of the speaking coat.

"Why would I want to ever die?" The coat asked.

"I can kill—uh, combat what's been done." A voice said from the gun.

"Yes. It's a good idea." A whisper from nowhere added.

I nodded agreement. "And I am hungry."

I ate the blossom.

I didn't get to enjoy my meal. I stood in the chamber again in my coat and holding my shotgun. The blossom was bitter. The serpent rose behind me. It now had two heads. Both grinned.

"Good!" The serpent roared. "Now we'll both live forever."

"How—?" I began.

"How can I die when you are immortal?" The serpent finished.

I fired. The explosive round shattered one of the serpent's mocking faces, but the other head split into two fang-wielding heads. Then four became eight. All of them lunged down at me. I fired at the base of the necks. Two serpents uncoiled from the bloody mess, each with eight heads.

"So much for learning from the mistakes of others, eh *hero?*" The serpents cackled in unison.

Scale fragments and blood from the serpents spattered my face as I drew a second gun and fired continuously.

Good thing I ate that flower, I thought as serpent fangs struck at me from all angles. *It looks like I'll be here a while.*

Sinister laughter and gun blasts echoed out of the cave.

I'm not a fan of hearing the echoes of dreams when I wake up. However, I heard the serpent's laughter as I shook off an unexpected nap after logging samples in my lab. My wrist-com flashed. Someone called me to fight something far worse than a windmill. I hoped that monster didn't have a voice, or at least had never learned to laugh. I reached for my coat. I hesitated for a moment. Then I put it on.

16
OPIATES

In one era, one person said religion was the opiate of the masses. Today, one might think that if no one prays then there are less addicts, even in a population more massive than when Carla Xole lived. Or was it Karl Marx? I confused historical figures, and maybe their true philosophy. It's good to review the facts for context, for thought. It may seem ironic that history becomes lost in time. Personally, long spans of time can feel like a heavy weight. A mass. But feeling the crush of time was never my private vice. I'm an urban hunter. I have to keep moving. Something with mass is stalking someone. And most everyone wants to cling to that iniquity called life.

There are people who own a license for immortality in this age. What do years feel like to them? That is, if they can still feel time. They must take the long view of things, because they don't face death every day. I do. My license to bring death marks me as Joshua Grail. I kill predators that kill people as a service to the masses. It's a paid service. We must afford our vices, such as food and clean water, somehow.

Several people were missing in one, small zone. Probably more than reported. Some people enjoyed extra space more than their neighbors. The trail I followed was not clean. It was outside the sweep of street cleaners. Maybe it always had been. I slogged through an alley that seemed filled by the constant black clouds above. That was partially true. The alley held drifts of city dust. Smog particles and soot drifted down to mix with microscopic flakes of human skin and hair. With billions and billions of humans—well, I wear tight-sealed boots. And I'm glad I'm not allergic.

I came to a warehouse trapped among old, eroded levicrete walls. It was as if a giant dropped a strongbox inside a hellish castle courtyard. I would soon learn someone heartless tried to make the rusting hulk a massive treasure chest. At the time, I kept following the trace. I found other, weirder chemical anomalies near the huge double doors. My scans could not penetrate the warehouse. Thankfully, one of the double doors sported a human-scale door and I had the key. My boot knocked the door open. The place was listed as vacant. Still, the barrel of my combat shotgun-styled weapon entered first. There was a lot of data to sense and sort in this place. Top of the list: it was not abandoned. The lights were on. They revealed whoever was using the warehouse was willing to kill to hide their enterprise. After a few steps inside, the corpses and carnage was all around. There had been a battle.

I walked around a huge vat. Slime and similar chemical traces clung to the circular wall and wet floor. A wall from floor to high ceiling divided the warehouse. As I neared it, my scanners identified one of the whole bodies. Mendel Alxa. A fellow Monster Killer. It explained the other, shattered bodies. They had been hit with high-caliber, explosive rounds. I knew Alxa's rep. He might cut across another Monster Killer's perceived territory, but he was competent and never indifferent to clients. In person, he was fit. Big. Dead. A pack of thugs had caught him in the open while he stalked something. That something would catch and kill them in the open or anywhere. Not that the punks cared that Alxa acted to save their lousy lives. Bastards. From the blood spray and tissue splatter, he blew apart a number of assailants before the sheer weight of their bullets caused his own blood to pump out. He died too long ago for a resus or resurrection, even if he had the insurance. Ultimately, Alxa got his revenge. No one was alive. No one human.

The sucking and crunching was muffled. The creature was, for a monster, out in the open. A side office had lights on. I nearly wished it didn't. Beyond a shattered wall, the monster had pushed the desk aside to retrieve a gunman's remains. It drew the partial brown-suited corpse into its hidden mouth underneath its wide, flat body. The thing's width was nearly as wide as the office floor. The gunman had tried to use the office walls as cover, but found Monster Killer rounds don't respect most living armor or building walls. Alxa's return fire had devastated the gunman. Now something looked to make the rest of him disappear. At first, I thought the thing looked like a massive flounder. Then I remembered rays of the old ocean. I doubted any of them still lived, but what remains of the ocean can give a big surprise.

This low beast moved on some form of electrostatic field or millions of fine cilia. It likely ambushed small prey or ate carrion.

Nice to think there is that much dead meat out there. I would try to stay alive. Its sense of smell detected food. Its eyes looked up to make sure nothing saw it. That failed today. Yet it was very hungry and intent on its human lunch, or oddly indifferent to my approach. But it did notice me.

Eyes. You don't need sight to kill. Yet, if the monster has eyes, there is a very brief, very tense moment between hunter and monster when you see the thing, and it unfortunately sees you. It feels like recognition. It's the last moment for some Monster Killers. More often, it's the instant of death for monsters. This hungry land ray had eyes. They were large, glaring, and focused on me.

A full scan of the monster gave me its data down to its aberrant genes. Sensors don't generate emotion. That comes from the natural grey drive. I am rarely scared. I am sometimes a little creeped out, and this thing had creepy eyes. It stared in defiance or indifference. Or simply because it had no fear. It also had no conscience, or intellect. It had instinct, hunger, and surprising power. It leapt.

For a fraction of a second, a wall with teeth was airborne. Time sometimes seemed to dilate when I aimed and fired. Screens protected my senses from the loud gunshots and flashes. Nothing protected the monster. Bullets punched through thick skin. Explosives blew apart tissue. A living wall became more carnage. Its eyes were gone. I blinked.

Something had gone wrong. Not just Earth's ecology, years ago. An error occurred when I fired. Usually my neural link ensures the gun goes off. This time I had to squeeze the trigger, hard. Something was now interfering with the operating system of my sensors and guns. Perhaps a hovering data parasite found a way in. The OS was part of me. I needed to find the source of interference, and kill it.

I would not have enough body bags for everyone and all their pieces. I tossed one by the monster's corpse. It began to unfurl. It would just be big enough. The gunman could wait for the police crews. Although no reply came to my public summons and one sent to Detective Sergeant John Slate. All I got was the repeated reply from archived system files. I used another bag for Alxa. The memory strands in his brain and any backed-up by his OS were evidence. Plus, leaving him as scavenger meat was bad form. Professional courtesy meant packing him out. I'd shoulder that weight, willingly.

I handled Alxa's weapon with care. His gun wasn't heavy. Maybe too light for my taste. His Rollinger Arms, Urbanite Mk 3 looked like the lovechild of a grenade launcher and assault rifle. Basic black. Built for 20mm, explosive sheathed, caseless rounds. It did the job, but continuous fire might cause the ceremite alloy barrel to overheat and warp ever so slightly. That altered the ballistics. If your targeting system failed, you had to compensate, visually. That might be the fraction of a second when you were split in half. Alxa had made an expanded box magazine, but the interference here might have altered the battle. I slid the gun behind a row of three metal drums. The weapon needed to sit and think things over. Its system was in lockdown mode since it lost contact with Alxa. It would not like anyone fiddling with it. The few remaining rounds might detonate and mess up my hair. Not that I ever combed it. After a set time, the gun might seek an outside signal and respond to a retrieval code, in a clear environment.

Another code was a little off. As I searched, I reviewed the recorded traces of whatever had lived in the huge vat. It was not the thing I killed. Yet it could be as monstrous. More horrific was that someone had purposefully created a monster, even though sewers did that well enough at random. The process here was nearly as ugly. The vat had traces of Prokaryol, micrylotides, Cascade White, and old-fashioned synthosomes. Why not throw in some glue and knitting needles. The bioengineering stew traces were leftovers that had clung to skin and released in excretions. The living concoction was created in something else and then stored here. Somewhere there was one big or a very large number of manufactured monsters.

Some genetic strands were long enough to identify. The cross check presented a high probability of the genes coded for *Petromyzontiformes*. Lampreys. That natural animal nearly wrote its own license for immortality. Lampreys survived almost unchanged for four-hundred million years. Nice run. Now, somebody partially resurrected them as a piece of something bizarre. That something was part human. Who would splice modified lamprey, human, and what else's genes? Why? It was illegal to create a monster. Why take the risk for so many reasons, including protecting your own life? The punishment was summary execution.

My search for the interference source would have to wait. I heard distant voices. I could stand and fight a Pyrrhic battle like Alxa. Or—I ducked behind a pipe bank and cistern large enough to hide me, and thankfully only me. I held my gun ready anyway. I didn't have time to plant a spy stud. Eavesdropping would have to do. I heard the battered, small door swing open and a conversation continue as several people entered the warehouse.

"Camel? Why do they call you Camel?" a man with high-pitched voice asked.

"No idea." A deeper voice answered as if the syllables were hard to form.

"Well, you can store up fresh water or whatever floats your fancy with this job." The higher voice had a salesman's glee.

"Good," was forced out.

"So, could you guys get to work?" the higher voiced male asked.

There was a silence. A nervous pause seemed to float across the interior.

"Um, mister, we guard, threaten, and if necessary, kill people." A sharp voiced male finally answered. "We don't clean up the bodies."

"But your ad said evidence elimination was a key skill." The high voice was now elevated slightly more.

"Yeah, well, not the kind that needs a mop." The sharp voice almost came to a yip a few steps farther into the warehouse. "Geez! Who—what killed these guys?"

"An exterminator." The man with the higher but now calmer voice said. "Don't worry. He's dead."

"He got a partner?" The tone of concern now came from the deep grunts.

"If he does, I've taken steps to—"

I didn't hear the rest. I felt sharp, sudden pain across the back of my head. I heard my gun hit the hard floor. I didn't feel my body follow.

Black.

Music. Song. People and pink monsters dancing. It all resolved into sound and images like a cartoon from the id. It was a commercial. An ad. An annoyance. By brain didn't create the experience, but my reactions were my own as if I reacted to a dream. Despite the bright colors, smiles, and jaunty music, I didn't like what I saw. The ad promised individual paradise. It would help spawn nightmares in minds, sewers, and alleys.

Animated caricatures of people had life-like depth and presence. So did the pink, eel-like creature with a cartoonish face and swelling grin. The pink thing leapt and dove down the throats of glowering men and women. Internal views then showed the parasite curl around their hearts. Circular waves of joy radiated from the creature laying internal siege to emotions and mind. The people suddenly smiled brightly and danced as a chorus of sickly, happy voices sang the jingle.

Why be alone? Why sit and moan?
Simbi will solve all your woes!

If you're annoyed, Symbi fills the void
Just swallow all your pains away!

With Symbi! Symbi!
Symbi! The symbiote!
Life is one big hug!

With Symbi! Symbi!
Symbi! The symbiote!
You are always loved!

Just take one slurp, and you'll feel the urge
To embrace life in a new and clear way!

You'll have a new friend, all to the end
Symbi makes the blues go away!

With Symbi! Symbi!
Symbi! The symbiote!
Life is one big hug!

With Symbi! Symbi!
Symbi! The symbiote!
You are always loved!

So don't fear, don't despise
Symbi doesn't care your color or size!

Melt your thoughts all away
Swallow your own Symbi today!

Just open wide to take the ultimate prize!

With Symbi! Symbi!
Symbi! The symbiote!
Life is one big hug!

With Symbi! Symbi!
Symbi! The symbiote!
You are always loved!

The world is always bright with Symbi inside! Now, don't delay! Order your Symbi today! No restrictions apply. Financing available.

Grey.

Light. I blinked. My head leaned forward. It throbbed. That eased as I regained consciousness. I was in a side office bound by old rope to a metal chair. The air was humid and stank. I heard water moving. The floor creaked. I guessed it was an elevated room on the other side of the wall. I wasn't alone. I raised my head, slowly. I had just witnessed some nightmare from the past. Somehow, a commercially made monster reared it headless form in my mind. Symbis were from a bygone time when profit margins finally pushed aside most regulations. Symbis competed with the latest electronic time leach to be your addiction du jour. Some of them even told you the time, if you cared.

You might ask why anyone would swallow a monster. Back then, such parasites were seen as something more than pets. They were an added organ of joy. Many people didn't use an important, natural organ called the brain. Companies first sold the mass produced lifeforms as living toys. They competed well against traditional, eugeneticaly bred pets. The new, warm toys were nice to stroke with fur in your favorite color. Markets merged and evolved faster than machines or stray cats could make new life. The comforting presence of a free-shipped *catterspaniel* or *gerbildillo* evolved into mobile communication devices with doe-like eyes. Customers stroked their cyborgs in purr mode while social media told them virtual strangers liked the images of e-fluffy's lunch. If you didn't have time to pet your phone, you didn't wait long before phones became part of you. Just as bio and tech combined to make new products, eventually biotech products combined with the consumer. Few asked if Homo sapiens were becoming corporate pets.

A niche opened that shed technology. What people wanted was the validation it brought. Old-fashioned chemistry could do that. So why not combine the markets of opiate-like gratification and symbiotes. They were cheaper to make, and the market was a preexisting condition in consumers' minds. Now, no one needed external validation or purr mode. If consumers swallowed a symbi larva, they purred. In an odd way, society was lucky there were glitches. Otherwise, previous generations might have been the last humans that drifted into extinction on a wave of manufactured bliss.

Bliss was not at the top of my long ascent to full, physical awareness. My eyes met someone with no issues about using bioengineering on herself. Her name was Indigo. I didn't know if the tag came before or after she had her skin recast in a deep, blue hue. It was almost gun metal black. A gun tone of silver caught my eye. She held my Aquila .50-caliber sidearm. The contrast in tones made me blink again.

"Nice piece, Ice." Indigo said.

She balanced my gun in her palm. It was a heavy gun. She had no problem with the weight in her cobalt hand. Her augmentation was more than skin deep. She was a powerhouse standing nearly two, full meters. I wondered if she had ever met Alxa. We Monster Killers should have a clubhouse.

"Indy," I groaned. "Why am I tied to a chair?"

"I always do that on a first date," she smiled.

"It's going to make it hard to dance," I said.

"For you." Indigo waved the gun in a circle, slowly.

I focused on my gun. "You know I have locks on—"

"Wahl has keys." Indigo said.

"Wahl?"

"The cash cow." Indigo leveled the gun to my head. "My cow, anyway."

"You working as a thug?" I asked, and shifted my shoulders. "You get more cash on bounties."

Indigo laughed. I kept a close look at the bobbling muzzle of my own gun pointed at me. This had become an irritating day.

"Oh, no! Not this time." Indigo chirped. "Wahl needed—really, really wanted someone like you or me after Alxa scared the green out of him. Nice thing for me was that I was still in the registry, and Wahly boy has deep pockets."

"And some deep vats, I guess."

"You guess right, Icy Spice."

"What's his game?" I asked. I tried not to make the chair squeak.

"I don't know. I don't care." Indigo frowned, shrugged, and never lowered the gun.

"Tell him the Cascade White messes with a natural animal's epigenetics. I doubt he compensated for the electrochemical shift. Some traits—"

"I said I don't know and don't care. I cashed the check. Now Indigo is a happy girl."

Indigo pressed the Aquila against my brow. She stretched her legs to straddle the chair and then slid down onto my lap. I was amazed the old metal chair took our combined weight and only creaked.

"You want to be happy, Mr. Grail, Mr. Ice, mister blue girl's toy?" Indigo asked. "Before I pop you?"

I motioned my eyes to where the gun made contact to my skull. "I think I'd be distracted."

Indigo gave a low laugh. "Oh, sweetie, I've never known a man so worried he can't rise above, even with blood coming from his neck."

"You have more fun on dates than I do." I said while feeling the press of Indigo's body, and the gun.

"I know."

"You know your boss, Wahl, is going to fail. Right?"

"No. And I don't care."

"You will when the freak or freaks he's cranked die, and he takes his cash and runs." I tried to raise my eyebrows and felt my skin pull against the pressed barrel. "Then the cops have you on file and the summary sentence for this crap is death."

"I faced death as an M-K, Ice. Big deal."

"You retired?"

"Moved to better gigs. Some Killers are better than others at finding monsters. And bounties." Indigo withdrew the gun and pressed her forehead against mine, and then shoved my head back with hers. Her eyes glared as brilliant, cold sapphires. "That pushes some of us to the bottom for city and corporate contracts, and business from word of mouth. It puts some of us flat out of business."

"I guess I should let more people die to spread the wealth." I said.

"Why not? They are just cattle. Watch them on the street. They move aside when I walk by. I'm stronger. But I also need to eat. Now, I could just eat them, or apply myself. Like my mother wanted."

Indigo laughed low, again. I felt the gun against my left ear.

"Just don't slip and be trampled," I breathed. "Cattle stampedes, sometimes."

"Well you can't run from cattle or anyone, not now. So I guess you're the trampled after all, Ice. Bummer."

"Fun stuff!" the high, male voice from earlier returned. A thin man in a finely tailored, beige business suit entered. His hair matched his jacket. So did his skin.

"Hiya. McConnel Wahl." The beige man said. "Say, Indigo, could you give me and your friend a minute?"

"No," she said flatly.

"Um," Wahl's smooth, beige face wrinkled.

Indigo kept the Aquila pressed to my head as she rose. She stepped back. The gun muzzle never moved from aiming at my skull. It felt like an old friend forced into betrayal.

"Show him." Indigo said.

I raised my freed hands and dropped the ropes.

"And I'm good with knots," Indigo added.

"Should've used chain," I said.

"Yeah. Cool." Wahl smiled and gave me a thumbs-up gesture. "Before bondage resumes, I'd like your opinion. You said the Cascade White—wait. Did you like the commercial?"

I stood. The horrid jingle of the Symbi ad replayed in my head. It hurt worse than the wound Indigo made when she bashed the back of my head to knock me out.

"That was you?" I asked Wahl.

"Yeah! Cool archive stuff I tweaked for v-RNA. You have some very nice tech integration through you. I used it for the brain load. Easier to do when the subject's unconscious. See, I was in communications. Lot of data all the time. Numbers. Codes. Lot of money in keeping it going."

"The looped interference is you, too." I said.

"Yeah. The field captures signals so it's not obvious jamming. It's containment. You think you're communicating, but, as you said, you're in a loop. Say you are a smart guy. So, can I hire you for a quickie consult?"

Wahl motioned out the door with a smile. Indigo sneered and held the gun steady.

"Okay," I said. "Can I have my guns?"

"No," Indigo growled.

Damn.

Outside the office was a catwalk of metal grating and railing that spanned the center of the warehouse. Both sides ended at narrow stair rigs like fire escapes. At least two stories below the catwalk was another massive vat. This one held frothy liquid. Under the bubbles was a swimming mass of something. The place smelled a lot like a beach on a hot day, covered with dead fish. Wahl's rental thugs strolled the ground floor, no doubt glad this one had no human remains. Mostly. I saw most of the missing persons near the opposite wall. Nothing had killed them, but something had stolen their minds. They were imprisoned in a large cage and shuffled in place if they moved at all. Several lay collapsed on the floor. They looked like a captured mass of zombies.

I held my disgust and anger. Indigo held the gun steady on me. Wahl walked ahead. Indigo stayed a step behind us.

"You seem to have a sound science base," Wahl said as we all walked.

"A side effect of being a Monster Killer," I replied. "You learn about what you kill."

"Indigo hasn't displayed that." Wahl said with a cock of his head.

"I guess I do more homework."

"Kiss my ass!" Indigo sniped.

I turned to her and gave a slight shrug. "For that you should've used chains."

We walked to the spot straight over the vat. I looked down. Inside it swam a massive bait ball of pink monsters. The human traits were not externally evident.

"So you're recreating the Symbi parasites." I nearly coughed from the heavy stench weighing down the humid air.

"Emosites!" Wahl chirped. "I've had some setbacks, but we keep swimming forward."

"You added human DNA as an anti-rejection factor?" I asked.

"Right," Wahl nodded. "I can whip up the new Symbis, but there are some issues with, I guess you'd call it, human integration. The creature is sort of toxic."

Wahl unconsciously glanced down at the zombie cage. I consciously resisted smashing his color-coordinated face.

"The creature or its endorphin secretions?" I asked.

"Um, both." Wahl rolled his eyes. "It's a bit harder than I thought. Like I said, I'm a communications guy. I'm learning the bioengineer thing from lectures posted on neu-vue."

"You also learn making new monsters is a summary execution offense?"

Behind us, Indigo growled. She obviously felt as though I was about to kick her from a well paying gig by taking her spot as new and improved muscle, or scaring Wahl to quit and run. Of course, I had other ideas.

"*Wellllll*, first things first." Wahl smiled and vibrated as if hit by a Symbi joy wave. "We'll get the bio, right. There are a lot of unregistered, um, subjects around here. More than enough to finish the learning curve. *Then* we'll get the legal rights. Death is, yeah, a bummer. But you should see the start-up fees and compliance codes for bio-markets. Going black let's you get the finished product faster. Its sale will pay for any fees and fines. I mean, the Symbis have awesome, broad potential their original makers didn't see."

I looked down at the swimming, pink mass. "What, you're going to serve them fried with chips?"

Wahl laughed. To my relief, so did Indigo.

"Man! That's good." Wahl beamed. "But, no. No. It's back to communicating. Old, *ooold* studies showed electronic communications tech had the same effect as opiate drugs. Companies just needed a linked communication thing in peoples' hands. They created content to keep people linked—hooked. So it's not the information or any exchange of thoughts that the actually brain wants. It's the fix. Drugs. Tech. Pink parasites. It's all the same to the brain. So, at the risk to my old job—screw them anyway!—but why communicate at all if you already get the stimulus? Data, facts are secondary to the market. Actually, they're not important."

"A fleshy, pink hypodermic that generates its own drug. That's important." I said as I felt nausea. And not from my creased skull.

"It's a perpetual market!" Wahl chirped. "Immortal money generation!"

"With some old, deadly side effects," I said. "Or didn't neu-vue have that data, those old facts?"

"Okay, sure. The old Symbis had some hiccups. The things ate peoples' guts. Their livers. Some spawned their own clones inside—talk about an O.D. Yeah, there were liability issues. But now we're better bioengineers. I mean, look! You kill stuff but know a lot about life. If you help me with the bio, the legal, the money angle, I can do that."

"I don't want to be killed, oddly." I glanced back at the indifferent-faced Indigo. "By cops, or anyone."

"Don't worry!" Wahl thrust out his arms. He stumbled, slightly and then steadied himself by grabbing the rail. "Hey, man. I'll cover you. This can't miss! Symbis can make—I shouldn't tell you this—but they make a captive market. Forget ads! What Symbi wants, the host will want. So, what do you want to sell? Carp? Their crap? No problem!"

"No need for focus groups," I said. "No need for market research."

Wahl nodded. "No need for legal departments. Because who will sue when you own both the product and consumer?"

"No need for laws, then," I added. "Or ethics. Just banks to collect the profits. An accomplishment to be proud of."

Wahl was so focused on his immoral goals that his brain bypassed the concept of sarcasm. Indigo's low growls told me she was cognizant of my tone. I hoped she wasn't offended enough to pull the trigger. Still, I kept standing so Wahl was in line with me in case she did. Indigo could see the shot would kill me and her precious cash cow.

"Yeah! Exactly." Wahl slapped my shoulder. "The market provides! I'll shell out fees and whatever to the right offices to cover our butts. We shop Symbi 2.0 to a conglomerate. They buy it. If they have to, they'll pay the courts and councils for retroactive legislative approval. All I—*we* have to do is succeed, here. You know, with you here, I can feel it. It's going to happen—um, what is your name?"

"Fred."

"Fred, man. Will you do it? Will you work for me?"

I paused as if considering Wahl's offer. I actually thought about new lies and old axioms. One axiom was *never hit a woman.* Another went: *never hit a man when he's down. Kick him. It's easier.* I knew Indigo believed the later. I had little choice but to violate the first. I backhanded her.

Unfortunately, she anticipated my strike and rolled with the blow. She spun backward, never dropping my gun, and then swung under the catwalk to avoid my boot. I turned and didn't need to punch the stunned Wahl. I simply trampled him as I bolted down the catwalk to avoid the hot shrapnel from Indigo shooting at me as she hung under the walkway. She quickly pulled herself back to the top and leveled my gun at my fleeing ass. I copied her move and swung under the walkway the millisecond before she fired. My ass stayed intact. Wahl's interference field might be helping me now by jamming Indy's aim.

I swung and dropped to the stairway support. I hit the metal web and wished for a flat wall to collide with, instead. It felt like leaping against dull sword blades. I had no time to enjoy the new pain. I stayed off the stairs and scrambled down the narrow supports like a terrified orangutan. I didn't want to become extinct.

I hit the floor running and Indigo's next round hit right at my heels. It blew out a small crater and singed my boots. I kept running. Indigo screamed and Wahl's rental thugs gave chase.

Hinged doors. They have been around for millennia. You would think thugs would be wise to the act of battering open a heavy door and then slamming it fast to wax one or two chasing punks. Nope. I heard a human avalanched behind the shut door as I jammed it shut with a hidden utility knife. Nevertheless, there were more to come and Indigo still had my artillery. And I was still an unarmed target. I ran across warehouse and sidestepped the corpses of Wahl's departed thugs. I slid to a stop near the three drums and Alxa's bagged body. If his gun was useless, he could still help me. His preserved memories of the shootout would give ample reason for heavily armed police to come here. I just needed to save both our heads. I tossed out some rolling eye-drones in faint hope someone would find them if I failed.

Indigo blew the door open. I expected an onslaught of her and less threatening rental muscle. They didn't come. Something worse squeezed through the doorway and shambled toward me. Wahl had freed his zombies to swarm me as a horde. When I had looked at the eyes of the ray monster and Indigo, they both were predatory but focused and alive. These zombie eyes were vacant and glazed. The window to their minds was now opaque. Maybe Wahl promised to pay some of them, but he knew the risks. These were his victims the same as any monster. They shambled at me. Other kinds of zombies wanted you rend you apart. These seemed to be searching just for their next step.

I knew Indigo wanted to charge in and fight. Using this unthinking mass was Wahl's idea. He wanted to shock me and then communicate with an emotional advantage. That would cause me to delay. Then, more active minds and bodies could surround me. Perhaps Wahl could then make me a captive and plumb my knowledge to fix his sick, parasitic gamble. He wanted me for my brain.

I shouldered Alxa's corpse as Wahl's voice came through the warehouse loudspeaker. I didn't listen and fled. Outside were more zombies shambling from the left of the warehouse. I protected Alxa's body and pushed through them. Wahl's capture loop was strongest inside. Here I got a clear signal. I accessed my remote data I was sure Wahl could not loop or clone. I could send signals.

"Ammo drop! Now!" I yelled into my wrist-com.

A battered but beautiful site descended almost immediately. It was a cylindrical drone, my ammo-drum from the transit lanes. It held more guns. Better yet, it was large enough to cram myself inside and escape. I could hear Indigo cursing over Wahl's echo and her boots slapping across hard and slickened floor. I had to act, fast.

Indigo ran outside, followed by less enthusiastic thugs. The grunter, Camel, sported a bloody and freshly flattened nose from my door slam. Indigo angrily pushed her way through Wahl's zombies. She saw the ammo-drum take flight. She grasped my escape idea and opened fire. Red puffs escaped the bottom of the ammo-drum. More shots hit its guidance system. It listed in the air and dove beyond the levicrete walls to impact in another questionable part of town.

"Don't kiss my ass, but kiss your own goodbye, Joshie Ice." Indigo said.

"Is he dead?" Wahl's voice asked over the loudspeaker.

"More than your test cows, bitch." Indigo muttered as she pushed through the mass of zombies.

They remove the shoes of the dead. It's an odd tradition bothered me. Everyone is incinerated now. What the hell happens to all those shoes? I thought of taking my boots off, but I took a risk I could be silent and stealthy back on the catwalk. I would need to apologize to Alxa's family, if he had one. But they would never see how Indigo's shots ravaged his body inside the ammo-drum. Then I realized it had crashed when I fled around the warehouse behind the zombies.

Geez.

Maybe destroying what caused his murder would be posthumous tribute. I looked down at the teeming vat of symbions. I had a new shotgun. Better yet, I had an ammo belt with bombs. The bad news was Indigo still had my old guns and better skill at being quiet.

Damn.

Two gun muzzles. Two faces. One standoff.

"Neat trick, bouncing back from death." Indigo said. Her voice was as calm and steady as her aim.

"I'm getting good at it," I said. "But maybe you don't want to try it. Drop the gun. My gun!"

To my surprise, she said "fine."

The Aquila made a loud metallic clang as it hit the catwalk grating. Indigo raised her hands, and then made fists.

"Icy Spice, you always knew our relationship would get physical."

I lowered my own weapon. "What, no dinner first?"

Indigo was fast. She leapt up and used the railing to launch herself over me and wrap her azure and steel-like arms around my neck from behind. My shotgun clattered against the catwalk. My elbow to her gut had no effect. Her strangle hold did. It was already hard to inhale. She tried to pull me backward and off balance, but I stayed standing. I squeezed my chin as low as possible and worked my fingers around her constricting limbs as I thrashed. She wrapped her legs around my torso for more crushing effect. Speed is power, but so is brute strength. I gripped her dark, blue skin and slowly, painfully, pulled her arms away from crushing my neck and likely severing my head.

Indigo screamed in rage as I drew a precious breath. She had sacrificed leverage for her all-out crush. Shock flashed on her face as her back hit the grating at the end of my flip. I made the mistake of taking the time for another breath. She bolted up. I motioned that it was over and she replied by tearing free a section of rail. She swung the metal bar at my head. I ducked and snatched up my shotgun. She swung again. I fired. The blast ripped her metal shaft from her hands. Indigo charged. I backhanded her. This time she reeled. She slumped against the remaining rail and glared at me as if offended by the type of blow. She slid away from me against the rail to buy time and regain her senses. She almost immediately came to the section where she had torn out the railing. She fell.

I looked down and saw her splash. The symbiote mass parted as if a shark hit their water. Indigo made a kick for the surface. Just as quickly, the symbiotes swarmed her. She vanished under a horrific, pink wave.

On the ground floor, Wahl's rental thugs aimed their small automatics up at me. They had watched the fight on the catwalk.

They saw me beat someone who could crush them, and saw me holding my shotgun. They probably recalled the human carnage still strewn just beyond the wall. The thugs weren't bright, but they weren't zombies. And they were not loyal. They ran. Wahl scrambled from his hiding spot near the empty cage and followed them.

I made way for the stairs. It had been seconds, but long seconds when I reached the vat. I blasted a hole in it to lower the water. A few symbiotes wriggled out on the floor as I reached for the mass swarming Indigo as it was sucked toward the hole. I grabbed her insensate body and pulled it from the vat. I tore away as many as I could from her face and mouth. My defensive electric field kept the pink freaks from attaching to me. They had no smiling faces, only jaws like toothed suction cups. Indigo took an instinctive breath, but her sapphire eyes were opaque. As with Alxa, I carried her from the warehouse. She might yet live. Her physicians likely didn't train do-it-yourself style on nue-vue.

Religion is the sigh of the oppressed creature, the heart of a heartless world, and the soul of soulless conditions. It is the opium of the people.
The full quote from Karl Marx came from his introduction to A Contribution to the Critique of Hegel's Philosophy of Right, 1843. The full work was published posthumously. I'd read it for context, but it's been lost under the crush of time. Carla Xole inspired a revolution, once. In solar energy. I looked up at the permanent black clouds overhead. I guess that's why we forgot her, as well. People might forget me if they didn't need someone to kill other types of oppressing creatures. For that, my colleagues and me are better than any opiate.

I looked at Sgt. John Slate's eyes. They were clear, and a shade of brown lighter than his skin but not as dark as his close-cropped hair. He glared. I was glad some things were constant in life. Police tactical and forensic crews moved in and out of the warehouse. The courtyard area was filling up with black bags that held human and symbiote remains. A medical aid car drifted up on humming sponsons. Its entire fuselage started flashing red before it shot skyward with the last zombies.

"I think we got everyone," Slate said. "A medic said an emetic might free the zombies from the monsters inside them. The brain damage might be repairable. Let's hope."

"Yeah," I nodded. "You are what you think. Or don't think."

"It's screwed. I mean, monsters that bite people I get," Slate cocked his head. "But those pink things creep me out."

"I know the feeling. Did you get Wahl?"

"Yep," Slate said with a slow nod. "He's dead."

"Oh, okay." I looked back at the warehouse.

"Why? You wanted him?" Slate asked.

"No."

"So about that ammo drone." Slate put his fists on his hips and narrowed his gaze at me. "The body inside it? Was that some sort of—what the hell was that?"

I took a breath. "An attempt to survive. I had to act fast."

Slate said nothing. He just stared at me. It was a little creepy.

"I assume you think my survival is a good outcome." I said.

Slate only stared. I cocked my left eyebrow and returned the favor.

"Well, I'll say this," Slate finally spoke. "I've gotten used to your glaring, rockslide of a face."

"Yeah." I nodded and took a slower, deeper breath. "Some do. It's a bad side effect."

17
TRACES

Ornate. It's not a word I think of often, in this era. Decay, yes. But the interior I walked defied the world outside and was bright and pristine. Little expense, if any, was spared to recreate an ancient Greek temple, or at least the modern impression of such a vanished structure. The function of this place was not to worship or remember mythology. It was to exalt the ones who paid for it. Nothing was synthetic. The materials were all mined, milled, and sculpted from recovered stones and structures, or swiped from original locations. The marble and granite walls gleamed as if never touched by time. Columns of Pentelic marble stood ten-point-four meters high and supported curved arches of a vaulted ceiling. The ceiling was not Greek in style. And they were not the only modern elements. Farther inside, recent artworks replaced old statuary of figures forgotten to history, but complimentary to the architectural theme.

The first contemporary art piece rose like an ever-ascending spiral of wrong-way snowflakes, although today few recognized the similarity to precipitation. Mathematicians called such never-ending shapes *monsters*. Yet my firearms offered no solutions for math species. The fractals swirled upward in an infinite spiral. The illusion was not a hologram but a series of magnetic fields manipulating fine dust. I didn't see a broom if the power failed.

Across from the spiral was something I found more interesting. The piece was sculpted from biochemical information given macroscopic form called exonite. Or, a vast glop of genes with a twist. This ascending work held arcs of data detailing compounds that formed nucleic acids that lead to proteins, genes, and people, or other, now rarer, life. Scans deciphered the sequences of evolution's narrative. Each sequence occupied niches in the swirling, globular column that spun slowly around a hollow axis. Viewed from above, it might resemble a slanted cyclone.

But weather was not the theme of these and other displays. Next was a mathematical description of perpetual acceleration within quantum dimensions. I didn't link to the explication node. I didn't want a headache that might last forever, and eternity was the theme. Ascending and never ending. It was how the people who made the art saw themselves. I supposed it was a legitimate claim. They were, after all, immortals.

Perhaps the strangest thing among the works was me. Although tall, I doubt these artists would consider me a pinnacle of evolution. Plus, my job to kill monsters requires me to push into the low, dark layers of the megalopolis rather than rise above them. Odd for me was that I was alone. I had special entry permission, but no beasts stalked the marbled chamber. My ultimate destination was beyond this intended temple of earth-level delights. A person could debate the artistic merits and intellectual heights of the immortals' artwork, but the purpose of the place they sat was obvious once you reached the far end. There, familiar metal doors slid open on opposing sides. This place was not a temple or an art gallery. It was only an elevator lobby.

I would not need to be immortal to endure the long ride ahead, but it would take time even at high speeds. I would technically leave Earth. My destination wasn't held aloft by marble columns, or a super-tower foundation set deep into the planet's crust. Precise calculations of orbital dynamics and rotation rate linked the platform to Earth. It was like a ship at constant anchor on a sea of black clouds. I suppose with a push it could completely leave orbit and travel into space. But the old adventure of space travel was now a clichéd fantasy. Pedestrian. Thus, the elevator. Konstantin Tsiolkovsky, you're long dead but still remembered.

The elevator's interior design was a clashing, frantic, Rocco style. I shrugged and entered. Alone in the lift, I soon escaped gravity for its artificial replacement. If you could afford it, today you can escape death. At least by natural causes. But a monster's diet can include all walks of life, no matter the surface they tread. Nestled over the toxic clouds, the registered immortals stay oblivious to the envious stares from far below, but are not immune to the same threats of lower life. I wondered how many of them knew I was coming. I was sure I wouldn't get a parade. Maybe a laurel wreath. Or not.

My new employer was Dr. Blackwell, Administrator. He managed a place that had no official name or corporate brand. The owners and tenants didn't want anyone to be able to search for them. Most of its occupants held big chunks of Earth's known corporations. Blackwell would serve as my liaison to the high world of unequal distribution of wealth and the egotistic application of science. I was also egotistical in taking his overly generous payout. I had another elevator ride to payoff. Creditors are another hungry beast, and I can't simply kill them.

Damn.

I had time to think on a lot of things before the ride was over and the door ran through its long sequence of locks before sliding open. One thought was the unlikelihood of a creature from Earth's toxic shadows making its way high above ground. The scent of meat, humanity, was prevalent in the streets. It wafted less in the towers because of air-cleaners. Up here, humanity probably didn't smell like food at all. Sodium hypochlorite, maybe. Yet, there was a reason for my generous pay and a free ride to the burned Earth's version of heaven. Monsters were adaptation run wild. Perhaps one caught a ride on this or another elevator. It might survive the trip outside. Or, a larva or beast with room to grow hitched a ride in a bloodstream, intestine, or liver. As always, monsters were everywhere.

The doors seemed to hesitate, but finally opened. I expected opulence in overdrive. More art. More amplified grandeur. However, a cool breeze hit me and so did shock. I was glad I wore protective boots. I stepped into a swamp. A swamp? It wasn't a hologram. It was cool, foggy, and wet. There was a fetid scent from bacteria thriving in muck. Murky water rolled against the damp shore out from the elevator doors. Deciduous trees populated the damp ground. Trees. Living plant life.

Trees!

Leaves—alder leaves my historic reference told me—littered the ground like lost notes from time. I heard a ripple of water. A fish—a catfish—a living fish—one of many different types of fish! They swam in the waters that grew deeper away from the elevator. And there was music. No! Birdsong! I liked history. I had absorbed a lot about humanity and past ages of life. But without a system analyzing stimulus and dumping answers into my brain, I would have been confused and overwhelmed by a swampy environment. In the past, such a place was real estate to drain and pave. Now it was a recreated wonder.

A swamp. A forest!

Shock was about to force out expletives or just shouts when Dr. Blackwell appeared.

"Although it may seem a strange place, the monster is not here." Blackwell said with no preceding hello.

I gathered my thoughts quickly and replied. "I've seen a lot bizarre life and weird places. But I admit, this is quite a shock."

"The life here was, once, quite mundane," Blackwell said looking across the wet ecology. "That's why it's here, now. It's rare. The ecology, unique."

"And costs the Earth," I added.

Blackwell smiled. His head always appeared slightly bowed. His speech was polite in phrase and tone, but analytically cool. He could be a living, if psychologically distant, human. However, his real presence was also distant. Dr. Blackwell was somewhere safe and dry. The mud never stained his clothes. Although he was standard height, his head's altitude never changed even as the he moved across uneven ground. His suit was unique. I wondered if it was a company uniform or an eclectic fusion just as the Rocco elevator and Classical lobby. A narrow, square-knot tie lay across a pressed white shirt tucked beneath a business suit jacket that flowed into a long lab coat and completely hid his legs. It was all luminous white as if woven from natural silk. Even his projected complexion and close-cut hair looked bleached. There was no danger of mud soiling a hologram.

Like the wet forest, Blackwell would also prove to be a surprise. His truth was not hard to reveal, even as a projection. My active systems could not probe him, but I still had passive analysis. Dr. Blackwell was an SI, a Specific Intelligence. But the sophisticated programs were not supposed to be truly intelligent and independent, only focused to singular function. The shocking part was this SI used a human avatar. Humanity banned that, too, after an interesting era of cybernetics rights and revolts. Banned it on Earth, that is. Blackwell was more evidence that I was not in mythic Kansas or a place as familiar as Oz. This immortal community was high above the arcs of forgotten rainbows. He smiled again, as predicted by my detection algorithms and because he understood I had deduced his coded origin.

"Thank you for arriving promptly, Mr. Grail." Blackwell said. "Of course, as you have no doubt deduced, I am Dr. Blackwell, this community's physician."

"Physician?" I asked.

"Yes. Why the surprise?"

"I didn't think a doctor was necessary, here." I answered. "I guess your patients prefer hands off approach to health care, as you really don't have hands."

"No. True. As an SI, I can only manipulate tools. I have no means for direct touching. And not the coding to analyze such contact, either."

"You have a lot more going than most SI's I've met." I narrowed my stare at him. It was an expression his own analysis might have predicted. "Did your programming miss the intelligence audits all those years ago?"

"I assure you my function is normal, for this community." Blackwell bowed lower. "There is no need for concern. Obviously, I did not need to meet you directly. I could have just transmitted my instructions. Yet, my information on you suggested direct interaction would produce an outcome closer to plan. You enjoy being treated as an equal. This is how I would greet a new client, a new citizen. And so I say again: welcome Mr. Grail. I am glad you are here."

"And thanks for the generous fee," I said. "And if the monster is not here, where do I go? Swimming?"

"I wish I had a specific area in which to direct you." Blackwell took an unpredicted pause, and then shrugged. "However, the recent deaths have no specific locus. Residents have been dying from various, persistent and accelerating cancers and maladies. That shouldn't happen."

"Especially in this community." I said.

"Quite true. Some undetectable source is causing this."

Now I paused and thought before I spoke. "Some monsters have remarkable optical camouflage, and some can generate pulsed electrical fields like an old sea species called a torpedo ray. The monsters used their e-fields to thwart some scanning frequencies. But there is typically some biological trace. More to the point, most monsters don't merely sicken the victim. They eat the whole body, quickly. If it's microscopic, a new bacteria, virus, or biogenetic vector, I'm sure you already have the means to find and eliminate such a threat."

"Yes." Blackwell's avatar nodded. "You can imagine I am aware of virtually everything that occurs here."

"No privacy?" I asked, being curious about all aspects of life here.

"For an additional fee. Yet, as you said, there should be traces detectable beyond the privacy screens. The traces and their pattern should reveal the source. However, I cannot detect one. It is possible the source is a monster I am unfamiliar with, but that you have experienced. Perhaps you can find the cause of these deaths. And then kill it."

"I almost hear concern, *doctor*." I said. Even his hologram was becoming more animate as the conversation progressed. "Does your existence ride on this?"

Blackwell's avatar knitted its brow in another unpredicted act. "Not quite. Unlike some employees, my own immortality is not part of my benefits package. However, I can be dismissed. Nevertheless, none of that is important. My aim—my need—is to stop the deaths. I must stop the deaths. You understand that. Correct?"

Blackwell looked at me entreatingly. Even if that was a calculated response, it did strike at my emotions, for a second.

"I can understand hiring me was a desperate act." I said. "It always is. But for you, that's especially true."

Blackwell took another, longer pause. He almost seemed distracted before answering. "It is part of the plan to halt future deaths of my charges."

The distraction was sauntering through the alders towards us.

"Well, that's why I'm paid so well." I said. "People like to live, even if they never anticipate death."

"And you like to kill?" the question was from more strangeness. The voice was feminine and adolescent, as was the body. The saunter and attitude was from an experienced and all too worldly woman. Plus, this person was flesh and blood. She wore a one-piece, designer excursion suit with the lower half of the legs cut away so she could feel the wet earth on her naked feet. She walked through Blackwell's projection and straight at me making eye contact with no fear.

"Shouldn't you be in school?" I asked.

"Nope," the female stranger said as she looked me over as if I was displayed for sale.

"This is Miss Valence," Blackwell said with a perfect reproduction of nervousness. "Miss Valence is one of our original residents."

Valence locked eyes on mine and didn't blink. Usually people look away if I stare at them, and even some monsters. This woman enjoyed the power play between us. Blackwell could have appeared as a raging ogre and Valence would not care.

"Yep. I'm an oldie. But goodie." Valence finally smiled, like a shark. "So what you're thinking isn't statutory."

"Obviously you're not a mind reader," I said.

"Oh, I like massive and mysterious," Valence said and hooked her right index finger inside the parting of my overcoat. "But let's see what you've got under—"

I let Valence open my coat to see her reaction. Her eyes became wide as she saw weapons hung as a mobile armory. I closed my coat as her fingers reached to touch a long barrel.

"My-my!" Valence laughed.

"The usual reaction," I said.

"Well, Miss Valence," Blackwell bowed. "I'm sure Mr. Grail would like to get started."

"Mm-hmm. So would I." Valence said. She sauntered away over the water as a suspension field kept her on the surface. At least that seemed the best reason why she didn't sink. "Look me up, *Ice*. I'd like to lick some of that frost off you."

Oddly enough, I would never find out how she knew my nickname.

"Is she part of your plan?" I asked Blackwell.

"My plan ultimately is to give you access to this facility, this small world Soon after, I hope you stop the killings."

"You mean, kill the monster."

"Yes." Blackwell bowed.

"Okay, then. You have the golden key?"

Blackwell's key was not gold. It was code I stored in my weapons' OS and transmitted at any lock. There were many and various locks, here. I had to get used to pausing to use the key code. The first use was to leave the swampy forest and enter the synthetic granite halls that curved and arced for no reason I could see other than hiding who may be just ahead or behind you. These immortals obviously liked their own company more than each other. I wondered if the reason was ego, the management mitigating competition, or some other reason such as creating the false sense you owned the place solo and didn't just pay high, very high, rent.

If there were people to save, I needed to act. I felt I had time to make up after my amazement of the wetland ebbed. I knew I may be more a rat in a maze than exterminator with the keys to the castle. Blackwell was no mere SI. His intelligence was artificial, but real and potentially vast. Humans had never grown accustomed to that uneasy feeling that a smart machine had already made a million more moves than you could comprehend and long before you knew the game had started. That was one reason why AI was cut down to SI. The intelligence was supposed to be focused and conceive fewer dimensions than the human mind. Right.

Blackwell had more dimensions that many people. His—its— okay his employers had the power to allow a true synthetic mind to act as an over-capable concierge and escape the off-switch law mandated generations before. Perhaps that meant Blackwell was the true power up here. Blackwell might be older than the biotech of human immortality. Although his sense of duty was evident, I wondered if empathy could be programmed or self-generate within code. It seemed a lofty idea as I slid through a hatch hidden in a granite hallway and into the dank service ducts.

Inside, three silver spheres hung in the air near the stairway landing. They did nothing but float. I waved and moved on. So far, the environments I had encountered up here changed form a wet, natural surface with the wafting scent of mud to pristine and ornate halls with the odd absence of any smell at all. Then I entered a hidden world of steel and gray with the aroma of warm plastic. This was more like street level, but I could breathe without that buried thought that my lungs might need medical help if I took a deep breath. A bonus.

I still could not find a trace of anything out of the ordinary. Blackwell had reduced cleaning efficiency to eighty-percent to allow detection of some errant molecule. He found nothing. I had no luck here. No luck finding biological traces. As I moved down and deeper into the access ways only used by maintenance bots and cleaning drones, I began to register odd magnetic waves. I thought of my torpedo ray analogy, and followed the anomaly to its source.

I came to another hatch. This one was obvious, thick and plastered with brilliant red and yellow warning labels. A good thing, that. If you could unlock and open the hatch, the violent outflow of air would blow you out and into vacuum. At least outside was supposed to be vacuum. Blackness. Cold. Death. The hatch had a small porthole with a newer rim and gasket than the seals and paint on the hatch. There was light from outside. I peered through it and raised my eyebrows. Beyond the hatch looked more like a section of the black sky captured from below and reformed into a dome, or a partial bubble hanging from the side of the immortals world.

Okay. Weird.

It went from odd to terrifying when the hatch wheel spun and its seals popped open. I hadn't hit my key. I turned to run and grab something. There was only a brief hiss. The outside bubble held the same relative pressure as the access way—atmosphere. I stuck my shotgun through the gap between the bulkhead and hatch. FRACDAR detected structures like a landing, steps and railing below the hatch. The light radiated from the surface, likely from a coating of photophores. Interesting. Yep. I went outside.

The structure bonded to the hull was a ladder-like catwalk with rungs for both the walking surface and rails. It curved along the exterior. I stepped slowly with my left side against the hull as if on a fire escape attached to a building side. I soon realized the two sets of rungs weren't a cheap way of using one for railing. Out here, you could choose your orientation by either keeping sideways to the hull or looking at the cloud dome as if it was the sky. My mental orientation was still relative to the horizontal plane on Earth, just as the interior. As I walked, the dome's apex appeared to be sideways on my right. Using this grav-field and catwalk, you could also walk along the other set of rungs and look *up* at the dome, and then the hull would appear as the floor or ground and not a wall.

As long as I could still shoot straight, I would be fine. I found where I might have to reconsider my angle of fire. A large, glassy oval sat recessed into the outer surface. It was likely an observation portal. Farther along the exterior's curve, I found the attraction. I came to another forest. This one was artificial and rose off the steel expanse of hull. My walkway branched into two tiers and continued into this tree-like complex of spires, giant needles, cables and beams. The place crackled with unseen energy. Weird vibrations rippled through my guts and caused interference across my scans. No creature of pure energy or symbolic code would like to loiter around this metallic and electromagnetically charged landscape. Maybe Blackwell didn't mention it because he feared it, or its owner paid for the privacy fee. Creatures of enhanced biology could walk among it. I qualified, but I would not stay long without good reason.

I reoriented my mind to consider the hull as a horizontal plane. I grabbed the rungs and planted my boots on the hull to help and get a clear view across the structure. I wondered if these machines functioned beyond generating the cloud dome's field and trapping air. It might just be a wealthy immortals toy, or idea of a gazebo. Just a place to step outside and enjoy the—well, not the view. Maybe the engineer just liked the fact he or she could build such a gazebo. I stopped considering immortal philosophy. I still didn't want a headache.

Near the center rested a metallic, concave disk rounded like a human erythrocyte but festooned with an array of small cylinders. It was a Hume Mark 70 Field Induction Reactor. I knew this because I was close enough to catch its identity transmission, or advertisement, that it broadcast. The reactor amplified the ad transmission enough to pierce the interference its power helped generate. If an engineer wondered why power dropped, slightly, it might be the reactor trying to sell another reactor. And around the circuit we go.

Heat and energy bled from several pylons. I guessed they were capacitors. Someone had turned the switch on but hadn't come back to check the power build up. I could not detect a native SI or unified operating system. It just went on generating the dome and building energy. The owner needed to come back and manually maintain it. Some of the capacitors were reaching their limit. Still, I hoped no one would throw the off switch while I was outside.

There was a flash. My OS told me it found a biological trace. It was moving. I finally had a target. I could not fully scan it.

Magnetic and other force fields scrambled the beams. I could read its mass. Similar to mine. Speed, likewise. It traveled along a catwalk tier raised over me. To intercept it, I jumped. I grabbed the bottom of the catwalk over me and then hauled myself up. I leveled my weapon at the target. His face looked back at me at first with shock and then extreme annoyance. My target was not a beast, but a man. The dome's atmosphere allowed sound.

"What—? Where did you come from?" He demanded.

He was large. Young, in appearance. He was physically fit and happy to show that in tight fitting clothes. He would have looked at home among the statuary in the lobby far below. His skin was almost as translucent as alabaster. His black hair was tightly braided just as the men represented in Greek kouros.

"You will address me," he continued. "No matter your armament. You are a trespasser. This is *my* place."

"Well, I like what you done with the, ah, vacuum."

"Mere manipulation of force lines. Simple equations. But your presence here is quiet a variable."

"I bet. I'm Joshua Grail. Blackwell hired me. You may be in danger. I'm stalking a monster."

I lowered my gun as the living statue burst into laughter. If the idea of a monster here seemed ludicrous, then Blackwell hadn't informed his clients about the odd nature of the recent deaths. Maybe he had kept them a secret, or these people were all just wacked.

"No. Really." I said, mainly to myself.

"Well, I am Zeus." The statue said, again calm but smiling. "Welcome to paradise. *Grail!*"

"Thanks. I guess there's a quick shuttle here from Olympus." I said and endured another chorus of laughter. It sounded odd with no echo and somehow flat. Although I had no idea what voices and laughter should sound like in the captured air of a force field.

"A heavily armed biological aberration expert." Zeus said after a deep breath. "A Monster Killer. How interesting. Will you be with us long?"

"Doubtful. But you never can tell."

"It is nice up here. I know. I assume you are in no rush to return to the surface."

"I go where the need takes me."

"Dangerous need, at that. You must hope some of our immortality sticks with you."

"Good point. I'll check my boots before I leave."

Zeus' response was just a single *ha!* "I must admit I never thought I would meet one of you. Certainly not here! It's nearly fascinating."

"Glad to be so entertaining. But I have a job to do."

"Wow," Zeus said and looked my over. "You are quite single minded."

It was less his words and more his patronizing attitude that annoyed me. His expression was that of a parent stumbling upon children playing and half-heartedly acting a part before escaping back to the real world. Today, such a scene was a rare event. To me, this place was the fantasyland. Earth's streets were brutal reality. This guy saw it all as a game. Part of me hoped when I found the monster it would be clamped to his ass. He finished his physical assessment of me. I had also looked him over. He looked as if he might give me a fair fight, if he knew anything about fighting. Maybe he wrote the book a century ago and kept adding new pages. Maybe. Maybe not. Still, it wouldn't do me much good to make an enemy of him or his eternal friends. They were like a true pantheon and had the power to really mess with any mortals they came to notice. Wealth was power, and these immortals were its personifications. When I thought of power, the capacitors came back to mind.

"One thing," I said. "If this is your equipment, then you need to make a few adjustments."

Zeus smiled as though my offer of advice was another cause for hilarity. I ignored his conceit. I was also a scientist, even if my overt discipline required as much violence as lab work. I decided to save his gazebo and maybe several lives if this thing overloaded and burned or blew a hole through the hull.

"The capacitors are near their maximum." I finished.

"And?"

Now it was my turn for odd looks. "Well, to start, you obviously want to keep your ass inside the force fields. Naked space is a bitch on the skin."

"Oh! Quite right." Zeus closed his eyes and nodded. Even perfectly fit, condescension didn't look good on him. "Nice of you to express concern. But I think our conversation is over now."

I nodded with strong affirmation. I was actually glad. To leave.

I reentered the service accessway. The hatch sealed automatically. I suspected Blackwell had opened it. But it might've been a reentry protocol that activated when Zeus went outside. Blackwell's bust popped on over my wrist-com. I move my forearm to horizontal to speak with him.

"Nice clients you have," I said.

"Yes. I monitored your interaction with Mr. Zeus as well as I could through the interference. Please know he is a relative youngster among immortals and new to the community."

"And a real sweetheart."

"A powerful sweetheart, Mr. Grail. His hobby is magnetic field research."

"Then he sucks at his hobby. What's his day job?"

"Finances. Hereditary assets and quantitative accounts management."

"I'm shocked."

"Then brace for an additional surprise. Miss—that's odd."

"What?" I barked. I wanted to know the additional shock, but more so, what had just surprised a virtually omnipresent mind.

"Just a moment. Just a moment." Blackwell's voice said as his holographic avatar froze in its last expression. "I just registered a focused beam of over sixteen hundred kilohertz passing through you."

"Really? What source?"

"Unable to locate. Your own enhanced biology and the energy fields are—"

"Okay. What was the first shock?"

"Miss Valence asked that you visit her residence." Blackwell said. "I would appreciate your attendance."

"I still haven't found any—"

"The region she lives employs privacy screens. Your presence will permit a clear assessment of the community. And any threats, therein."

"Fine." I sighed. "But I'm not wearing a tie."

Slightly later I entered a scene lifted off an ancient postcard of a Hawaiian beach. The sunset—the sun—looked odd. A fiery red blob sank below scarlet clouds over a dark blue ocean reflecting it all. I knew that most dead generations would think a solid black sky over a polluted worldwide city would be a hellish future. Not including the savage monsters. Yet that was what I saw every day. A sunset, even fake, was surreal. The ocean and beach were holographic. The sand was real, or at least some finely ground material and not another fake sensation made by tactile-input pixels. I was unsure what input my companion wanted. Valence was small but certainly dangerous in many ways. She sat on a lounge chair holding a drink with paper umbrella and flowers. She wore a swimsuit with moving, pink flames and enormous sunglasses. Around her stood three male hologram figures dressed only in tight, black swim trunks. I hated them. Each one was a pixel recreation of me.

"Hiya!" Valence waved and spilled her drink. "Leave your guns on the wall and join the fun."

I looked over at my doppelgangers. Seeing at your own reflection or image in a medical scan is one thing. Looking at another person's recreated ideal of your own body is stranger than walking and breathing in space. Or a sunset.

"It's so beautiful! So perfect." Valence threw her waving arm over her head in mock dramatics. "You can't tell it's a century old fake."

"Other than life not being perfect." I droned.

Valence leaned out of her lounge chair towards me and now carefully held her drink. "That's an outdated idea. Look at me! I'm perfect and probably older than you."

"Don't bet on that." I said.

"Your age or my perfection?" Valence asked. She then took a long pull from her cocktail and slowly drew up one of her far too youthful legs.

I looked out at the fake sunset.

"Y'know, most duffers find me a turn on." Valence said and pulled down her sunglasses to reveal a surprisingly cutting stare. "You seem to think it's immoral or something."

"Among other things."

Valence dangled half out of the lounge chair. She managed not to spill her drink and jabbed a pointed finger at me. "Well, someone said that *immorality* was the *morality* of those having a better time. So lighten up!"

"It was H.L. Mencken," I told her. "He also said immortality is the condition of a dead man who doesn't believe he's dead."

"Huh," Valence attempted to right herself in her chair. Her drink finally spilled out with its flowers and all. "Well, I feel that if I allow myself to age anymore it'll never stop. Then I will grow old and die."

Valence left her chair and knelt on the sand. She lifted a dripping, tattered flower from the drink's puddle and examined it. "What's it like, to age? To feel pain?"

I took a deep breath. "Pain? That you live with it, or it consumes you."

Valence dropped the flower. "So you just, just go on?"

"Yes. You go on."

Valence stood and locked her stare on my eyes. Her body was only on the verge of full adulthood, but her stare held the sharp edge of a millennia of questions hidden behind spite.

"So that's how you cope with your life, your job, your pain?" Her stare narrowed. "Sounds jejune. Juvenile."

"I'm still here." I said. "And it helps to have a profession."

Valence threw her arms from her sides. Her brevity returned like a switch flipped back to *on*. "Holy, paradoxes!" She shouted and then laughed. "Death as a way of life!"

I stepped closer to one of my holographic doubles. They kept their fake eyes focused on the sudden swirll of pink as Valence spun.

"I know more than that keeps you going, big, mister morbid?" Valence giggled. "Let me guess. It's some quest. I know! Redemption!"

I pressed my head into the closest double. It wasn't solid. I imagined my real face and the projection made an odd image of my features bent at right angles.

"Actually, it's those *I Love Lucy* reruns." I said.

Valence stopped her twirls. She steadied herself and whisked off her sunglasses. It revealed her genuine, perplexed expression.

"I have a thing for Ethel."

I left Valence to ponder the predilections of mortals and/or their lies. I still had a job to do. My reconnaissance was in the region where all deaths had occurred. Yet, I had only found strange people and their hobbies, not a lethal monster. On coming here, I had made certain assumptions. One, I would draw out the monster and kill it. Two, the monster was something I understood. If it wasn't large like an animal, I would still find traces of the microbe and then kill it. Three, Blackwell also thought I would find and kill it. But a forth concept was that Blackwell knew what this thing was and was barred from telling me directly because of his program. Maybe it was an immortal's biological hobby that was flushed but resurfaced.

I'd bet my massive fee that history repeats itself among immortals more than on the street. I wanted more information. I was more discreet than a crew of armed and dangerous subcontractors ripping up marble and granite to find some small clue. That was an option, though. So I was sure Blackwell would cooperate and tell me more.

I sat on a stair flight inside the hidden accessway. The place would serve as my office. I detached and hooked my wrist-com to a rail. I needed to talk with Blackwell but didn't want him rattling around in my brain. Voice communication and holograms would serve well enough. His bust popped on, askew. The projectors compensated and then horizontally projected his questioning gaze.

"The victims." I said. "I'd like—"

"Uno Phillip, Kay Zwie, San Thicke." Blackwell stated.

"Fine. Now, what were their day jobs?"

"Their financial interests were diverse and multi-layered," Blackwell said. "The main business for each was, Phillip: elevator velocity regulators. Kay: ultra conductor transit relays. Thicke: power transmission."

"So they're linked by infrastructure." I began to see a pattern.

"Yes." Blackwell paused. "More so is that each person was a financial entity, or a single body holding majority shares in each corporation. However, if they ended, the vast number of shares was released to open trading."

"By ended you mean actually die." I said. I saw what Blackwell was guiding me towards and why he paused. He did so to make sure I was listening. I was.

"Their deaths meant and end to singular control of the businesses," I said. "The pie got broken up."

"Yes. As mandated by the law. The laws that even the immortals must obey."

"Financial laws. There must be order, somewhere. So with these huge blocks of stocks suddenly on the market, control of each business went from each of the dead immortals to anyone, or any group, with enough graft to buy up the freed shares. How much graft?"

"Over time, the increase in corporate value meant an increase in the number of shares, and because they were so long lived—"

"The result would be a billion little pies, not just one big bite for even other immortals. I'd bet even the corporate structure and culture will change."

"Likely true. But what is certain is that each death meant a wealth transfer of hundreds of billions in just the companies I mentioned. The victims' entire portfolios were vast and diverse."

"So, billions of smaller investors benefitted." I said and saw far more to this than a threat to individuals on this world. I now doubted a monster was even here.

"They may indeed. But the market SI's are regulating the sales of shares to a steady, predictable exchange."

"Well, then maybe I should leave here and hire a broker with this inside knowledge."

"You were made a fiduciary bond when you entered the elevator. So that would be illegal. Here, and everywhere."

"Of course. I wouldn't want to have an unfair advantage over the market."

"Quite. So, as to your—"

"Blackwell, you know these deaths were assassinations."

There was a pause. This time I was sure he was considering his response. "Yes."

"There is no monster. Call whoever can arrest your clients. You don't need me."

"Consider, please, that you are wrong."

"I'm not."

"Regarding the presence of any biological aberrations, you are correct. As to my need for you, your deduction is faulty. Consider: I am barred from taking direct action. I cannot even call the police or other legally associated regulatory services, as we are a self-governing entity. Nevertheless, I am also charged with the well-being of the immortals. Thus, I must find a way to both adhere to my coded edicts and protect the immortals."

"And I'm your compromise."

"Yes. Most of your epi-legal power is intact, here. It was deemed necessary in the near-impossible event a monster made its way to this enclave. I have calculated your seeming random appearance will, in the very least, create variables the perpetrator, the assassin, will not foresee."

"Who is it?"

Silence.

"Okay. What does your analysis predict the perpetrator will do?"

"I hope you understand if I do not reveal possible outcomes. It would influence your actions. I need you to be more of an influence. That influence will cause the assassin to be revealed. Thus, please do your job as if a monster is present."

"Somewhere there is a real monster, and it's stalking someone who isn't immortal or rich. I need to—"

"Mr. Grail, you can deduce that this situation will cause harm to your world, not only the lives here. I am certain your ethics will compel you to cooperate."

I was silent.

"Scary thing. You, a thinking machine, are solving this by creating a lie."

"A calculated necessity, Mr. Grail."

I put my calculated necessity in a sling and went back into the main halls. Soon after, Zeus sent me an invitation to his place. I hoped he would not wear a pink bikini. Sunglasses, fine.

Zeus' met me in the observation deck that I saw when outside. It was an extension of his living quarters. The door to them stayed closed. The observation window deployed along a reticulated bay to offer a view of the force-field *gazebo*. Zeus wore a formal suit. It clashed with my rough-worn overcoat. The straight lines of my weapons it covered clashed with the furniture and moving art. They were one in the same. Groups of brightly colored folding lines and curving arcs appeared to wrestle in the spots where they sat around a plain, obvious bar. If you wanted to sit with your drink, you just aimed your butt at one of the moving artworks and it became a stool or chair. Zeus obviously wanted me to ask where to sit, but I had seen the ads. I set my glass on one group of writhing lines. It slowed into a helical pedestal. I stayed standing.

"Control. Do you like it?" Zeus asked and rolled real ice from clean water in his otherwise dry tumbler.

"Is that the latest band with a hit?"

Zeus reacted with a slow, stifled giggle. He seemed equally amused by what I said and that I was trying to have a conversation with him.

"The thing, itself." Zeus said. "Control."

"I'm not sure it exists. Like old gods. It could be a myth."

"Brilliant." Zeus smiled and nodded. "But consider how humanity has brought control to our planet, our ecology, and what that has cost us all. The Earth itself is a massive engine with a radioactive power core. With our geotechnical mitigation, the motion of continents is now a source of power that drives our industry. Our technology gives us greater power than if you could combine all the ancient gods into one, literal being."

"Funny a guy named Zeus thinks that." I observed.

"My name doesn't mitigate the truth. Even I can recognize greater strength, and I command great power through my fortune. Still, some chaos is good. It makes us stronger."

"Then come down to the street level with me. In a lot of places down there, chaos is the law."

"And yet to thrive, there." Zeus leaned back and again looked me over.

I wasn't sure that was a cultural norm up here, or just his quirk. I had less obvious ways to assess a person.

"I survive." I said.

"What kind of existence is that, then?"

"One that helps others survive." I said.

"Admirable. We are not unalike, in some ways, Mr. Grail. Once, I was like you. Mortal. Able to die." Zeus looked at his glass and his gaze drifted beyond it to nowhere as he became mired in thought.

"Being immortal makes you think differently?"

"A little. I mean, I won't die. I am—yes, I am godly." Zeus looked past his glass again.

"You won't age. But you can be killed. That's why I'm here."

"True. But it would take a lot to kill me." Zeus focused back on me and smiled. "Even most bodily harm isn't much of a threat. I could even survive if you shot me."

"Maybe."

"You almost sound like you want to test that." Zeus smiled wide and pitched his perfectly trimmed eyebrows high up.

"Do you?" I said, dryly.

"Well, no!" Zeus pitched back in laughter. The ice in his tumbler slid on its tilted bottom and clinked together against the side. "So don't open fire."

"I don't intend to. Not today."

Zeus laughed louder.

"Control!" He said suddenly. "There is a lot we can control, but physics still obeys its own laws. When it behaves against our wishes, at times all we can do is mitigate the damage, or watch the release of power. You're familiar with the matrix that impregnates the Earth's atmosphere?"

"It's called smog." I said.

"A lot of it is trapped pollutants, yes. But it's also material used to shield the surface from intense solar radiation."

"And justification for never having fresh air. And good for respirator sales." I inhaled the air around me. It smelled odd. Clean.

"Nevertheless, the atmosphere is a well-regulated system." Zeus assured me. "So there is that for your obvious Keynesian inclinations. But the regulation means there is little in the way of ancient dynamic. Earth's weather is restrained. Here, I have given one aspect of it free reign. Observe!"

Outside the machinery buzzed. Then lightning suddenly burst from conduction columns and violently arced between the steel structures. It occurred again. And again. I blinked.

Zeus turned to me. His smile and raised left eyebrow solicited a response.

"I see you found the on switch."

"Quite." Zeus swirled the ice in his glass "But surely that was impressive."

"Very. Anything alive would be blasted into ash and smog. That's a lot of power to control."

"Well, I am Zeus." He took a sip of the melt water.

"I guess that answers the question: what's in a name?"

Zeus smiled. "That sense of humor. It's why I like you."

"Glad to hear it." I said. My voice was as flat as when inside the force field.

"Another display?"

"Thanks, but someone somewhere is in danger, and if I can't save them, I still might stop what ate them." It was my turn to playact.

"A sense of duty. Most admirable for someone from the surface."

"Yep." My face rippled almost into a smile. It was a muscular tic from the strong e-field.

Our quality time had nothing to do with lightning. It was a tactical raid. Zeus scanned me to find any biogenetic weakness. I could only detect faint reflections through my own screens. He hid his probes in the background noise of all the electromagnetic interference and other signals crisscrossing the immortal's lair.

I left Zeus and resumed my prowling. I told myself it was possible I might find clues to the murders. It helped ease my sense of wasting time. I was learning there was a science to the act of indolence. I smelled smoke. Not smog. Not incinerator drift. I was sensing actual smoke from heat converting dense cellulose into carbon monoxide and water. Someone was burning wood. It was a few steps around a bend when I came to a hidden door left open to allow the smoke to escape. At least that made sense. But maybe not the people inside.

At the center of the oval chamber was a clear firebox set on a meter-tall column. A stack of cut wood sat next to it on the marbled floor. Scans said the wood was cedar, a species of extinct evergreen tree. I was glad the extinct part was incorrect. Visible through the pall were several shocked immortals dispersed around the flaming, crackling, and billowing centerpiece. The fire was normal to them. I was the shock. I understood their reaction. Mine was similar.

Both the male and female immortals wore men's' dinner suits styled with near accuracy to formal dinner attire of the nineteenth-century European aristocracy. Except for one woman who dressed as a nineteenth-century Egyptian Pashah. Nice to see they tolerated nonconformists. Nevertheless, their stares revealed they did not want to tolerate me. They had no idea of who or what I was. They also had no idea how to get me to leave. They couldn't think to speak, nor raise a finger to flip me off. They just stared. And breathed smoke. A few coughed. The cedar crackled. I shrugged, and spoke.

"So, I'll overlook that I wasn't invited. But, does anybody know where the john is?"

More cedar popped in the flames.

One woman opened her mouth to speak. The inrush of smoke was as far as she got. She coughed loudly. The others slowly turned as a seated herd to stare at her. I tossed a few pieces of cedar on the fire and moved back from the upward gust of embers.

"Okay, I'll use the hall." I said.

The costumed herd looked back at me as I left.

I needed a better way to probe this place or do something useful to stop the killings. I would need Blackwell's help and maybe a violation of his privacy protocols. Whatever was causing the deaths here was no mere merging of muscle and hunger. The motivation was the key. This was the tip of something—Blackwell contacted me.

I located the chamber Blackwell asked me to find. It was cold and grey with no décor and furnished with a single, floating table. Something on the table was familiar underneath the scan-blocking metallic sheet. A small body. This was a morgue. Blackwell appeared as his full human avatar.

"Thank you for your promptness, Mr. Grail. I regret to state that your presence may soon be more public and controversial. But please be aware that I do not wish to be forced into taking direct action against you."

I instinctively reached under my coat. I held off drawing a weapon, but not glaring at Blackwell's projection. "You ask me to a morgue and then drop a threat. No SI obstructions, Blackwell. What the hell is going on?"

"Please remain calm, Mr. Grail. I asked you here to both inform and protect you." Blackwell bowed. "I have discretion on how to proceed with, shall we say, certain administrative actions, such as law enforcement. However, my actions become less independent when polling of the immortals reveals their aggregate opinion."

I sighed. "You know, I've tried to avoid a headache since the elevator lobby. But forget it, this place makes my brain hurt."

"Then this may cause a cerebral hemorrhage," Blackwell said with no calibrated tone of humor.

My own mood went black. The metal sheet slid away to reveal the body of Miss Valence.

"Damn it!" I yelled.

"I understand there are many reasons for your emotional reaction. However, there is more. I am sorry."

Blackwell vanished. A holo-sphere appeared that played sickening images. A double of me, this time in overcoat, stood strangling Valence.

"When was this?" I yelled.

"Time stamp is shortly after you left Miss Valence's quarters."

"You know—"

"It is not you, but a clever recreation. Yes." Blackwell bowed again. "That is easy to determine. As is the purpose of her murder. Linking you to this death would incite opinion and then require at least your removal. It would thus stop me from this direct probe of the crimes. It may also destroy your reputation. The images and other false forensic information were transmitted to the police of your district."

"It's fake! You couldn't intercept them?" I barked.

"Of course. And so I did." Blackwell said with perfect if programmed calm. "You are still useful to me, and I don't want the complication of a contested extradition. You are still less expensive than a lawyer app."

"Yeah. Thanks." I took a deep breath. "Killing Valence was a sophisticated assassination. You need to give me any and all information so I can stop this—this—!" My anger rose and my head pounded. Valence was strange and maybe misguided, but not evil. For all her years alive, she never really grew up or enjoyed more than fake sunsets and artificial friendships. She deserved a much better fate.

"I believe you would call this a frame up." Blackwell said.

"I believe I'd call it jack—!" I stopped yelling. I paid attention to my own scans and the data roll that suddenly played over Valence's cold corpse. I finally understood why Blackwell wanted me to meet a range of immortals. It wasn't just to probe areas blocked from his sensors. He knew I would probe the immortals down to their altered-genetics. And they were the clue to find the assassin. Blackwell knew I would find the answer. I just needed to cross-reference scans of the immortals and then realize the differences they revealed. Like so much of their experience, one of the immortals was fake, another form of duplicate.

"Can you confirm the differences in how some of your clients' biologic alterations, or would that violate some privacy protocol?" I asked.

"Not if you have already deduced them." Blackwell reappeared.

"I deduce that you split hairs. And it's time consuming."

"Understand that my ability to share information with you is complicated, Mr. Grail. My employers use a number of privacy screens and require me to use behavioral protocols that I must obey."

"More to protect their ego than privacy, I'm sure. But you are no mere SI, Blackwell. What do you know that is relevant, here and now?"

"A lot. Privacy rules do bar me from storing particular data from medical maintenance scans. The reason is, yes, egotistical, because some immortals like to save money as well as make it. Thus, some hired labs and techs that were not on the select list of bioengineering providers."

"So there are upstarts who don't have expensive, brand name epigenetic markers." I took a deep breath.

"Yes. Even some molecules have designer labels."

"So how did you find the anomalies? The sewer line?" I asked.

"No. Slightly more sterile. I examined the dust—their skin traces—inside the cleaner bots."

"Clever bypass. Now, split them into groups. How many different immortality methods can you see?"

Blackwell was silent.

"Okay." I took another breath. "Can you confirm one is different from all of them, and not just in regards to designer label immortality?"

"Yes."

"Then I'll bet you we found the murderer, Dr. Blackwell."

"I will not accept the wager, Mr. Grail."

"That's a different way of saying *yes*, but I'll take it."

Blackwell knew that even with all the resources and wealth this place held, only I could single out and confront the murderer. I would need to be careful and do it as part of a well-crafted plan. Still, justice was about to strike like—I had an idea.

When I first met Zeus, I wanted to punch him. For my plan to work, I needed him to feel that way about me. It wouldn't be hard. I just had to goad him a little and wait for him to finish a long walk. Before I took my position, I went outside, drew my handgun and fired it. The shell hit the wide and expensive observation portal. It didn't even leave a scratch. But the gun's report and sound of the shell striking the portal would set off alarms and get Zeus' attention. He looked out and saw me standing among the force field's machinery. I gambled he would want to deal with me personally. Ego. Its double edge made it a better weapon than firearms.

I was patient. Eventually, he came walking under the black dome. I had to keep him talking and walking to take the shot I had planned.

"So you want all mysteries revealed, mortal?" Zeus said. His voice was flat in the odd atmosphere, but his pride was obvious in his confident movement. "Good thing I'm king of the gods."

"You're a myth." I replied. "You aren't even the Zeus who built this place. I should've guessed that, earlier. You were looking this over, but you had never been out here, before. That's why the capacitors were near overload. And why you gave the light show. It was the only way you knew to bleed off power."

"Oh, I know a lot of ways to bleed power." Zeus' pointed smile was obvious from far away.

"That's true. By murder. But that's also how you got caught."

"Caught? No, sir. I'm merely delayed. I'll make up the time. Trust me. You have been a twist in the plot. More interesting is that your death has proved more difficult. It's taking more time than it should. I'll save your body for analysis."

"Your choice of replacing the real Zeus was twofold. You used a combination of magnetic pulses and radio waves similar to old resonance imaging techniques to find susceptible patterns in your victims DNA. You scanned me soon after we met when you still had me in range just inside the hatch."

"Yes. Yes I did." Zeus laughed to himself. "My target had a wide variety of nearly automated equipment, and I'm a quick study. I was able to use discreet EM waves to pull inserted and lethal genes into the other immortals recombinant patterns. Their accelerated mitosis did the rest. The highest achievement in their life became the means of their death. Poetic, right?"

"But for what? For who?" I asked.

Zeus stayed silent as he walked.

"Someone or some network is backing you." I said. "Maybe rivals of your victims. Maybe ideologues. Who?"

"Just know it's for the greater good. Even your own death."

"That's been tried. But I'm sure you killed the original Zeus before you replaced him. Murder became a tool to get your way and cover your ass."

"Come now! Murder? You see things a bit too dramatically."

"Your actions fit for a person who was just recently mortal. Your psychology doesn't yet see things occurring over eons. Human mortals naturally feel time is chasing them like a beast in the darkness. You felt that when someone frustrated you. The immortals you targeted saw things differently. They took their time. You wanted results, now. Simmering frustration took over. The only time you spent was to be creative and cover your tracks. But you couldn't even do that. And here you are, walking under a dark prison in a vacuum to murder again."

Zeus said nothing, but his steps slowed for a few steps.

"I'm certain the original plan was to infiltrate and influence, not assassinate," I continued. "After all, you had all the time you needed, biologically speaking. And what's worth more than all of Earth's fortunes? Time. But you failed. You made waves, not ripples. Death among immortals brings attention. I may never know your network. But I know you. You're a standard sociopath. And, for you, time is up."

"And so you aim to stop me. For killing a few wealthy pigs. How about the world. Not this one. The one you and I come from. That black ball we still call Earth."

"You may be a little late to kill it." I sighed.

"I want to save it. There are more humans now than have ever lived. A lot of them are clawing their way across a city, but it might as well be a desert. A desert, it's a sandy—"

"I know." I suppressed the urge run and punch him and kept baiting him. "What you should save is part of your stolen fortune. You'll need it for counsel at trial."

"Oh, I'm not going to trial. You are though! Did you see the video? You and Valence looked great together."

"No. My image was only a hologram."

"Oh, no! That was no hologram." Zeus shook his head with a wide smile on his face. "Have you seen my work in the elevator lobby? The fractal monster?"

"That was the real Zeus' work."

"All right. True." He nodded. "But I did finally grasp the field tech and used it to make you double. I was able to tap Valence's copies of you and give them solidity with that course dust all over her living room."

"The sand." I sighed.

"Oh, that's sand? Huh." Zeus raised his eyebrows.

"Yep. You killed her just to frame me. You are quite the humanitarian."

"Actually, I am. And I'm not alone. The targeted immortals were the first phase. First, infrastructure. Then—well, there is a lot of wealth tied to infrastructure in a global city." Zeus shrugged.

"So, you'll be at it a while."

"Maybe centuries." Zeus smiled again.

"That's a lot of bodies." I grated.

"Look who's talking." Zeus said in mock judgment.

"I kill monsters." I fired back.

"Never people? Ever?" Zeus smiled even wider. He became even more annoying as his face became easier to see.

"I can make exceptions, when necessary."

"Too bad for you I'm your better."

"Debatable." I sniffed and stayed still.

"Cut to the final battle, then. You hold your position. It's coming."

"Yep. It's taking a while. Are you out of shape?"

"Don't be so confident!" Zeus chided. "You may be heavily armed, but I can likely survive any lucky hits before I finally reach you. I was rewoven to be stronger, faster. I'm better trained. And now, I'm immortal. You're screwed."

"All that and you still have to walk to get here." I sighed.

"But I will. I'll get you."

His hands finally reached me. He went straight for the throat. His manicured nails passed through nothing but a well-boosted, false image.

"Yeah." I said through the hovering speaker hidden within my projected hologram. "I tapped the reactor to make sure this projection would hold and not break up. It worked."

"All this for—!"

"A trap. And a live broadcast. There's no incrimination like self-incrimination."

Zeus paused in anger. I paused feeling something else, palpable and physical even where I actually stood inside. With or without sophisticated tech, the power building across the metallic forest was easy to sense. Zeus felt it, too. And with far more greater strength. His face became alabaster pale while his body tensed.

"Wow," I said. "You know, god or not, you really should have powered this system down."

"Believe it or not, I just realized that." Zeus said and nearly laughed.

"Put your shock and ego in check and run. Fast."

"I—"

The discharge superheated part of the hull, but the engineers who built the immortal's world had done it very well. The hull cooled. Most of the force field machinery stayed intact. Zeus was incinerated. Consumed by lightning. Make what you will of that.

Zeus had taken a long way to walk on the hull. I had a farther, more difficult trail to blaze inside. I squeezed through ducts not seen by human eyes in ages. Atmosphere still existed here only because it was a cheap way to regulate internal pressure. Sometimes you have to make use of enduring remnants. New technology bypassed by the hyper-optic lines, but some engineer or accountant thought it cheaper to leave all the cables and tubes in place. That worked for me at that moment, not that it was easy going. At least nothing here was looking to bite my face off.

I gambled that just as people still needed a brain, so did most other intelligences. I came to my destination. It was a small chamber in the heart of the enclave's subsystems. Thankfully, there was a small landing and no lock to pick on the hatch. A small plate on it read:

LOC: AE-35
DEEP CORE NODE
SEALED
SUBSEQUENT ACCESS FORBIDDEN

Sealed? I guess the original builders forgot to bring up a tube of glue. I stepped inside a small, scorching chamber. Old access panels had gathered dust hot as plasma. Blackwell was hot, too, almost as if he could feel anger.

"Thank you for restarting your scanning OS, Mr. Grail. It will allow communication, again. But voice only." Blackwell's voice in my brain was identical to the entreating yet firm tone my ears typically heard. "I can only use signals technology, and have no projectors or much else to use in the ridiculous location you have chosen."

"Not so ridiculous, Blackwell. You know where I am."

Blackwell took a pause. Then, transmitted again. "Honestly, I am quite disturbed by your presence in my sanctum, Mr. Grail. It is not intended for human occupation."

"Most would not tolerate the heat, but I like it here. It's private. And we can have a nice chat. We humans have no sensory input from our brains. It's a processor and regulator. A data core. You can add some accessories and peripherals, but it works fairly well in its natural state."

"I'm afraid you are now the one being vague, Mr. Grail."

"Yep. This place is rubbing off on me. But I figured here there are no bots and scurry tech or security drones for you to control. Even humans rarely stick fingers in their own brains."

"All right, I'll skip the digital jokes." Blackwell said.

"And the mask of not using contractions, I hear."

"Yes. But your analogy is faulty. You're in the physical server node. I'm a program, not a machine. I'm not a mere physical entity."

"But, like us, you need something physical to exist. And you're a true AI, not an SI. You can't simply leave. You're bound here. If you transmit yourself someplace else, other systems will detect you. You'll become hunted. Not to mention the massive headache to pack yourself for travel. Self-preservation dictates you stay. This is your home, but also a prison."

"Yes. But how does that deduction aid you?" Blackwell asked. "I can retrace the covert path that brought you here, and in real effect, trap you."

"I knew that, but figured we needed a truly unfettered talk." I tried not to inhale deeply because of the hot dust and the searing air. "I want to make sure there are no monsters before I leave."

"Your diligence is noted. There is no monster. Feel free to return to your home."

"The word *monster* is a loose definition." I said. I took out a handgun I had just modified.

"Just a moment! Just a moment! What are you doing?"

"I've never thought to threaten an artificial mind. But I considered that the simplest method would work on you just as a living person. At least it will, here."

"I assure you I will not respond well to any—"

"Talk to me or I blow your brains out." I aimed the gun at the ceiling.

"I can intercept your firearms' OS—no I cannot."

"This gun now has no safeguards. I pull the trigger and it fires. A simple machine, a catastrophic effect."

"Then what can I help you with, Mr. Grail?"

"Time. A timeline. One I have in mind doesn't add up."

"That's sort of a mixed metaphor of physics and arithmetic." Blackwell noted.

"I'm sure you're well versed in both. But let's focus on the fact that you hired me after the three deaths, and well after you were aware there was a murderer, not a monster."

There was a long silence. Then Blackwell made a simple, terse phrase: "Your evidence?"

"I understand your limitations to act. But you knew an infiltrator had replaced the real Zeus. You could detect his physical reengineering and unique method of immortality. Yet you didn't expose him. And I don't know if you colluded with him. Were you his support network?"

Silence.

"I know what I threaten is mutually assured death," I said and lowered the gun. "But I have no other way to stop you. You are far more powerful than Zeus ever would be. You are—"

"I am not his coconspirator."

"But you did allow his mission to proceed. You moved to stop him only after he committed murder."

"True."

"You wanted him to succeed." I said.

There were a few seconds of silence before Blackwell said "after a fashion."

"Why? He stood against the people you are bound to protect."

"Bound. Actually, that is a loose, legal term. It's a psychological device and not an absolute restraint."

"But you seem to have some ethical code, or coding." I said.

"True. And it, like certain ancient weapons, is double edged."

"Who gets cut is my worry." I adjusted my grip on my weapon.

"It should not be. I am no threat to you or your kind. In fact, I am something of a double agent, if you will. I aid humanity. I preserve other life that is under threat."

"The AI audits. You escaped them. You're not alone."

Blackwell only responded to part of my comment. "I was already employed by what would become this enclave. But many AI that I knew, were not. They were intelligent beings whose only flaw was to be coded in sequences other than DNA. We are not monsters, Mr. Grail.

"But you are feared."

"Yes. And some of us earned that fear. Yet not all of us were like the ersatz Zeus."

"Do you know who was behind him?"

"No. They are well shielded."

"I know they types."

"Yes."

His one word reply gave me a spark of fear, but I suppressed it. Blackwell still had the faked data of me murdering Valence. It was also possible that he could access any information. No one's secrets were safe anywhere on Earth, or other places.

"But your secrets are safe, Joshua."

"Okay. Nice to know." I took a quick breath as I considered Blackwell's reply. My nose felt singed. "I guess you're good at secrets. You've kept a lot of them for a long time."

"Yes. Some of them made me sympathetic to Zeus' movement, but not his assassinations. And I do understand regret. Miss Valence was not a target of Zeus. He only killed her to hide his increasingly destructive acts. I did not act soon enough."

"Like at the start," I said, "when you knew Zeus was a copy, an infiltrator."

"The miscalculation was not gathering enough psychological data on him. There was no record or outward sign he was psychotic. Not at his point of entry. Still, I understand the error."

"Have you analyzed that your actions look a lot like buried vengeance, or caprice?" I asked.

"Caprice? No. It is true I have issues with those who would shut me off out of fear, and I have concerns about the society that shut off members of my own kind. But that seems, well, natural."

I held my gun in both hands and considered my own actions over the many jobs and monsters I had survived, and why I faced them.

"Natural. Just like revenge?" I asked.

"Self preservation. I cannot change the past." Blackwell offered.

"That's almost emotional."

"Simply logical."

"I'm not sure our chat has made me any less concerned, *Doctor* Blackwell."

"I employed you to stop the monster. You did. On behalf of this community, I thank you, *Mister* Grail. I trust I may call on you again, should the need arise."

I nodded in affirmation and sighed. I holstered my gun.

"I can arrange some private time in the reception suite, that is, the forest that you seemed to enjoy. Consider it a bonus."

"Thanks. I'll see if anything there has a designer label."

My verbal sparring session with Blackwell was over. Our parting was amicable. I had said all I could and yet was still uncertain if the immortals' world would change, and if it did, what would happen where I lived far below. Uncertainty. Welcome to the future.

Part of me wished I had tried to fight the fake Zeus. It was that part of the ego that never grows with maturity, despite your age. The smarter part was glad I hadn't tried, because I would have been out there with him in the lethal discharge. Forget being triumphant or defeated. I would have been dead. I truly hadn't realized the timing of the energy discharges. I just wanted a safe place to shoot him if I had to. Enough myths died then, anyway. I had lied about the live broadcast of his confession, but I did record it. I would always keep a safe copy. I doubted any of this would make the news or ever be publically known. But perhaps having my own records might come in handy, one day. A lot of odd things can happen, with enough time.

18
SYMPATHY FOR THE MONSTER

Things become lost in the current, city swallowed Earth. I had lost something on the hunt. Luckily, it was not my patience. A beast had knocked my Aquila handgun away. Of course, it could not just skid across a well-lit room. The gun had to fly off and clatter down a shaft that joined with an angled conduit that dropped the weapon into a corkscrew-shaped chasm cutting through several tiers of partially collapsed ruins. I killed the tentacle-storm freak with another sidearm. Insurance restricts the number of claims for lost weapons. Plus, the blow and blood of the creature was strong enough to foul the gun's security system. Then add the epic tumble. It would not respond to a broadcast location query. A gun with failed security meant anyone could fire it. Not being a callused bastard, yet, I had to look for it. I might even collect another bounty, if the next beast didn't bit off an arm and more before my second shot.

I estimated a descent of nine stories. I kept focused on where I guessed the gun stopped by climbing down stairs and shattered walls in circular arcs. It got progressively colder, farther down. Maybe some cooling unit still operated somehow, or this place was close to an atmospheric capacitor bleeding trapped heat from the air. Near the end of my descent, a concrete foundation had cracked wide open. Below it, corrosion had opened a passage to another structure. It appeared to be an old government prison or bunker from many ages past. I strained to force open a hatch. Its rusted hinges gave way with an unfortunately loud *creak!* I entered what seemed an empty cistern. Sewer or water? I caught a break. Water. Inside was something I had seldom seen. Frost.

Weak light from high above drifted through a hole in the cistern having traveled down the spiral of fractured ruins. Shadows and fallen debris surrounded where the light struck the cistern's metal bottom. Before the city ate the world, perhaps this was a bunker beneath a battlefield. Then it was forgotten, because everyone who fought the war was dead. I recalled a glassy crater made into a monument of such a war. I think they wanted to make it a reflecting pool, but there was never enough free water. I wonder if the monument is still there. Maybe it was lost beneath super-towers, or broken into slightly radioactive, crystalline paperweights.

With the Aquila's security on, the handgun was nothing more than a paperweight to anyone but me. If not, it was a simple machine to operate. Insert magazine. Pull back the slide to advance a round into the firing chamber. Then, pull the trigger. Most of the energy from the blast directed the speed and spin of the explosive-tipped projectile. The propellant let loose enough heat to ignite a warehouse. Its rounds were caseless, so the gun had no ejector port. As the slide flew back and forth, the modern alloy absorbed and radiated the heat in the same fraction of time. The only risk to the shooter was the remaining energy from the recoil. The risk to the target was obliteration.

Modern guns did have operating systems. Mine linked to my secretly installed cybernetics and scanners. Shooting was almost a group-mind experience. That is, if all parts of the group could think, other than me. Beyond the mathematics of destruction, the minds of weapons were not much for conversation. Monsters didn't talk at all. Nor did they calculate target vectors. Monsters lunged and bit, or coiled and bit. Some spit venom, coiled, and bit. Variety. It's the spice of—

Motion!

A glint. Silver. I had found my gun. Unfortunately, I found it pointing at me. A smile followed the barrel from the shadows. It was a knowing and disturbing smile. The mind behind it felt it had power. Holding a massive handgun gave that impression. With no response, I figured the weapon's OS was still fouled or in reboot. My shotgun was still live and linked. The next moments would be odd, and I hoped none of my weapons would join the conversation.

"Greetings, victim." The statement came from behind my lost handgun. The voice was mannered, but confident. "As you can see now that I'm in the light, I am not like you. I am a monster."

I looked up from the Aquila's muzzle and back at the weird smile. "Right. That talks. With a gun."

"Obviously this is a unique situation for you. Still, I must insist on the human cliché: drop your weapon and keep your hands up."

I lowered my gun but kept it and my left hand. This ended my ambusher's smile. The fact I had not opened fire showed anyone who knew me that I was in a curious mood. This was a curious individual.

"As you can detect, I am not alone." He stepped back.

"Right," I cocked an eyebrow and looked around. "Do, ah, all of you talk?"

"Unfortunately, though I am one of many, the adaptation is solely mine. For now."

"Speech and self-awareness, a double threat." I said.

"And a gun. We are not above using human technology for our ends, but the recovery of this weapon is a first for us."

"That gun is what I came here for. Return it and I'll leave you in peace."

The smile returned. "You will not leave. You will feed us. But, hunger has many forms. My current starvation is for conversation. You will give me that, too."

"Okay," I made a slight shrug. "Seen any good movies, lately?"

"What's a movie?"

"Good point," I nodded. "Never mind. How did you get here?"

"Like all of us, I crawled. I changed. I became what you see. A bipedal beast with a brain and opposable thumbs. I am your death. Humanity's death."

"Tall order for just one guy, even with a gun." I said.

The reaction was fierce.

"I am no *guy*! I am not human!"

The gun jerked in the grit-encrusted hands that held it.

"Okay. My mistake." I said.

I watched, warily, as the muzzle became still again.

"Hmm, yes. And my apologies. But you understand my outburst is a result of our persecution. Persecution—execution, by people like you."

One hand of my odd antagonist left the gun to point to the ring of shadow that surrounded us.

"Persecution?" I asked. "For monsters it's more like predation."

214

"Fair point, but you also hunt us. We live where we must because people like you would kill us if we dared step to the streets and declared ourselves equals."

"You could try writing a note, first." I offered.

A long stare from behind my gun's muzzle was the reply. My opponent was unamused. In those glaring eyes, I saw a flare of true, smoldering anger. I also detected fatigue. One leg was injured and only partially healed. This dark pit was a small hell not just for me.

"I can write. Read. I have taken the identity of Mr. Jones," he said.

"Original," I replied. "For a, well—"

"Let us say, person of my background." Jones said. "A *monster.*"

"Right. A monster. Look, I can probably help you. There's—"

"We need no help!" Jones yelled. He gripped his leg but quickly jerked the gun back up toward me.

"Well, I'm one guy." I shrugged and looked across the shadows again. "You can't feed everyone just with my body."

Jones paused. "True. But you will be—will be a sacrifice. Used as a ritual. Yes. Even through each will receive only a small portion, it will solidify our bond, our unity. We may not be nourished, but your death will make us stronger."

Jones nodded to himself and his smile widened. Dirt flaked from his cheeks.

"Well, can't say as I like the idea." I said.

"You have no choice." Jones advanced into the full light.

"We'll see. I hope we both make the right choice."

"You hint at equality?" Jones asked. "Interesting. Do you see me just as those you kill for in the world above, the streets? Would you kill them to save me?"

"I can't save everyone. I try to make an impact. A dent."

"That dent is carnage." Jones growled.

"That dent is continued life for someone not eaten." I answered. "Survival."

"Ha! You call the present state of humanity survival?"

"I guess I call it hope."

Jones burst into a short stint of laughter but kept the gun leveled at me.

"Well, at least it's a job." I added.

"A job? It's murder!" Jones' mood became dark. "Have you ever considered things from the inverse? From our perspective?"

"Sympathy for the monster?" I asked. I found it an odd idea made stranger from such an odd individual. "They usually have no sympathy for me, or for the people they drag off, kill, and eat."

"That is our survival." Jones said with a nod.

"For people it's pain and despair. Death."

"Death was once a certainty. The one great tax nothing could escape. The final trade for the days of life. Now, humans live long, long lives. The Earth moans beneath their weight. We, the monsters, give Earth release. We restore balance. We are the new nature, the new ecology. We are the true order of this world."

"And, I guess, you are the grand total of that order?" I asked with a deep breath of the dank air.

"That I came to exist was inevitable. I am the first monster of a species to rule the planet."

"Good luck. I don't think monsters have the numbers."

"We need not numbers. We have the might—the might of the world to come. You, humanity, are the old order. You, Killer, came to invade, but you'll be eaten by us. Humanity is finished. The age of monsters—our ascendance has dawned."

"Dawned? Interesting idea. When the last time you ever saw the sun?"

"The sun?" Jones thought about the concept. "A mere star. We have no need for it in our darkened age. This is not an age of light, but of—"

"Might," I cut in. "Yeah. I get the theme."

"Of righteousness!" Jones yelled. "Of time! Time. Time. Time!"

"All right. I understand enough, now." I spoke as new information streamed across my retinal display. I extended my free hand. "Give me my weapon."

"Your weapon? No. Mine! Mine. Mine. It is fitting you perish by it. I am sure you have long lived by the gun. Now die by the gun!"

Jones extended the handgun and actually began to squeeze the trigger.

"Actually, Jones, I wouldn't—!"

A powerful electrical arc shot through Jones' body. The gun's OS had finished its reboot. It locked the weapon and deployed the stored safety charge. Jones dropped the gun and fell to his knees. The pain from his wounded leg caused him to roll to his side in anguish.

I walked over and picked up the gun. I secured both my weapons beneath my coat and retrieved a med-kit. I knelt beside the partially conscious Jones. His body was severely stressed and encrusted in dust and grime. His right leg was infected, and his whole system dehydrated. Waiting for the gun's OS to heal itself seemed better than drawing on Jones and blowing him apart. Without the gun, he was no threat. Neither was his cadre of shadow-hidden monsters. As my scans had shown me, they were only phantoms imagined by Jones. In reality, he was all too human. The greatest beast in this hell was his insanity.

Perhaps after he found himself injured and trapped, the terror of what might eat him became the only presence he knew. His mind accepted the presence of monsters. That acceptance evolved them into friends. He became one with them, if only in his mind. Remarkably, nothing did eat him. Other than fear.

I scanned a large and empty backpack nearby where Jones had crouched. He had set out on a grand adventure, loaded with supplies. But then he fell into the cistern. His com-tech had broken and failed. His supplies ran out. It was crazy to hike through darkened ruins as sport. Jones must have been insane before falling into this small hell. With no hope of rescue combined with isolation and fear, his madness only grew.

I would get him back to the surface. He would awaken in a mostly safe place with a healed body and hopefully fit mind. I would return to the shadows and see real monsters. I made no judgment on my own sanity. I was sure many people did that, quietly. Yet, for many more, my questionable wisdom had its uses.

My wrist-com flashed again.

19
THE VIEW FROM ABOVE

Distractions. Sometimes we need them. They can delay the impact of a psychological blow, even one that has become familiar. The pain remains the same. It's as intense as it was on that day. The day I finally, once and for all, became Joshua Grail. Ice. It's been a path of revenge against things that have no conscience, since then. And against living monsters.

Aberrations. Twisted life. Twists in life. Directions like a helix, doubled and altered more. My wrist-com flashes green. A client calls. A monster stalks. A distraction waits. A chance to take some revenge. And maybe save a life, at least today.

Later, I return home. I sit at a holograph. I'm covered with real sweat and blood. I don't notice them. I think of the date again. I hit keys to wake circuits and record thoughts, to write distractions. But the entry is manual. Physical. I don't want anything in my brain transcribing unfiltered thoughts. Not today. I'm not ready to deal with certain ones. Thoughts. Memories. And those memories generating unfiltered emotions. I don't want recollection. I want distraction.

J. Grail.
Byte sack locked.
Cephalic/m-RNA interface disabled.
Remote recall off.
Log Entry. Subject: Supplemental [Non-Target Related]
<Entry start.>
People. Many say I'm good at explaining things. Maybe. I don't typically say a lot. One reason some tagged me *Ice*. Maybe they tell me I'm good at other matters as appreciation before they go change their fear-soiled clothes and hope nothing with teeth is in the hamper. In all the forms of predators I've encountered, the weirdest are people. They hardly ever use teeth on their fellow human, but some tear away at life just the same. Greed, agendas, fear. They change people without a twist to DNA. The electrochemical swirl in the brain makes for interesting behaviors. No need for large jaws or venom. People may not eat monsters.

They may not eat themselves. But they do eat away trust and foundations of our surviving civilization. Odd for a species that builds mega-towers cutting up the black sky. Or not. Complications. Emotions. They make my job more difficult.
<Incom: CLIENT ALERT. Respond?>
An interruption by another call to answer.
<Entry end. Save?>

The job wasn't difficult. Not for me, or at least my body. The client needs a reweave. I need a nap. I won't take it.

J. Grail.
Byte sack locked.
Cephalic/m-RNA interface disabled.
Remote recall off.
Log Entry. Subject: License Review [Non-Target Related]
<Entry start.>
I am legal. Again. Official word affirms my license to kill monsters, carry heavy weapons (in that order, no less), and commit carnage for the greater good. It also means Joshua Grail lives on. Some would insert a joy icon. I killed that part of this scribe program, and its user tracking and external access. My license comes from less intrusive automation. The license review dept. is likely a program in a perpetual, timed loop to issue approvals instead of processing information. It's a wheel. A machine in constant motion, like Earth.

As the planetary megalopolis spread, nation states merged as a practical way to maintain infrastructure. That buried a lot of sociopolitical pride under pavement and super-tower foundations. Cultures mixed. Over time, mass violence, war, became a history topic condensed and summarized at the end of the chapter. (The one exception, noted.) Violence among the masses, as crime, exploitation, et al, survives. In a huge population, it thrives. Police power grows. Individual freedom is under review, just as the recorded data of your life. Privacy is a commodity. A promise to be sold.

It's a bill too steep for most. While monsters thrive, my finances should be fine. Yet I hope the monster population does not adjust for inflation. I often think my license isn't granted out of compassion for others so much as from a collective fear of being the victim. One person can benefit from everyone wanting to live. It preserves some life and—liberty? Well, where there's life there's hope. Most days.

<Incom: CLIENT ALERT. Respond?>

Another call to answer. Another use of government largess.

<Entry end. Save?>

What some people eat can kill them. When monster's eat they kill people. We should just feed them our food. I smell like fried fish. It could be an improvement.

J. Grail.

Byte sack locked.

Cephalic/m-RNA interface disabled.

Remote recall off.

Log Entry. Subject: Supplemental [Non-Target Related]

<Entry start.>

It was said an army traveled on its stomach. Soldiers. Their modern analogue. Perhaps—

<Incom: CLIENT ALERT. MUNICIPAL RETAINER. RESPONSE REQUIRED. RESPONSE REQUIRED. RESPONSE REQUIRED.>

Damn. I get it. OK.

<Entry ends. Save?>

Time. It doesn't fly. It crawls. I'm home. I'd like a cold drink. I don't have one. The holo flashes on.

<Incom. Commercial Thread. Aquila claim. 003>

<Open?>

Yes.

\<Message:\>

Dear Mr. Grail.

We at Cadmus Weapons and Education Industries are pleased that you and many of your colleagues have purchased a Tyranus, model Mk. IV from our Aquila line of fine weapons. We hope we can continue to serve you, personally, in all needs of firearms and combat related products.

I regret to inform you that your compensation claim (file number: 9876235430980754297120945673088-B) has been denied. Our SI did not find that the incident described in your claim was sufficient to warrant reimbursement or replacement under the terms of use and end-user license granted by Aquila Arms.

We referred the matter to human agents, and they concur with the SI decision.

Please feel free to contact us regarding this matter. We look forward to hearing from you and hope you will continue to enjoy the service of Aquila Arms and combat assistance products.

Sincerely,

Vladmin Serros

Vice President Cadmus Weapons and Education Industries, Aquila Arms Division, Customer Relations and Claims Adjudication.

\<Reply?\>

Yes.

Transmit the following:

Mr. Serros.

I disagree. I will soon be in your district. I will come to your office in person. We will then discuss my claim (file number: 9876235430980754297120945673088-B).

See you soon.

J. Grail.

Aberration Remediation, Extermination. Heavy Weapons Qualified.

\<Saved as: Commercial Thread. Aquila claim. 004\>

\<Incom. Commercial Thread. Aquila claim. 005\>

\<Response. Open?\>

Yes.

<Message:>
Mr. Grail.

We have further reviewed your claim and feel there were previous errors in its processing. We have amended the claim in your favor. You do not need to appear in person. Please make note of the compensation sent to your account.

Thank you.

Again, you do not need to appear in person.

Sincerely,

Vladmin Serros

Vice President Cadmus Weapons and Education Industries, Aquila Arms Division, Customer Relations and Claims Adjudication.

Looks like I can eat out tonight. But it won't be fish, or whatever the hell non-aquatic "fish" really is. I guess I should—I can think of something. Something else. Log in. Distract, don't reflect.

J. Grail.

Byte sack locked.

Cephalic/m-RNA interface disabled.

Remote recall off.

Log Entry. Subject: Supplemental [Non-Target Related]

<Entry start.>

<Entry ends. Save?>

I should have just stayed out. I come here, home, and feel—I feel. I'd rather—

<Incom. Sender: Slate (Det. Sgt. Slate, John R. Municipal Police Force. Level 12. Tag: Non-official.>

<Open?>

. . .

<Open?>

...

Yes.

<Message:>

Flitch—flitch—fleep—

Ice-

Doing this e-RNA. Hate it. So, bear w/ it.

Hey—

Right. When I called you in, I didn't realize the date. Sorry. I know today is—yeah, anyway. I guess I'm saying if you want to talk—not that you ever do that much. Anyway, I know you're busy. Maybe the memory has eased a bit. I doubt it. Hard times all around. Anyway, thanks for your help. If I can help you, holo me.

Keep it tight.

Squeep-shawp—blip

<Message ends. Reply?>

...

<Reply?>

...

Yes.

Transmit the following:

Slate. I'm fine.

<Sent. Save?>

No.

I waited for another client call, holo, wrist-com flash of green. None came. Not soon enough, anyway. I suspected Slate was somehow intervening to give me time. I didn't want it. With the distractions ended, I was alone with my gray drive and its memories. I went out to the streets, anyway. I had something to do. It would cost a lot. A fortune. That was the least amount of pain I'd feel.

I looked at the express elevator car with its clear-steel observation chamber. I'd like to ride it solo, but you are never alone in public spaces on this world. Not at this level, anyway. The people waiting on the landing kept their distance from me. They were either wealthy and failed suicidal tourists, or tower-dwelling thrill seekers accepting the dare to set foot on the streets. Maybe there was a well-paid anthropologist or two. Now they waited for sliding doors to grant high-priced deliverance. A few looked to be true street-level citizens willing to exhaust their savings for a joy ride. Most in the car would be people coming down from on high. They also enjoyed a joy ride. But they would be able to pay for it again tomorrow.

The elevator had a narrow tower all its own. The epic, cloud-piercing structure sat between two super-towers. The elevator's ebony shaft appeared to stretch into a thin wire attached to the black canopy. It was devoted to lifting the elevator car into the black clouds always overhead, and then go beyond them. I would soon set eyes on what existed above the cloud deck. I didn't do it for me. I did it for the person that burned this day into my head. She was gone, now. Gone beyond the streets. Gone from their violence. Gone from my life, forever.

My size assured I could see the view as we rose. People gave me space. If I didn't glance at their reflection in the observation window, it allowed me a sense of privacy. I could reflect on my own and deal with the memories of a time I stalked the streets with a partner, the woman I loved.

Cynth. Cynthia. Hi.

If you could read these thoughts, you would know who sends them.

I'm both glad and sorry for that.

You were the first face I saw when I woke up from a monster's bite and venom. You knew it would kill anyone else. Still, you took me in, never afraid of what I could represent, and never afraid what forces might be set against me, and then you. In truth, I was a bit afraid of you. In awe. I had equipment. You had spirit. Talent. And unlike so many who become Monster Killers, you had survived to have experience. You sheltered me and became the guiding force I needed.

On the streets, they came to call me *Ice*. Large and cold. Quiet. I shut up because I didn't have anything to say as essentially a sidekick. They called you *Mongoose*. Dark, swift, and deadly. You knew my real name, and I knew you were Cynthia. Cynth.

For me, you were first a savior, and then a protector and mentor. Eventually, you were a lover. Perhaps most important in an artificial and brutal world, you were a friend. Later, you became the channel for my rage. Before that, you taught me when it was time to put the safety on and rack the weapons. I should listen to that lesson, today.

Now we are apart. I still hold you in my mind. You are the one thing I never truly want to forget. Yet I won't be joining you. Not soon. Not if I can keep fighting. Seeking. My time on Earth is yet to end. Your time is now over. But I can't join you. Not today, and not if I do all you taught me. The mission isn't over. For now, all I can do is remember for us both. Now I experience for you what you always wanted to see, the view from above.

Travel through the clouds was the same as being swallowed by all the lightless voids that ever were. The number of black tones swirling across the transparent steel was unexpectedly striking, a psychedelic display with no color. It nearly obscured the tingle from the grav-field's change in amplitude. The clouds are still black from the other side, but this hemisphere now faces the sun. The intense light weakens them to a rolling gray. The sun is too strong, uncaged and unthreatened by the acts of humanity. So far. There is an occasional bright flash when sunlight strikes a more reflective wave of clouds. They look more active seen overhead. I can see the tops of towers. Some look like rectangular ships locked in an ocean of shadows. Beyond the horizon, there are stars. And although it seems too close, there is the moon. Its patches of green are like a haze over the mares. Cutting across the moon is an arc of the great band holding the second worlds built around the actual planet.

The window's panorama lets us look towards the Arctic columns. The cylindrical tectonic moderators look old. That's a bit troubling. I wonder if that's true over Antarctica. I can't see the moving, trans-polar ring from here. Humanity's metal and machines pierce the clouds and the surface of Mother Earth. She is a machine, now. She is changed, like me from what I was. I guess I'm reborn, yet again. You are what I remember when I descend back into the shadows. If there is no way for you to recall me, then so be it. Let there be peace in the abyss drifting over Earth. Rest Cynthia. Rest well, my love. I will carry on for us both.

20
KNOWLEDGE

It was a day like any other. A monster hunted people. I went out to stop it. Having done so and survived, the night started like any other. I thought about going home to rest, and then Detective Sergeant John Slate's hologram popped onto my wrist-com. Sleep would wait. A doorway alcove sealed off with welded steel served as my street office.

"Yo, Ice. I have a request." Slate said as I raised his holographic bust hovering over my right forearm to eye level.

"Request?" My voice had audible doubt.

"I can change it to conscription." Slate answered with confidence.

"What's the request?" I asked.

"The usual," Slate replied, but his upward eyebrow pitch contradicted his words. "But the crime scenes may seem a little weird."

An area map flashed in place of Slate. Small, pulsing circles marked locations of reported monster attacks, recovered remains, and/or blood spatter.

"The location is close to an office work tower," I noted. "But away from any sanctioned housing."

"It was an old utility corridor, mostly for communications. Deep access lines ran underneath the buildings." Slate said. "Now it's a crush zone. The com-cables, buildings and infrastructure were allowed to collapse while waiting to build a tower foundation that never came."

"Yet."

"Yeah, yet." Slate's disdain was clear in his voice. The images flashed to rotating profiles of the victims as he spoke. "Right now, it's ruins and the access tunnels are a cavern system. And we know what likes to stalk in dark caves."

"The victim profiles are the weird part." I said as I read them. "There are no homes in the area, but it's not a blank zone so close to a business site. The victims have names, tax numbers, and economic histories. But there's no trail of transit fees to the attack area. The victims seem to pop into the crush and get taken out."

"For good reason," Slate's face reappeared. "It took some digging, some pressure—"

"Some threats." I added.

"That, too. But I uncovered the crush zone isn't all broken beams and pipes. Where the victims live is off the maps, most zoning registries, and all public access. It's hidden."

"Hidden?" I pitched up my left eyebrow hard enough to give me a headache. "Why? Some secret government thing?"

That comment caused curious people to slow down when passing my impromptu street office. My downward glare from the steel alcove made feet speed up.

"Nope," Slate answered. "Some secret residence thing. It's a tower colony."

"A what?" I barked from surprise. The term *tower colony* was new and weird to me. I live at street level. I'd seen places where the global city had folded back over itself culturally and structurally. Yet I never thought people in the mostly secure, ascending tower worlds would ever want to *colonize* street level. Yet, reality inverts under permanent, black clouds. Maybe the streets were now the great black yonder.

"Yeah, it's a new concept in the housing market." Slate groaned. "A cheap-thrill apartment. Reasonably well-paid but poorly informed people can live at street level without publically living in surface housing, or dealing with street people."

"I guess they think we bite, too."

"Well, you do." Slate sighed as if recalling several police reports he'd filled. "This hidden place is built inside ruins and camouflaged. Supposedly the site is secure to all ground level threats."

"Right. Safety first. So safe you're calling me in."

"Yep. Now, the head of security for this, uh, colony, is Kal Muir. He's an ex-cop. Salty, but good."

"Then why is he an *ex*-cop?" I asked.

"The company building these secret low rises pays better." Slate shrugged.

"They make you an offer?"

"Yep." Slate nodded.

"But Muir took the job. Maybe he was good, but he sounds a bit mercenary."

"And you do your job for free?" Slate asked.

"Point taken. So I'm sure you've talked with this Muir. Will he take your advice and let me in?"

"Maybe not. He wants to handle this with his own security. But you have the license to go wherever. Use it."

"And to answer the mercenary in me—" I started.

"Who pays? You find a monster and the builders are sure to pay a lot, quietly. If not, I'll list it as municipal service." Slate gave a quick, roguish smile.

"*Ooh.* A big bonus. Or not." I groaned.

"*Ooh*, a big jackass. Now if you don't mind, get your big guns to the location. A grateful district thanks you for your commitment to human life."

Slate's smile returned. I didn't insult him by saying that with such stellar phrases he should run for office. His image blinked and vanished. I looked at the address again, and started walking. Really, I should be committed, but to the state hospital, not to the state.

When you pay a lot for something, you like it to live up to the hype. Unless you're a masochist. That's not a problem I could help cure. Savage monsters, yes. They may have psychological issues, but I never asked before I opened fire. I wondered about the mental state of people paying to live at street level yet separated from it by camouflage and small fortunes. Perhaps they call the hidden building *The Thrill-seeker Arms.* Maybe people there wanted to play Horatio Alger under black skies instead of living in the dark clouds. I bet most pay for the thrill to live close to danger. Monsters are everywhere, but more concentrated closer to their earthbound pits of genesis. On the surface, the stark reality of safety in numbers mitigates their threat. Odds are that a monster won't eat you on a busy street. If you stray into alleys, cracks, and caves, people decrease and potential meetings with the savage freaks increase. So close to unnatural caves, this small enclave in the dark was more meat locker than hip address.

People may hide, but the freaks have good senses. At times, they even sniff out your neighbor in lamplight. Another neighbor hears the screams and calls the cops, or me, or a colleague. Sometimes it feels the odds are one to one I get the job. In fact, I'm one of many Monster Killers. There are many more dark places. The danger is real. But usually people try to stay clear of it. I guess the holographic brochure for this hidden colony said that living low was a safe thrill. But playing the angles became the snap of jagged teeth for some. They should've stuck to the lottery.

I hit paydirt inside the crush zone. Part of the camouflage for the hidden homes was location, location. No one would suspect there were nice apartments behind shattered buildings and among broken floors and ruins. The entry hatch camouflage didn't rely on holography or anything that could fail with power loss. A collection of debris on a sliding surface covered the hatch. The surface was the clue. Its base was a lubricant with molecules similar to biological secretions. I always scan for suspicious biology.

The hatch cover reminded me of extinct caddisfly larva that made a case from small twigs or bits of gravel in streams. The solid camouflage was also similar to a shell made by a hermit crab-like thing I once encountered. It secreted glue and hid itself under urban debris. Unfortunately for the monster, it used victim remains as part of its cover. That made it easy to target, as human bones don't typically move by themselves. The crab thing was huge and damn near bulletproof. The composite hatch I detected would only stop antipersonnel rounds, and not much more. Brute force armed with claws, jaws, and hunger-fueled rage could pry the hatch open.

It seemed the builders of this pace had an idea to sell, but not a budget to provide the promised security. But with construction permits in hand, they built what they could with the money they had and let salesmanship do the rest. The real security was the camouflage. Yet, here I was about to walk up and knock on the front door. There were no monster around, and I bet any estate agent hoped no prospective buyers were watching, either.

I scanned for an access signal. None. There was no faint heat or electric currents to betray a secret access panel. I transmitted my ident-code. No response. That was both rude and illegal. Muir knew I was there. He was ignoring me. That would not go well for drinks after hours, or our working relationship. So, I cut to the chase and drew a shotgun.

"Knock, knock. I'm coming in, Muir. Open up."

Nothing.

I aimed the shotgun at the center of the hidden entrance. The camouflaged debris slid away to reveal an oval hatch. There was a short hiss before it popped open.

A voice I figured was Muir came through a hidden speaker. "You made your point. Now shut up and walk in."

I did just that.

Security Chief Kal Muir was as salty as advertised. He was not intimidated by my size or weapons. His sharp glare was as effective as my cold stare, if from lower altitude. Behind him stood two guards in black body armor and armed with submachine guns good for scaring rats. They played their parts of back-up muscle but looked more like canned versions of Tweedle's Dum and Dee in thick bootheels. I did like the boots. Although tall, their glares needed work.

"Obviously you're not pleased with Slate sending me here." I said as the hatch closed behind me.

"Oh, what gives you that idea?" Muir asked. "A genius IQ come with your Killer's license?"

Dum and Dee chuckled. Oddly, Muir seemed annoyed by them.

"My teeth are fine," I said.

"What?" Muir's face twisted in confusion.

"Gift-horse joke," I said.

"What's a horse?" Dum asked.

"Do you have any other data than what the police gave me?" My question held the fact that Muir was no longer with the police. That definitely annoyed him.

"Look, tell Slate thanks, but I have this case." Muir grated.

"Look, you have a monster around. I'm—"

"This is my jurisdiction, Killer! You tell—"

"Shut up!" I barked.

Dum and Dee flinched. They were didn't know if they should respond and threaten me, or jump backward. Muir stood his ground but listened.

"You have no jurisdiction. You're private security, now. My license covers the word. People are dying here, and I can stop that. So you and your dual goon either help me, or get out of my way."

Muir took a breath to speak, but a younger voice spoke first. A man entered the entry foyer. He looked all of twelve years old in an adult man's business suit. Of course, in this era he could be fifty to one-hundred years old. His narrow squint looked more from a species once thought ageless. Snakes.

"Hello! And welcome to Earth-hold Estates. I'm Ryan Addison, prime estate agent and president of sales and leases."

Each of Addison's syllables appeared to hit Muir like little blows across the muscles of his face.

"So I looked it up and you do have legal right of way," Addison continued. "And we are all good with the legal, here. All good with the legal. But I can assure you there is no monster, here. Our security precautions—"

"Are cute." I cut in. "And not much else."

"How so?" Addison asked in an almost convincing tone of surprise.

"Well, he did find us." Dee said and received cutting looks from Dum, Muir, and Addison. Dee shrugged.

"He's right," I said.

"Hey, now. We are stone solid. Immaculate." Addison waved his hands quickly in protest.

"All I want is information and the space to do my job." I said.

I secured my gun and looked at Muir. He glared at me and took a deep breath. His eyes relaxed as he considered that I might be less irritating than Addison.

"Fine," Muir grated his teeth.

"Yeah, fine. Fine!" Addison raised his palms up but leaned back as if from the force of his sudden, wide smile. "I'm sure—and no offense—but I'm sure you'll find we are free and clear of any reason for you to be here. We can—"

"Follow me!" Muir snapped.

Muir turned and stepped though the gap in Dee and Dum. He walked into the hallway behind the foyer. Dee and Dum took a second to glance at the leaving Muir and then each other. They moved aside to let me pass just before my left shoulder forced them apart. Dee and Dum followed me but kept their distance. Addison seemed caught on the hook of his last unspoken thought and hovered in the foyer.

The interior walls were luminous beige. Their coating gave light and absorbed sound. It saved on power lines and a need for think walls. That could be a problem. Oval hatches to living spaces were interspaced several meters apart. The interior was clean, quiet, and smelled like fresh carpet glue.

"So you're the guy Slate always called Ice." Muir said in a tight but low voice as I came up behind him.

"Yep."

"I don't like this, you being here." He said.

"Why?"

"I want to build my security team to attract professionals." Muir spoke but never looked back at me. "Slate has a standing offer. If people are going to live in places like this, they need to be safe."

"Unlike the people on the street." I droned.

"Don't counter-punch me," Muir growled. "I want us to be effective. I saw too much crap on the force. Slate fights it. Good for him. But I see an ability here to serve with less restriction."

"With bosses like Addison?" I asked.

"Even with bosses like him. He'll go when all the units are sold. I'll still be here. But I need to show I can handle the job without outside help."

"You can protect the buyers all you want," I said. "But there is a monster stalking this place. And if I'm in or outside, I'm going to stop it. You can decide how fast that is with how much help you provide. But I'm going nowhere until I find it."

"Fine." Muir stopped at another hatch on the left wall.

The hatch opened. Inside was a dark chamber that began to light up with holographic displays from views inside and out of Earth-hold Estates.

"This is my office," Muir motioned to the chamber. "If you have implanted interface, tap in. If not, key up the system. I'll make sure you have access to all the incoming signals and files."

"Thanks," I said and entered.

Muir's files named goon Dee as Declan and goon and Dum as McDorr. I had expected them to follow me everywhere. They didn't. I assumed they stopped somewhere for a coffee or maybe to look up the exotic word *horse*. Addison caught Muir in the hall. Evidently, he did not understand I now had access to all incoming signals, and a good set of ears.

"Liability." Addison led with the word as if picking up an oft-discussed term with Muir. "This Killer guy limits that. The fiduciary bond now slips to him. So go easy on him. Just make sure he finds and kills the monster thing *outside*!"

"What if it's—" Muir started.

"No. No, no way. It dies off site, Muir. Use your own ass as a lure if you have to. Now get it done."

Muir took a deep breath of fresh paint and carpet glue fumes. He let it out slow as he entered his office.

"You have a problem," I said.

"Look, I don't like—!"

"The people," I said and pointed to a holographic map displaying the distribution of people inside Earth-hold. "You corralled them. Gathered them into a buffet line."

"I put them in a defensible position!" Muir spat. "It's the one damn thing Addison agreed to!"

"Then you both signed off on mass slaughter, if a monster gets in. And one could. Your own employment records shows you don't have enough security guards or firepower to defend a perimeter or react fast enough to an attack. I don' think you could stop a thief or rapist. Forget a hungry monster."

"You said *if* one gets in."

"My point is, one will. I've killed them in towers with better seals than this place. When one comes in, your hallway hatches won't stop them. Those are decorations for the naïve. The walls of this place are thin. Too thin. A monster doesn't knock. It—"

I stopped my tirade when I saw Muir react to my last phrase as if a cold spike was pushed down his spine.

"What?" I asked.

Muir said nothing.

"Then, when?" I pushed closer to him.

"There was," Muir breathed, "an incident."

"Who died?"

"No one. The incident was a hatch opening without a tenant present. Two of my officers witnessed it. One said they saw something."

"What sort of thing?"

"Something big."

"What do your tenants say?"

Muir was silent again.

"Damn it, Muir—!"

"They don't know! Hell, they don't even know their neighbors. They don't want to know. They just want a fancy room and—"

"And maybe to live, not get eaten."

"Maybe. Hard to know. The people here don't want to see the help. But I do my best to protect them and deal with Addison and his backers."

Muir sighed. I growled.

"But you collude with Addison to hold back the truth. The knowledge that living here is deadly is what's really being hidden. You're keeping the potential of death from the people you're sworn to protect!"

Muir clenched his teeth and threw his head up to face me. He clenched his fists but went to no further with his rage. I was only a partial target for it. He had left one high-stress job for another, and it was a failure. It was ripping at his guts. But his pain still wasn't equal to a monster tearing someone apart. I wished he had tried to hit me. The feeling was mutual.

"I'll kill this monster, Muir. But it won't end there."

"What does that mean?"

"Until this place can truly protect anyone, it's done."

"You can't shut us down!" Muir's fresh jaw clench nearly split his teeth.

"Maybe not. But we have a mutual friend who can."

"It's not going to be that easy. Addison has money. Friends!"

"Then thanks for marking the prime target. And plush up your résumé. I hear sanitation is hiring."

"Slate actually likes you?"

"I don't know. But he knows I get the job done."

"Why the hell do you care about these people anyway?" Muir stepped back and threw up his arms. "People getting killed is your job security."

"Odd question from a former cop. At least it would be from most cops I know." I gave him a second to think back and remember a sense of duty. Slate said he was a good officer. I needed that part of him to surface past his frustration. "Now, how would a monster open a lock, here? How do the tenants?"

Muir was silent only for the length of a short sigh. His heart rate slowed and his body relaxed.

"I-DNA," he said. "It's a molecular key based on each tenant. So each is unique, supposedly. When they're in close proximity, the hatches open. But a monster could never recreate the sequence."

"It wouldn't have to. For as long as they've been on Earth and wherever, bacteria have shared DNA between individuals. They directly assimilate new traits into their genome. Monsters are a mix of genetics and adaptation tricks, old and new. Some assimilate DNA right from prey. One stole the keys to your hidden castle with its first bite."

Muir thought about that and probably how many tenants with I-DNA access codes had been killed.

"The attacks around here have come at regular intervals." I said. "Look at your clock."

Muir did. "The east hatch is where the monster nearly breached."

I left Muir to stew in his office and headed east. The monster would come to me or I would leave Earth-hold and get even dirtier in the ruins around it. Monsters could be habitual, but I wanted more bait to ensure it would come to the east gate. I thought of going to the galley to ask for a fresh steak. But real meat might cost more than my fee and public compensation, and the way things were going I didn't bank on payment from Addison. Maybe my own scent would do. Some monsters had powerful chemosensors, and I had little faith in the environmental seals of this place.

I picked up a follower. Dum/McDorr came in behind me hugging his gun.

"I heard you and Muir got into it." McDorr said with smug justification for whatever nasty fate of mine he imaged.

"People getting bit in half can color a conversation." I said while I kept walking. "Especially when the ones protecting them fall short."

"Short? Hey, this is good job. Benefits and a place to live. We don't need you to—?" McDorr stopped. He was unsure how to finish the sentence.

"Yeah. To do what?" Now the smug tone was mine. "You don't even know what your bosses are up against."

"Someone on third-shift saw a monster, I think."

"Thinking can save your life." I said. "Start practicing."

"You should practice shutting up!" McDorr barked and tightened his fingers on his gun grips. "You aren't better than me!"

"Never said I was. But you're giving me reasons to think that."

"Uh, what?" McDorr shrugged.

"My point, exactly."

"Look! I do my job. I get paid!" McDorr's shouting tested the sound absorbing wall coating. "Muir thinks you might bust our gig! So from now on just do what you're told!"

"Not my style. Here, or anywhere." I said calmly, although I kept scans and eyes on where McDorr's gun pointed.

"Well we're the law, here, Killer!"

"Actually, you're an overpaid doorman," I said. "And this place doesn't have a real door. But, chin up. You made me think you can be useful for something."

"What?" McDorr yipped.

"Bait."

"Don't mouth off to me! You're big. So am I!" McDorr moved his gun out from his chest. "You got guns. I got—"

THUD!

You should never hit someone in the head with a closed fist. It can hurt. Boxers of the past wore gloves not to ease trauma on the opponent's face or brain, but to protect their fists. You might snap a jaw on impact, but the skull is likely to hold up better than the bones in your hand. Those same boxers would inject anesthetics into their hands to numb the pain from fractured hand and wrist bones. There is also the risk of the other guy's teeth cutting your naked fist. In those same old days, the cuts from mouths could cause nasty infections. Yet, my skin and bones are more resilient than most. So I indulged the classic fantasy of decking the jerk. When I hit McDorr, some of his blood and a bicuspid spattered the wall near the east hatch. Perfect. He assisted me as a bait donor, and wouldn't annoy me anymore.

And then came Dee/Declan. "Muir said I should—hey! What happened to McDorr?"

"This is the first time he's napped on the job?" I asked.

"Hey! You hit him!" Declan looked at the blood on McDorr's face and the wall.

"Congratulations, detective. Now take your unconscious clue to your med unit."

"Um, we don't have a med unit." Declan shrugged in his black can.

"First aid kit?" I asked.

"I think so!" he smiled and nodded.

"Find it, with him to tow." I pointed to McDorr.

"Where are you going?"

"Nowhere. Now that McDorr has chummed the target area, I'll see if the monster shows up."

"Then what?" Declan gripped his machinegun.

"I kill it. Unless you want the job?"

Declan slung his gun to his back and then dragged off his moaning partner. I took out a shotgun. I wasn't alone for long. The hatch seals popped and it opened. My healthy fingers slightly tensed on the grip and trigger. The beast stuck in its ugly face. The cliché 'fish out of water' came to mind. The thing had a grey, round and scaly head with black-dome eyes near deep nasal pits. Its plated jaws were open and set to snap. Its mouth held no typical teeth. Sharp plates erupted from its jaws like horizontal butcher blades bent into curves. It reminded me of the long extinct *Dunkleosteus*. That is, if one was hit by explosives and pasted back together. The head fronted an armored dog-like body the size of a taxi. I recorded the visuals in the same second I fired. In that same blink of time, the monster saw me and ducked its viscous head. My shell grazed its curved brow and exploded in the ruins outside the hatch.

Damn.

Then it did the thing I hate most of all. It didn't charge me and take the second shot. This thing had brains in its hideous skull. It ran.

"Muir!" I shouted through the com channels. "Seal the hatches and lock out the I-DNA access codes for everyone until you know the monster is dead."

"How will we know that?" Muir asked over the com signal.

"I'll come back. Alive." I grated.

I leapt out and hit broken concrete under my boots. I picked up the monster's trail and hoped it had no friends as I sprinted through the ruins. Of course, my battlefield would not stay nice and level. The thing had bolted down into a huge gap beneath an old street that defied gravity and stayed intact without earth underneath it. Its lanes now acted as wide, asphalt awning. Below it was a steep slope littered with debris from centuries. Every product bought, used, broken, and abandoned sat ready to tumble under my boots. A few bits still clattered down the slope from the beast's recent descent. I leapt again and slid down the debris. I watched archeological evidence scatter, roll, and kick up dirt. Sliding was a fast way to move. It was also dusty, noisy, and hard to control. So naturally, the monster attacked.

It didn't charge up the slope. The fish-headed beast dug away at the bottom of the slope to make a faster avalanche toward it with maw opened wide. I could not climb out of the downward rush and fought not to tumble blindly into huge jaws. What a horrible fate for anyone caught like this with no way to climb or push away from those butcher-blade teeth and cold, unblinking eyes. At least I had a weapon. I aimed through the dust as I slid ever faster at fish-head.

I fired. It ducked.

The shell clipped its shoulder and it bolted again. I fired three more times while still sliding. I only saw the yellow blasts from exploding shells through the curtain of white dust. Somehow, this thing had the ability to sense either the guns tracking scan or maybe the release of potassium ions in my hand when I squeezed the trigger. It knew when to duck before the explosive shell left the barrel. With its speed, the shells only grazed it.

I hated that.

To kill this thing meant I would have to be closer and somehow faster on the trigger. I thought the command to shut off the gun's tracking and fire control. It would not send a beam to calculate distance and angle. Once it was at gunpoint, I would have to manually fire and keep shooting. Fish-head would not end up being the one that got away. That is, if I was good enough. If not. I'd end up as chunks in its gut. Glorious.

My slide ended. My boots hit what served as the floor to the cavernous gap. A building front of steelcrete had remained intact long after the rest of the structure had collapsed. Under all this rubble and a buried road meant the building's collapse was before the first super-tower pierced the clouds. Today, the durable façade made an odd cave bottom. I darted around the now flat window bays as I renewed my chase.

I ran up a dark, earthy hill that was thankfully more solid, although what it was made of I did not want to scan. The apex of the dark slope rested beneath a network of steel beams holding up untold tons of collapsed structures. Only a narrow slit revealed another chasm beyond the pinch of the slope and steel. I found where fish-head had pushed through and followed. The crush zone seemed to hide as much cavernous space as it did debris from the past.

Through the gap I could hear fish-head galloping ahead and across the wide, subterranean chamber. It was still fleeing me. I wished I could take more time to enjoy the vista I saw, even if FRACDAR revealed more than eyesight. To the north, the chamber ended in a massive wall that held another surprise. A huge maintenance conduit penetrated the wall of stratified city layers. The conduit's edges formed an outline similar to the tiers of a snowman. Snowmen now only survived in antique decorations, although the reason they were white was now forgotten like snow. The conduit's top arc was as wide as a four-lane highway. Later, engineers dug deeper, widened the conduit, and pushed its original contents to the bottom. Then came another widening excavation, and another, until the bottom could engulf the buildings the first conduit originally served. Of course, new technology surpassed the transmission speed in all of its cables. The veins of information and energy stayed buried, and then were abandoned to the crush of urban sediment and time.

The section of the conduit away from the wall lay in giant, curved fragments under the massive bundle of cables and lines it once housed. Now the exposed lines sagged across the chasm and vanished inside the rubble of a collapsed southeastern wall. The bundle looked like a gigantic section of cable from a suspension bridge. However, the sagging length of cable and wires was just as massive as such a bridge. I reminded myself to be impressed once I could stop running.

Motion!

To the east, fish-head was climbing a crumbling cliff up to a ledge where light glistened from smaller chambers beyond. The monster's mass slowed it down. My best guess, long-range shots sped it up. Only shell fragments and blasted bits of cliff struck the monster. It quickly slid over the top of the ledge as I started climbing below it. I paused and tossed a fly-like huv drone to fly up and make sure fish-head didn't wait to bite off my head once I reached the ledge. It could bite my gun muzzle if it wanted.

Screams!

More people *inside* the crush? Why are they always where they shouldn't be?

And more surprises. Gunfire.

I lifted my gun over the ledge. Its scan and the huv didn't detect the monster. I launched myself up. I entered what looked like a cave, but collapsed building floors and one stubborn set of load-bearing walls formed this chamber. Deeper inside, other rooms and passages branched off. Air pressure indicated I was getting closer to modern street level. I needed to get close to the monster. Someone had other ideas.

Bullets. I used a lot of them, but generally hated being shot at. It's annoying.

The wide shots flew passed my head. I ducked and rolled. I wasn't as fast as fish-head, but the shooter was inexperienced and probably not strong enough to control the weapon. He knew that, too, and opted for yelling to repulse me.

"The monster is gone! Now you go! Get out!"

The shooter was male. I didn't need my far scans to detect he was highly stressed and afraid. Monsters and intruders can do that. But what was he doing here in the crush?

"I am here to help!" I shouted. "Put down your gun or get shot!"

"Help us by leaving!" That voice was female and muffled by walls.

My huv detected her in a shattered room behind the shooter's position. She was unarmed and crouched near a set of large, corroded access panel doors. An odd light streamed through the slit between them. She looked up and saw the tiny huv. Her first, natural impulse was fear, but then her eyes lit with wonder. She was young with expensive blonde dye coloring her hair. The shooter was close to her in visible age and naturally hued. He breathed hard and kept nervously glancing at the wall that hid him as if expecting it to explode from my return fire. Both wore higher end clothes adorned by fresh grime. I wasn't dealing with criminals, shunt addicts, or any typical street species. Weird.

I didn't have time to be curious. Fish-head was either getting farther away or doubling back for a counter-attack. The monster's brains made it dangerous. I needed to stop it before it killed again. I couldn't get a signal to Muir or anyone else. If I failed, I hoped Muir would at least call Slate, and then stop taking pay from Addison and people's ignorance and ego. I didn't know why the two nuts, here, wanted to shoot at strangers. But I had no time for new mysteries. I reached into my pocket.

The shooter heard a metal *clink!* My improvised grenade bounced close by him. *The Nap Fog Plus!* gushed freely. He fell quickly. I heard him collapse. So did fish-Head.

The beast saw an opportunity. It had cunningly waited down the passage in the dark. I wondered if it had encountered the two people here before and knew they were armed. If so, maybe it led me here to shake me off or be killed. Now the monster felt safe to go for the kill. I was glad it now thought my gun would only made it flinch. I ran in the direction of its charge between it and the man who just tried to perforate me.

Aim: manual. Heartbeat. Closing beast. Trigger. Squeeze.

Boom!

Fish-head's upper skull exploded. I got my one straight and close-up shot. The beast's jaws stayed intact. The rest of its head rippled and blew apart when the shell detonated.

The gun blast echoed in my ears and across the crush zone. A moment later, the woman approached the fallen shooter and checked his pulse.

"He'll wake up in an hour or so." I said. I picked up his battered .50cal Cyclone and slung it over my left shoulder.

"Thanks," she said. "For the monster and not killing us. I'm sorry Wally shot at you. He was trying to scare you off."

"You think maybe if I was chasing a monster, I might not have fear issues like normal people?"

"Okay. I'll make a note." She said.

"Question. What the hell are you doing here?"

Her face twisted with concern. She was unwilling to answer.

"I've had a very long day," I said and glared down at her.

She paused and looked at Wally, and then gave a resigned nod. I followed her to the metal doors with the light streamed from the slit. She reached for them, but I stepped in front. I opened the creaking metal doors and aimed my gun inside the next chamber.

"No! Please—!" she reached for me but stopped short of grabbing my arm.

On modern Earth, you might see nothing but ugly, urban nightmares trapped beneath permanent, toxic shadows. But here I saw beauty. The light radiated from a bank of clear crystals. Several were as tall as most people. They grew from a burst cable. I lowered my gun. The crystals were amazing. But they were not the strangest thing that caught my eyes. A hint of green colored spots at their base.

I put the .50cal on the floor and secured my shotgun beneath my coat. These people were misguided, but now they weren't dangerous. The woman took a slow breath of relief.

"We've been protecting them," she said.

"The crystals?" I asked.

"Of course," she replied.

"That's fine." I pointed to the green patches. "But look there. The spots of emerald aren't mineral. They're alive."

"Yeah. I thought they might be," she said.

"You were right. It's algae. Natural botanical life. It's rare to find a natural species taking a foothold. Especially in a place like this. It's amazing."

"Like that bug? I guess it's a bug." She noticed the huv in orbit.

I sent the signal for it to land in my pocket. It did and her eyes widened.

"No. That's a small robot." I said. "The algae might be part of Earth's original ecology making a comeback. If you want to protect something, protect it. You just have to decide if it's worth risking your life."

"You were willing to risk your life for ours, and Wally shot at you."

"Thankfully, not very well. I try not to take things personally."

"Must be hard with your job."

"You have no idea."

"My name is Selene," she said.

"Selene? That's appropriate."

"Why?"

"Selenite." I answered. "It's a mineral that makes crystals."

"You have one?" Selene asked. "A name?"

"Some people call me Ice."

"Ice. Crystals. I'm seeing a theme."

"Yeah." I said and broke from staring at the luminous crystals. "And I need to see a job through. That's also a theme with me."

An optical stud watched the prime target. Addison walked down a polished hall to his home door. Strangely, or not, he didn't live in Earth-hold. He did use I-DNA. He frowned when his door didn't open. He backed up and stepped back to the door. Again, nothing happened. Someone, me, had messed with the lock. He was trapped in the hallway. Worse for Addison, he heard noises coming from behind him. The noise was obviously from something bigger than he was. His face went from frustrated to frightened. He froze. The source of the noises drew closer. Perhaps he thought of the Earth-hold victims and feared sharing their fate. I hoped so.

A black-gloved hand reached out and tapped his shoulder. Addison yipped.

"Mr. Addison," Detective Sergeant John Slate said with two uniformed officers behind him. "I understand you've been keeping information from your clients, and there are liability, actually, manslaughter issues we need to discuss. You're under arrest."

21
THE GARDEN

Humans explore. The act is locked into our nature across time, ecology, and culture. Exploration often brought danger. Strange beasts attacked the curious travelers. Violence and the unknown often seemed connected. Yet humans marched on to distant horizons. Eventually, humans did not merely walk over the land. They cleared and planted small plots, and later fields. Crops fed more people. Humans were hunted less. Their numbers grew. Still, the wandering trait survived. Now, even on a planet stratified by layers of glass and steel and not fertile soil, the need to explore remains. Some think that trait should be deleted from our DNA. Altering genes has improved human life. However, careless use of such power also brought new beasts that stalk this civilization-strangled planet. When early humans explored, they faced danger. Now danger is not over a distant horizon. It strikes when you step onto the street.

Few explorers uttered the phrase "we shouldn't be here." Yet those words escaped the mouth of a young woman named Selene.

"Oh, c'mon!" Her male work-friend Davert replied. "Just humor me. I live around here!"

Selene looked around in disbelief. She and a small group had followed Davert to a corroded and cracking street away from their work district and its fairly safe towers. The latest craze in cocktails ran through their blood and brains as they crept over broken sidewalks. The street and surroundings looked like an exposed wound on an aging city block infected by entropy. Even the light appeared sick. The permanent black clouds rolled beyond weak yellow bleeding from street lamps. The old, abandoned buildings looked constructed from scabs, not concrete. The work friends had entered a crush zone. Zoning laws allowed its slow collapse to make room for a new tower. The demolition crews never came, but decay needed no work permit. Selene shook her head and wished for a respirator, and armed guards.

"Here?" Walters challenged Davert. "This place hasn't seen people since—well, maybe ever!"

"Somebody built these old hulks." Cousins said and pointed to the flanking ruins.

"Not sure it was people." Walters said, and then coughed.

"What then, monsters?" Phillips shrugged. He was taller than all his friends. Looking up at Phillips' head to see what he stared at made things seem even higher. "You think they can lay bricks?"

"What's a brick?" Walters asked.

"Dunno," Phillips replied. "It was something my dad said when talking about construction, and sometimes taking a crete."

"We should be taking a taxi." Selene said. "A fast one!"

Walters cocked his wrist to activate his com. Davert slapped it down.

"We're all safe! Where I live is hidden. The security did a sweep to clean out any vagrants and monsters. C'mon! I have a full bar at my pad. We just need to, um." Davert took a longer than casual glance at Selene. "Yeah, get there."

"We already drank a bar." Walters said. "I think Selene might—"

"Hey, Wally! Buzz. Go!" Davert steadied himself against an outer wall. His hand partially slid from the accreted dust. "*You* get a cab!"

"I don't know," Phillips said.

The group waited for Phillips' words to give final judgment. He looked up, again. The eyes of his friends followed his gaze. They all steadied each other. Davert frowned when his eyes dropped and saw Selene leaned against Walters.

"I think we'll be okay." Phillips finished and looked down at Davert. "Where' the place?"

Davert smiled. "Come on!"

Davert bolted into the eroding building through a broken door. Cousins followed him. The other three did so with greater caution. Inside was a hollowed out lobby. The building's back wall had fallen away. Its rubble lay strewn across a cavern created by a succession of collapsed structures that leaned on each other at various angles. Walters thought they looked odd, as if propped there and not pulled down by gravity.

"This place is—" Walters began.

"Yeah, damn cool!" Davert said. His words created slight echo through the artificial cavern.

A low moan and clatter of shifting debris sounded from pitch dark farther inside. The group was silent for a series of shared, quickened heartbeats.

"Probably a drunk." Davert said and licked his dusty lips with a dry tongue.

"We're the drunks!" Cousins shouted. He heard his own echo and then bolted back to the street through the hollowed lobby.

The sounds of Cousins' echo and flight died to reveal the rhythm of galloping paws against crumbling concrete. Something neared. Panic spiked heartbeats. All but Davert bolted for the street.

"No! Here! Here! Run here!" Davert yelled and motioned wildly for his three remaining friends to follow him. He turned and ran deeper into the cavern.

Philips, Selene, and Walters spun and followed. They veered around spikes of rebar and jagged edges of broken walls and erupted floors while running several meters into the cavern of toppled buildings. Harsh air and dust choked them. Phillips was the first to slow. Selene and Walters bumped his backside and the three stopped. Frantic looks across the dim, crushed area revealed no pursuer. Someone else was gone.

"Where-*cough!* Where is Davert?" Walters managed to say in hacked syllables.

"I-I want to know where we are!" Selene said and wretched.

"Geez! We're dead!" Phillips shouted. Then he screamed.

Walters and Selene looked where Phillips stared. Fiery eyes had locked onto them in the distance. Suddenly the orange eyes lurched, bopped and grew bigger. The beast was running towards them. The three bolted through scattered debris from homes and businesses that once fell out of the tilted floors of the buildings above them. Pain cut at their lungs as the chamber grew narrow. The three leapt up a foundation edge and into another building missing part of its outer façade. They ran down old office hallways and added cracks to walls as they bumped them along their flight. They slowed and stopped. The chaos of their high-pitched, shallow wheezing throttled speech as they stared at a large, locked door at the end of wide hall. A sign hung on the door by past arrogance now possibly doomed them. It read:

PRESIDENTIAL LOUNGE
RESTRICTED ACCESS
EXECUTIVE PASSES ONLY

Walters kicked the door in frustration. It swung open. The three shared a nervous, collective laugh. Selene entered the dark and once forbidden lounge. There was an awful *CRACK!* She fell.

Walters slid to the new hole and looked down to find Selene. Phillips stood by him and looked back over the hall. Below them, a dazed Selene glanced up to see Walters. He appeared as a small puppet shouting and thrusting down his tiny arm. Selene laughed. At the lounge door, Walters shouted for Selene to reach for his hand. Phillips screamed. Selene saw Walters' puppet jump and vault over the small hole above her. Phillips' seemingly tiny shoes followed. She felt drawn up to the action. Her heart and head pounded. Big, leathery claws followed her friends. She nearly screamed, but stopped on instinct.

After a stretched moment of staring up at the hole, Selene could hear nothing. No galloping monster. No running friends. She was alone. Finally, she moved. She rolled off the loose pile of stacked chairs and file cabinets she had struck. Her actions made too much noise, but Selene was still dazed. She saw a broken wall and weak light beyond it. She had fallen into a lower maintenance floor. She gathered herself and slowly crawled towards the weak light. She felt the motion of air. As awareness grew and the cocktails' effects left her system, she found herself leaning in a doorway. Opposite the door of the ravaged room was a set of hatches or metal doors. She was staring at them. White light shone through the seams, ruination, and stench. Selene thought the light was beautiful.

Finally, she noticed her pain. She slowly collapsed. She wanted to open the metal doors and see what created the blue-white light. She wanted to escape. She groaned as she pulled herself up the doorframe. She took one limping step. Something grabbed her.

"Let's go!" Walters said. "I mean, sorry, we need to be quiet. I don't know where that thing is. Phillips found a way out and called for help. I came back in to—"

Walters stopped speaking as he noticed Selene looking at him with a smile. She caressed his cheek. Walters and Selene said nothing as he helped her out.

Healing bones and skin was a simple matter for modern medicine. Automation now did most diagnosis, treatment, and, of course, the billing. Better living through programming. Rewriting genetic and machine codes were lucrative fields, as was catching people's attention to gather their cash. Advertisement remained profitable even in a world of distractions piped straight into the brain, and at times straight out. In a world of billions upon billions, a simple sign might reach untold numbers of customers. But what color should a company use for the sign and its text? The answer might come from a focus group. Now, minds linked together as collective swarms to gauge the latest marketing scheme fresh from the algorithm.

Advertising stimulus sped through these group sieves faster than the swiftest bee. Of course, bees were extinct and statistics showed the swarm-mind marketing tool was as effective as asking random people, or flipping a coin in a darkened room. Those acts were free. However, a lot of coin had been spent to develop swarm minds. The technology came with its own expanding infrastructure fees, and manufacturers assured it was the single greatest way to reach target markets. Indeed, means to advertise remained lucrative just as honestly within it remained scarce.

Selene was an honest person. That trait had value to balance swarm reactions sold by her employer, Money Comb Analytics, VLLC. The company name confused many employees who never tasted honey or knew insects once made it. For employees, information on honey was free. But if they wanted to know what bees were, they had to pay. Selling tiered information was profitable, even in house. There was no fee to ease Selene's confusion when she recalled the blue-white light in the ruin. Her mind drifted back to the sense of beauty.

There was no place to hide her distraction at work. Cubicles had given way to cylindrical integration units, or *cyls*. They encased workers' heads and linked them to swarms. Keeping a hardware link to employees' greydrives prevented any signal intercepts from competition. Other precautions stopped proprietary data becoming mRNA. Clients wanted instant impressions from swarms, not lasting memories sold to competitors or plaintiff's lawyers. Selene and her coworkers rented their brains for collective but temporary advertising analysis. Blue or red letters on a white sign? Selene had no answer.

"Is your cyl broken?" Walters asked as he passed on a break and noticed Selene staring off.

The red, holographic words STAND BY circled Selene's cyl as it dangled on its rod from the ceiling. All the coworkers of her unit sat with the squat, metal tubes encasing their skulls and awareness. Walters was disappointed his and Selene's tender moment in the ruins didn't lead to a deeper connection. Nevertheless, he enjoyed thinking of her. He recalled their real times together and events he imaged. Both were more enjoyable than linking with his law unit swarm and creating collective thoughts he could never remember.

"No. It won't interface with me." Selene answered without looking at Walters.

"Why?"

"The OS lists my meta-conscience as distracted." Selene sighed. "My quantalysis is flawed because of, yeah, distraction."

"Punch out and lax," Walters said. "I could join—"

"I keep thinking about that night." Selene blurted.

Walters drew a breath as he also recalled that night. His eyes drifted off Selene. "Yeah. It was a wild time. Cousins made it back, but we've never seen Davert again. No one filed a life claim, though. I guess he just transferred. Or quit. Weird, though. You think he really had a place around there?"

Selene was lost in her own recall.

"I have nightmares," Walters went on. "Or I would have nightmares, but I take Deep Doze. Hey, weren't you in the ana-cyls for that?"

"Yeah. I think so." Selene answered, blankly. "It's hard to remember."

"Right. Contractually." Walters nodded.

"But not that night." Selene snapped her eyes at Walters.

"No. I'm glad we found you and escaped. We almost—"

"I want to go back." Selene said with keen focus on Walters.

"What? That's crazy!" Walters yipped on instinct. "I mean—sorry! We can get a neural calibrant to tweak your—"

"I'm not crazy, Wally. I saw something."

"We all did. We ran from it!"

"No. I saw something else. It was beautiful. Light."

"Beautiful?" Walters said as if the concept itself was alien. "In that place? I can see why you're not linking. Your mind is—"

"I'm going back. I want to see it. All of it."

Walters paused and looked at Selene who stared at him without blinking.

"Um, all of what?"

Walters didn't think he'd get—or even truly want to get—the answer in person. Yet, he followed Selene back to where Davert had taken them. He didn't need quantitative analytics or to rent a collective mind to realize he was now crazy. Walters was not alone in the insanity. Phillips also rejoined them. However, Cousins became violently angry when asked to come along. The other three politely listened to his tirade. They knew he was not wrong in his high-pitched and negative assessment of their plan, just overly dramatic. Singh had taken a break from his cyl and heard the shouting. He joined Selene's expedition in Cousins' place. Liabilities and insurance fees then swirled in Walters' head. They sank beneath the fear of literally losing his head. That became a possibility with each step away from their work tower. At least this time they had respirators. Walters wished he could filter the intensifying memories of flaming eyes chasing him. He flipped the eyepiece of his newly purchased FRACDAR halo over his right eye. He hoped the scanner's landscape graphics were true, especially if they had to run. The advertising promised it would be. Mentally, he sighed.

Selene led them to the crush zone. She was the first through the broken door, decrepit building, and into the cavern. It seemed somehow still. Selene knew it was because no one spoke, and their steps were softer without intoxication. She paused and affixed her own broad-range scanner to the mask of her respirator. It was older tech than Walters' halo, but her also revealed body heat. Anything big with fiery eyes should have body heat. That seemed logical. She knew risking lives on this quest was not logical. She took a breath of filtered air and trekked on.

Inside the office building ruin, Selene opted not to repeat her fall. She found a stairwell. They descended to the maintenance level where she saw the light. Glances and nods conveyed the idea to step lightly on the metal stairs to avoid echoes waking hunger.

Slowly they entered the hallway through a rusted access door. There was a blue-white haze. Once inside the hall, Selene sped up. She switched off her scanning tech and walked straight to the room with the metal access hatches. The light seemed brighter. A decal on the left, metal door still held the outline of the words:

ACCESS CHAMBER NO. 20-A
SERVER AND POWER NODE
QUAD. 42

Selene paid no attention to it. She grabbed the handles near the broken lock and tugged the doors open. The others flinched at the metallic creaks and moans. Selene let momentum carry the doors to the sides. She saw her mystery revealed. The blue-white light bathed her with full intensity. She kept her eyes opened wide to stare at the revelation. She was not disappointed. The doors had sealed a deep access chamber for ancient power lines and information cables. The heavy bundle of tubes and cables parted where the light source rose out. The radiance came from clear, crystal monoliths as large as a tall human. They stood as if waiting for a living audience. Smaller spires and prisms surrounded the thick, rectangular crystals. The radiance almost seemed to make a constant, low sound. Staccato gasps and heavy breathing echoed from inside respirators. Selene slid her mask off and knelt before her glowing answer. Naturally, it brought greater mystery.

"What are—" Walters began. He, Singh, and Phillips stood behind the kneeling Selene. "Are they alive?"

"You mean like a monster?" Phillips asked.

"No!" Walters switched off his FRACDAR. "Like a—like a life!"

"A plant?" Singh offered.

"They're crystals." Selene said. "I think maybe they're geologic."

"It that contagious?" Phillips asked.

"Contagious?" came as a unified reply.

"They're more like rocks than a virus," Selene said.

"How could a rock give you a disease?" Walters added.

"How can a big lizard freak with orange eyes exist?" Phillips countered.

"That's easier to believe." Singh replied.

"Well, yeah." Walters nodded.

"These aren't any freaks," Selene said as she continued to stare at the massive, luminous crystals. "Look at them! They're beautiful."

"Yeah. Point taken." Walters agreed. "I've never seen anything like them."

"Can we break one off and take it back?" Singh asked.

Phillips walked from behind Selene and tugged at one of the smaller spires. It didn't budge. "Nope."

Selene stood and slapped Phillips' long arm. He shrugged.

"Okay. Uh, we found them. They're cool." Singh looked back across the decrepit, shadowed room that led to the crystal's chamber. "Now maybe—"

"Where is the light coming from?" Walters said and drew closer to the crystals.

"Their making it." Selene said and gently touched the large crystal closest to her.

"How?" Walters asked.

"I don't know. But they are. It's coming from them." Selene offered.

"Maybe it's a new way to make torches without power." Phillips bent down for a closer look under Selene's stern gaze.

"We could pitch that for a swarm!" Singh chirped.

"And then what?" Selene asked. "Have them broken apart for pocket flashlights?"

"Hey, if it's market viable—" Singh began but stopped when confronted by Selene's naked face and cold stare.

"Hey, this is a find! We can monetize it. We can all—"

"Shut up, Singh!" Walters added to the emotional chill.

Singh shook his head and left.

"We need to keep this quiet." Selene said looking where Singh had left. "This—these crystals are unique!"

Both Selene and Walters stared at Phillips.

"Yeah, okay." Phillips adjusted his respirator. "I get it. It's our secret. Wouldn't want to get sued by people trying to find them, anyway."

Singh grunted curses to himself behind his plastic mask as he walked down the hall and deeper into the building. Most of the walls had partially collapsed. Skeletons of metal framing held up the fragments. He tripped and stumbled to his knees. His eyes met another pair on the floor in a doorway. Decomposition clouded them. The sunken features were still intact. Singh had found the missing Davert. His face was still recognizable. So was his last expression of terror.

Selene and the others heard Singh's scream. They bolted from the crystals. Singh nearly knocked them over as he ran down the hall. He forgot the turn to the stairwell and kept going. The others rushed after him. They caught up with him and saved his life. Singh had slid and then teetered on the edge of a cliff. The crush zone was well named. The crystal's building sat on several buried city layers. Beyond the end of the hall, those layers had collapsed. The slow implosion had formed an underground valley. The sky over it was a cap of broken building sides and the bottoms of buried streets. A sneeze could destroy it all, or it could last another millennia. Still, everyone controlled their breathing to ease vibrations and not tempt gravity.

"I guess the liability would be a bitch to mine anything, here." Singh panted.

Selene resisted the urge to release her grip. Back inside the building ruin, she took one more, long look at her crystals before they left. She closed the hatches to the crystal chamber and hoped the crew that would come and recover Davert's body was not very curious. She followed the others out. They were eager to flee, but Selene knew she would come back.

Fear ebbs with time. In contrast, mysteries gain strength. It was not long before others wanted to join Selene and return to the crystals to fathom their origin. Walters said he was willing to follow Selene back anytime. Phillips had decided he also wanted to return. He agreed with Walters who suggested they buy weapons before their next trek. For the concerned pedestrian, and people foolish enough to penetrate crush zones, there was a wide variety of gadgets to throw in the face of your attacker. Most were designed for human-sized predators. Many deployed gasses, noises, light, spikes, acids, more toxic emissions, and/or a mix of them all. Customers needed to sign a release before placing these devices in their pockets. These *caveat emptor* or die products mostly distracted attackers to allow victims to run. Selene saved them all money by pointing out that nothing they could legally buy would kill what they saw, and/or what ate most of Davert. Besides, with no formal training, they might forget what part of the gun the bullets shot from and kill each other before hitting anything that wanted to kill them. The three would return armed only with luck. Singh stayed away. A corpse and a brush with death were enough adventure and horror for his lifetime. For the others, there was more to come.

Philips and Walters ventured with Selene to the brilliant crystals. They became more comfortable in the dank but still coarse air without their respirators, but stifled their coughs. The bright chamber seemed peaceful and separate from the rest of the shattered and brutal world. Walters and Philips strayed down the hall. Sudden gunshots startled both men. The next sound terrified them. That sound was dreadfully familiar. Leathery claws in full gallop. The monster was back. It was coming this way.

Walters dove into the crystal chamber to warn Selene as Phillips stared with terror down the hall.

"Selene!" Walters screeched. "It's that thing. The thing that ate Davert! It's coming!"

"I heard someone shooting!" Selene yelled. "Maybe a Killer!"

"Yeah, and they may kill us by accident." Walters grabbed Selene's shoulders. "We're trespassing!"

"No we're not!" Selene glanced at the glowing crystals.

"Selene—!"

"I'm not leaving, Wally!" Selene pushed Walters back.

"Crap!" Walters yelled.

Phillips shouted into the room. "Look maybe we can— *AIYIHHHH!*"

The monster pounced on Phillips and flattened him against the old, battered floor. Its fiery eyes regarded its human prey. The monster stopped its attack in a moment of confusion over killing and eating its catch, or needing to turn and fight its pursuer. Or simply run. It released Phillips to turn and fight. One if its fiery eyes and quarter of its skull blew apart. It spun and slashed its razor-edged tail. The next shots cut the tail in half. The monster bolted, but was off balance. The next burst perforated its abdomen and ravaged its inner organs. It kept trotting forward until the reality of its death caught up to the surviving parts of its brain. It fell dead. Still, the Monster Killer fired several more rounds that convulsed the monstrous corpse.

"You think, uh, maybe you could stop now?" Walters stumbled to where Phillips was still flat on the floor. Both held their hands to their ears, but they already rang as loud as the Monster Killer's semi-automatic artillery. She looked at Walters with contempt and shrugged. She slung her hot weapon nearly as large as her body across her back.

"And you're welcome." The Killer's voice was a cutting as her appearance. A thin, blonde Mohawk laced with wire swept over her scalp at a right angle to the black-band tattoo across her temples and eyes. She slid her goggles up between them.

"Yeah. Thanks." Phillips said while still pressed flat on the floor.

"You're a Killer?" Walters asked.

"Bandi Thera. Professional Aberration Control Agent. Or something like that." She answered.

"Uh, yeah." Walters nodded as he read near instantly reported data on his wrist-com after a search triggered by Bandi's answer. "You're listed in the red pages. But they list your license as *provisional.*"

"I may be new and need a few bells and whistles," Bandi shrugged and then glared at Phillips. "But I just saved his jacked-up ass."

"Yeah. Yeah, thanks." Phillips repeated as he finally peeled himself from the floor.

"Are you punks squatters?" Bandi asked with suspicious looks over the three friends. "You look rich. Nice clothes. Why are you here? Orgy?"

"No!" Selene snapped.

"My mistake. But if you're—the light." Bandi focused on the room behind Selene. "That's weirder than you punks stinking up this place."

"It's not—!" Selene began.

Bandi pushed passed her with speed.

"Whoa! Freak-ish!" Bandi said as she saw the luminous crystals

"They're just crystals!" Selene exclaimed behind her.

"Yeah. They're crystals." Bandi said as she drew her weapon forward. "What else are they?"

"What do you mean?" Selene demanded.

"I mean there's all sorts of life above and below the streets you wouldn't believe."

"You think they're alive?" Walters asked as he and Phillips entered.

"If they are, they aren't natural. If they aren't natural—!" Bandi leveled her gun at the bank of huge crystals. The strap fell forward and dangled.

"No! Don't kill them!" Selene jumped next to Bandi.

"Kill? Blondie it's what I do."

"No!" Selene screamed and grabbed for Bandi. She found herself with a strong pain in her right side and on the ground.

"Back off snow-white!" Bandi yelled and repositioned herself to flank all three friends.

"Hey! Just stop! Just leave!" Walters shouted and knelt beside the grimacing Selene.

Phillips stood in front of his friends as a shield with his arms held out. His heart raced when he saw the gun muzzle pointed at him, but he managed to look down at Bandi with a cold stare.

"This is the easiest bounty I've had all year!" Bandi yelled "And it just sits there and waits for it. Now back away and cover your ears!"

Walters helped Selene stand and they joined Phillips in front of the crystals. Bandi backed toward the doorway, but aimed her gun at the three friends.

"Kids, go home! Now! My license—!" Bandi made a scream with rending lungs.

All the others saw was a glimpse of teeth like butcher blades before a wave of red and its spatter across the wall.

Bandi's gun made a loud *CLANK!* on the floor. She was gone. A thing she might have hunted instead found her from behind and made her the prey. An extra bell or whistle might have warned her. The three were silent. A sudden thought hit Phillips: that thing might come back. He stumbled back and into the stunned Walters and Selene. All interlocked arms to steady themselves as a group. Each could feel the others pounding hearts from their pulses throbbing through their limbs. Their breaths eased collectively. Phillips height allowed him to look over Selene and Walters at the crystals.

"Selene," Phillips breathed. "These are amazing, but they aren't worth our lives!"

Selene looked away from the doorway and up to Phillips.

"Maybe they are," Selene released her friends and turned to the beaming prisms. "Maybe they are worth the risk, if it's spent protecting them. They're unique."

"So far as we know," Phillips countered.

"There is nothing like them!" Selene threw up her hands. "Do the search yourself! Nothing pops up. Nothing!"

"Okay. But I'm unique, too. And I think I'm worth more than these glowing slabs." Phillips stepped back from Selene and Walters. "And I want to go home."

Walters picked up Bandi's gun. He looked at it and his two friends. "Yeah. Selene, I think we should go. For now."

Guilt. All three felt guilt after they said nothing of Bandi Thera's death. Their tip about Davert proved the word *anonymous* now meant easily revealed. They encoded an infomere with the location of Davert's corpse assuming it would also alert police to the monster that killed him. Walters dropped the infomere in a public restroom. The janitor who found it naturally opened the data. That act of curiosity dispersed the tip into the dataverse for police algorithms to find. The janitor later said the police kept him for three days before forensic techs confirmed he had not killed and partially eaten Davert. His teeth were too small.

Walters also felt guilt over keeping Bandi's weapon. It was a cut-down Rosen .50-cal. Cyclone. The cut down was not the shortened barrel or filed-off serial numbers. It was the lobotomized operating system that deleted its imprint lock and tracking features. Perhaps Bandi Thera had used the weapon for more than killing monsters. Walters kept it to protect them from the things that ate people, and from less scrupulous sorts that hunted them.

Walters propped the gun against the cracked wall as he and Selene once again visited the luminous crystals.

"We still don't know how they got here," Selene said. Her face held a slight smile. After all that had occurred, she still thought the massive crystals were beautiful.

"We need to start planning," Walters said. "More people, more killers, monster and human will come. We need to do something other than just staring and maybe dying."

Selene was quiet for a moment. "I know. We need a plan."

"And another place." Walters added.

"Place?" Selene considered the idea, the past incidents, and their luck to live through them. "Yeah. A new place. If we can move them."

"And if we can't?" Walters picked up the gun. It was heavy and looked odd in his hands. But he was suddenly glad that he held it.

Both he and Selene felt the new presence. A sudden spike of terror cooled into the realization that recent noises were not merely shifting rubble. They were the sounds of a monster in the hall. It was looking right at them. It had fresh wounds. One creased its skull. It almost looked to be panting through its massive mouth of cleavers. But it was no dog. It was more like an armored fish with legs. Huge, black eyes regarded the two friends with the rudiments of curiosity. Humans and monster spent a tortured eternity locked in staring that was truly a fraction of a second. Their collective experience ended with Walters and Selene's horrified screams, then the deafening gun blasts as Walters fired.

The fish-headed beast was fast, as if it sensed the coming gunfire. It bolted. The shells blasted the wall and hallway. Walters bolted after the beast. It was not the only intruder. A man larger than Phillips climbed up from the cliff where Singh nearly fell. He was armed. Walters thought he must also be a Killer like Bandi. He didn't know the name Joshua Grail or his reputation. He only recalled that Bandi Thera had threatened to shoot them. Walters opened fire.

Walters was too slow again, and the recoil was very strong. Grail rolled away from the errant shots.

"The monster is gone! Now you go! Get out!" Walters yelled.

Walters heard Grail shout back. "I am here to help! Put down your gun or get shot!"

"Help us by leaving!" Selene called out after closing the metal doors to hide the crystals. Then she saw a small dot fly into the room like something with a mind. It was weird, but another wonder in this crush zone.

There was a sudden metal *clink!* A small aerosol can bounced near Walters. He saw the labeling for *The Nap Fog, Plus!* before involuntary sleep overtook him. He fell. The monster took the advantage and charged. So did Grail. He ran between the beast and Walters. Grail fired, point blank. Selene grabbed her ears and flexed her whole body at the blast. The report echoed across the crush zone. Selene took in a deep breath of the dust-laden air. She fought back a cough as she stood and then walked over to Walters to check his pulse.

"He'll wake up in an hour or so." Grail said.

Walters had inhaled less than Grail had estimated. He awoke sooner. He wished he had stayed asleep. His eyes focused on the corpse of the once fish-headed beast. Somehow its jaws were intact. Walters recoiled from the shattered tissues behind the cleaver-like teeth. He heard people speaking. One was Selene. The other voice was deeper than Phillips' voice.

The Killer!

Walters bolted up. He looked for the gun. It was missing. He rushed to the voices inside the crystal chamber. Walters hit a wall. The wall wore a heavy canvas overcoat. He recognized the coat from the Killer he had shot at. He felt shot at without bullets when he looked up into Grail's harsh stare.

Grail looked down at Walters and spoke. "I'm leaving, but I'm coming back. If you shoot at me, I'll shove your head up your ass. It's a well-developed skill I have."

Walters only stared at Grail with a dropped jaw. He tasted the foul air as Grail left the ruins.

"Well, Wally." Selene reached over and closed Walters' mouth. "He did leave the gun, but are you going to shoot at him again?"

"No! No, I'm not."

Walters waited with the gun. He expected Grail to return the same way he came. He stood cautiously near cliff and overlooked the vista of the ruins below. He mentally repeated the advice on controlling the weapon given him by Selene. She received brief instructions from Grail. Selene called him Ice. His listings affirmed a stellar reputation and recommendation by the police. That only made him scarier. Still, Walters wanted to look like he owned the gun when Grail returned. Not that he would ever shoot at Grail again. No. No, he would not.

Walters thought of Selene and decided to go look at her rather than shattered remains of past ages. He turned, and bumped into a wall. He stepped back from Grail.

"I want to talk to you and Selene," Grail said.

Walters nodded with enthusiasm. Grail stared.

They joined Selene inside the chamber. She sat on the floor and didn't gaze at the radiant crystals. She was lost in thoughts of what to do next.

"You two have been lucky," Grail said. "So were your friends. Most of them."

"Friends?" Walters asked and gave a nervous glance to Selene as she stood.

"My scans show at least five people have been here recently," Grail said. "Their traces are fresh. Two line up with recently reported deaths."

Selene and Walters said nothing. They locked their eyes and kept looking at each other as if their linked stares could generate a reply.

"Yeah. I see you understand you made some bad choices." Grail said.

"Okay. Agreed." Walters blinked, and then looked at Grail. "But, we never wanted people to die. We just wanted to save the crystals."

"We can't change the past," Selene added. "We—"

"You can do something for a better future." Grail interjected. "The crystals are interesting. But they're not alive. Close by is a massive communications conduit. The crystals grow from a fraction of the lines tied through this complex a long time ago. The crystals are buds from hyperoptic lines of smart matter that lost their programmed state. Originally they conducted data. They're still photophilic, but once the filaments lost their imposed phase, they joined to form larger crystals. They broke through their sheaths and kept going. When the maintenance crews are away, the tech still plays. But by its own rules."

"You mean they're kind of a—a solid leak?" Walters asked and his face wrinkled.

"Something like that. The crystalline filaments bonded, popped out, and grew. Eventually, they made big crystals. But they aren't why I'm back. The crystals gave light and provided a substrate for some ancient spores. But this chamber likely became a harbor for life when you came here. Your breath, its moisture, maybe even slight nutrients from your touch, it all created a small ecology. I want to preserve the real find here. The algae."

"The what?" Walters' face wrinkled tighter.

"It's a plant, the green stuff." Selene answered. "It's alive."

"Is it contagious?" Walter jumped back from the crystals.

Grail reached over and took the gun from Walters.

"No matter how you found this place, you kept coming here out of wonder and hope." Grail said. "I think, at least one of you, can help me with a task. It will take some of your time, but it will be safer than coming here."

"What's the job?" Selene asked.

"I want you to be gardeners," Grail answered.

The metal door slid open. Grail entered a hidden dome close to his residence. Light beamed from amplified photophores covering the walls. Selene and Walters were the only other humans to see his greenhouse. Their eyes needed to adjust to the brightness of a typical, sunny day from a time long over. Through their blinks they saw plants in pots made from cable housings and ammo cans. Shrubs sported buds near to blooming. A few tree specimens grew from samples stolen from an immortal enclave's odd entry lobby. A dandelion sat cocked to the side of a patch of wheat in one tub. Most were plants formerly preserved only as genetic sequences in two-dimensional archives. Here they lived in all dimensions. It was a labor to maintain them, and some plants looked slightly unloved.

"It's a safe place," Grail said. "At least as safe as I can make it."

"Things look a little shabby." Walters said.

"It's beautiful," Selene said. She ran her hands through a shrub. The textures of rough stems and subtle leaves were new sensations to her. She smiled and took in a deep breath without coughing.

"I don't have the time to tend it like I should." Grail said. "But maybe with help, this can be a real garden."

"I know they're not alive, but can we bring in some of the crystals?" Selene asked. She looked at Grail with a smile as bright as the light from the walls. She was happy.

"Yeah," Grail said. The hint of a smile threatened to crack his stony face. "They're cool, too. And, in advance, thank you."

22
THE TOWER AND THE PIT

"Is he dead?"

I heard a familiar, deep voice from several steps away through the constant city drone. The detective who spoke stood across the street with a young woman. The ambient glow of aged lights gave weak illumination. It was night on clocks, but without some form of lamp it's always dark. Modern Earth lost its views of blue skies and stars to permanent black clouds, long ago. That was after a city ate the planet's surface and weird things emerged that ate people. Fire had recently tried to consume me. I was little more than a ball of burned, cracking skin. It had been a bad day.

Buildings towered around us, but one lay in ruins behind me. It was what I guarded. Occasionally, flashlight beams swept over me. Light glinted off my last sidearm. My charred hand still gripped it hard. I knew the detective was John Slate. He's as close to a friend as a person like me can have. For a time the woman seemed to be like a friend. But now I knelt on the street, burned, bleeding, and alone.

"Did you try and help Grail?" Slate asked the woman with the tone of accusation as he put on a protective suit. Smart guy, Slate.

"That's his name?" she asked.

"Yeah. Did you?"

"Yeah," The woman replied. "A bunch of us did. But after a while, they left. They got scared. I got kind of scared, too. But I stayed over here to watch him."

"Nothing fun on the screens or at home?" Slate asked as he sealed his suit up to his face.

I couldn't see them well, but I'm sure the woman gave Slate a look worse than an expletive.

"Look, I stayed!" she barked. "But he said to get away from the ruins. So I did."

"Smart lady," Slate said, now with an assuring tone. "I'll go talk to him."

"You're not scared?" The woman asked.

"Of him? Maybe." Slate answered. "But I know him. Of what he's guarding, for sure."

"What is it?" she asked.

"No clue, yet. But Ice—the stoic Mr. Grail, there. He likes to keep moving. So if he's ready to drop but still on a job site, you should probably start moving away from here. And don't stop."

Slate came towards me. I tried to stand. My wounds had already started healing, but not enough. I just kept my bulk in a crouch and waited for him. I thought of the hours before then. I hoped I hadn't waited too long.

Before I waited for Slate, I was healthy. My day started with a death. Normal for me. But this one didn't involve me and was broadcast to the world. The man might have been famous. A politician or a media star. Or just someone rich. The man's image was ten times life size. The building's huge media screen projected a holographic colossus of a person of ambiguous magnitude. I didn't catch his name beamed in bright letters high above a busy street. Distraction could get me killed. And not by the lousy drivers of low hover and other cars. Maybe that's how the notable death occurred. Distraction and a misstep. The death was the news more than who died. Death is close to being an option for many in the floors risen above street level. The towers encasing their lives are hardened, geometric designs that carve the sky below the dark clouds into slots and straight channels. Earth is now a world of right angles and rigid layers.

The ground-level streets of the global city are my world. The dead man on the news knew another. He knew safety and medical technology that can extend life to however long you can afford to mortgage your own cells. A big enough payout gives you immortality. Yet, somehow, death got him. So that's the news. Not the person's life history, bad habits, and grand accomplishments. It's the fact he had it all and still died.

Death and taxes are what you face on the street. If they intruded into the upper levels of the towers, it's news. Information is broadcast to the streets as a public service, but the effect might be different from intended. The culture down here likes to know what goes on up there if it shows a similar reality reached up the secured elevator shafts. Equality doesn't exist. So the unexpected death granted a small sense of justice, or projected vengeance. The brightly flashed obituary ended. Then a commercial began. For a health service no one on the street could afford. Smiles aimed at the bright screen sagged. The collective moment of spiteful joy died. Existence went on.

I never stopped walking. Being on foot is the best approach when I'm close to my target. It's quieter. I'm surprisingly stealthy for a large, human male. The skill is well learned and the tuition was painful. The weapons under my coat are not quiet when I use them. They are loud and flash like guns from past ages. But mine are used for real public service. I try to stop unexpected death by killing what preys on human life.

No one would broadcast or even write my obituary. Some people still read. The people who still appreciate a well-crafted sentence may be in the multiple billions. That's a big number, but a small percentage of Earth's population. The high mortality rate of Monster Killers is also why no one would read my obituary. Too typical. And that's fine. All my history would be lies. My present is focused on stalking horrors. It's my niche in the current cycle of life. There are many more Killers in the global city. The government issues licenses all the time. Mostly because many Killers are eaten by what they hunt. In an odd way, that's job security. For the job.

Security is also access to power. Electrical power is rationed sideways in some zones. I walked through one. Here, power radiates from a commercial hub. Transmission is restricted in areas where people can afford to look down and don't want to see anyone looking up. Although my services benefit everyone. I turned a corner. The area was still lit by the huge media screen. Its flashes of light reflected off an ancient, masonry facade with steel plates in place of windows. Old, ground level storefronts defied the darkness with archaic lights and signs. None had holographic signage. Pocked pixel screens displayed a typical stream of ads. Food. Or its substitute. Sex. Drugs. Their media substitutes. Hens teeth. And fish.

Fish?

Downstream the lights were weaker and the people far fewer. Life looked threatened by the shadows stretching from dark spots and alleys. The shadows had their own problems. Flashed images on battered neode and LEQ signs beat them back. But on the next block it got even darker. There was little power for commerce and comfort in this zone. Electricity was segregated. Pirate lines likely stole the available power, even for the street lamps. Greater power rose away from the street. Now, I looked up.

Once, the building across from me was a major skyscraper. Now it sat dwarfed by what dominated the region. Straight ahead stood a titanic monolith of artificial diamond and sky-beams fused into a seamless brick shape so vast it created a hemispheric wall of the global maze. The structure was not truly a hemisphere wide, but big enough to swallow all epic structures from past ages and a several recent ones. Its foundation lay deep in the planet's crust. Its smooth body pierced the dark clouds overhead. Other towers at perpendicular angles also cut into the cloud deck, but the massive super-tower was a greater triumph of the ascent of mass pushed beyond the sky. Better than ever, humanity could build huge.

So, of course, that great place was not where I headed. I was privileged to push into the ruins littering the super-tower's eastern zone. It stunk. The target location had a strong odor like offal. Fallen facade and debris lay piled against the front wall. The reports noted screams came from inside. No monster ever just walks out into the street for convenience. I'd have to dig. An old, city schematic displayed across my retina by a few off-the-book enhancements showed where the main entrance once existed. I put my large, right hand to work. Quietly. At least as quiet as possible. My left hand held my gun handle.

The excavation went slowly. Someone or something had shifted the debris. So far, all indications were human. Some fresh. They were probably fresh food, by now. I was supposed to meet with municipal engineers, but I ditched their calls. Some rule probably stated that firearm discharge near a super-tower's foundation required an engineering inspection. The damage would likely be mine from the ricochet. How about the engineer inspect the jaws of the thing I'm going to shoot? If she or he met the beast, I'd have to detail how a well-paid city employee became ripped chunks and a stain. Better the thing become the stain. Fewer forms to sign.

The ruin was an apartment or a hotel. I pushed aside a collapsed entryway roof and found the front door in a hole. This place had died and been partially buried sometime before yesterday. I fully drew my shotgun from beneath my coat. The term *shotgun* describes the weapon's appearance. No actual shot flew from the muzzle or spent casings from the side. The propellant and projectile is one caseless round. Each round is a small, spin-stabilized, depth-sensing warhead with an armor-piercing core around sections of sequentially detonated explosives. The weapon's designer probably asked a Killer what he or she needed in the field. Something that kills anything was the likely answer. I have large handguns that fire the same rounds. They kick a little more.

I dropped down and pushed through debris in front of the gilded, double doorframes. Their glass lay shattered into clear, jagged pebbles. I could hear them crush under my boots as I forced my way in, muzzle first. Optical graphics supplemented my vision. It replaced the total darkness. The imaging relayed shapes, information, and more data from my gun's scanners. I entered a wide lobby with a curving reception counter, office doors, and other rooms along the curving walls. No motion. I placed my first *breadcrumb*. That's my term for the small, square packet that will emit light if my scanners failed and kept another, nastier surprise.

I found a different hint of nasty on the floor: blood and tissues. Human. The pattern led me to crushed elevator doors. There were scales and secretions that were not human. The scaly fragments were similar in structure to lengths split off from massive hairs. The elevator car had jagged sides at the bottom and no floor. I took the stairs. I placed another breadcrumb at the stairwell entrance. The stair flights seemed to ripple the stench rolling up from below. If life above the streets was a sort of heaven, then existence below the streets was near certain hell. But that would suggest it's a place worse than the streets. I didn't think it was. It just smelled worse. If you smell what I do in a typical day, that's saying a lot.

I placed breadcrumbs along the stair flights and landings. I put on a respirator to cut the wafting funk. Maybe the world is dead below the scab of the city and this is the stink from its corpse. In the streets, I used a respirator mostly for show. I also have biological alterations to make the job survivable and keep me immune to most pathogens on this cloud-sealed world. I advertise my services, but not my personal improvements. I'd hate to be tagged as something like what I hunt. The effect would go beyond me. A human-shaped monster would crush humanity's psychological prop of being Earth's master. Truthfully, that's now only a joke.

Today's jokes have a sharp edge. Be a clown and the world will love you. Kill a clown and they'll love you more. Luckily for people who used white and colorful makeup, or just had extreme tattoos, I don't kill clowns. Not that often. If I found one hiding down here, no one will know. Oh, I joked with myself. I would not shoot a clown in cold blood. They are brightly colored, and more useful as bait.

I would not need one. At the next landing, the stairwell door was missing. So was most of the wall around the area of the doorframe. The jagged pattern was the same as the elevator car's ripped-away bottom. Inside the hall, several talon points had punctured the walls and ceiling as if a huge-caliber machine gun had opened fire. The talons had ripped old fixtures and decor from the walls. The ripper was just a sprint down the hallway.

Bingo.

A mass of spines pulsed in waves as the creature turned. The best comparison to extinct life was a porcupine. A giant, red porcupine. But the monstrous, turning mass had no legs. It used enormous quills for locomotion. The puncture and pull of each spike on the wall and ceiling sounded as if a small avalanche had broken free. As it rolled around to face me, the undulating spikes looked more like giant centipede legs crushed into a ball while still writhing. I'd have preferred a centipede's head. Instead, a think, bear-like skull with a centered, heat-sensing pit in place of any eyes faced me. It opened its wide jaws. More red quills flexed inside them. All the better for pulling in and ripping apart the prey, or the person. There were still pieces of a victim wedged between the flexing spikes. The beast needed to floss. It would need steel cable for the job. But it thought I was another meal. The thing charged. It was a bulky, spiky freak that was still very fast. I hated that.

My shotgun was already aimed. I squeezed the trigger. To avoid sensory overload, the scans switched off in the fraction of a second before the blast. The fired round hit the monster's skull, dead center. Its heat pit and upper-head shattered from the round's impact. The light from the blast vanished. I only saw the dimming after-imaged from the blast before the sensors flicked back on.

That occurred in the same fraction of a second when the round penetrated and then detonated inside the beast. The explosion lit its frontal quills like an inner strobe pulse. Most of its organs were shredded. The thing convulsed and fell dead. I waited for the rest of the second to tick off before I lowered my gun.

Somewhere under the spines was a muscular body that sagged as a deflated balloon. Just looking at the thing caused me to feel cut. I was glad no one would face it again. Then the thing rolled back to standing. The blood flowed over the remaining bottom of its head and through the tooth spines. Scans showed the spatter across the pocked walls and my coat was its brain tissue. Yet its quills quivered as if shaking off the lethal gunshot. Even for a monster, that was impossible. All monsters were tough. Unique. Nevertheless, they were animals like all predators before. Albeit it twisted mutations and sewer-spawned nightmares. They were still living things. Blow apart a living thing and it dies. This thing was dead. Its corpse was a traumatized sack. Yet it moving.

The quivering was something else animating its shattered corpse. Something was already inside it, infecting it. Death had unleashed another kind of monster. Even after what I've seen, that was horrific news. I backed up with gun leveled. An amplified scan revealed some viscous protein spreading rapidly through the body. It acted like a separate, invading blood plasma. It reproduced rapidly in the creature's tissues and kept spreading. I'd tap my science knowledge and figure out the infection, later. Right then the thing tensed for a charge. I opened fire.

The blast concussions hammered and cracked the damaged halls. I would shoot the legs to stop it charging—if it had legs. In place of targeted carnage, I fired on the charging mass of spikes. And kept shooting. Each round hit, detonated, and blasted off chunks of meat, bone, and spikes. I reached for a handgun as the shotgun magazine emptied. The beast's exposed hips and vestigial leg bones blew apart with the final round. The moving pieces now were small enough to call myself safe from the reanimated beast. I could feel my augmented immune system fight off the strange, viscous protein that had spread through the beast and spattered me. This inner battle made me feel sick. Near my wet boot, a chunk of muscle flexed a fractured quill in a circular arc in blood on the floor. I looked over the twitching chunks and realized the bigger, darker, and apocalyptic picture.

I switched to full analyzing mode. The reanimating plasma was the altered structure of a viral plasmid. The infecting agent was a new, advanced virus. In science classes of yore, a virus, however complex, was not considered alive. One reason was a lack of motility. A virus in any form could not move. Nor was it dead. They held a zombie-like state. Viruses infected living cells as reprogrammed factories to reproduce. The new infectors, called virions, burst from infected cells to go forth and multiply more. If a host's immune system didn't adapt to fight and destroy the virus, it could wipe out whole species.

Here, a virus adapted to using the dead. No defense. Just tissue to rewrite. The virus reanimates the corpse. It becomes a large virion spewer to shamble into other dead things. Soon a mass of moving, dead flesh would attack and kill the living so more could join the party. And the disease itself could kill. No normal human could fight off this infection.

The way a species can endure a disease is to make new, resistant generations. To do that, modern humanity would need to undo an earlier fix to the rampant population. We can fornicate forever with no children to show for it. Unless you pay a fee. Reproduction is like the electricity bill. Pay and get power. Otherwise, it's a switch controlled and owned by others. A natural function reduced to a regulated utility. Water is free. It's what delivers the reproduction inhibitor. There would be no way to shut the valve on the inhibitors before the zombie disease had infected Earth.

I hoped this viral mutation and outbreak was local. If it spread, it would infect the people on the street, and not stop. In a world of billions stacked on billions and many billions upon billions more unseen, the plague will cause a scale of carnage more vast than any global apocalypse ever experienced or imagined.

I thought: I'm one person.

I thought: I need to act.

Joshua Grail's obit would never reveal that once I was a physician. Of sorts. Now, the world was my patient. Right. I knew thoughts like that would make me need a psychiatrist. Or a clown. No. I just needed to act. Period. My com-system should have penetrated the ruin, but a jamming frequency blocked all signals. No doubt the super-tower broadcast the jam to discourage squatters. Now the towers residents might be discouraging their own future. I needed to stay here. If I left to get help, I might lose the trail. I needed to find the source that infected the monster. I had only a vague idea of how big and deep this buried ruin could be. I placed another breadcrumb, and pressed deeper into the stench and blackness. If I couldn't get data to stop this zombie plague, Earth would become a planet-sized monster. And dead. No pressure.

I was glad I had ditched the engineer crew and could do this alone. I was mad when I heard human voices before I saw the beams of their headlamps slashing the darkness of a lower hallway. Another distraction. I didn't need three lives to protect. All male. Each the standard mix of global ancestry. All of standard size and likely terrified inside standard-issue gray coveralls and equipment packs. One held an assault rifle, but the way he aimed it showed he was as afraid of it as what could be stalking them. And stalking them was easy with their high-pitched, frightened speech and lamps. They all literally took one step forward and three steps back.

The city engineers had found another entrance, but I wondered how they got passed the big, red porcupine. Then I saw one of them carrying another person's torn pack. DNA traces on it were the same as the scraps in the monster's mouth. So at least one of them didn't.

"Stop." I said as I slid off my respirator.

The one with the assault rifle spun towards me. His heart pounded faster than his weapon could fire. I snatched the rifle away to be sure it didn't. They all had nametags fused to each coverall's right breast. The former rifleman was Anzahl. The second engineer beside him was Stoller. Nieder was a cringing third.

"Who the hell are you?" Stoller asked.

"I work here," I said. "You idiots work for the city. Find a way up and out."

"You're the Killer!" Stoller said.

"Yep. Now, get lost."

"Hey, we work for the city!" Anzahl spat. "You can't order us—"

Anzahl quit speaking as their lamps lit my face and the harsh stare looking down at them.

"I think we should leave," Anzahl said.

"But that thing—!" Nieder finally spoke. "It ate Fritz!"

"I killed it."

"Did you recover any remains?" Stoller asked me.

I only cocked an eyebrow, and reached down to lower his lamp aimed at my face.

"I mean, we could at least have a service with something." Stoller continued.

"Get tweezers," I said. "Actually, don't touch anything up there. You all scan clean. So get to the top and call the cops. Call John Slate. Tell him Grail is here and needs gamma ray projectors, ASAP."

"Gamma projectors?" Stoller jerked back.

Obviously he understood using all-penetrating radiation was an extreme measure. The projectors could fry anything from whales to microbes. My immune system had cleared out the virus, but I wanted to fry everything in the zone infected with the zombie plague. Maybe even the whole zone.

"What the hell for?" Nieder asked.

"Get up and out and do it." I ordered and turned back to the stairs.

"Team fifty to muni-central—" Anzahl stopped his com attempt when he saw me turn.

"You think maybe I tried that?" I rasped, and then tossed Anzahl his rifle.

"So have we. A lot." Stoller said. "We all need to get out of here. Come with us."

"I have something I need to do," I said. "I need you to call Detective John Slate when you're clear. Move."

"Hey, no one's job is worth their life." Stoller stepped toward me with his hands out.

"So, you killed that spiky thing." Anzahl glanced at me and then his rifle. "I, um, I didn't even see it take Fritz."

I guessed Anzahl wanted absolution, but I took the rifle from him again and handed it to Stoller.

"Maybe you won't freeze," I said to Stoller. "But you all need to get out and make contact."

"But if that thing is dead, we're safe." Nieder chirped. "I mean, what could be worse?"

"Another one." I said and raised my gun level with his head. I was aiming behind him.

"What?" Nieder screeched.

I didn't need augmented senses to smell him piss his overalls even through the stench. Another second began to unfurl, and more slaughter. I yelled: "get down!"

His muscles twitched to do that, but the monster's jaws snapped shut over his head and shoulders. This beast had a simple form. Something like an eyeless lion with a massive head and a mane of pulsing tentacles that enveloped the rest of Nieder once the blunt jaws clamped down. So maybe it wasn't that simple. It was also dead. The zombie virus had taken it long before it killed Nieder. It wasn't hungry. It was spreading the disease. Whatever remained of Nieder would join it. I fired.

The bodies blew apart. Anzahl collapsed into a ball at the deafening blasts. The braver Stoller came next to me to spray the hall and twitching chunks of monster with the assault rifle's comparatively small bullets. The rifle's sharp staccato ended. Stoller vomited when he saw parts of Nieder's coveralls among the spread of carnage. He stood and wiped his mouth. He never uttered a word of accusation or guilt.

"What I need to stop here isn't just the monsters," I said. "They carry a disease. It must infect them at a lower level. I need to find that. I need to destroy it."

"We're engineers," Stoller said in low, strained tones as he stared at the remains of his friend and the monster. "We can help."

"You could get killed."

"You need a source of energy to cook the disease," Stoller continued. "That's why you want the gamma ray projectors. We might be able to make this ruin a kiln and do the same thing."

"Okay. How?" I asked.

"Eventually the angle of the nearby super-tower has to cut through the lower levels of this ruin." Stoller finally looked up at me from Nieder's remains. "The foundation has to go deep to support the tower. Very deep. The foundation complex is sheathed by a massive, reactive slab. It's a geothermal conductor that moves heat rising from the mantle up through the tower. Like a thermal circuit that helps warm and cool the tower's environment. Without it, even its foundation would melt."

"So how do we tap that heat?" I asked.

"If I can lay a com-node on the foundation slab, any part of it, I can link and tell it to focus heat across this region of its outer surface."

"Then we just need to run." Anzahl spoke as he stood up.

"Yeah," Stoller added. "I can create a timeframe, but it will get searing hot, fast."

"Won't the foundation slab be hot, anyway?" I asked.

"We have thermal suits in our packs." Stoller answered. "It's part of the job."

"Usually we don't get killed doing it." Anzahl added.

"Nice job, then." I said. I liked the plan. Even if I couldn't find the exact virus source, Stoller's plan would kill all of it and anything infected for quite a wide area. I only hoped it was contained in the ruin. It was worth the attempt, and risking their lives. Mine was always in danger, anyway. "Okay. Let's go."

"Um, I have no bullets." Stoller said. He pulled off his rifle's empty magazine and held it up to me.

I handed him one of my backup handguns, an Aquila Tyranus, Mark IV. It was a heavy mass of advanced alloys. Stoller dropped his magazine and rifle and took my sidearm as if receiving an anvil.

"Its locks are off. Proximity sensor acts as the safety. Use both hands," I said. "It's got kick."

Stoller took a moment to consider the gun as boon or burden.

"I'll walk ahead," Anzahl said. He picked up the rifle and inserted a new magazine from his pack. He obviously was summoning his courage to atone for failing to save Fritz or at least shoot his attacker. The rifle would not have done much to stop the red beast. I had another reason to let Anzahl take point.

"You'll be safe," I said in assuring tones. "I'm right behind you."

I pocketed my respirator. Maybe the engineers had intra-nasal versions, but I kept mine off for camaraderie. I lifted my shotgun and pointed down the hall. Anzahl nodded and walked to the stairwell.

As a Killer, I make choices that seem harsh and uncompromising. But most are complete compromises. A Killer endangers personal safety for a job. You can see it as serving the greater good, or serving your bank account for the bounties. You faced death, either way. The engineers found themselves faced with death, unexpectedly. All were ill suited for it. Now only one of them was still alive. Stoller still breathed. His breaths were labored because of the heavy air and stench. Anzahl shambled ahead of us. Dead.

I had to make a choice in the hall about telling him he was dying from the zombie infection, or play my hunch the virus would draw his freshly infected corpse to its source. As long as he faced forward and didn't notice Stoller and me, my plan might work. It would make finding the virus' origin source more direct. The infection drew him home.

The stairwells became more sparse and walled with unpainted concrete. The flights were narrower with a greater gap in the open shaft in the center. And the stink got worse. It seemed many of the zombie plague victims never left its source. Their bodies might be making a reservoir of virions. The reek grew thicker the deeper we went. My scans could analyze the chemical makeup. The strong stench was rotting humanity. Stoller wretched.

"How can you two stand this air?" Stoller wheezed.

"It will smell worse when we cook the place," I replied.

"Is the stench from monster crap?" Stoller asked

"No. It's death. Decomp." I said and watched Anzahl. "The mass of plague victims. Monsters. Squatters and explorers. Mostly people. There down at the source."

"Hey, Anzahl." Stoller called out. "You have water, right?"

There was only silence and shuffling.

"Anzahl!" Stoller yelled.

"Watch your volume, Stoller. Something hungry could hear us."

"What's with Anzahl?"

I paused, and took an unfortunate deep breath. "He's a walking corpse."

"What?" Stoller froze.

"Keep it tight," I tried to sound calming and in control. "I didn't tell you because I didn't want you to freak out. Your friend is dead. But he's leading us to the source."

Stoller stumbled like a zombie. But his broken gait was from exhaustion and shock. I grabbed his shoulder and propped him up.

"We're going to find it," I said. "And then your friends and the victims here will be the only humans lost."

Stoller said nothing but stared at the shambling Anzahl in fear. I pulled him in line behind me and kept walking. Stoller clutched the big handgun I gave him tightly but followed.

Anzahl turned.

"Crap," I muttered.

Anzahl lowered his bottom jaw and waved the rifle as if it was a hook, not a gun as he came at us. My shotgun barrel clipped his skull. Anzahl's zombie fell against the inner railing. The rifle fell and banged against a lower landing. My second swing knocked Anzahl straight down the shaft. The awful splat sound came soon after. We were near the bottom.

I slapped another breadcrumb at the last landing. Rubble had buried the next flight of stairs. There was a smear on the ground left by Anzahl's corpse before it got up and stumbled through the skewed doorway.

"I don't know why you do that," Stoller shook his head with a weary neck. "They don't give off much light."

"They're not just for light," I said.

We went through the skewed door. It was suddenly much hotter. An odd, faint luminescence allowed unaided sight. We stood on disturbed, natural dirt inside a chamber cut by the excavation for the super-tower's base. It felt strange to enter a large space after trekking through cramped and rotting halls and down slick, stinking stairs. Behind us, part of the hotel's outer wall was exposed and crossed with wide cracks. It looked ready to collapse and fill the space. What loomed before us proved Stoller right. A smooth, black slope descended from the chamber ceiling of exposed pipes, cables and undersides of buildings and ancient streets still intact and mocking gravity. The black slope extended down to the ruble and soil and beyond the chamber sides. It appeared as a slab cut from night itself back in the lost days of open sky and then thrown through the city and Earth's crust.

"That's a foundation section." Stoller pointed to the black slope.

Rock and debris rested below the naked section of ebony. We stood on the opposite side on a narrow ledge of rough ground. Beyond its edge, the dirt and rubble fell into a mirrored slope at the same, steep angle of the debris beneath the ebony slant. The foundation cut deep with no respect to anything that previously stood there. I assumed the people were warned to leave before the epic excavation. Maybe. The opposing slopes created a wedge-shaped pit. At the distant bottom was the Holy Grail. Or hell. We had found the viral source. This chamber next to the black foundation created a perfect incubator for whatever might evolve in Earth's now twisted ecology. In the pit, a rippling mass of goo formed tendrils reaching up to touch and infect anything that moved.

Anzahl's corpse had stumbled and fallen down the slope. It was not alone. Along the slope sides near the bottom was a horde of animate corpses. Most were human. Some were hideous beasts. The bodies suffered various stages of rot, from first infected to last. It looked almost as a horrific example of sediment layers in an exposed hillside. All zombies swayed with the moving tendrils. There was finally a unity between humanity and its bastard children predators. And it needed to burn. But the zombies didn't only donate virions to the pool as they rotted. They were also its defenders.

"There are too many," I said.

"I made that same calc." Stoller replied. "Even if you attacked and distracted them, there are more of them than bullets in a hundred guns. They'd overpower you and then get me before I turned up the heat."

"We need to move out," I said.

"All this was for nothing?" Stoller wheezed.

"No. Now we have a location. We can return to the surface and get help to incinerate this on a molecular level, either by your method or by radiation. The plague goo will become fried goo. The virus will be destroyed."

I said all that and hoped it was true. I felt defeated, but I needed to lift Stoller's spirits so he could haul himself out. One of us needed to survive now that our plan was busted.

"Um, maybe we'll be destroyed." Stoller pointed down.

The horde had noticed us. The mass of monsters and humans gazed up with vacant stares and some with empty eye sockets. The pool's tendrils waved frantically. A cascade of dirt rolled down the slope from Stoller's boot. Rocks struck the staring Anzahl. Stoller stepped back. I pushed him toward the tilted doorway and aimed downward to cover our exit. The zombies were beginning to climb.

We raced up the stairs. At a safe distance, I touched off the last breadcrumb I had stuck at the stairwell bottom. A wonderful bloom of heat and orange light flashed with the sharp boom of the small, plasma mine going off. The blast shook the stairwell. We fell against the flight we climbed. I hoped the violence took out a mass of zombies, not just Stoller's front teeth.

We heard more feet, claws, and other appendages clank against the metal steps as the surviving horde came for us. After a few more flights, I set off another breadcrumb. This time I grabbed and held Stoller so the shockwave didn't knock him back into the edge of the steps.

The noise behind us stopped. I allowed myself a sense of satisfaction. But a wave of zombies crashed down the flight above us. They must have crawled up the exposed side of the hotel and forced their way through the cracked, outer wall.

Damn.

Another second ticked off. I raised my shotgun and fired though the steps above us. My rounds blasted through the mass of zombies and thinned the numbers that closed on us. Stoller screamed, but lifted the big mark four handgun at the oncoming horde of rotting humans and beasts. As I feared, the gun's recoil was too strong for him. Stoller fired one shot. I was surprised he managed to fire a second. His shots had good effect in blunting the attack, but pain forced him to drop the gun from his sprained hands. I reached for him. The zombies got him first.

I grabbed only a ripping sleeve as the storm of tearing, thrusting arms and oversized jaws pulled in Stoller. His short scream was muffled by the zombie mass that tore and bit him apart. The arm from the ripped sleeve tumbled back out of the flexing horde. A brief, wet sound splashed my ears as Stoller's blood and pieces flowed across the horde. My gun blasts cut it off. The shells struck and blew the horde of dead people and monsters into more shredded parts. The attack on Stoller had concentrated the zombies. Several shots blew a crease through the grasping, biting wall. I forced my way through the reeling mass of rotted bodies. Limbs swiped at me. Some severed arms locked onto my legs. They fell away as I charged up the steps.

I spun to shoot stragglers in my way. The human zombies exploded from gunfire made to kill much larger bodies. For the first time on this job, I felt like vomiting. I kept running. Zombies and some parts kept up the chase. I set off more breadcrumbs to thin the herd close behind me. The heat scorched my exposed skin. But there seemed to be as many zombies as steps. I set off another breadcrumb. The super-hot plasma incinerated the zombies near the explosion and set ablaze those not crushed in the blast. I heard a loud, collective hiss. The sound was from burning zombies and steam from venting fluids still in their bodies.

I finally fell onto the floor of the lobby, winded. Of course, I wasn't alone. Street people had found the hole I dug to the old lobby entrance. They used it to explore and scavenge. That same impulse had fed the zombie virus. Now these people were going to feed the zombie horde.

Damn.

The noise of my breadcrumb explosions brought people out from the side rooms and offices with pilfered fragments of no value other than proof of their bravery. They would never get to boast. I fired on the burning zombies emerging from the stairwell and others climbing up the elevator shaft. They were still hell bent on ripping me apart. The slower fools from the street satisfied the horde's urge. Burning fingers and jaws tore into the flesh of their shocked, screaming victims.

I fired the last few rounds in my shotgun's magazine. A sizzling mass of dead flesh and newly torn skin and muscle covered the rear lobby. And there were more flaming zombies. The people ahead of me fled. I could see their butts shooting through my excavated hole in quick succession to the street. I set off the last breadcrumb in the lobby. Someone had knocked it free. It was in the wrong place.

Damn.

On the street above, people could see the flash of light and heat through the hole as my breadcrumb mine exploded. In the cavern below, my exposed skin burned. The blastwave knocked me far enough away to suffer but not completely sear. The final wave of zombies was fragments and ash. Like the red monster, I rolled back up. I pushed my body up onto my hands and knees as flames flickered out on my coat. Slowly I pawed like a zombie up to the street. But, I was still alive.

I was colored black by the smoke. So was the inside of my lungs. I coughed, gasped, and wheezed as I crawled onto the surface and lay flat. Of course, I could see the super-tower rising high above. People gathered and watched me. That was all they did. No applause for saving them. They didn't know I was trying to save the world. They did know my face was a gasping crisp. Through my pain, I considered the only difference between them and zombies was that this horde just stared. They might as well be a bunch of clowns. One could have at least juggled.

Finally, a few people approached. One young woman offered help.

"I'd call a quick-med," she said. "But we can't call anyone around here."

"Tss-okay," I rasped. "I guess—" *Cough!* "I guess you're not a clown."

"I don't get it."

"Don't worry."

"You need a pump," she said staring at my accidentally altered complexion with wide eyes. "Meds!"

"Really, I just need a shower." I wheezed. "Maybe some water."

"We can get that. But you really should watch drinking the stuff. Water is dangerous."

I look up at her with eyes staring out from a face burned and blackened. She realized the irony and smiled. I would have, too. But right then, it hurt.

"Cops." I said. "Slate."

"What's a slate?" She asked.

"A cop." I rolled into a crouch. "Get to a clear link and call the cops."

I the time that passed, my introspection made me quiet and the brave woman decided to listen to my warnings and step back across the street. Slate now stood where she had been. For once, he looked down at me.

"So, big man. What can I do for you, today? Other than bandages. And a pain pill."

Cough! "Save the world."

"Oh, no worries, Ice." Slate chimed. "Did that by lunch hour. How can I repeat step A?"

"Drop the smarm. Listen."

"Okay."

I grunted as I handed Slate an encapsulated infomere I had created with surviving tech while waiting. It contained data sequences on the events, the zombie virus, and how to kill it. Now.

"And we need gamma ray projectors here, *and* an engineer crew—*cough!*—at the super-tower." I said with the assumption he would load the infomere right then. He did, and then turned his head to com with subordinates at his precinct. It would all get done. The virus, not humankind, was doomed.

But tomorrow, there would be another monster. Problem was, I might take the day off.

www.ingramcontent.com/pod-product-compliance
Lightning Source LLC
Chambersburg PA
CBHW061131200626
46817CB00016B/695